In the Shadow
of the Sphere

An Adventure of Heart and Spirit

Thomas Youngholm

Creative Information Concepts
San Diego, California

Published by:

Creative Information Concepts
P.O. Box 1504
Lemon Grove, California 91946
E-Mail: Creativeic@aol.com
Web site: http://www.tomyoungholm.com

This book is manufactured in the United States of America.

Author: Thomas Youngholm
Cover Design: Graphic Minion Studios
Painting depicted on cover: Helene Brossel
Interdimensional Art: Zon-O-Ray

Library of Congress Catalog Number
99-90749

ISBN 0–9642488-8-3

10 9 8 7 6 5 4 3 2 1

Other books by Thomas Youngholm

International Best-Seller
The Celestial Bar

"The dynamics here provide for a great read, and a wonderfully educational one at that! Grab it and read it. Meet the wise and whimsical characters... and learn about yourself in the process. You can if you hang out for awhile at *THE CELESTIAL BAR.*"
The New Times

"This is one exciting book to experience, and I love it! If you want a book that you can't put down—run, don't walk, and pick up a copy. You'll be glad you did."
Inner Self

"If you've read *The Celestine Prophecy*, you'll enjoy *THE CELESTIAL BAR*. If you haven't, try this one first."
NAPRA Trade Journal

"... energizing, riveting, enlightening, and intellectually stimulating, filled with concepts and truths to be pondered, and then accepted!"
Metaphysical Reviews

"Read it once, then read it again and add it to your library. No doubt you will want to visit many times."
Pathways to Wellness

"Tom Youngholm strikes pay dirt... a dazzling array of well conveyed, extremely visual experiences."
The Awareness Journal

A portion of the net proceeds from the sale of this book
will be given to hospice organizations—"Keepers of the Gate"—
throughout the country.

Acknowledgements

For those who have influenced me on this incredible journey of writing, I wish to express my gratitude and thankfulness; Suzanne Dewar for telling me of the "stone spheres" and arranging my accommodations in Costa Rica, Kevin Killion, Karen Popowski, Pat Schwier, Sue and Mark McKeigue, Debbi Gillespie, Stephanie Gunning, Cecilia Perucci, J.T., Joseph Downey, the focus group, and the Visionary Writers' Circle for their invaluable feedback, Rani and Tracy for teaching the "dance," Helene Brossel for her dynamic painting depicted on the front cover, Zon-O-Ray for her inspirational interdimensional art, Jake for showing me the child within, Marc Duggan for his computer help, Lorraine Gonzalez for her "Costa Rican word-smithing," Autumn Lew for her talent and creativity on the cover, "Blue," my constant companion through the wee hours of the night, who illuminated and danced within my dreams, on my manuscript, and on my keyboards—computer and piano (maybe you'll see him), and all "the others" I haven't mentioned who have supported me during this chapter of my life.

Special thanks to Lianne Downey, an incredible editor, who squeezed out the hidden writer within me and taught with a parent's patience, understanding, and discipline, who coached on the sidelines when appropriate but also "challenged" me (whether I wanted it or not). But she always, always nurtured my "in-born" storyteller.

Heart- and soul-full appreciation to Debbi who stood by me through this sometimes agonizing yet always creative three-year process. Her compassion, love, and belief—in me and my passion—carried me through my time in the "shadow."

I would also like to thank the "collective unconscious" or "creative pool" or whatever one wants to call that "ethereal reservoir" which every artist dips into. Thank you for providing me with creativity, information, and truths that stretched beyond my wakeful consciousness.

To My Mother

Who now sits at the Celestial Bar.
I wish you love on all your journeys.
Thanks for encouraging me to the reach for the stars.

In the dark womb where I began
My mother's life made me a man.
Through all the months of human birth
Her beauty fed my common earth.
I cannot see, nor breathe, nor stir,
But through the death of some of her.

John Masefield, "C.I.M."

Author's Note

Wherever rivers run, they bring opportunities for change, growth, and life. Earth is on the shore of one such river.

At special times in our history, the heavens are in a unique alignment and the tides reach their highest point. A rare, wonderful, and unsettling melding occurs between land, water, and sky. At this crucial point, cultures, civilizations, ideas, and beliefs stretch their boundaries and share a common place. We have the opportunity to see more clearly than ever, because the light shines brightest at these times.

But if we turn away, all we see is our shadow. In that moment we truly witness our death.

That death is our consciousness looking back at the old: old beliefs, old ways of doing things, old relationships, old perspectives of yourself and the world. We must face, welcome, and hasten this death in order to survive, indeed to live.

Living in the shade and the light, our vision is then filled with paradoxes of challenge and enlightenment, violence and beauty, despair and hope. It is only our commitment to the Light—our spirit—that will enable us to move out of the shadow. This isn't attained by the shouts of a revolution or the explosion of a gunshot. It is simply accomplished by the silence … the silence of turning forward, changing a belief, expanding an idea, glancing within and knowing that you are of spirit and truly connected to one another, this planet, the stars, and the Divine.

We are standing on that river shore and in that light. The tides are at their highest and the light is at its strongest. We have looked at our shadow too many times and much longer than needed. Turn back to the light. The time is NOW.

Enjoy your journey,

Tom

November, 1999

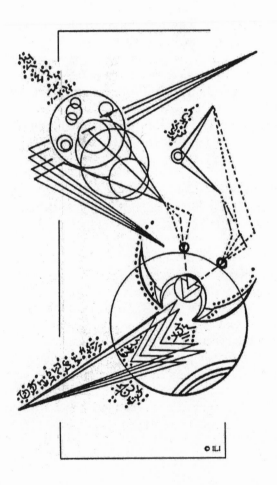

© ILI

Chapter 1

"A rhythm played within the jungle—for those who cared to listen."

The notes of death had followed Digger more than three thousand miles into the Costa Rican rainforest. Now they reverberated around him as he stood within the lush jungle enveloping him in an array of colors, textures, smells—and sounds. As the realization seeped into his consciousness, he chuckled to himself: there was no escape. Closing his eyes, he listened with the ears of a trained musician. He heard again the persistent sound of falling leaves tearing from their branches and brushing against limbs on their journey to the rainforest floor. There, amongst all the other leaves, they landed gently, with a soft, brittle rustle. The sound of death. Digger mused about the variations of that sound, and how it occurred in cities and countrysides all over the world.

Then for a brief moment the jungle held its breath and became still. Waiting. Waiting for the inevitable. It was all part of the cycle of light and shadow, inhalation and exhalation, life and death. The jungle expected it; in fact, it needed it to survive.

A gust of wind rustled the forest canopy. Digger opened his eyes as more leaves tore from their birthplaces, then twirled overhead and landed at his feet.

A flash of lightning filled the sky and outlined the rich foliage that thrived along the riverbank. Instinctively, like when he was a little boy, Digger counted the seconds before he heard the thunder to determine how close the storm really was. "One-thousand one, one-thousand two, one-thousand thr…"

The thunder crashed and rolled over the canopy of the tropical rainforest.

"*Venga! Venga!* Hurry, come into the tent," yelled Francisco, one of the two river guides leading Digger and five others on a rafting trip down the Río Pacuare in central Costa Rica.

Digger saw the others quickly drop the work they'd been doing to set up camp and hurry over to the main tent. He followed them, huddling inside to listen to the guides.

"*El río* might be too dangerous with all this *lluvia*—I am sorry, rain," Francisco was explaining. The slim, dark-haired young man was the senior guide for Wild River Excursions, with long experience on the Río Pacuare. He probably knows what he's talking about, Digger thought. "We have been getting more rain than usual the last few days," Francisco continued. "With all the water runoff, the river will be running high and fast. If this storm hits us with a lot of rain, we might be able to run the river but it would be a wild ride. As you know, the last part of the trip is the most difficult, with major rapids—including Caliente Falls and Dos Montañas. We want to know what you all think about continuing." Francisco and his helper, Danny, a blond-haired guy from Denver, scanned the mixed group of amateur rafters carefully to gauge their responses.

A tanned woman in her mid-twenties spoke first. "Well, as you know my boyfriend is not feeling so well." The young man sitting on a cot next to her had his head down and hands on his stomach. Montezuma's revenge had taken another victim. "So we wouldn't mind cutting the trip short." The couple reminded Digger a little of himself and his girlfriend, Mary Bendetta Porcelli, whom he'd nicknamed Bendi. Though he hadn't been sick—physically—Bendi was always trying to take care of him.

"I've already fallen out of the raft once..." It was the rugged-looking guy from upstate New York whom Digger had helped fish out of the river earlier that morning. The river had treated the strong and healthy man as if he were some helpless, floating debris. "I don't want to take any more chances," he admitted.

Outside Digger could hear a big gust of wind sweep into the campsite, bringing with it a wall of rain. As the rafters continued their debate, the popping-thud noise hitting the top of the tent drowned out the usual dull background roar of the river.

It certainly doesn't rain like this in San Diego, Digger thought, his mind wandering away from the group as it had been doing throughout the trip. In San Diego, a light mist was called "rain" and would be noteworthy enough to mention on the eleven o'clock news. San Diego weather was mild—no thunderheads, rarely lightning, no gale force winds—just beautiful, boring weather. Not like when he'd lived in Chicago or the Florida Keys. Those storms were exciting and would get the ol' heart pumping. Digger loved the sunshine, so it was a small price to pay, but every once in a while he would wish for a good old-fashioned storm with blinding lightning and knee-knocking thunder. Sometimes it was needed. It could even be exciting. Most certainly it was a change.

Be careful what you ask for, he admonished himself, you might just get it.

Focusing on the elderly couple who were shrugging their shoulders indecisively, Digger tried to remember where they were from. The woman finally said, "Well, if it keeps raining like this, maybe we shouldn't go." She turned to Digger and waited for his response.

At that moment the ground moved. As the earth began to undulate, Digger looked across at the terrified faces of the other rafters. The tent rolled violently from side to side.

He'd never expected to be in the middle of a remote rainforest, listening to the constant tumbling of the river, hearing the rain slapping at the tent, and now to have the jungle move beneath his feet. What next? Locusts?

First, his mother had died, but not before he'd witnessed her slow, painful death. Then, after the funeral, his girlfriend picks a fight with him. So he did what any intelligent male would do: he retired to the safety of his cave. Well, this time he had taken a long trip to find his cave, and now he wasn't so sure that it was all that safe.

What he didn't know until much later was that the entire eastern central section of Costa Rica had been violently shaken by a major earthquake. The epicenter was located east of them, in a sparsely populated area known as the Caribbean Lowlands. Energy that had been stored for centuries finally released and changed the look of the land.

Along parts of the Costa Rican fault line the earth rose several feet. Miles away from Digger's camp, landslides slipped into canyons and riverbeds as rivers flooded, scraping away shorelines. Estuaries rose and washed their brackish water into the lowlands, threatening the vegetation and contaminating freshwater lakes. The living coral reef along the southeastern coast of Costa Rica was pushed out of its watery habitat, only to merge with the deadly unfamiliar air which laid to waste hundreds of years of creation.

Digger tried to surf the undulating earth. Living in California, he had experienced several types of earthquakes: the "slammers" that lift you up and then bring you back down—hard, the "shakers" that throw you from side to side, and then there were the "rollers" that made you feel as if a lolling terrain were speeding beneath your feet. He smiled nervously at the elderly couple. "It's a roller."

The tent continued shaking for a few more seconds and then as quickly as it came, the quake stopped.

Some of the rafters turned pleading, childish eyes to the guides for comfort. Francisco and Danny glanced knowingly at each other, then placed practiced smiles on their faces.

"Don't worry, that was just a little tremor; it happens all the time," Danny smiled. Digger thought he looked a little nervous.

"It is just Costa Rica putting on an *espectáculo*, how do you say it in English? Ah... show... ahh... for your entertainment," Francisco added.

The elderly man looked at his wife and proclaimed loudly, "We're ready to go home."

"I think we'd all better go back tomorrow," Danny agreed. "Given all the runoff from this new rain, the Río Pacuare will rise and probably make most of the rapids Class Five, which would be a hairy ride. I don't think we should continue." He looked to Francisco for support.

"Besides, it sounds like all of you are ready to leave," Francisco added. "I will radio to Manuel at the Wild River Excursions office in San José. He will send some people and a couple of Jeeps to pick us up."

Digger's immediate impulse was to agree with the plans. But something prevented those words from spewing forth. Even though he was frightened, something from deep within spoke instead, "I'd still like to go down the river."

They all turned to him in surprise.

"Well, it sounds like you are the only one, Digger," Francisco replied. "But if by some miracle the river is not running high tomorrow morning, we can reconsider."

As the group broke up, sliding in the mud trying to get back to their dry shelters, the rain continued to pour. Digger stopped momentarily when he saw the tail of a long black snake lying in his path. The wet and shiny reptile turned and looked at him, darting its tongue in and out. Digger had always been afraid of snakes and had gone out of his way to avoid them. But with all his personal tragedies of the past few months, with all the rain, thunder, lightning, and tremors of the present moment, he only gave the creature a moment's thought before he pushed on toward his tent.

Finally reaching the small shelter, Digger unzipped the front flap, turned around, and then fell backwards into the opening, leaving his feet outside. He slipped off his sandals and then speedily zipped the front flap back up. His wet clothes dripped onto the already moist floor. The smell of mildew permeated the tent; many of his clothes were still damp from the previous days of rain. Grabbing a towel from his sports bag and slipping out of his wet swimming trunks, he dried himself off before putting on some clean shorts and a T-shirt.

As the wind continued to whip down the mountain river's sharply-cut valley, the tent swayed from side to side. He felt stuffy, hot, and a bit claustrophobic as he lay on the cot, the top of the tent only a couple of feet from his head. He looked up blankly into the darkness.

How did he ever land himself in the middle of this rainforest? And why did he hesitate to head back to San José? Why would he want to continue when it was clear to everyone else—wisely, he thought—that it was safer to return?

As the noisy duo of the clamorous thunderstorm and deafening din of the river were underscored by the chatter in his head, he laughed at himself. My mind, he thought, is stronger than a locomotive train, faster than a speeding bullet, able to leap tall buildings, and louder than—

The tent filled with a bright light that was immediately followed by a thunderous clap.

—than the voice of God. He laughed out loud and said to himself, "You've lost it, Digger."

A quiet, almost imperceptible thought bubbled up to the top of his consciousness. Before it broke through the surface, he realized it wasn't so much a thought as a voice. A voice from somewhere deep within him that said, "No, you haven't lost it; you're just lost."

As the rain continued to beat down, he allowed that sad realization to move through him. His thoughts drifted back to the audition in Los Angeles that had given him his first shot at composing music for a film score, the audition that had changed his life from starving artist to successful composer. While he was playing on the stage that night—an original piano concerto—he had flashed back on vague bits and pieces of a mystical, dreamlike experience he'd had while meditating in the green room, trying to calm his nerves before he was called to play. He remembered feeling lights, meeting familiar people, and seeing some kind of symbol. But that was all. He knew that the forgotten symbol was somehow important but he had no idea why, and he couldn't quite bring the image back to mind. It was like waking up in the morning only to remember the vague, unrelated images and sounds of a dream that you know is important, but you just can't recreate. That veiled, mystical experience had vanished from his conscious mind. His attempts at meditation since then had been unfruitful, unrewarding—and they never took him back to that mystical place he couldn't quite recall.

A crash of thunder brought Digger back to the present. Why was he willing to go on the last leg of this journey? He didn't need any more excitement in his life. In fact, that was why he'd taken this so-called vacation, to get away from all the turmoil back home. The multitude of emotions he'd experienced during the last six months had been almost too much to bear—the guilt, relief, sadness, hope, love, anger, and resentment. He didn't want to think about the fight with his girlfriend, Bendi, or that he couldn't make any headway with his musical compositions. But most of all he didn't want to think about—no, he corrected himself, he didn't want to *feel* —the death of his mother.

His throat began to choke up ever so slightly. The tiniest hint of a salty tear began in the corner of his eye. He hadn't cried at his mother's funeral; he sure wasn't going to let it happen now. Quickly he swallowed and replaced the wetness with a deep sigh.

As the night wore on, the rain eventually washed away the outpouring of Digger's mind and heart. The dance of wind and trees, lightning and thunder, river and land moved throughout the spectacular ancient landscape. A rhythm played within the jungle—for those who cared to listen.

* * * *

A mile downstream from Digger, the swollen river severed the trunk of an old eucalyptus from its roots. The Río Pacuare, the most remote river in Central America, carried its victim along what would have been the last leg of the river rafters' journey if they had decided to continue the next day. The fallen tree was carried eight miles before it flipped over the treacherous, boiling water of Caliente Falls and crashed through the ensuing rapids. Three miles further down, the old eucalyptus reached the place where the mountain river was squeezed together by the steep and narrow walls of Dos Montañas Pass. The impressive, sheer granite walls rose twenty stories high on either side of the raging river; a split in the mountain caused perhaps by an ancient earthquake of even greater magnitude than the one now changing the Costa Rican terrain. The pass was only a football field's length and twenty yards wide, but it had bruised and broken many a rafter who had challenged it.

Just as the floating tree entered the pass, an aftershock undulated the jungle terrain. Like a house of cards, a small section of the granite walls loosened from its stronghold and began to crumble. Several huge chunks of rock fell into the narrow opening, shattering the old tree into giant shards, creating a dam of granite and wood. The angry river crashed violently into these stubborn obstacles as it tried to enter the pass. More boulders fell onto the new dam as plants, bushes, debris, and dirt that had been washed into the river tightly packed the makeshift barrier.

The agitated water swelled at the blocked entrance to Dos Montañas Pass. Ol' Man River looked to find some other place to discharge all of his massive energy. For him it was simple. He knew no other way but to follow the path of least resistance.

On one side of the opening to Dos Montañas Pass was an old dried-up riverbed, an ancient route of the Río Pacuare. Hundreds of years ago nature had locked out this old riverbed, but with the force of a small tsunami, the Río Pacuare now joined with its forgotten, timeworn partner. Now with a freedom and release of energy, the river flooded through the rainforest, uprooting bushes, rocks, plants, and trees.

The wall of water running straight through the ancient waterway dismantled everything in its path. A centuries-old ceiba tree bent over as the raging waters flooded onward. Then the wall of river slammed into a steep rocky bluff. The crushing force of the water was only temporarily delayed before it moved to the right and continued its journey deep into the jungle.

Meanwhile the raging waters beat relentlessly and slammed jungle debris against the precipitous stone barrier. It wasn't long before earth and rock shed into the tumbling river. After several hours of hammering, the water finally split a fifteen-foot-wide opening at the base of the bluff, exposing a semi-circular cavern that was ten feet high. Inside were eleven perfectly symmetrical granite balls that ranged in diameter from two to seven feet.

As the torrential river swept into and flooded the dark cavern, the stone objects were quickly swallowed up. The churning waters lifted all but the largest sphere, playing with these ancient stone sculptures like beach balls, tossing them out of the long-forgotten chamber and into the raging current.

* * * *

"Jonathan. Jonathan Taylor?"

Digger thought he was dreaming. He barely heard his given-name being whispered above the din of the river.

"Jonathan Taylor," a female voice called softly.

"Yes, I'm Digger," he answered groggily. Opening up the tent flap he peeked outside. Silhouetted against the hint of early morning light was a female figure, about five-and-a-half-feet tall. The woman stared at him in a way that made Digger uncomfortable. He'd always felt at ease in his lean body. His girlfriend Bendi said he was in pretty good shape for a 41-year-old. He ran his hand nervously through his sandy-colored hair. Heck, nobody looks great when they first wake up, he rationalized. Then he realized she wasn't really looking *at* him but *into* him.

"Are you ready to go?" she asked with a Spanish accent.

"It's too early; nobody is even up yet." Digger rubbed his eyes and strained to see this early intruder more clearly. She had features of a Meso-American Indian. "Besides, who are you?" he added.

The woman bent over and looked at Digger again with those penetrating green eyes. "I am Angélica," she replied, pronouncing the name in the fluid melodies of Central America, "Ahn-HEL-ee-ka." She put her arm out and clumsily shook his hand. "I am here to take you the rest of the way... down the river."

"I thought it was going to be too difficult," Digger hesitated.

"*Ningún problema.* The rain has stopped. We will do just fine," she answered. "Let us hurry; we need to get an early start."

"What about the others?" he asked.

"No, it is just you," the slim, muscular woman added forcefully. "I have everything we need in the raft."

Digger, still half-asleep, lazily rubbed the whiskers on the side of his face.

"We need to leave now. You do want to go, no?" The words were put in the order of a question but Digger felt a hint of command in the tone that she used.

"Uhhh... yeah. I guess so."

"*Fantástico*," she said quietly. "Just bring a few dry clothes and leave everything else inside your tent and meet me in *cinco minutos*." She pointed toward one of the rafts at the river's edge.

"Will someone bring my stuff and then meet us at the end of the day?" Digger asked with concern.

"*Sí*, do not worry. There will be people who will meet us. Now please be very, very quiet, so as to not wake any of the others." Angélica turned quickly and walked toward the river.

Digger stared after her for a moment. Then, sleepily, he grabbed an extra pair of shorts and a T-shirt, changed into his swimming trunks, and stumbled out to follow her.

Chapter 2

"Digger felt a recognition that they needed to overcome this moment not just for themselves but for...for what, he didn't know."

"Ssshhh," Angélica cautioned. "We do not want to wake anyone." Her dark skin glowed warmly in the early morning light, set off by the lime-green, one-piece bathing suit she wore. Digger nodded sleepily.

In the stern of the boat were two water-tight containers and an extra paddle. Digger handed over his clothes and wallet to Angélica. She placed them inside one of the containers and checked to see that the other one, filled with fresh water and light snacks, was tightly closed. She tied them both securely to a metal ring. Then she strapped on a light-blue, Wild River Excursions life jacket and tossed one to Digger.

Silently, he helped her push the raft off shore. When they were mid-thigh deep in the river, they both lunged on top of the inflated sides and flopped into the raft. The swift current quickly swept the raft downriver as Digger and his new guide positioned themselves slightly towards the forty-five degree "V" of the bow. Digger side-saddled the left side of the raft while Angélica did the same on the right. Footholds were glued to the floor of the raft and Digger slipped his sandaled right foot into the closest one. The foothold would help to keep him inside the bouncing raft when they hit the rapids coming up. He dipped his paddle in and matched Angélica's slow pace.

The air was humid as the low overcast clouds held in the moisture of the rainforest. Digger searched the floor of the raft. "Where are the helmets?"

Angélica's green eyes grew bigger as she looked around the raft. "I thought they were here. They must be in the other raft." She took a breath, "No problem. We will be okay."

"No problem?" Digger questioned. He looked at the river-swept shoreline and noticed the damage of the previous night's rain—uprooted bushes and trees were strewn everywhere. He gave his life jacket an extra tug, checking to be sure it was fastened securely.

"Pay attention!" Angélica warned him.

Bubbling whitewater stretched across the river several yards ahead of them. Before he knew it, warm water slapped him across the face and temporarily blinded him. When his eyes finally cleared, they only brought the vision of a bright blue patch of sky as the bow of the raft flew up in the air and landed partially on a boulder.

"High side!! *Empuje!* Push off!"

He could barely hear Angélica over the river's roar even though she was shouting next to him. But he leaped to her side of the raft and tried to push it off the rock. He knew this was one of the most dangerous positions to be in. It was called a "wrap," where the river literally wraps the raft tightly around an object. If you happened to be on the "low" side, the side closest to the water, you could easily be thrown into the river with no raft to cling to, or worse yet, get caught by the raft and pinned underneath.

Angélica crawled to the back of the raft and back-paddled, frantically trying to swing the stern of the raft to the left so the river would then pull them off the rock. But the force of the water continued to seal the raft to the boulder.

She was still yelling "*Empuje*" as Digger's muscles strained to push them off the obstruction.

Then, like a magnet, the river slowly started to drag under the side of the raft where Angélica was still stroking. The top of the inflated side was just inches from the white-capped river.

"Up front! Up front! Further up front!" Angélica shouted.

Digger scooted as far as he could to the bow of the raft and, with his paddle, tried again to push them off the rock while Angélica back-paddled frantically. He leaned into his paddle so hard he thought it was going to break.

Miraculously, the raft started to slip slowly off the boulder. He kept pushing. And then, with one strong backstroke from Angélica, the river spun the raft off the boulder. They rushed downstream again, but now the raft was facing backwards. Both of them stared at the boulder that they'd just been stranded on and Digger's mind started to catastrophize about all of the things that could have happened.

Angélica quickly took a new position at the stern. She twisted her body to the side and plunged her paddle into the water at a forty-five degree angle. Acting as a rudder, it turned the raft 180 degrees. They were facing downriver again. Finally a calm stretch of river gave them a little reprieve.

Digger turned around and looked into Angélica's eyes. They both laughed and yet knew that nothing was funny. It was the kind of laugh that came from nervousness, a release of fear, and also from a happiness that they were still alive.

Angélica moved up front again and sat on the right side. Slim but powerful, she paddled rhythmically. Digger noticed that her long black hair made a stunning contrast to the lush green shoreline. He shook his head and said with a slight laugh, "*El río esta muy loco.*"

"Maybe he is not so much crazy as he is playing with us. No?" Angélica smiled.

"*Muy* rough play," he added seriously.

Digger was fascinated by the way humans gave objects or aspects of nature a gender and personality. At first he thought it was just human ego spilling over onto other species or objects. But in recent years he'd discovered that his piano, in fact, any instrument, really did have a personality. If he'd never played his piano, he would never have discovered its essence. So he supposed that a person who always lived in the desert would consider a river to be just water. But for the lovers of water, the ocean was a "she" and the river a "he," along with whatever personality traits the water-lover wanted to bestow.

His attention suddenly shifted as a dazzling array of colors flew out of the jungle. A flock of macaws with their bright, long tails flew high overhead and then disappeared again into the dense rainforest.

Digger and Angélica paddled lazily, keeping the raft headed straight downstream. His thoughts drifted back to his piano. Though he had not given it a gender, he called it the "Maestro," the Teacher. Together they created magic. In recent years he'd been able to share that with millions of people. But lately his relationship with his piano had suffered. He'd hit a composer's block, so to speak. He'd convinced himself that one of the reasons he'd come to Costa Rica was to get inspired. Digger laughed sadly to himself as he reflected that his piano was the least of his "problem relationships."

Angélica lightly skidded the tip of her paddle over the river. A spray of water hit Digger. "*Atencion!*" she yelled as she quickly plunged her paddle back into the river.

Digger heard the rumbling of unseen rapids in the distance.

"*El río* feels different today." Angélica sounded concerned.

"Maybe because of the rain last night," Digger suggested.

"No; it is different. So we must be very good to get through all of these rapids safely. The rapids will be a preparation for Caliente Falls, which is coming up soon. If we are not in complete unison, there can be much trouble."

Digger could see that directly ahead, the river dropped about twenty feet over the span of fifty yards. In the middle of the river were five barely-submerged boulders, one every ten feet. As the river moved swiftly over these boulders, it created a cascading, watery staircase. And after that—the treacherous Caliente Falls.

Fear tightened its grip in the pit of his stomach. He knew there wasn't any safety net out there in the river. No one to magically reach out a helping hand if he fell in. The consequences were immediate and potentially deadly.

"Stroke!" Angélica yelled, as the river's roar increased.

"Forward or backward?" Digger yelled back.

"Forward!" Angélica responded, not looking at Digger.

"Of course," Digger sarcastically repeated under his breath. Well, how would he know? The other river guides gave precise instructions. Angélica had been very general so far.

The bow of the raft lifted up as they slipped over the first boulder. Plunging back into the tumbling waters, the bow lifted up again as they swept across the next boulder and again slammed downwards into the whitewater. The Río Pacuare simply pulled them through this roller-coaster ride, while water sprayed Digger and Angélica from all sides.

As quickly as they'd entered the rapids, the river suddenly became quiet and serene again. It was much like life, Digger thought. At times you were almost lulled into complacency and then the next thing you knew, you were working hard just to keep your head above water. Then, after a while, life would slow down again so you could enjoy its beauty. Even if you were drenched.

"Look!" Angélica pointed to some low overhanging trees.

Grasping tightly to a branch, with huge claws and long legs and arms, was a sloth. It remained totally motionless amongst the leafy branches. Long, greenish-gray hair covered its body—the result of tiny green algae—giving it the appearance of a big chunk of moss.

Digger spotted the mammal only as the raft passed directly underneath the low-lying branches. As he continued to look upwards, the sun began to peek through the clouds. He welcomed the sight. He was tired of the smell of mildew within his nostrils. All the days of his trip it had rained, broken only by brief appearances of the sun. He was told that this was the dry season but they were in a rainforest, so rain was never unusual. Francisco claimed that in a year, depending on the region, it could rain anywhere from two to four hundred inches.

The river grumbled louder now. The noise grew deafening as they entered the next set of rapids. Digger's muscles tensed, ready for the next flurry of activity.

This river trip was supposed to be fun but it had turned into something else. At first he thought it was just his inexperience that made him feel this way, but he could sense that Angélica was feeling something very similar. That left him feeling even more uneasy.

"Remember to continue to paddle as we go through the rapids,"

Angélica yelled. "It is the only way to get through them. If you stop paddling, we will lose control."

The white of the boiling river filled their vision. Digger firmed his position by squeezing his left foot between the floor of the raft and the inflated side, while shoving his right foot into the foothold in front of him.

"Hard left!" Angélica yelled.

Digger stroked deep and hard on the left side of the raft.

"Back left!" she changed her command.

He immediately started back-paddling. His adrenaline was pumping full steam ahead as he wondered how much the body could produce in one day. He was pretty sure that he was close to his limit. But the jungle had a way of shattering one's perceived limits.

The raft glided over a boulder and plunged into white foaming water. Digger bounced hard and almost flew out.

"Forward left!" Angélica screamed. Several seconds later she yelled, "Stop!" Digger pulled his paddle out of the water while Angélica continued paddling. The raft turned to the left as he heard the loudest grumbling yet from the river.

"We need to move cleanly between those two boulders ahead," Angélica shouted over the roar. "The raft has to be facing perfectly straight—downriver. This will allow us to be in the best position to safely maneuver over Caliente Falls."

The river narrowed as the strong current swept between the two firmly entrenched boulders. Several yards further down, the river spilled over a seven-foot drop-off into white boiling water—Caliente Falls. Then after the falls, the Río Pacuare broadened but was studded with more boulders and more rapids.

"Left forward! Hard! Hard! Hard!" Angélica yelled.

As they approached the boulders the strong current tried to push the raft sideways. Straightening out temporarily they slipped through between the two obstacles. But then the back of the raft hit one of the boulders and turned them around. They were headed backwards as they came upon Caliente Falls.

Angélica frantically back-paddled on her right. Digger knew they were in trouble when he heard the deafening rumble behind them. He panicked and stopped paddling. Leaning forward towards the bow, he pitched himself to the center of the raft.

"Stroke! Stroke!" Angélica yelled at Digger as she paddled furiously. The raft turned slightly. "Paddle. Pad—"

Angélica paddled air as the raft dropped over Caliente Falls sideways. She leaned into the raft as her side crashed at the bottom. Digger's body then smashed into Angélica's.

Out of control, the raft bounced hard and high as it continued through the rapids. Angélica, stunned and in pain, sat there for a moment, holding her arm while she yelled in some unknown language. Digger grabbed his paddle and scrambled back to his position. He tried to control the raft as water splashed them in all directions.

Churning through the whitewater, the raft turned completely around several times and again gave them an upstream view.

In an instant, Digger flashed on how the last several months of his life had been exactly this perspective: of life turning him around, seeing only quick moments where he had been, his focus not on where he was going.

The river quickly funneled them toward a couple of whitewater-crested boulders about eighty yards ahead. The raft was still turned backwards. Angélica instinctively grabbed her paddle and plunged it into the water. She grimaced in pain and clutched her wrist; the paddle slipping from her grasp and dropping into the river. It floated several feet away, traveling at the same speed as the raft. She reached for it desperately, but the paddle stayed teasingly inches from her grasp.

Suddenly a submerged boulder grabbed the bottom of the raft and brought it to a complete stop. Digger flew forward and landed on the side of the raft while Angélica flipped over into the water and floated downstream. Digger rocked the raft back and forth a couple of times, helping the river pull the raft off the boulder. He clumsily paddled as fast as he could and quickly came up close to Angélica. He stretched his paddle towards her as she reached up and tried to grab it. She missed. Digger leaned out a little further until Angélica finally, with her good hand, clutched the paddle. The raft moved sideways down the river as he pulled her closer.

Then Digger spotted another huge boulder coming up, just a few yards ahead. He quickly stood up, grabbed the back of Angélica's life-jacket, and tried to heave her into the boat. In that moment the raft hit the side of the boulder and squeezed Angélica between the boulder and the raft. Digger was thrown forward again, as if the emergency brakes on a train had locked. Still holding onto Angélica, he was now more on the boulder than the raft. And the current was beginning to pull her under.

Digger dropped down to his knees inside the raft and again grabbed Angélica's life jacket. In that moment, their eyes met. A bond between them—a bond stronger than one built over lifetimes—was instantly clear. Digger felt a recognition that they needed to overcome this moment, not just for themselves but for... for what, he didn't know. He just knew it was more.

Angélica gave the smallest hint of a smile.

Chapter 3

"Death was always in the shadows and didn't care whom it took, the old or the young, the rich or the poor, the river guide or the composer..."

Grabbing the shoulder section of Angélica's life-jacket, Digger gathered all his strength to free her from the river's hold between boulder and raft. With a mighty heave, he flipped her into the center of the raft as it shifted to the left and then dipped down and around the rocky obstacle. They bobbed, turned, and bounced their way through the next hundred yards of rapids.

Whenever Digger tried to get up, water gushed in from all sides and blinded him. Finally able to open his eyes, he grabbed his paddle and stroked frenziedly. They barely missed the last of the boulders.

As the river calmed, Digger looked and listened for any more signs of rapids. All he could see downriver were peaceful waters, with a few lazy eddies. Behind him the sound of the churning whitewater began to diminish.

Angélica still lay in the middle of the raft, moaning and holding her wrist. He quickly paddled over to the riverbank. Jumping out, he used all of his six-foot frame to drag the raft as far as he could onto the shore. Then he climbed back in to help her.

"Your leg is bloody," he said, reaching instinctively to probe for breaks.

"It is not broken," Angélica snapped.

He looked up into her eyes and reluctantly pulled his hands away. "Well, what about your wrist?"

"Why did you stop paddling?" she barked at him. "I saw you. When you should have been paddling, you were in the middle of the raft! I told you to stay on the side and paddle! Why did you stop paddling?" she demanded again.

"I don't know. I suppose I got scared and thought I was going to flip out. I didn't do it on purpose. It was just instinct," he added weakly.

"Well, your fearful instinct nearly got us killed."

Digger knew, even from his limited rafting experiences, that she was right—he should have kept paddling. That's how you get through rapids safely; otherwise the river takes you where it wants. He had seen many a raft flip over because one or several people didn't paddle through a rapid. He felt guilty—and confused.

Shouldn't she be a little bit grateful that she was even alive? If it hadn't been for him pulling her out of the water, she might not even be here. He didn't know what to say. All that came out of his mouth was, "How is your wrist?"

"All right. I think it is just bruised." She sounded hostile. But she hadn't made any move to get up.

Digger opened one of the closed containers and took out a first aid kit. Before she could protest, he gently wiped an anesthetic wet-nap over her bloody leg. "Looks like a couple of nasty cuts but nothing that needs stitches," he said.

"There is a plant along the shoreline that I need. It has a broad green leaf," she moved her hands to show the size and shape, "with a white stripe down the middle. I need just one. You shouldn't have to look far."

"Why do you need that?"

"Please, just look for it." Her voice had softened a bit.

He remembered seeing such a plant around the campsites. So without another word he headed downstream, searching for the unusual leaves.

The riverbank was swollen with greenery from the encroaching jungle, making the path difficult. Squeezing between two low palm trees, Digger heard a rustling at his feet. "Damn it!" he yelled as he felt sharp, needle-like pains in his leg. He looked down to see a small porcupine with a long, rat-like tail waddle quickly into a nearby hole. Several quills dangled from Digger's calf. Sweating, he tried to pull them out. The pain was throbbing as each quill broke off an inch from his leg; it must be barbed, he thought. He rubbed around the stinging area.

Damn it, he cursed again. He'd better be more careful where he walked. Or with whom he walked. Still bending over to examine the wound, he spotted the white-striped leaf a few feet away. Limping, he made his way over to the tropical plant and started to pull a leaf off one of its branches. He hesitated for a moment and then broke off a stem that bore several leaves.

When he stood up, he noticed a cecropia tree at the river's edge, its roots protruding into the water—and Angélica's lost paddle neatly tucked between them. He leaned against the hollow, bamboo-like tree as he reached over to retrieve the lost paddle.

Paddle, he thought. It wasn't my fault that I didn't paddle! I'm not an expert at river rafting. I just came out here to have fun. Well, that's not really true, he chided himself. He grabbed a low-lying branch and pulled himself back up.

As the limb shook from his weight, a colony of azteca ants dropped onto his head. In an instant he felt hundreds of hot, stinging bites cover his entire body. He slapped his back, face, neck, and arms to no avail. The ants continued to attack their intruder ferociously.

In a panic, Digger threw his body into the shallow of the river's edge and rolled along the rocky bottom. He didn't stop rolling until the biting stopped. Slowly standing up, he wiped himself off. Tiny little welts covered his body. This was not why he had come to Costa Rica.

With a sigh, he pulled himself back out of the river and carefully picked up the stem full of leaves and the paddle. He held them with crossed arms against his chest, as if they were his "Elphie," the little musical elephant he took to bed with him every night when he was a boy. The wind-up, tinny sound of Brahm's lullaby played in his head as he made his way back upstream, toward Angélica and the muffled rapids of Caliente Falls. His arms and legs throbbed from the ant bites and the porcupine quills, but his mind was busy playing over the events of the day.

He should never have taken this little walk to look for a stupid plant; in fact, he should never have come to Costa Rica...

Several birds chattered loudly overhead. He looked around for evidence of the winged creatures but saw nothing.

He should never have left Bendi behind.

The chattering continued. He looked again for the source.

He should have loved his mother more.

He stopped. Now the chattering sounded to him as if it came from deep within the rainforest.

He should have told Bendi where he was going, he should have...

"Stoppp!!!" he shouted with a throaty voice that could rival the howler monkey's. Birds flew from their trees and crossed the river, fleeing from this unknown creature with the strange, loud call.

Suddenly Digger realized the jungle was indifferent to all that had happened to him. In fact, such things were part of its everyday existence—an endless cycle of movement: rivers moving downhill, leaves falling from their branches, *ants biting*, rain pouring down from the clouds, day creatures retiring before dark, and mysterious creatures stirring in the night. There was no meaning to any of it. What happened to Angélica or Digger or anyone else was not considered to be good or bad. The river, or the trees, or some mighty animal did not sit in judgment about events that had occurred. The jungle didn't worry about what had just happened or what might happen or what should happen. The jungle simply was. Only Homo Sapiens placed arbitrary moral judgments and expectations on life's events.

Finally he reached Angélica and the raft again. She'd changed into a pair of blue shorts and a short-sleeved white blouse. She glanced at the tiny red welts covering his arms and legs. "What happened to you?" She could see for herself, he knew. But he played along.

"Nothing," Digger replied.

"Well, you should change into something dry. By the way, what were you yelling back there?"

"Nothing," Digger said again. "How is your wrist? And the cuts on your leg?"

Angélica gingerly rotated her wrist. "It will be okay. Did you find the plant?"

He handed the branch to her.

"I said a leaf, not a branch!" she exclaimed.

"I didn't know. I thought several would be better than one. I didn't know what you would be using it for, so I thought more was better, just in case."

"I told you one, just one. What is this, 'more is better?' I guess I should expect that from someone of your culture, but I do not get it!" Shaking her head, she turned from Digger to focus her attention on the branch. Gently, she pulled one leaf from the stem. A soft green ooze leaked out as she folded it like an accordion. Then she rubbed the folded leaf into her cuts.

"What does that do?"

"Many things. The leaf heals but also takes the pain away," she answered tersely. "It can also stop bleeding." She looked up at him thoughtfully, her gaze so penetrating it made Digger uncomfortable. He escaped by walking back to the raft, turning it over to empty out all the water they'd taken on. He unclamped the dry container and pulled out a dry pair of tan shorts and another of his favorite T-shirts. It featured a big red poisonous Costa Rican tree frog sitting in a tiny raft, its long dangling legs with large suckers on the ends of its webbed feet, holding a paddle. "Have Fun Rafting in Costa Rica!" the caption read.

"Is that the only kind of shirt you wear?" Angélica smirked.

Digger ignored her question and slipped behind a tree to change. He made sure that he didn't touch any part of it.

"What happened to your leg?" she asked when he came out again.

Embarrassed, Digger described his first-ever meeting with a porcupine.

"Come here," Angélica ordered. Sheepishly, Digger walked toward her. She pinched her fingers around one of the quills and pulled it out. "See? Here, inside the quill, there is a spongy material that absorbs moisture. So as the quill becomes swollen it is very difficult to rip out.

But once the quill has been broken, it is much easier to remove. Without even knowing it, you have done the correct thing."

"Great! It's nice to know that I've done something right," he said sarcastically.

"We should stay here for the night," Angélica announced, ignoring his sarcasm.

"Why?" His experience of the place so far hadn't endeared him to it.

"We still have a ways to go and would never reach the final landing before dark. I hope that you did not have to be anywhere tomorrow?"

"No, not really," Digger answered, wincing in pain as Angélica pulled out the last quill. "But wasn't someone supposed to pick us up? Will they wait for us?" Digger lightly scratched his arms where the ants had bitten him.

"Do not worry. The right people will be there. By the way, you are a mess. Take the rest of these leaves and bend them like I did," she ordered. "Then rub them over your bites and wound. It will help take the scratch away."

Irritated, Digger obeyed.

Angélica reached into the dry container and pulled out a couple of ham sandwiches and Milky Way bars. She threw one of each to Digger. "You should be used to this. This is an American dinner, no? Sorry I do not have, what you call it, a Pepsi? But we do have this," she reached over and unscrewed a canteen filled with water.

Over the next few hours Digger lay exhausted as Angélica bombarded him with a myriad of questions. He skillfully dodged most of them. Just before the sun disappeared, spreading a soft layer of darkness over the rainforest, Angélica stood up and announced, "I will gather wood for a fire to keep the mosquitoes away. You can towel off the raft, so that we can sleep in it." She hurried off before he could disagree—or offer to help her.

Later, as the two of them sat near the fire, Digger watched quietly as a soft breeze blew the embers to an orange-yellowish glow.

"So why are you called Digger?" Angélica asked softly. Her earlier irritation with him seemed to have cooled considerably.

"It's a long story." He glanced up for an instant, then returned his gaze to the burning fire.

A few moments passed. Then Angélica said more gently, "I have time."

He realized she would not be put off. Finally he answered, "Some of it has to do with baseball." She gave him a curious look. "You've never heard of baseball?"

"Very little," she admitted.

Hoo-boy, he thought. He wasn't going to get away with a simple answer.

"Well, so tell me, what is baseball and what does your name have to do with it?"

He explained the game as briefly as possible and then added how sometimes you dig the cleats of your shoes into the dirt to get a better stance, in the batter box or when you're trying to steal a base.

"Well, where does the rest of the meaning of your name come from?"

She seemed genuinely interested, so he continued. "Well, I took many philosophy courses in college and have a tendency to be reflective and dig, so to speak, to get to the bottom of things. I want to understand the whys."

More silence. She's waiting for me to be polite and ask her a question, Digger thought. He knew she wanted him to ask her something, anything. But he refused to play along. That's how it's done. That's how useless conversations are born, from fear of silence and feelings of guilt that are only satisfied by reciprocating with a silly question.

He thought back to Key West, where he'd owned a floating houseboat restaurant—before it sank to the bottom of the ocean. One holiday season he'd been invited to a Cuban Christmas. Digger generally liked to spend his time—especially his holidays—quietly. But the man who had invited him was an excellent customer and Digger thought it would be a new experience.

It turned out to be a festive affair where the food and booze flowed freely. All the customer's relatives had come down from Miami and baked a pig in a closed pit. After Digger sampled what he believed to be a tamale, he'd gone over to compliment the hostess. Then he'd made the drastic mistake of being polite and inquiring about how she made the delicious concoction. Taking his arm firmly, she ushered him to a corner of the yard. He knew he was in trouble when the elderly lady looked him in the eyes and said, "Well, *señor*, first you kill d' pig." Forty-five minutes later she finally finished answering the question. Angélica could probably put this lady to shame if he gave her half a chance.

"Are you not going to ask me anything?" she finally urged.

"No."

"Why not?"

"Because if you haven't already noticed, I'm not much of a talker," Digger said.

"Why not?"

"Uhhh…" Digger responded.

"Well, let me help you. Ask me about my name."

"I believe the literal translation is 'angel,'" Digger said, fixing his gaze again on the burning fire.

"Yes, you are right, but it means so much more." Undaunted by his curt attitude, she persisted, "What do you do back in the United States?"

"I play the piano and compose music." Digger's tone betrayed a bit of exasperation.

"A piano?" she questioned, ignoring his signals.

"You've never heard a piano?" Digger was perplexed. She doesn't know what a piano is? Nevermind baseball! He played an invisible keyboard. She still looked confused.

Suddenly he had the feeling she was doing more than just making conversation. In one day, Angélica had talked more than Danny and Francisco put together during the previous five days. Who is this woman, he wondered, and why is she asking so many questions?

As if on cue Angélica stood up, gently rubbed her wrist, and said that she was tired. Stepping into the raft, she pulled on an oversized sweatshirt from the dry pack and settled in to sleep.

Digger stayed by the fire until he was sure she was sleeping. Then he doused the dying embers with handfuls of dirt and snuggled into the other side of the raft. A gentle breeze blew down the river, warming his skin and bringing with it the scent of an unknown orchid. Tossing his empty arms over his chest, he looked up into the night, just as he always did at his favorite perch back home—the end of the Mission Bay jetty in San Diego.

The darkened jungle blocked out the sky except for the area above the swift water. Slowly drifting clouds exposed a dazzling river of starlight, which triggered many responses within him. At night his thoughts somehow felt lighter, as if they rose into the heavens. It was a time of letting go and receiving. The stars were vaults of music, he once told Bendi. He was particularly attracted to one of the theories of light: that light was actually waves of energy. Somehow that soothed his pragmatic mind as an explanation of how he received the inspiration for his music. In some mystical way, he believed, he could hear those unheard notes and melodies arriving on waves of starlight.

Out of all the heavenly bodies the three bright stars of Orion's belt found his attention and directed his sight to the Seven Sisters, the Pleiades. That cluster of stars had always intrigued him. He remembered reading about them; that they were considered a "star nursery." A place where ancient stellar explosions, from near and far, deposited their star matter. Over vast amounts of time, the raw materials of the universe changed, recycled, developed, and eventually gathered. In the gathering, the interaction of the interstellar stellar gases formed the beginning of new stars. When he looked directly at them, he could only see three or four of the Sister stars before they disappeared, but when he turned his head slightly, he could see all seven of them twinkling.

That night he found more comfort than usual in viewing the small grouping of stars as they played hide-and-seek with his eyes. Surprising how at times the simple things can make such a difference, he thought. The Pleiades were always there, no matter where he was or what he was doing.

He thought back to his first music audition in L.A. He'd looked up through the roof of the limousine on the way home afterwards and had seen the intriguing star cluster. In that moment he'd known he had to call Bendi. That was the real beginning of their relationship. With her, he had opened up his heart—at least a little more. He liked that; he liked it very much. But he also knew now that she wanted more from him. She wanted him to feel toward her the way he felt toward his music. She also wanted marriage. He didn't know if any of her dreams were possible for him to fulfill.

Dreams, he mused. That meditation he'd experienced before his audition that night was like a dream. The only way he could describe the feeling was that it was a release, a feeling of freedom. Something had shifted within him, because when he played at that audition, the music flowed from him like never before. He got the job; no more being poor, no more being a waiter. That night Warner Brothers contracted him to compose the score of a new film and catapulted him into a new career. A career where he could actually live his passion: music.

"What are you smiling about?" Angélica asked quietly.

"Nothing." He was perturbed that his silence had been broken. He'd thought she was sleeping.

"Well, it is good that you smile. We will need it for tomorrow," she said, tucking part of her long black hair behind her ear.

"Do you think we'll have any problems getting down the river tomorrow?" he asked hesitantly.

"I don't think so. The river is quite wild but I believe we will arrive at our destination. So tell me, what is that smile? Are you thinking of a *novia*, a girlfriend?"

"Not really, I mean I was thinking of a time when I first fell in love with her but now… I don't really want to talk about it."

"*No entiendo*, Digger. For one who likes to dig, you do not care much to share your findings."

"I guess not," he chuckled. "I never really thought about it that way."

"Let me begin with something basic. How did you come to Costa Rica?"

"I flew," he grinned, knowing full well what she meant.

"No, I mean why did you come?" she persisted, ignoring his joke.

"Ahhh," he thought for a moment. "I came to be inspired. I had a kind of creative block with my music."

"No..." Angélica sat up and mimed playing the piano, exactly as Digger had done previously.

"*Sí*, no piano," he laughed. "*No hay música en mi cabeza.*" He pointed to his head. "Do you play guitar, or drums, or flute?" He mimicked each instrument as he spoke.

"No, I do not, but I do know of instruments and music. My tribe plays much music. It is a very noble calling, no? It is highly respected to be a 'Keeper of the Sound.'"

Digger was confused; she didn't act or talk like the other river guides. She mentioned a tribe she lived with. She didn't even know what a piano was. And then there was that "thing" that happened between them when she had fallen out of the raft and they looked into each other's eyes. He was hooked. He had to find out more.

"I assumed you lived in the capital, San José," he said tentatively.

"No, I usually live with my tribe," she answered warmly.

"Where is your tribe?"

"They live in the heart of the jungle."

"Is it far from here?"

"That is not an easy question to answer. It depends. For some, it is just around the bend of the river. But for those who do not know how to travel, which is many people, it is so far that they can never get there." Angélica's green eyes peered through the darkness and looked deeply into Digger's. He gazed back at her for a moment, then grew uncomfortable and changed the subject.

"Have you been a river guide for a long time?"

"I have taken many persons on trips," she replied. "As you said, one of the meanings of my name is 'angel.' But to me the more correct definition is 'traveler.'"

"Traveler. Traveler from where?"

"It is not so much 'from where' but rather 'between where.' You could be said to be a traveler because you are able to hear the unheard notes from the heavens and play them for the people of this world."

Did she know what I was thinking just a minute ago?

"Now, could you please tell me why you really came to Costa Rica." Angélica again looked deeply and softly into his eyes.

"I told you it was to get rid of a creative block." He stopped as each word scratched his throat before it vaporized into the night air. It was hard not to speak the truth when he looked into her gaze. There was something different about this woman. He had known that from the start, when he'd first seen her in the early morning haze. Her slightest glance seemed to seep deep within him, in a knowing sense. Slowly he took a deep breath and closed his eyes before speaking again.

"I just needed to get away," he whispered. "Nothing seemed to be working back there. Everything I did or said didn't turn out right. I just felt I needed a break." This time the words tickled more than they scratched. He opened his eyes again. "Why do you need to know?"

"Because it is important." Angélica's gaze hadn't left him. "To live to the fullest, you need to reflect on what thoughts, emotions, and actions of your life brought you to this moment. That reflection can unlock the mystery of the present. So what brought you here?" she probed again.

Digger wasn't sure what she was trying to get at, and even if he did know, he wasn't sure he wanted to go there.

In chorus, the sounds of the rainforest suddenly erupted around them as the wind changed direction. Dark, billowy clouds passed beneath the sliver of moon, casting a darker shadow on the jungle below.

"I brought myself here," he decided to say.

"*Sí*, that is true, but you know what I mean, *señor* Jonathan," Angélica said firmly.

"You mean what kinds of things happened to me before I ended up here?"

She nodded.

"Well," he began reluctantly, "things in my life were going fairly well. My music was selling and the money seemed to be rolling in. I bought a great home on the ocean and Bendi, my girlfriend, spends most of her time with me there. We were getting along pretty well—that is until about six months ago, when my mother was diagnosed with cancer."

Angélica squenched her face a little.

"Breast and lung cancer. She was a heavy smoker." He mimed smoking. Angélica nodded slightly. "She was a difficult woman to be close to, nevermind to have as my mother." The emaciated face of his mother flashed through his mind. She had been beautiful even into her seventies, but when the cancer took hold, it quickly deteriorated her body. "That's when trouble between Bendi and me started. She said I had changed, and that I was hard to talk to. I wasn't"—his voice scratched slightly as he saw Angélica looking back at him—"that hard to talk to. Besides, I had a lot going on in my life. I also felt pressure from Bendi about getting married; it wasn't the time to be dealing with that issue. Then, a week ago, my mom died. After the funeral, Bendi started cleaning my house and throwing away a few things. I know it was silly but I didn't want her to do that. I wanted to keep some of those things from my past. Well, we got into a heavy argument. I told her I needed to get away and that I'd talk with her when I got back. I didn't even tell her where I was going. So if that was what you meant about 'bringing me here,' that's it. I need to get some sleep now." Digger turned around and nestled into the side of the raft. Tucking a towel around a damp life preserver, he laid his head on the makeshift pillow. Angélica's voice cut through his pretended slumber.

"You can't go to sleep yet."

He turned over to see her climbing out of the raft and grabbing a rope they'd left near the fire.

"What are you talking about?" Digger was perturbed.

She stood scanning the river's shore intently. Above them, the rainforest canopy began to sway. Then a gust of cooler wind swept down the river valley. Digger shivered.

"We will need some protection."

Angélica quickly tied the rope to two O-rings at the bow of the raft. The wind, filled with moisture, began to blow hard as the two of them dragged the raft to a nearby tree.

"Take out the containers and life preservers and put them on that boulder," Angélica ordered.

Digger quickly did as he was told. At Angélica's signal, they flipped the raft over and she lashed the bow to a low-lying tree limb hanging over the large, flat boulder. A flash of lightening crackled above, followed by a clap of thunder that shook the ground. Just as they crawled underneath the raft, huge drops of rain pelted down.

Hunched over under the musty raft, they spread out their dry clothes on the cool rock and tried to get as comfortable as possible. Digger didn't want to engage in any more conversation, so in silence he curled up again. He could hardly see, but he could feel the attention of Angélica's eyes. She was clearer about his past than he cared for her to be.

It was difficult for him to sleep with all the internal and external noise. He also felt a little claustrophobic, with the mildewy rubber just inches away from his body, nevermind the hard rock underneath him. He felt a spray of water as wind blew into the makeshift shelter. As he listened to the rain beating down on the flimsy raft, the realization of his predicament soaked into his mind and body. Fear and a little panic overtook him.

He'd felt secure with the other river guides and rafters as they'd camped out every night along the river's shore. But now, even with Angélica next to him, he felt alone. Alone with the sounds of a jungle that never slept. The various sounds that meant to whoever could understand: Here I am, where are you? This is my territory, let's mate, come here, go away, I see you, beware…

It was amazing how a big part of him loved to succumb to the unseen. His mind would conjure up real and imaginary monsters, like when he was a kid. The dark shadows of a closet were a hiding place for many forms of creatures. But those monsters never really went away, even when he got older—they just changed hiding places. Yep, that part of his mind loved to mess with him. It tested him over and over again, and just when he thought he had it under control, it would reappear—magically transformed. There he would be again, a frightened little boy, clutching his stuffed "Elphie." His tormenting mind would then step slowly up behind his child's consciousness and whisper, "Gotcha! Again!"

A rustling of bushes startled Digger. He lifted the side of the raft and peeked out. All he saw were shadows. A soft snore echoed under the raft. How could she sleep? he wondered.

His thoughts kept racing as he lay back down on the cool boulder. The death of his mom and the damaged relationship with Bendi were things that would take time to heal, but his present situation had to be dealt with once the morning came. Here he was, in the middle of the most remote jungle in Central America. Tomorrow he would be rafting the most difficult part of the Río Pacuare. Even though Angélica didn't seem worried, he was still concerned. How were they going to manage the Class Five rapids? They didn't even have helmets. How could she have forgotten them? Could they make it through without injury? Heck, he thought, injury was just another thing that time could heal; what about making it through the rapids alive?

Death was something that was hard to rebound from, he joked to himself. Death was something that you spent your whole life running from and you weren't even encouraged to talk about it. You always tried to escape the faceless, sickled, black-robed figure. Death was always in the shadows and didn't care whom it took, the old or the young, the rich or the poor, the river guide or the composer...

"Aaaarrroooo-ooo-ooo-gahhh..." The deep, gravely bass notes of a howler monkey echoed in the distance. The mixture of its low, guttural sound and the gurgling of the river reminded Digger of his mother's gasping for air. The river had nearly claimed Angélica's life, he thought, as the male howler monkey sounded its call twice more. Doesn't death come in three's? He hoped that he and Angélica wouldn't fill up the quota the following day.

Each drop of rain seemed to stretch time as the night wore on. Time had a way of becoming distorted, slowing down during certain circumstances in your life: when you were away from a loved one, when you were going through some painful tragedy, when you slept in nature—Digger chuckled to himself—when you were sleeping next to some woman from the jungle with a stare that could melt stone... For Digger, this seemed like the longest night of his life.

Not far from Digger's restless musings, a dark figure moved stealthily through the jungle. Its nose twitched as it contacted the pungent smell of humans. Long whiskers brushed against branches as it moved, practically invisible, through the drenched foliage. With a confident stride, it slipped between two saplings and sat on its haunches. Rain dripped off its oily coat as it gazed with hypnotic yellow eyes at the river's edge.

Chapter 4

"He was losing consciousness, he thought, and that would be his death."

The busy chatter of the early morning jungle woke Digger under the darkness of the raft. He stretched his long, lean body along the coolness of the rock. Angélica was already gone, he noticed. Then he screamed. Something big and scaly had brushed against his leg.

He bolted out from beneath the raft and bumped into Angélica, who'd been stretching just outside.

"There's something big with scales and..." Digger pointed toward the raft "... and a long tail."

A ctenosaur the size of a large dog waddled out from beneath the home-made shelter. With scaly skin banded with stripes of blue-gray and black, and a huge, spiny, crested head with slurping tongue flicking out of its immense mouth, it looked like something that had escaped from Jurassic Park. The mini-dinosaur slowly slithered back into the jungle.

Angélica laughed. "So, did you enjoy sleeping with your new roommate?"

"What the hell was that?" Digger's voice shook. "I've never seen anything like it!"

"Just a big lizard," she answered gleefully. "Are you ready for what the day brings?"

His heart was still pounding from his encounter. "Yeah, sure. I'm ready to challenge the river," he lied.

"I would like to think of it as *dancing* with the river. The river is not anything to overcome. The river is more of something to move with. Is that not true for everything in life?" She turned and looked at him.

"It's just my competitive nature to look at things that way," he shrugged.

"With your sound, your music, do you compete or dance?"

Digger just smiled back at her.

The air was thick with humidity as the previous night's rain evaporated off the rainforest vegetation. They untied the raft from the tree and turned it over. Angélica opened up one of the dry containers.

"We only have two Milky Ways and apples left," she announced, handing Digger his share. After they finished eating Angélica asked, "So are you ready?"

"Do I have a choice?" he smiled back.

"There is always a choice, Jonathan Taylor," she answered seriously. "As unpleasant as many consequences seem to be, there is always a choice. You just make many of them unconsciously, and then you wonder how you got where you are."

Oh, this is going to be a fun trip, Digger thought as he helped her push the stern of the raft into the river. They pulled themselves in and then allowed the current to move them gently along.

"Okay, let's dance!" Digger raised his paddle eagerly.

Angélica just glanced at him from beneath raised eyebrows as she dipped her own paddle into the water.

He could hear the distant, low rumbling of rapids. As they rounded a bend in the river, he saw the white foam bubbling up ahead of them. His muscles tensed as they prepared for the first test of the day.

The raft moved sideways. "Back left!" Angélica yelled.

They bounced off one boulder and just missed another.

"Forward!" she yelled as they entered a series of rapids.

The bow of the raft bounced high and then slammed down into another rapid, bringing a shower of water upon them. Digger spit out a mouthful. They bounced through the set of rapids and back to flat water again.

Not so tough, Digger thought.

"I can dance!" he yelled, bobbing his head and mimicking a rapper. He knew these rapids were easy compared to what they'd gone through yesterday. But no mishaps this time. That was good.

Several morpho butterflies flitted by, showing off their huge, electric-blue wings. Digger and Angélica stopped paddling for a moment to watch as the beautiful creatures entertained them with haphazard flight patterns. One circled around Digger's head, but before it could rejoin the others, a small brown-and-white bird flew from a nearby tree and snatched the brilliant creature, then flew off, pinching the iridescent wings between its beak. The others darted down the river, a host of flapping blue, unaware or unconcerned about their fellow's fate. Digger watched as they flew between two canyon walls.

A barely detectable smile came over Angélica's face as they approached an earthquake-spawned dam blocking the entrance to Dos Montañas Pass. It faded as soon as she noticed the remains of a fallen eucalyptus tree among the tightly-packed boulders. Several branches poked dangerously towards them.

"Paddle! Hard back left!" she yelled as the treacherous currents slammed the raft against the freshly-fallen boulders blocking the pass's entrance. They paddled hard but the current was too strong; it shoved them into the new dam.

"Watch out!" she hollered as several branches jabbed them and the raft. One branch dug deep into the inflated side. They pushed their paddles against the dam and leaned. "Push hard! We do not want to sink here!" They threw their weight into it, moving the raft slightly.

"Now back left!" Angélica's voice echoed off of the canyon walls.

As the tumultuous waters rushed in and around the scattered boulders, they spun the raft several times in a huge eddy. Digger felt as if the river couldn't make up its mind. First it wanted them to continue straight through the dam, then the swift current shoved them to the left. The raft dipped violently as the river thrust them into the ancient waterway, now filled with raging waters seeking a way around the dam. They were thrown about helplessly and their extra paddle flew into the river.

"Don't worry about it now," Angélica shouted. "Keep paddling."

They plunged through another set of rapids before the river became very quiet. They looked around for the lost paddle but it had vanished.

The river was narrower here, only ten to thirty yards wide. Heavy vegetation grew on either side. Digger noticed that the "shores" consisted of submerged bushes and half-drowned trees, as if it had been recently flooded.

"This doesn't look like the rest of the river," he said quietly.

Angélica motioned upwards. "The heavens."

He thought of the previous night's rain and shrugged his shoulders. They paddled on in silence.

For the next few miles they hadn't encountered any rapids. He was relieved, but anxious. This was supposed to be the toughest part of the river, yet there had been no rapids since Dos Montañas Pass.

They paddled slowly through the flat waters. At times the encroaching rainforest created a canopy over the calm river. He watched nervously as a red-, yellow-, and black-banded coral snake slithered along the surface of the river and made its way to shore. Along the shoreline, different varieties of birds flitted among the trees. The mimicking song of a mockingbird echoed through the dense jungle. As they rounded a bend, Digger spotted several large bird nests hanging thirty feet above the ground. They were suspended from thinly-woven, ten foot strands attached to the tallest trees. From this precarious "swing" hung a three-foot-long nest with one small opening.

"I've never seen anything like that," he remarked.

Angélica looked up. "The male bird is the one who builds it, while the female sits in some nearby tree and watches."

"I imagine it would take a good bit of time to build a nest like that."

"When the male is through with his work, the female inspects the new home. If she doesn't like it, she cuts the strand with her beak. The male bird then starts all over again," she smiled.

"Well, I see that some things haven't changed through evolution of the species," he chuckled.

Angélica glared at Digger momentarily, clearly unamused, before she continued her paddling.

The time passed slowly, and Digger could feel them going deeper into the rainforest. We should have seen some roads by now, he thought. And a real shore line. He calculated that they'd traveled about three hours yesterday before they put ashore. And today they'd been traveling for—instinctively he looked at his wrist—no watch. He remembered he'd packed it in his sports bag.

"Angélica, are we almost to the take-out point? Shouldn't we have been there by now?"

"Just relax and enjoy the scenery."

That should have been easy, but he had this feeling. (Oh, no, not a "feeling!" Watch out, world, Digger has a feeling!) Of course, he didn't say any of this out loud. But he couldn't shake it. First of all, Angélica had been very quiet all day, the total opposite of yesterday. Secondly, this part of the river just plain felt different. Not bad, just different. Thirdly, the end of the river run was supposed to be the most dangerous and this water was as smooth as ice. Fourthly, —

Several drops splattered on his head and back. He looked up into sky and saw darkened heavy clouds. A clap of thunder reverberated down the ancient waterway—

Fourthly, they should have been at the end of the trip by now or at least seen a road.

"Back left," Angélica muttered, as she paddled forward on the right. The raft turned slightly sideways as they attempted to move around a recently-fallen, centuries-old ceiba tree.

"Forward left. Be mindful. We do not want to puncture the raft with any hidden branches."

They maneuvered carefully around the light gray barked tree which still had termite nests, bromeliads, and orchids attached to its branches. Suddenly Angélica whispered loudly, "Stop!"

The jungle was deathly silent. The only sound came from leaves falling on the debris of the rainforest floor. Small whitecaps instantly covered the length of the river. A rumbling began from behind them. The rainforest started to shake off its unwanted foliage as another major after-shock rippled through it.

Out of sight, several miles behind them, another piece of granite loosened and fell into Dos Montañas Pass, splitting open the biggest boulder blocking the entrance. At the same time, the land beneath the ancient bypass Digger and Angélica had taken now jutted up several feet, cutting off this alternate route. The Río Pacuare, swelling like a pregnant woman, made one final push to break through the pass again. Finally, the raging water tumbled the damming debris—trees, bushes, and boulders—through the steep canyon walls, returning the river to its previous path. Digger and Angélica were now completely cut off as the ancient riverway disappeared once again beneath the jungle foliage.

Huge drops of rain pelted down upon the isolated rafters as black clouds opened up and cleansed everything that lay below. The uplifted fault line that had forced the Río Pacuare back to its previous course had also catapulted tons of water into a wave. Now a five-foot wall of water was headed down the old riverbed towards Digger and Angélica.

A shiver surged up Digger's back. Turning around he wiped wet, sandy-colored hair from his eyes and absently stared upstream.

"*Attencion!*" Angélica yelled.

Digger turned back around. Up ahead, at the base of a rocky bluff, boulders and sharp pieces of rock stuck out of the river in front of an exposed, fifteen-foot-wide cavern. The river was slamming into the semi-circular cavern, washing over a large, partially exposed boulder. Water then gushed out to the right and churned over debris and rocks.

"Remember, keep paddling!" Angélica shouted over the roar.

White foam bubbled everywhere as the river swept over the rocks. They tried to steer but the raft turned every which way. All their efforts proved futile. Meanwhile, the rain continued to beat down on their faces, making it impossible to see.

"Paddle! Paddle!" Angélica screamed as she spit water from her lips.

Suddenly a low-lying boulder grabbed the raft's underside and dragged it to a halt. The force threw Angélica into the churning water. Now, with less weight, the raft broke free from the rock and headed downstream. Digger dove to the bow. He reached for Angélica's outstretched hand. But the current split in two directions outside the cavern, sending Angélica downstream to the right and Digger hurtling into the cavern. The raft was caught in a huge, bubbling eddy, bouncing off walls and spinning around. He tried to push off with his paddle. He had to get out of this dizzying "tea cup" ride! But the raft threw him against another wall, an exposed shard slicing his left arm. He grabbed the bleeding wound instinctively and the paddle fell into the funneling water. This threw him off balance, and nearly out of the raft, but he landed on the inflatable's side.

The mind is a strange instrument, Digger thought. In the midst of this life-threatening predicament, his attention suddenly went to an oddly shaped stone in the cavern with him. Only about a foot was exposed, but it was perfectly rounded. Time slowed as he looked at this out-of-place rock.

But what about Angélica? his thoughts snapped back. He tried to peer outside the cavern. All he could see was boiling water and pouring rain. "Angélica!" he shouted, but his voice was lost in the roar of water beating against the cavern walls. Then the horizon disappeared. A wall of water was headed straight towards him.

Digger ducked as the wave completely filled the cavern, slamming the raft into the back wall. As quickly as the wave hit, it gushed back out to continue its ravaging coarse down the waterway.

Digger managed to cling to the raft as the immense Jacuzzi bounced him around the cavern like a little toy. He coughed up some water, then a surge sent him flying up and his forehead hit an overhanging rock. That knocked him on his side as the river decided it had had enough fun with its passenger and shot the raft out of the cavern. As it plunged and spun down the river, Digger lay gasping for breath at the bottom of the raft. He felt a five-foot drop, then the raft's side landed hard, throwing him out into the white cauldron of foam. The force of the current drove his body to the bottom of the river.

He had no idea which way was up or down; it was like being in a washing machine. Finally he was able to fight his way toward the surface. Hoping to breathe soon, he felt instead the impact of a solid object hitting the top of his head.

He'd come up under the raft. Now, desperately, he struggled to get out from underneath it. Every direction failed. He was racing downstream, pinned between the bottom of the raft and the bottom of the river. His legs bounced along the riverbed. Then his shoulder hit a rock. It was at that point his lungs ran out of air. Panic pulsed through his body. Craving for oxygen, his lungs burned inside his chest.

The raft began to roll over him, digging him further into the rock-studded riverbed. Finally, his lungs couldn't hold out any longer. In one quick suction, they expanded.

At that instant, the raft completed its roll over Digger's body and he quickly popped to the surface. He coughed and inhaled in great gasps, water out, air in—water out, air in. The raft spun away as the river dragged Digger back to the deeper part. Still dazed, he somehow remembered to turn his body and position his feet downriver as he bounced through the rapids, gasping and coughing.

The boulder he hit was perfectly round—and it knocked out what little breath he'd managed to capture. He reached instinctively to grab hold of it. Near the top his fingertips found a gouge and dug in. With every ounce of energy he could muster, he held on. Miraculously.

The drenching rain washed clean the thin streams of blood flowing down his face and arm. Time stopped as his fingers clung to the stone ball. Had it been hours? Or moments? He couldn't hold on forever, he knew that. But he was afraid to let go and let the river take him.

"Angélica!" he yelled weakly. He looked from side to side, hoping to see her safely on the shoreline. But all he heard was her voice ringing in his head, "There is always a choice."

After a while the strange-looking stone felt wonderful under his body. He realized that this boulder was similar to the one in the cavern. A soft, warm, tingling sensation began in his fingers. Then in his chest. Soon the granite ball seemed easier for him to grip, as if there were more rock beneath him. The river can't be receding, he thought. But then he switched his mind-set to believe that the river was indeed receding. He was choosing to believe that. It was hope. It was all he had besides that round rock.

The rain splattered incessantly as Digger kept his grip. Images and thoughts flashed through his mind's eye: He saw himself as a little boy running for a fly ball. He felt the music pour through his fingers as he played at a concert. He heard the fumbled notes of his new composition while Bendi's legs were wrapped around him. He watched his mother's frail body on the edge of death, still refusing to let go. In a strange way, none of that meant anything. There was something more. Something just beyond his grasp.

The clouds continued to dump their life-giving sustenance upon his body. The longer he lay on that boulder, the more he felt in some strange way a kinship with it. It appeared to be only a rock but yet it was so much more. He was tired. Digger took a couple of deep breaths as his body became lighter. At first he felt as if he were melting into the stone but then he had the sensation of falling into darkness. I'm losing consciousness, he thought, and that will be my death. He took one more breath and let go.

Chapter 5

"… she just somehow knew things."

Bendi bolted straight up from her couch. She took a breath and ran fingers through her long, brown hair, her much-needed nap abruptly disturbed. Rubbing her eyes, she still saw the distressing images of the nightmare, a dark variation on a long-forgotten but pleasurable childhood dream, where she was a little girl playing with floating, luminescent bubbles as they disappeared into a richly-painted jungle. But this time, strewn along a hiking trail, the bubbles had turned into colored balls which varied in size from baseballs to huge beach balls. Beside one of the smaller balls lay the body of a man, face down, blood on his head and arm. She didn't know if he was alive.

The dream both disturbed and annoyed Bendi. This was the first nap she'd been able to take in months. She'd been grading papers till all hours of the night, and lately she hadn't been getting much sleep worrying about her relationship with Digger.

After his mother's funeral a week ago, they'd had a fight. She'd been trying to help out by cleaning his house, throwing away a few things he didn't need anymore. Digger had gotten angry, told her he was going to get away from it all and that he'd see her when he got back. She told him he wasn't angry about her cleaning the house, he was just upset about his mother's death. The fight continued from there.

She'd met Digger several years ago, when she was still going to school part-time and waitressing the graveyard shift in Ocean Beach. Digger would come by late at night, after working on his music, and they'd talk. Early on, she discovered that he was charming, handsome, and talented, but somewhat aloof. After a few dates, though, she realized that he had a difficult time expressing his feelings. Whenever things got tough for him, he clammed up.

But when he made that first breakthrough with his music—his first successful audition in L.A.—he changed. He became more open about his thoughts and feelings, and he walked with an air of confidence. It seemed they might have a chance together. But their romance turned out to be sporadic.

Digger had moved to L.A. for his new job, composing and arranging music for a Warner Bros. soundtrack. And she'd gone back to school full time to finish her teaching degree. They took turns driving to visit each other. In the beginning, it worked. Then the trips between L.A. and San Diego became less frequent. Digger was putting in extra hours on weekends to meet deadlines, or she was busy studying for an exam. Engrossed with their careers, they had little time for each other.

But they didn't date others. They still got together on some weekends, or special occasions—school functions or film openings or parties. This went on for a year and a half.

Whenever they were together, things were great. But she wanted more from their relationship, more from Digger. Once she brought up the idea of living together, but she could feel his hesitation. She'd even told him she'd transfer to U.C.L.A. But his answer was always the same: "Things are going great the way they are."

After she graduated, she told Digger she needed an extra degree to get a better-paying teaching job, an ESL degree—English as a Second Language—from San Francisco State. She'd be moving *north*. (It was true, but she knew it was an excuse to make a break from Digger for her mental and emotional health—and maybe to get his attention.)

He never tried to stop her. She was gone for two years.

During that time, Digger's career skyrocketed. He recorded several CDs after a couple of songs from his film scores hit the charts and occasionally arranged songs for popular vocal artists.

Then one day, out of the blue, Digger had phoned and asked her if she'd like to go to Mexico with him, to the Club Med in Cancun—"just as friends." At first she hesitated. What should she say? It would be too easy for her to start caring deeply again. She didn't want to open up the old wounds. But on the other hand, he did say "just friends." She quickly convinced herself that it would be a great getaway. Besides, she'd just finished her last semester and was ready to celebrate. So she went, just as a friend.

During the trip they visited the newly discovered Mayan ruins in Cobá. Standing on top of the tallest pyramid in the Yucatan, she stood watching a flock of birds glide over the rainforest canopy. Digger surprised her from behind and took her into his arms. She remembered goosebumps covering her body as his breath warmed her ear and his heart beat gently into her bare back. She felt the embrace of his firm body as his crossed arms tenderly squeezed her breasts and his long fingers lightly touched her belly. Time froze, as together they watched the orange sun slip slowly into the emerald-rich jungle. That was when she fell in love with him all over again.

When they returned to California, she found a teaching position in San Diego's Pacific Beach area. She moved into a cute apartment on Sapphire Street, but spent most of her time at Digger's beautiful new oceanview home in nearby Cardiff-by-the-Sea...

The low, throaty voice of radio DJ Art Good abruptly brought Bendi back to the present. He was introducing a song, "Here's a beautiful piece by one of our local talents, Jonathan Taylor." Soft violins and piano swept into one of Digger's compositions. Bendi began to cry softly.

Since his mother's illness, she'd watched Digger totally withdraw from his music, from her, and from everything in his life. In a way, their fight over her housecleaning was probably good: at least by yelling Digger expressed some of his feelings! But going away to sulk, or whatever he was going to do, wouldn't solve anything.

Intuitively, Bendi knew his reactions were more than a response to a parent dying. Digger had a fairly open mind, except when it came to dealing with his mother. His demeanor would change, but he'd never admit it; Bendi, though, could see it clearly. Every time they visited his mother, she'd watched Digger's shoulders drop and his posture stoop ever so slightly. His voice got higher, and his face took on a boyish look. It was all too clear—but not to him.

Now she knew Digger was in trouble. The dream-image of the brightly-colored balls and the man's body came vividly back to her; she knew it was more than a dream. When she was a little girl, she just somehow knew things. But her parents and friends had made fun of her, so after a while she stopped telling anyone her dreams and insights. After a while, she started to believe that there was nothing to them. After a while those dreams and insights stopped. Until today. She shuddered.

She reached over and turned the radio off. Picking up the phone, as she'd done so many times that week, she dialed Digger's number. Again, no answer. Just his voice mail. Where could he be? It's been almost a week. Wherever he went, he should have been back by now. Or at least called.

She fumbled through her purse and found her keys to his house. Hurrying down the steps of her apartment, she got into her Honda Civic. Bendi didn't know what she was going to do when she got to Digger's place, but she felt she had to do something, anything. As she turned onto Highway 5 heading north, the images from the dream returned: the bubbles, the colored balls, the limp body. Pressing down on the accelerator, she sped to Cardiff-by-the-Sea.

Pulling into Digger's driveway, she parked behind his Nissan Maxima. She fumbled for her keys and unlocked the door, hoping to hear a familiar sound. All that greeted her was the sight of a week's worth of mail under the slot. She looked around the house—for what, she didn't know. Absentmindedly, she opened the refrigerator and looked inside: a half gallon of souring milk, margarine, mineral water, a six pack of beer, lettuce, and onions.

As she walked by the white oak baby-grand piano, she played a couple of notes, just like Digger. He always said, "Walking by a piano is like trying to pass a candy jar. I always need to have a little taste." Heading up the stairs, she went into the master bedroom, where she opened up the drapes. Digger hated having the drapes closed at any time. He always wanted to look out at the sea. The room was a little stuffy, so she cranked the windows open. Immediately, the sound of the surf and the smell of salt air filled the room and reminded her of the Yucatan.

Bendi took a deep breath. She'd always hoped someday that she'd be a permanent resident in this beautiful home. She wasn't naive; Bendi knew the challenges this complex man brought to a relationship, but she still wanted to spend her life with him. She always envisioned him as a white gardenia that had just begun to bloom. She'd almost lost him once and wasn't going through that again. She took another deep breath.

Walking into his study, she found his desk drawers halfway opened, papers and pamphlets strewn around the desk. She thought first that maybe somebody had broken into the house, searching for valuables. She glanced around to see if anything was disturbed or missing. Nothing seemed to be. Sitting down at his desk, she gathered and stacked the loose materials absently. Then she noticed that all the information seemed to be about Costa Rica.

Digger kept a file of places he wanted to go, so she went to his file cabinet and looked under V for Vacations. All the other countries and cities were still there; only Costa Rica was missing. She went back to the clutter and started to rummage through it, hoping for another clue. Costa Rica is a small country, but it's still a big place if you don't know where someone is. Maybe an airline reservation? Or better yet, a hotel phone number? No luck.

On an impulse, she picked up the phone and dialed Digger's brother Jeff, explaining the whole situation to him. He was surprised to hear about the fight between the two of them, but not about Digger's lack of communication. "That's the ol' Digger, keeping everything inside," Jeff said. But he didn't have a clue where his brother had gone. He asked her to keep in touch, let him know if she found out anything

As Bendi hung up, a thought struck her. She went back to the vacation file. Sure enough—Digger's passport was nowhere to be found.

Okay, she thought. He's definitely in Costa Rica. But I know the airlines won't give out passenger names. A red pamphlet on the desk caught her eye: "Whitewater Rafting with Wild River Excursions."

Digger loved anything to do with the water, she knew. Any time he felt down, he'd swim, dive, sail, or raft. It was the main reason he'd bought this house—even though at the time it was a little out of his price range. When he was around water, he felt better about himself and his music, he'd told her.

She dialed the number on the brochure. It turned out to be a Miami number and they knew nothing about a Jonathan Taylor calling for reservations. They gave her the number of the main office in San José, Costa Rica. She called the long-distance operator and was put through.

"*Hola! Este es el Excursion de Ríos Salvajes. Cómo le puedo ayudar?*" a woman answered.

Bendi, who'd learned to speak fluent Spanish for her ESL degree, informed the woman of the situation, hoping for a positive response. The woman asked Bendi to repeat the name.

"Jonathan Taylor; he is an American. He might have signed up for one of your trips a few days ago."

Bendi heard muffled voices as the woman put her hand over the phone and repeated Digger's name to someone else. Then a male voice came on the line. "Hello, how can I help you?" the man asked in broken English.

Again, Bendi told her story. The man, like the woman, asked her to repeat the name of the person she was looking for. Exasperated, Bendi tried to remain calm as she said, "Jonathan Taylor; sometimes he goes by the name of Digger."

Again she heard a muffled conversation, and again someone new came on the phone.

"Hello, Miss Porcelli, I am Manuel," the man said cordially in English. "Yes, a Jonathan Taylor did sign up for one of our five-day trips."

"Great!" Bendi exhaled with relief. "Can you please tell me if you know what hotel he is staying at? I urgently need to reach him."

"I am sorry, Miss. There is a little problem that we are having," Manuel apologized.

"What do you mean, a little problem?" Bendi sat up in her seat.

"He has not returned yet."

"When was he supposed to return?"

"*Ayer.*"

"Yesterday? Well, where is he?" Bendi fidgeted in the chair.

"I do not know if you heard the news in the United States?" Manuel asked.

"I haven't heard anything in the last couple of days."

"We had a major earthquake two days ago," he explained calmly. "There was little damage here in San José, but it did cause some landslides. The highway we would travel to pick up your friend and the other rafters has been blocked. The rafters have hiked to the nearest village. I hope that we will be able to get through tomorrow."

"Why don't you take another route?" Bendi asked.

"Miss Porcelli, Costa Rica has very few roads and only two that go east." Manuel added carefully, "I do not want to alarm you, but I need to ask you something. Is Mister Taylor... impulsive?"

Bendi was confused. Why was this man being so evasive and asking strange questions? "*Por favor*, just tell me what has happened!"

"We have had much rain. This made the river very difficult, so the guides canceled the last day of the trip. But when the guides awoke the next morning, they found that Mr. Taylor had taken one of the rafts—by himself. That was *muy loco* for him to do, Miss Porcelli. Because of the landslide, we have not been able to pick him up at the take-out point."

"You mean none of the rafting guides have gone to look for him?" Her voice quivered.

Manuel responded authoritatively, "As I have said, they have hiked with the other rafters to the nearest village. Their responsibility is for the safety of those rafters."

"What about the safety of Jonathan, of Digger? Where is he?" Bendi insisted, trying not to become hysterical.

"Please, Miss Porcelli, as soon as I can get through I will go down there myself and look for him. Do not worry. Give me your phone number and I will call you the minute I hear anything."

She gave Manuel both her own and Digger's phone numbers and then hung up. Her stomach felt as if someone had just given it a hard kick. As she paced around Digger's house, her thoughts whirled and catastrophized about all the terrible things that could have happened to Digger. The dream-image of the lifeless body burned into her mind.

When her thoughts came back to the present moment, she discovered she was sitting on Digger's piano bench. Despite her alarm, that made her smile. It reminded her of when she was a little girl. Because her dad spent much of his time at work he'd given her a puppy—to keep her company. Her mother had told her that when she went away to school, the puppy would snuggle next to Bendi's favorite sweatshirt. Now she stared at the piano, realizing this was the closest she could get to Digger, at least for the present.

Digger was fairly private about his life, especially his music. When she was around, it was rare for him to play a composition he was working on. His music never seemed good enough for him. He always wanted it to be perfect before it was presented to the world, to anyone, to her.

She had to admit she was a little jealous about Digger's special relationship with his music. But he told her it was when he played his music that he truly expressed himself to the outside world. How could she deny him that?

But as reserved as Digger was, when he made love to her, he played her like his stringed instrument—with feeling, emotion, and passion.

One night, after a passionate episode of love-making, Digger said to her, "This one's for you," and then told her to stay in the bedroom while he went downstairs. She heard the haunting, sweet melody of his new composition drift up the staircase and into the bedroom. Wrapping a satin bed sheet around herself, she tiptoed quietly down the stairs. Softly, she pulled up a chair directly behind Digger and let the bedsheet fall to the parquet floor, exposing her naked body. Sitting down, she wrapped her bare legs around his waist and her arms around his chest. When he missed a few notes, she noticed that he tried to regain his composure. Feeling him take a deep breath, she turned her head to the side and pressed her cheek against his cool, moist back.

Bendi wanted to be inside him. She wanted to feel what he felt when he played his music. The music swirled around the walls and then she felt the vibration of the notes resonate through Digger's body onto her hands, face, breast, and stomach.

Digger missed several more notes. Abruptly, he stopped playing. "I thought I asked you to stay in the bedroom!" he barked, leaping up and glaring at her. Then he stormed back upstairs.

She just sat there on the bench, dumfounded. What had just happened? She couldn't believe her ears. Why was he acting that way? Just because he missed a few notes?

Now, slowly brushing the piano bench with her hand, she took a deep breath. Since that night it had been tough going for the two of them; the next morning Digger had gotten the news about his mother's cancer.

Well. She couldn't just sit here. She went back into the office and called the airlines. The next flight to San José was a red-eye that left L.A. at midnight and landed in Costa Rica at 7 a.m. She would have to take a commuter plane from San Diego to L.A. at 10 p.m. in order to catch it. She quickly gathered up the brochures from Digger's desk and locked up the house.

When she got home, she called Digger's brother and told him her plans. He sounded relieved that she was going in person to find his brother. As she packed and made arrangements to get to the airport on time, visions of her dream kept haunting her thoughts. The little girl, the bubbles, the colored balls, the man's bleeding body...

Chapter 6

"Pura vida —the good life"

Bubbles floated into a cavern and transmuted into painted balls that were splashed with cobalt blues, shimmering greens, and iridescent pinks. In amazement Bendi watched as they turned into stone. The ground shook and rolled the stone objects out of the cavern and onto the deserted hiking trail. Next to one of the smaller balls lay a man with an infected redness around wounds to his head and arm. No movement came from the body.

She jumped back when a huge black cat mysteriously appeared amongst the stone balls. The animal twitched its nose and slowly scanned the area. Bendi realized that she was somehow invisible to the monstrous cat. Strolling in and around the strange objects, its graceful tail switched back and forth, lightly touching each ball. Then the feline leaped on top of the biggest stone ball, gazing lazily at the surroundings.

Bendi couldn't move. All she could do was just stand and watch.

The big cat looked first in her direction, then stared back intently at the still figure on the ground. It jumped down lightly and then, as if the balls were made of air, batted the heavy stone objects with its huge paws. A constant low rumble reverberated in the distance and the ground shook as a seven-foot, luminescent green ball rolled directly towards Bendi. Frozen, unable to move, she let out a silent scream. The ground lifted up. As the orb was about to roll over her, the ground slammed back down...

Bendi's eyes popped open as her body jostled in her seat; the only sound was the low hum of the airplane. Her heart still pumped forcefully as she took a deep breath. Seeing those large colored balls or spheres within her mind, scared but also fascinated her. They were heavy yet light. And what did they have to do with the cat or the injured man? Stretching her legs, she reviewed the last twelve hours of her life. Her first dream had given her the confidence to arrange this trip, but now that she was actually on a plane, that certainty had definitely waned. Digger was probably fine, and even excited about doing something really stupid—like rafting alone down the river. He'd probably already found his way back to the village, where the river guides had taken the other rafters. She pictured him drinking a *cerveza* as she showed up. He'd be upset with her, thinking she was trying to rescue him.

The old childhood feelings of embarrassment, shame, and stupidity overcame her. When she was a little girl, Bendi's family and friends had teased her about her premonitions and dreams. Her father, whom she had wanted more than anyone else to believe her, had ridiculed her unmercifully for having an overactive imagination.

She looked at her watch. 4:40. One stop and several more hours to go before she arrived in San José. She looked through the small window into the black night where several stars were visible. Was Digger looking up at the same stars? she wondered. Maybe he really did need her. She closed her eyes again and tried to make sense of her foreboding dreams.

A couple hours later, the plane made its way through the central mountains of Costa Rica and dropped steeply into the sprawling city of San José. After going through customs, she exchanged some dollars into *colones* and took a taxi straight to the Wild River Excursions office. The taxi ride was an adventure in itself. The *Ticos*, as Costa Ricans called themselves, lived two different lives. One as very calm, friendly, and relaxed people. But put them behind the wheel of a car and they turned into crazed drivers with no regard for lanes or stoplights, like Mario Andretti racing in a crash derby.

A bit frazzled, Bendi stepped out of the cab and gave the driver 2,500 *colones*. She walked apprehensively into the Wild River Excursions office. The girl behind the counter expressed a look of surprise when Bendi introduced herself. A handsome man in his forties apparently overheard the conversation. He walked over and introduced himself.

"Hello, Miss Porcelli, my name is Manuel," he said in fairly good English. "I talked with you yesterday... uhhmmm... we weren't expecting you...

Bendi started right in, "Have you heard anything yet?"

"I am sorry, we have not," Manuel replied, nervously combing his fingers through his thick black hair.

"Are you going to leave this morning?"

"No, I am sorry. They say that the road will not be open till tomorrow. I will go then. The moment that I know anything, I will call you."

"I can't just sit around while you go looking for him! I want to come along," she demanded.

"Miss Porcelli, the dirt roads can be very dangerous. We might even have to go down the river. Have you ever been whitewater rafting?"

Manuel asked.

"No," Bendi admitted.

A group of people walked in the office and looked at the company's brochures. They asked questions of the woman behind the counter.

Glancing at them, Manuel lowered his voice, "The river has been running high with all of the rains. It is now running a Class 5, which means the trip can be very dangerous. Plus, we do not know what trouble the earthquake has caused on the river. So for now we have canceled all our trips on the Río Pacuare."

"You mean the river where you lost my boyfriend!" Bendi raised her voice purposely.

"Miss Porcelli…" Manuel shot another nervous glance at the tourists. "Please…"

"I'm going with you!" The intensity of her proclamation surprised even Bendi.

Several of the tour group turned to stare at the distraught American. Manuel smiled at them as best he could, then turned back sternly to face Bendi's determined look. He took her by the elbow to urge her firmly toward the door of the busy office. But her feet were planted as she evaded his grasp by crossing her arms over her chest.

"Okay, okay," he hissed. "You can come along. Now, please…"

"*Gracias, Manuel,*" she smiled triumphantly up at him.

"We will pick you up at 6 a.m.," the frustrated man sighed. "Where are you staying?"

"I don't have a hotel yet."

"I will have someone take you to the *Hotel de Ambassador*… as our guest, of course. Is that all right?"

"*Gracias,*" she smiled sweetly at him again. This time she let him lead her to the door.

Bendi unpacked her clothes and tried to take a nap but all she could think about were the terrible things that could have happened to Digger and the real possibility that he could be dead. Maybe that's what the dream on the airplane was trying to tell her, she thought. She shook her head; that thought was too painful. Needing some kind of diversion, she walked down to the registration desk and asked if there were any museums close by the hotel. The clerk mentioned two and handed her a map.

She hailed a taxi. "*Cuanta cuesta ir al Museo de Jade?*"

"*Trescientos,*" said the smiling taxi driver.

Pedestrians dodged out of the way as the taxi sped through an intersection, only to come to a quick halt. The rest of the jerky ride was the same, with quick bursts of movement only to wait in traffic. Fifteen minutes later, the taxi pulled up in front of the *Instituto Nacional de*

Seguros. Bendi reached over the front seat and gave the man three hundred *colones.*

"*Gracias,*" he thanked his attractive passenger cheerfully.

"*Por nada,*" she replied.

"*No por nada en Costa Rica. Pura vida,*" the man exclaimed. He explained to Bendi that in Costa Rica, unlike other Spanish-speaking countries, one does not say '*por nada,*' which means 'you are welcome' or literally 'for nothing.' In Costa Rica one can greet or answer '*Pura vida*—the good life!'"

She thanked him for the Spanish lesson, thinking wryly of all those classroom hours she'd spent trying to learn the real language. Maybe she should have simply traveled more.

An elevator took her to the eleventh floor, which housed Costa Rica's famous *Museo de Jade,* boasting the largest collection of American jade. The sound of her heels echoed through the hallways as she wandered aimlessly through dimly-lit rooms, hardly noticing the beautifully sculpted Pre-Columbian jewelry and ritual pieces carved from gems. Nothing captured her interest, so she walked over to a window. Her reflection was silhouetted against the bustling city of narrow streets, heavy traffic, and several beautiful colonial buildings. She had read that seventy-five percent of the Costa Rican population lived in this central city nestled in the mountains. Looking again at the people below her, she wondered what they were doing: shopping, going to work, or just doing what people do during their normal day? They didn't know of her personal problems. Would they even care if they did? Would she care about theirs?

A few blocks away, Bendi noticed several levels of stone steps leading up to an old fort. Then she gazed off into the horizon where she could just make out the outline of the jungle. Her reflection stared back at her; it was missing something, someone. Digger was out there some-where. She had to find him.

As she neared the exit, Bendi was stopped by a showcase filled with several beautiful pieces of jade. The artifacts were mounted with a backlight so that the gorgeous gems glowed with a green translucence. It reminded her of the dream she'd had on the plane, the one with the colorful balls of stone.

Out on the street, Bendi made her way to the next museum, the *Museo Nacional,* the one with the stone steps she'd seen from the window. As she paid her money and walked under the darkened archway towards the main courtyard, she stopped suddenly in amazement. Several balls of stone lay sprawled on the green lawn, ranging in diameter from one to five feet! She stood and stared for several moments in disbelief, then walked deliberately among the perfectly symmetrical granite balls.

There were no plaques explaining the strange objects, and no petroglyphs or engravings on their smooth surfaces which might have given her some clue about their purpose—or about what, or *who,* had made them. Could erosion do such a thing? She'd never seen such perfectly round, smooth rocks in her life!

Looking for some explanation, she walked through several of the exhibition rooms that surrounded the courtyard. At the end of one of the hallways she finally found a huge, seven-foot granite sphere, the largest she'd seen so far. This one had a sign, which she bent down to read:

Las Esferas de Piedra
The Stone Spheres

These Pre-Columbian artifacts have mostly been found in the southern region of Costa Rica, known as the Diqui Valley. Their purpose is not known. How they were made or even transported through the dense jungles is not known. To this date they remain a mystery.

Do Not Touch

Bendi sank to a nearby bench. The colored balls in her dreams... was there some connection? She stared at the strange granite sphere. But this one had no color. Still, she couldn't help feeling there was some tie between her childhood dream of bubbles, which had lately turned into colored balls, these mysterious stone sculptures, and Digger. But what?

She had to find out. Standing up she walked over to a security guard to ask for more information about *Las Esferas de Piedra.* The young man shook his head, but told her to try downstairs in the *Oficina de Educación.*

Bendi used her Spanish to question the woman at the education office's reception desk. The woman handed Bendi a three-page photocopy of an article written in Spanish. Bendi thanked her and found a seat nearby where she could sit and translate.

She'd only gotten a few paragraphs into it when her concentration was interrupted by a smiling man who strolled in as if he owned the place. The portly man stopped to greet the receptionist.

"Are you back already, Professor?" the woman smiled up at him, exchanging words in Spanish. " I thought you were going to be away for two more weeks."

"I don't know, I just felt like coming back early. Maybe I will begin the outline for my lecture."

"By the sound of it, you had some success?" the woman inquired.

"We are getting more information every week," the man grinned. Bendi, completely distracted by the conversation, couldn't help noticing what a boyish face this older man possessed—especially when he spoke about his work.

"Well, there is plenty in your office to keep you busy here. I guess it would be nice for the new curator to spend a little time in his museum, no?" she chided.

"The knowledge might be stored within these walls, but the discoveries and the passion are to be experienced out there," he gestured dramatically as he continued past the woman to an office at the back.

Bendi returned to her reading. All the article mentioned were a couple of archaeologists and the location of several sites where stone spheres had been found. She returned to the desk to ask for more information. The woman just shrugged her shoulders. "Very little is known about them," she apologized.

Bendi stood there feeling helpless, not knowing what to do. She didn't even know why she was asking about these strange objects. But here she was, in an unknown place, with unknown people, and hardly any sleep in the last two days. She thought of Digger, lost in the rainforest. The grim possibility that he was injured, or dead, began to sink in and it became difficult to swallow. Finally, she lost control. The tears started to fall.

The woman behind the desk looked distressed. "Miss—is something wrong? Can I assist you in some way?"

Bendi brushed at her eyes and rummaged for a tissue to blot her runny nose. How embarrassing. But she couldn't help herself. In disjointed sentences, she started to blurt out all the events that had led her to the echoing halls of this lonely museum in Costa Rica. The stocky man, apparently hearing her tearful exclamations, looked out from his office doorway.

"Can I help?" he asked in Spanish. Bendi, engulfed in tears, didn't look up.

The receptionist interjected, "*Este, es sus conservador, el Profesor...*"

"Ortega, just Ortega. Are you an American?" he interrupted her in English. The fiftyish professor walked over to Bendi and extended a rough, callused hand in friendship.

"*Sí*, I mean yes, I am. My name is Mary Porcelli." She shook his hand. His strength was deceiving for a man barely taller than she.

"I went to school at UCLA for a little time," he said, trying to make her comfortable. "Do you know where it is at?"

"Yes, I'm from San Diego. I almost went there to get my teaching degree." She blotted her eyes and nose self-consciously.

"I am sorry. I do not mean to be, as you might call it, nosy. But I heard you mention something about *las esferas de piedra*, the stone spheres," Ortega ventured politely.

"Do you know anything about them?" She knew he was trying to distract her from her problems and she didn't mind. She was grateful.

"No one really knows much about those intriguing artifacts, but I know more than most. Many of my colleagues say that I think I know more than I really do," he laughed at his own comment. Bendi politely returned a smile.

"Maybe I can help you," Ortega continued. "Would you mind a stroll through the courtyard?" He looked back toward his office, where Bendi could see a desk piled with paperwork. "I know I feel better when I am outside. Perhaps you will, too?"

She agreed and they walked out to the courtyard filled with the stone spheres. Ortega, with a grandfatherly touch, gently patted each of the spheres as he passed them. Finally, he asked her if she wanted to talk about whatever it was that had been making her cry. Blushing a little, she told Ortega the whole story—including her conversations with the rafting company and her grave concerns about Digger's safety. She disclosed a little about their relationship, but she hesitated to tell Ortega about her dreams. She didn't want him to think she was crazy.

"I am sorry, Miss Porcelli..." Ortega interjected.

"You can call me Bendi. That is what my friends call me."

"Bendi. I do not understand why you are interested in the stone spheres. What do they have to do with finding your boyfriend, ahh, 'Digger'?"

Bendi averted his gaze, only to see a black cat scamper between the stone spheres and then slip into the archway. She took a deep breath and decided to tell him about her dreams—the young girl in the jungle, the floating bubbles that had turned into colored balls strewn across a trail, the lifeless body, the cat, and the stone balls that rolled out of a cavern.

Ortega's face lit up when Bendi talked about the colored balls. "So you think there is a connection between your colored balls and these magnificent stone spheres?"

"Yes, from the moment that I walked into the courtyard and saw the stone spheres, I knew there was a connection. I don't know what I know, but I know something."

"Well," Ortega chuckled. "You probably know more than the rest of my colleagues."

Ortega stopped walking near the largest sphere. He touched it gently.

"Here, feel it," he invited. "Close your eyes. Do you notice anything?"

With half-closed eyes, Bendi touched the stone. It felt smooth and cool. "I don't know. What am I supposed to feel?"

"Nothing, but maybe everything. Maybe the universe." As Bendi looked at him quizzically, he continued, "Archaeology is the study of the past. Standing from the present, we try to discover the old way of life. To do this, we need to focus on the relationship between the visible and the invisible; between form, the material objects of the past, and thought, the behavior and beliefs of the makers of those objects.

"Written records can help us but for most of history they do not exist. And if they did, many have been obliterated by the conquering culture. None have been so brutally efficient"—Ortega made a quick sign of the cross in front of his body—"as the past followers of my own religion.

"Given the complexity of the enormous puzzle that is before us, as a profession, we have done a great job in piecing together the picture of many cultures. Every once in a while, though, we come across a true mystery, such as the boulders at Stonehenge, the menoliths of Easter Island, or *Las Esferas De Piedra*, the Stone Spheres of Costa Rica."

Bendi heard pride in Ortega's voice as he stretched his hands before the various spheres in the courtyard.

"These mysteries tickle the minds of all who are aware of them. They are what stimulate the passion in my profession. They motivate us to continue our search and uncover more about our past. It is only through that awareness, that learning, that we can change our present.

"What is that statement? Ahhmmm… it goes something like, 'If we do not learn from our past, we are condemned to repeat it.' In that case, we as a species are most definitely on our last breath. So much of our history is already before our eyes, yet we do not see it; see it from the perspective of who we were back then and how we can be different now."

At the end of his breath, Ortega looked back at Bendi, as his boyish expression returned. "I am sorry. I will stand down from my soapy box. I have been preparing to speak at a conference in a couple of months. Sometimes I get carried away."

"No, please go on," Bendi urged earnestly.

"Okay, then. Archaeologists used to be happy just to find objects," Ortega spread his fingers and placed them on a sphere. "But today, equipped with the latest technology, we are actually trying to reach into the minds of the past peoples. Typically we go through the list of W's: who, what, where, when, why, and how. With our present knowledge of the spheres, most will agree that we know the what, the where, and the when, and some of the who and how. But no one really knows the why.

"The conference that will be here in San José is on Pre-Columbian civilization in Central America. A couple of my esteemed colleagues and I will be presenting lectures on the featured topic, *Las Esferas De Piedra*. But my theories are a little controversial compared to theirs." He smiled broadly.

"How so?" Bendi asked, as a gust of wind blew her long brown hair across her face.

"Without boring you with all the details, though I love to bore people"—Ortega laughed—"I agree that we do know the when. It is from 100 A.D. to the early 1500s. And I agree that no one knows the whys. But that is as far as I go with their assumptions for the W's. I believe that the 'how' and the 'who' are very different from what many think. Oh, we know the basics of how they made the spheres and the names of the tribes that probably shaped them. But I believe there is much more to the history. I believe those particular tribes merely mimicked the real originators of the stone spheres. I also think that there are still more spheres out there and that they are somewhere other than the Diqui region. But the biggest controversy is that of the most basic assumption, the what."

Ortega stood on one side of a large sphere, as Bendi stood on the other side. He stretched his arms out over the top of the granite.

"Most believe that this is just a rock; a stone slab that was sculpted into the shape of a sphere, an artifact that was used for a symbol of power or a religious rite.

"Archeologists, as scientists, try to remain objective as much as possible. The reality is that all of our theories are based on our cultures and our individual assumptions, prejudices, and biases of the past. Not only that, but how we conduct investigations are biased upon our own conscious and unconscious beliefs. If you believe this to be only a rock—a physical object that is comprised of certain atoms and elements, a rock chiseled into a stone sphere—that belief will lead you down a particular path of discovery. That belief will also then preclude you from other possible explanations. But if you also believe that this rock could be more than just physical, then you would possibly open yourself up to new avenues."

"I don't get what you're saying," Bendi interrupted. "So what is this stone sphere if not rock?"

"I know that I am not very clear. Think of it this way: if we were aliens who landed on this planet and came across the remains of some humans, if we looked at them as just a compilation of physical atoms, could we even come close to understanding them?"

"Of course not."

"Why not?"

"Because we are much more than just physical; we are also emotional and intellectual," she answered.

"Precisely my point. Our species and everything of nature is more than just the visible—the physical. Much of the essence of who we are is the invisible; that which you call the emotional, the intellectual, and I would also like to add the spiritual. And that reality is influenced by every connection we make on each of those levels. Therefore, we are a compilation of our own and each other's experiences.

"So archeologists and most people see this stone sphere, like many other artifacts, as just an object; something that was designed by human hands, something that is outside of us. I will agree that way of thinking may hold true for many of our findings. But I believe that this stone sphere is more than a piece of sculpture. This stone sphere could also be a compilation of all the invisible aspects of the people who worked on it—their dreams, hopes, fears, beliefs, and their experiences."

"Or it could be just a piece of rock," Bendi said.

"Yes, that is true. *And* it could also be much, much more," Ortega emphasized.

"Who is to say about any of this?" she asked.

"Who is to say about the meaning of your dreams, about the meaning of your life, about the meaning of your past? You are! You provide all of the meaning, not anyone else. The meaning is not found in the form—the physical artifacts—or even in the events themselves. Our culture, comprised of families, government, science, religions, technology, businesses, etc., tries to dictate a meaning to us. Our history books are full of that dictated meaning. But the reality is that the meaning is all interchangeable, depending on who is doing the interpreting.

"That is why mysteries are so appealing to our human nature. They allow each of us to decide their meaning. I strongly believe that at special times in our history, the earth unfolds keys to some of her mysteries. Those artifacts can help us to understand our past; like the Rosetta Stone and the Dead Sea Scrolls. The new information helps us get a clearer picture of where we have been. We can, if we so choose, adjust the way we see ourselves now, in the present. Adjust it so that we may learn, so that we may survive, so that we may truly *live*."

An attendant near the wrought iron gates called out that it was closing time.

Bendi extended her hand to the curator. "Thank you, Professor Ortega, for all your help. But I'd better be going now."

Ortega took her hand warmly. "It was very nice meeting you, Bendi. I hope that I did not bore you too much. I wish you well in finding your boyfriend." They both turned to leave, smiling over the deep conversation they'd just shared, two very unlikely strangers in a very unlikely place, Bendi mused.

Just as she reached the archway, she heard Ortega's heavy step hurrying after her.

"Miss Porcelli," he puffed, "may I ask you an imposing question?"

"Ahhh, sure." She couldn't imagine what could be so important that he'd chased after her.

"May I come with you tomorrow?" he asked breathlessly.

"You know that I am looking for my boyfriend," Bendi said instinctively.

"No, no, please—you misunderstand me. The thought of being inside my office and doing meaningless paperwork for the next few days is not appealing."

She looked at him questioningly. "So you want to come with me to get out of work?" She was confused by this odd professor.

"If you could indulge me for one more moment," he said, uncharacteristically shy all of a sudden. "When I was a little boy, my parents brought me here to see the stone spheres. I was totally fascinated with them. When it was time to leave, my parents had to drag me through this archway, kicking and crying. At that moment I knew I wanted to be an archaeologist." Ortega's head bowed a little, as his eyes scanned the sidewalk. "I never told anyone this, but I had dreams for three weeks before I came to see the stone spheres. I dreamt about colored balls strewn in the jungle next to a cavern." He looked up at her eagerly. "I know there is so much more to learn from the stone spheres. Something tells me that I might find some of those answers if I accompany you. I have learned in my profession to trust my hunches; sometimes they lead me much further than the cold-hearted facts. So you see, if you allow me to accompany you, I am not getting away from my work. This is my work," he added cheerfully, gesturing back toward the spheres.

"Uhhhmm..." she murmured. Maybe it would be nice to have friendly company on tomorrow's ride. He seemed harmless enough; besides, he was funny and informative.

"Okay," she said finally. "The people from the river-rafting company are picking me up at 6 a.m. at the Hotel Ambassador."

"I know where that is," he shook her hand energetically. "I will meet you outside. Besides, I still haven't told you everything about the stone spheres! So much has happened just in the last few weeks. *Muchas gracias!* And now I suppose I must get back to my endless paperwork. I will see you tomorrow, Miss Porcelli!" Smiling gratefully, he turned back toward his office.

After a few steps, he turned back and called softly to Bendi, "Do not let others smother your dreams. Those wonderful flittings of images have much to teach us all; it does not matter if your interpretation is correct or not, it does not matter if your dreams lead you to your believed destiny. Because many times, the treasure is different than what you believe you are searching for!" Ortega laughed out loud and then added, "*Pura vida.*"

Chapter 7

"How long have I been unconscious?"
"From the little you have told me, I would have to say most of your life."

High in the rainforest canopy, a breeze wrestled several leaves from their limbs. They twirled downward toward the nurturing soil of their past. Digger swatted a leaf from his face as he opened his eyes skyward. Quickly sitting up, he looked around. Twilight was about to usher out another day. How did he get off that round boulder? Where was the river or the boulder? And what happened to Angélica?

Surveying his surroundings, he gradually stood up in his now-dried blue swimming trunks and Costa Rican T-shirt. Thick foliage pressed the narrow riverbed from both sides. Pools of water dotted the rocky riverbed where the raging river had once been. He looked upstream and saw what looked like the cavern where he had been tossed around in the raft. The thrashing waters were gone.

Hearing a rustling of bushes several yards off to his right, he turned to hide behind a boulder. Before he could take a step, a female voice rang out, "It is a pleasure to see you up and around."

"Angélica! You're all right!" She was alive! He ran up to hug her, but hesitated about a foot away. Instead, he rested a hand gently on each of her shoulders, looked her in the eye, and blurted, "How did you make it to shore? Where did you end up? How is your wrist?"

She grasped his arms firmly and looked into his eyes without saying a word.

Embarrassed, he dropped his hands. "It's, um, it's good to see you again."

"You, too, Jonathan Taylor," she answered earnestly, "or I should say, Digger?" she added with a nervous laugh. A flock of noisy parrots flew into the air and they both laughed out loud.

That broke the tension and Digger was relieved to change the subject. "Where are we?"

"Well, we are here," she grinned, opening her palms.

Digger cocked his head and scrunched up his eyebrows.

"We are in the heart of the rainforest," she added matter-of-factly.

"Just because I've been vague answering your questions, don't you start answering like me," he wagged a finger at her.

"How do you like it when the slipper is on the other foot?" she beamed.

"You mean *zapato*, shoe, and no, I don't like it. How did I get here?"

"What do you remember?"

"I remember holding onto a round boulder. Then I got light-headed and must have passed out."

"Do you remember what you were thinking or feeling right before you passed out?"

"What I was thinking? What does that have to do with anything?" Her questions were beginning to annoy him.

"Everything," she said emphatically.

For a moment silence hung between them in the heavy air. Finally she added, "I ended up further downstream and then eventually found my way back here. And there you were."

"How long have I been unconscious?"

"From the little you have told me, I would have to say most of your life," she smiled.

Digger gave her a look that made it clear he was losing patience.

"A day, a year, a century. Does it make a difference?" she added.

He was not in the mood for her cryptic games, so he switched his line of questions. "I remember a wall of water coming at me. What happened to the river?"

"I have no idea," she shrugged. "All I know was that a wave of water threw me up onto the river bank."

For the first time, he noticed the tear in her green bathing suit. "Are you all right?" he asked with genuine concern, taking a step toward her.

"I'm fine," she answered, brushing him off.

"Then can we go now? I need to get back to San José—people are waiting for me, maybe they'll be worried ..." he began.

"It is not that simple," she interrupted. "Plus, it can be very dangerous."

He heard a note of concern in her voice—rare for this woman, Digger thought. That worried him. "What do you mean? Do you know where we are?"

"Right here, where are you?" she said with a little smile.

Digger scowled at her again.

She quickly added, "Here, is sometimes where one can find my tribe."

Birds squawked and trees shook with activity as the jungle's shift-change began. Digger looked around and noticed that the shadows of the jungle were encroaching; dusk was quickly setting upon them. He must have been unconscious longer than he thought.

He turned back to Angélica. "Can your tribe help us?"

"I believe they can, but we cannot leave until tomorrow. They are almost a half-day's journey further into the jungle. I will get some wood for a fire."

"I'll help you," Digger took a few steps and became faint. He stumbled down to his knees, as Angélica come over to help him.

"Just stay and rest. It should not take me long. I know where to go for dry wood."

He watched helplessly, feeling like a fool, as Angélica walked over to a puddle and half-filled a broken coconut shell. She brought it back to him to drink. Digger, still feeling woozy, took a few sips. He sat back against a boulder, sighing, "I'll stay right here." She nodded and then disappeared into the jungle.

When he moved, he'd felt a throbbing pain. Instinctively, he put his hand up to his forehead; he was surprised not to find any blood. He also felt pain in his left arm, but again, no signs of injury. He thought he'd gotten hurt when he was in the cavern, but now that he checked himself over, he couldn't remember.

Where the hell was he? Digger looked around again at his surroundings. The pain in his head continued to throb. Placing his fingers on his temples, he pressed and took a deep breath. When he looked down, he had a sensation of vertigo as ribbons of grass moved along the rainforest floor. With a closer inspection, he saw lines of leaves being carried off into the jungle. These must be the infamous leaf-cutting ants that he'd seen on National Geographic. The scene looked like an orderly L.A. highway—now that was an oxymoron, he thought. There were three lanes: one slow, one fast, and one for passing. He noticed that every third or fourth leaf had one tiny ant that rode on top; it appeared to be a lookout searching for any kind of trouble. Watching closely, he saw one of those tiny ants crawl off the leaf and check out a nearby colony of different ants. After a quick inspection, the tiny ant immediately moved to the passing lane and disappeared into the jungle.

The smaller, different-looking ants appeared to be not at all concerned with the tiny leaf-cutter ant that had checked them out, nor with the marching leaf-cutters just a short distance away. The smaller ants simply continued their normal busy activities.

Then, without warning, the warriors of the leaf-cutting clan, attacked the nearby industrious colony. From Digger's vantage point the struggle seemed benign. But as he leaned in closer, he could see the fierceness and brutality of the battle. Besides being outnumbered, the smaller colony could not protect themselves against the more brutally equipped and larger ants. With stingers and razor-sharp mandibles, the attacking ants decimated the smaller colony with ease; paralyzing them, decapitating them, and severing their limbs.

Digger felt sorry for the small ants, because they never saw it coming. If only they'd known ahead of time, maybe they could have saved themselves... and maybe if he'd looked where he was going, he wouldn't be here, slumped against this boulder in the middle of a tangled jungle, staring at these ants. He sighed and continued to watch the ongoing battle. Then again, he thought, maybe it wouldn't have made any difference at all, for the ants or for him.

"You're the only one who could screw up a two-car funeral," his mother yelled at him as he walked towards her, down the long, white, antiseptic hall. Her words punched the breath out of him. Digger had built protective walls around himself, but no matter how hard he tried to make them impenetrable, he was always surprised by his mother's x-ray ability to see the slightest opening. He wasn't surprised that his mother would talk to him like that—but under these circumstances? Even though he knew she had displaced her anger over the situation onto him, it hurt. It always hurt.

Mrs. Taylor had been seeing doctors all her life for a wide variety of illnesses and diseases: everything from the rare to the usual, from the real to the perceived, from heart problems to a brain tumor. Lately, she'd been having episodes of severe pain, but no doctor had been able to diagnose her present condition. Many times his mother had feigned pain, illnesses, and even suicide. So it was difficult for Digger to differentiate between when she was truly sick and when she was using it for attention or as an excuse to get him to do something. From growing up in the Taylor household, Digger and his brother Jeff had pretty much become immune to the whole ordeal. It wasn't so much from insensitivity as it was a protection; at least that's what Digger had figured out. Many times, their mother had used her illnesses to mask an invisible weapon that was used as a bidding for her needs and wants. It was a weapon used to control.

Through his own experiences and schooling, Digger fanatically believed that he knew the most destructive force in mankind's history. This weapon turned people away from their moments of joy, their loves, and their passions. It had destroyed more lives than any other 'one' thing. This destructive force wasn't the thunderous technologies of war, but the quietness and stealth of the penetration of a sentence, a word, or a glance. The effects of this weapon's painful and injurious blow could be felt for weeks, years, or even lifetimes. The most lethal insertion of

this weapon was the perpetrator's voice, quietly implanted during childhood. That whisper over time was mimicked and then dangerously
masked by our own voice, which now continually echoes down a maze
of internal hallways, searching for the slightest opening. This whisper,
this weapon, is called Guilt.

Digger had received his mother's phone call from the Arizona Mayo
Clinic. She told him she'd been diagnosed as having breast and lung
cancer; the doctors gave her no more than six months. For the first time
in his life, his mother actually sounded afraid.

Digger tried immediately to get in touch with her doctors, but it
wasn't until later in the evening that he heard back from them. They con-
firmed everything his mother had said. By that time, he couldn't get a
plane out until the next morning.

That night he lay there and couldn't sleep. He reviewed their lives
together, while that whisper of Guilt rattled amongst all the other
thoughts and feelings. She was a domineering woman who was bright,
beautiful, and talented. Throughout his childhood and adult life, their
relationship had many ups and downs. But he knew, at least in some
small way, like any other person who had done any soul-searching, that
despite all the outward appearances of behavior his mother loved him.
Albeit, she didn't really know how to show it.

Replaying their phone conversation in his head, he again heard her
frightened voice. It was alarming and a hundred times more powerful
because he knew that, for the first time, her true emotions had slipped
through her armor. He'd had a glimpse of the terror she was feeling just
by her authentic emotion, little as it was, which had seeped through. For
the first time that he could remember, he wanted to be with her; not
because of obligatory holidays or birthdays or guilt-laden phone conversations, but because she needed him. Digger was surprised at his initial
internal response; he felt true and deep compassion for this woman, for
his mother.

In a strange way, this ultimate tragedy had placed them on even
ground. A place where they were equals, where they could finally have a
real and honest exchange. So as he walked down that long hallway, he
was sad but also hopeful. He saw her body lying there and half expected
her to sit up with outstretched arms and tears in her eyes. Digger saw
himself going up to her and giving her a hug; wanting to give her
comfort, wanting to let down his walls and give to his mother whatever
she needed, especially emotionally. So he was shocked by the sound of
the weapon quickly slipping into an imperceptible opening: "You're the
only one who could screw up a two-car funeral."

His mother coughed heavily. "I've been lying here, by myself, for
the last eighteen hours reeking with the good news that the doctors

brought me. You first had to check it out with them, to see if I was lying." The blade now began to twist. "So by then it was too late to catch a plane." Digger heard the loud whisper as he reinforced his walls. He took a deep breath and tried to hear her frightened voice of the previous day. Leaning into her, he gave her a hug that was coldly received and not returned.

Digger sat there slightly slumped over, with his fingers still pressed onto his temples. He looked down at the industrious leaf-cutting ants; their production lines were still moving. The larger, attacking ants had apparently retreated back into the jungle, leaving no traces of the battle nor any remnants of the smaller colony.

"You haven't moved an inch. Are you feeling all right?" Angélica asked as she stepped out of the underbrush.

"Ahhh, yeah. I'm feeling better." He slowly got up, gingerly testing his limbs. Angélica laid down an armful of branches, some dried and a couple laden with berries. Within a short time she'd built a fire—with no matches.

"I'm impressed. Did you belong to the Girl Scouts?" he asked.

"What are Girl Scouts?"

"Nevermind." He rubbed his stomach. "I'm famished. I haven't eaten in a long time."

She handed him a twig of the reddish-purple berries. "Eat these. Even though they do not look like much, they can provide you with what you need. But please, eat them slowly."

She took a branch herself and began slowly chewing each berry. Digger, starving, stuffed them into his mouth and swallowed the bitter tasting fruit. Angélica shook her head. "Be careful. Eat them slowly," she warned again.

He quickly finished off the bunch and then asked, "What are we going to do? How are we going to get to the take-out point?"

"We will leave early tomorrow and try to find the village." She settled in comfortably near the fire.

"Why don't we just walk further down the riverbed? The take-out can't be too far from here."

"It is much further than you think. Besides, it is too dangerous," she warned.

"I know the jungle can be dangerous," he said impatiently, "but what is the difference if we walk down the riverbed or take a half-day's journey to find your village?"

Angélica gazed up at him intently. "There is no way you can make it back unless both of us go to the village first. You will just have to believe me, Digger."

"What if I decide to go without you?" he challenged her.

"That is your choice," she answered nonchalantly.

"But I don't understand," Digger whined.

"At this moment there is nothing to understand. All you have to do is trust. I know that is difficult, but in the end that is all there is. I could be wrong, but if you decide to walk back, you might not make it. And then again, if you go with me, the same possibilities await you. How do you decide? Ahhh, now that is a really good question," she leaned back, as if about to launch into a long story.

"I need more information to make a decision," he blurted out before she had the chance.

"Is that all you need?"

He ignored her response. "If I go with you, can your friends help me back to San José? Or to meet the others at the take-out point?"

"Yes, I think so."

"You think so! That's not good enough. I *need* to get back! Can they help us or not?"

"I think so," she repeated. "Do not worry about that now."

"Don't worry, are you kidding?" His stomach churned and gurgled.

"I am not what you call kidding. All that you can ever do is before you now, in the present," she said calmly. "Be thankful for all that has occurred to you. For your whole life has brought you here, to this moment, as is the same for all moments. Be thankful you are not face down in the river! Be thankful there are others who can possibly help you on your way. Be thankful that you are in the midst of a beautiful rainforest being warmed by a dazzling show of lights."

Digger let out a deep sigh and slumped down by the fire. He stared into the crackling embers. After a few minutes, he looked up and saw a few stars winking at him through the opening in the jungle canopy created by the ancient riverbed. He let Angélica's words sit with him, "Be thankful."

Eventually, she broke the silence, "So what are you thinking?"

"Nothing."

"Nothing? I don't believe that unless you are a *sukai*."

"Okay, I'll bite," he responded.

"You will bite what?"

"Nevermind, just tell me what a *sukai* is."

"It is what you call a shaman, or other cultures might call a holy man, or medicine man. They can do many things, and one of them is to think about nothing for a long time. They can squeeze between the tick and the tock." She moved her right arm back and forth like a pendulum. "You know, like a clock that is tall with a long arm."

"You mean a grandfather clock."

She looked quizzically at him.

"Nevermind. What do you mean between the tick and the tock?" he asked even though he felt as if he'd heard it somewhere before.

"There are hours, minutes, and seconds, all of which are explanations of time—which is an illusion, by the way. Anyway, I am talking about being between what you call a second. That moment can be after you inhale and just before you exhale. In the 'moment of between,' there is everything, there is all of eternity.

"We believe breath is sacred. Imagine if you could place yourself between the inhalation and the exhalation, the tick and the tock–for hours. Who knows where you could go or what you could do?" Her face shone with intensity in the firelight, which gleamed off her shiny black hair. "Have you ever felt that place?"

Digger thought for a moment. "I don't know if it's the same thing, but I might have felt it in my music; the time between two notes or between two musical phrases."

As he reflected on his compositions, anxiety and guilt rushed in about his present "composer's block." His flow of creativity had trickled down to nothing during his mother's illness. He felt stiff just thinking about it, and intricate lines of tension built throughout his body. That's the least of my worries, he chided himself. Pushing those thoughts out of his mind, he brought his attention back to times when he'd been writing music. Those times when the notes came to him on waves of starlight. His body swayed slightly as he heard his music and tried to replay those tick-tock moments.

"What do those moments feel like?" Angélica was watching him closely.

"It's hard to describe. There are many different feelings, some of which are seemingly contradictory." He paused for a second and then added, "It's the pure enjoyment of the note, right after it has been struck, the tick, like there never needs to be another note played. Yet there is the anticipation of that next note, the tock. You don't know what it's going to be, but yet you do. You relish the sound of it before you ever hear it. In that 'moment of between,' there's a peace of just being in that moment. And as a composer, you want to create that for your audience."

"True words spoken from the Keeper of the Sound," Angélica smiled at him.

He blushed slightly at her compliment, but also with embarrassment from his disclosure. He'd tried so hard to explain to Bendi that his expression of music was the "real" him she was always wanting him to reveal to her. He put everything he was into his music and it was all there for anyone to discover. But she never got it. Now this total stranger, Angélica, seemed to understand instinctively—even better than he did!

"*Gracias* for sharing with me," she was saying. "You are a difficult one to get to talk, but when you do... Well, it doesn't sound like you need more information when you are making a decision on what note to play next." She looked at him pointedly. He'd forgotten all about their earlier discussion about what he was going to do, he'd been so distracted by the thoughts of his music. "If you decide to, you may join me tomorrow to look for the village." She smoothed out a place on the ground to sleep.

Digger stood up suddenly as sweat beaded up on his brow. Bending over, he felt a wave of nausea sweep through him. Angélica just looked up at him with a slight but sympathetic smile, shaking her head.

"Damn berries," he said with a grunt as he ran off downstream, out of her sight. He leaned on a boulder as his stomach projected out everything he'd put into it. The smell of putrid, undigested food mixed with the hot, humid air and triggered even more vomiting. His intestines then cramped, and he quickly squatted. Again the rancid smells elicited more regurgitation. Everything that had been within him was violently spewed back into the jungle. The awful sound echoed down the riverbed.

Eventually the cramps subsided, but Digger was light-headed from the experience. As he walked slowly back toward the dying embers of the fire, he felt thoroughly exhausted. He stopped beside a puddle to wash up and then sat on a cool, granite slab. The moon seemed much fuller and brighter than he remembered it being last night. It reminded him of the end of San Diego's rocky Mission Beach jetty, poking out into the Pacific Ocean—his favorite place to be inspired, to think, to make decisions. Digger took a long, easy breath and held it for a moment before he exhaled. This place will have to do, he thought.

The mating calls of frogs and crickets filled the silence of the Costa Rican night. A small green frog with red webbed feet jumped into the puddle.

Digger flinched back as a splash of cold water covered his hot, tanning body.

"There's more to life than sports and music. C'mon, lets go! You'll love it!" Bendi was pleading with him, trying to get him off the premises of the Cancun Club Med to visit some of the Mayan ruins. "I promise you an adventure," she reasoned.

"I have all the adventure I need right here," he insisted stubbornly. "That's what I paid for." He was sitting on the edge of the pool with a Corona in hand, slowly kicking his feet in the warm water. She paddled closer to him and then stood between his legs, feigning a frown.

"Anything but that, please! Anything!" He was half-mocking her little-girl pout, half serious. He couldn't stand that look.

Bendi made an even bigger frown. He gently dunked her head under the water, but she managed to grab his feet and pull until he slid into the pool with her. She'd won.

So they rented a car and headed towards Chichen Itza, the most famous of the Mayan ruins.

"I talked with a couple who said the ruins were fantastic," Bendi chattered excitedly.

"I overheard them, but they also said it was really crowded," Digger added, his reluctance clouding his voice with grouchiness.

"Well, the brochure mentioned another ruin, but it's in the opposite direction. A newly discovered Mayan city, called Cobá, with ancient buildings, pyramids, and a ball field. In fact, it's the highest pyramid in the Yucatan..."

Digger sensed a pulse of energy move through his body as if he had just plugged into an electrical socket.

"... nobody knows anything about it, as of yet. So there are no plaques or explanations of what you're looking at. Consequently, the brochure said that there are hardly any visitors..."

Digger made a quick U-turn. "Sorry, do you mind if we go to those ruins?" He didn't know why, but he felt that he must see them.

"Ahh, no..." Bendi was a bit startled. "Why the sudden change?"

"I don't know," he fumbled. "Those ruins sound less commercial... besides, being around fewer tourists is more appealing to me."

They passed the airport and drove south towards the seaport ruins of Tulum, then headed west. Trees and plants reached out into the openness created by the narrow, two-lane highway. He wondered what prevented this path from being totally engulfed by the living, ancient rainforest. Just then, they passed a man swinging a machete. It must be the man's full time job to walk the road and keep the constantly encroaching jungle at bay, Digger thought—a lonely and exhausting job.

As they drove closer to the ancient ruins, he felt uneasy. The feeling was more than driving through a foreign country on unfamiliar roads, but he couldn't put his finger on it.

When they arrived, there were no tourist buses or vendors selling replicas or trinkets, just a few cars in the dirty, makeshift parking lot. A handful of tourists wandered around the empty grounds, looking at a city with no known history. To their right, a small, peaceful lake glimmered within the dense jungle. Several alligators glided lazily along its surface.

Digger's stomach churned as he stared at the imposing pyramid.

"Let's go to the top," Bendi chirped with enthusiasm.

"Uhhh, in a little bit, okay? I'm going to look around the grounds. Go ahead, I'll catch up with you in a little while."

He passed several two-story, stone buildings before he saw an open area about twice the size of a football field. On one side was a wall built into a grassy, sloping hill that was lined with stone seats in crumbled disarray. In the center of the wall, twelve feet up, was a half-broken, ornate stone ring.

While Digger stood staring at the ring, an elderly man walked up and introduced himself in broken English. He worked at the site as some kind of guide, Digger understood, and now he was trying to explain to Digger the history of the Mayan ball field.

From the man's halting description, all Digger could piece together was that there was some kind of game played there, which sounded like a combination of soccer, hockey, and basketball. The object was to hit a ball, made of a rubber-coated skull, through the not-much-bigger, sideways ring Digger had been staring at. The old man also told him the games were played at many of the various Mayan religious ceremonies. But on one special occasion, when a lunar eclipse followed a solar eclipse in the same month, there was a special event called The Shadow Game.

"Whichever team scored first, won. The game could easily go on for days," the old man nodded, as if remembering the scene.

"It looks pretty tough to get a ball through that stone ring—but days?" Digger questioned. "What was the prize for winning?"

"*Oportunidad,*" the man said assuredly.

"What do you mean, opportunity? Didn't they get prizes, or status—or women?"

"Oh, yes, for all the other ceremonies those were the benefits. But not for this game."

"Well, then, what was the opportunity?" Digger asked again.

"A reward. An opportunity to sit with the gods."

Digger still looked quizzically at the old man, who made a knife-like gesture across his throat and then said, "The winning team was killed before the dawning of the next day."

"That's terrible! No wonder it took so long to complete the games!" Digger joked.

"They played to win," the old man said seriously, looking into Digger's eyes. "They trained every moment of their lives to be the best at their game, the best at their life, so that they might have an opportunity to sit with the gods. How many people can say that about their lives? They think that the object of the game is to do anything to keep alive, to survive—while these warriors realized that the game was to do their best, so that they could move on to a better place."

The man then turned away and walked silently towards the other end of the ball field, disappearing as quickly as he'd appeared.

Digger turned around to see Bendi, in the distance, standing at the bottom of the magnificent pyramid. It was over fifteen stories high, with steps on all four sides. The Mayan pyramids were different than the Egyptian. They didn't form a pointed apex at the top. Instead, about two-thirds of the way up, the pyramid flattened out. At the top a room, called a vestibule or temple, was built in the center of the flat area.

Digger strolled over to her. "Have you been to the top yet?"

"No, I walked around to some of the other buildings. I thought that we could go up here together." She linked her arm in his.

When they reached the top, Digger noticed what looked like a washed-out, painted blue line. It began at the outermost perimeter of the top of pyramid and kept moving inwards, like a right-angled, squared spiral or a maze. He pointed it out to Bendi but she couldn't see it. How can she not see it? he wondered. She must be playing around with me. So he shrugged his shoulders, as if to shrug off her teasing, as they walked toward the rectangular vestibule in the middle of this high, man-made plateau. The room was approximately ten by twenty feet, and it had one open doorway.

Digger felt light-headed as they walked around the outside of the vestibule. When they turned the corner he suddenly had a sensation of falling into blackness.

The next moment, he discovered himself sprawled on his knees, the fingernails of his right hand digging into the wall of the vestibule while his other hand clung desperately to Bendi's arm. She helped him up, as a nearby cluster of tourists stared at the strange spectacle for a moment, then walked back down the steps of the pyramid, leaving Bendi and Digger alone at the top.

"What happened?" Bendi asked, with worry lines creasing her forehead.

He couldn't explain it, so he said, "Nothing. I must have tripped."

Bendi just shook her head at him in puzzlement.

She pulled out her guidebook to find out more about the vestibule. "It says here," she said, then read aloud to him about archaeologists believing they had uncovered only one-tenth of this ancient city of Cobá. The Mayas were an extremely advanced culture, the scientists believed, but their religious rites, by our standards, were very barbaric; it was thought they would cut the hearts out of dissidents and prisoners inside the vestibule and then throw the victims down the pyramid steps, while the heart thumped its last beat in the hand of the high priest.

Digger recalled what the old man on the ball field had said about death being an opportunity. Nervously, he looked down the steep, angling steps of the pyramid and shuddered.

From horizon to horizon, the rainforest stretched below them, temporarily held back by this newly-uncovered city. He thought about the death of this ancient city, the death that allowed the life-filled jungle to reclaim its hold, again.

Turning around, he stared back at the vestibule. Bendi then took his hand and led him into the rectangular room, built with blocks of limestone. A comfortable coolness filled the empty, hollow room. Bendi stood at one end and Digger the other. Without thinking it, Digger sang a note—"Ahhhhh..." The sound swiftly circulated within the vestibule, as Bendi joined in. The walls seemed to intensify the sound, not only in volume but in resonance. It was how he felt when he played his music, but ten times more powerful. Mesmerized, he lost himself within the sound as his entire body seemed to explode and implode simultaneously. In an instant, he became the sound and was everywhere in the room.

A sense of peace then overcame him. In the darkness, the sound still reverberating through him, a blurry vision of a symbol appeared. He tried to make out its form but couldn't. He knew somehow that this vague symbol was a key for him, he knew that if he ever saw with clarity this symbol, he would remember; remember everything he'd forgotten about that dream-like meditation in L.A. before his first film audition, remember everything of...

The heaviness of his day-to-day consciousness suddenly dropped back into his body. He didn't know how long he'd been in that transcended state. Looking around the darkened room, he saw Bendi had gone. Slowly, he walked out to a magnificent sunset view of her curvaceous figure facing out toward the jungle, her back to him, silhouetted by an orange sphere on the horizon. It was a gorgeous sight.

The early-evening breeze warmed his face as a flock of birds glided across rich waves of darkening greenness. He wondered how those birds knew at what moment to fly together or even where to fly. How did they know how to fly so perfectly in unison? He inhaled and took in everything before him: the birds, the rainforest—and Bendi. Walking up behind her and taking her into his arms, his heart pounded into her back as he tenderly embraced her. That was when he felt as if he'd finally fallen in love with her.

"Hey, are you trying to swim?" Angélica's voice broke through into Digger's soggy consciousness. He opened his eyes and stared into the puddle, which was only inches away from his face. "You must have been tired last night. Did you fall asleep and never wake up? Those berries can do that to a person."

"Thanks a lot," Digger said wryly, squinting up into the morning sun.

"Do not blame me. I told you to eat them slowly. Now drink some water. We need to hike up that rocky bluff above the cavern."

Digger drank, still feeling as if he'd just nodded off for a few minutes. His stomach growled as the two of them headed into the dense jungle. He was still mulling over his recall of the experiences with Bendi at Cobá, and his blurry vision of that symbol he couldn't quite bring to clarity in his mind. Still, the memory of it somehow triggered a sense in him of life being more than just this physical world, more of everything.

I haven't thought about any of that for such a long time. How could I have ever let my daily activities cloud that feeling? He remembered trying to tell his brother and his friends about his experiences at Cobá after he got back to the States. All he got were raised eyebrows, questioning looks, and lots of sarcastic questions. "How could that be?" "That doesn't make sense." "Did you bump into Carlos Castaneda and eat some 'shrooms?"

His new business agent wasn't any better. He warned Digger to keep quiet. "Now don't get all new-agey on me! Even though the industry expects artists to be a little off-kilter, it's damn hard to compete. If they think you're some kind of kook, well, there are ten thousand other musicians out there just clawing and fighting their way to get the ear of a producer, or a director, or a record company. I know I can't tell you how to live your life, but stick to what you do best—music—and keep the rest to yourself!"

After they had reached the top of the rocky bluff, Digger walked between two palms and winced in pain. The low-lying fronds were sharp and had given him several paper-thin cuts. He stopped to rub his legs, but Angélica's lean body was moving quickly ahead of him, so he tried to keep up with her.

Finally, she stopped and picked several cacao leaves and gave them to him. "Chew these. They will give you extra energy." Digger chewed them slowly and carefully.

As they slipped through the jungle. Digger's thoughts went back to the sight of Bendi, standing on top of the pyramid at Cobá. She hadn't experienced any falling, or melting into the walls of the vestibule, or seeing symbols. But she also didn't respond like the others. She'd at least listened to him intently and tried hard to believe that he had experienced all of those things. She believed in him; in everything that he did, she said. She was devoted to him. Bendi had told him that even though she didn't have any of his experiences, she knew in her heart there had to be more in life. And sharing his experiences made the world kind of magical and she felt more hopeful because of it.

For the first time since his ordeal with his mother, he thought about Bendi's love for him. So what is my problem? he questioned. How could it be going well and then fall apart? He didn't understand himself or her at times; how she thought, what motivated her, how she could get under his skin. Why was it at times he wanted to run away? Why was it so hard for him to open up to her, to anybody?

He slapped the back of his neck and looked at his blood-smeared open palm. A mosquito, the size of his thumb, lay squished. He brushed it off on his T-shirt. Digger hoped that God was not so nonchalant about His creations as Digger was about mosquitoes.

Chapter 8

"... so much of our history seems to be formed by the male ego, or should I say, the male—"

Bendi waited anxiously in the warm morning air outside the hotel on *Paseo Colón*. The early morning traffic had already begun. She watched as Ortega ran across the street toward her.

"Buenos días, Bendi," he said as he stopped in front of her, gasping for air and extending his hand.

Bendi put down her small travel bag and shook his warm hand, *"Buenos días, Ortega."*

When Manuel pulled up to the curb a moment later in a four-wheel-drive Jeep, Bendi introduced Ortega. The two men shook their heads as they looked one another over.

"Do you two know each other?" Bendi asked.

"*Sí.* How would we call each other, Ortega?" Manuel glared at Ortega.

"I guess you might say that we belong to the same side, but have different approaches," Ortega offered cheerfully.

Bendi ignored their posturing and stated flatly, "I would like Ortega to come along with me. Is that all right?" she asked Manuel in a tone that implied she would only take "yes" for an answer.

"I do not even want to know why," he sighed. "Besides, do I have a choice?"

"Of course you do," Ortega said, as he threw a backpack into the back seat and then slid in behind it.

Bendi sat in the front, passing her small travel bag back to Ortega. He squeezed their luggage amongst the neatly-packed camping gear.

As Manuel pulled from the curb, Bendi asked, "Is there any news?"

Manuel shook his head.

They headed east through the city, which was already awake. Cars darted in and out, totally disregarding pedestrians and the painted lanes of the road. As they headed out of the downtown section, Bendi broke the silence again, "How do the two of you know each other?"

"We belong to the same rainforest conservation council," the dark-haired driver said tersely. "Your friend Ortega thinks that I am, how would you say it in English? Aahhh ... pompous and arrogant, while I think that he is missing a few tools, so to speak."

"That is why we make such a good team," Ortega smiled genially. "I confuse them—and you roll over them."

Bendi quickly changed the subject. "Are we the only ones who will be looking for Digger?"

"No," Manuel said. "Several guides and three more Jeeps headed out just before me. We are all meeting at the small village where the rafters have been waiting for the last two days. Two Jeeps will take them back to San José and the other one will join us.

"Please try not to worry, Miss Porcelli," he added. "Your friend Digger is probably just tired and hungry. A road ends at the final take-out point, so there is only one way to walk and that is back to the camp where he started from. He is probably walking along that road now."

It took them two hours to reach beyond the sprawling limits of San José, home to several million residents. The epicenter of the 7.1 earthquake had been a hundred miles southeast of the capital, which sustained surprisingly little damage. But the road to the east coast had been closed and since this was the first day it re-opened, the traffic was horrendous.

Finally they reached a place where the traffic stopped altogether. Up ahead, they could see where a small after-shock had left enough debris to block the highway temporarily. It looked like several miles of cars and trucks were being held up, including Bendi and her two escorts, as bulldozers and dump trucks worked to remove the rubble of a fallen mountainside. When they finally worked their way past the landslide, the traffic improved but only slightly. Manuel had to maneuver around dozens of cracks and potholes.

Several hours later they turned onto a dirt road. Even though Bendi held onto the strap, her head hit the top of the Jeep several times. She hadn't eaten much for breakfast and was now glad for that fact as the Jeep bounced wildly down the winding dirt track. As the road curved its way through the jungle, every once in a while Bendi caught a glimpse of the Río Pacuare—sometimes splashing whitewater, and sometimes a deceptively calm and beautiful stretch of reflected light.

By early afternoon, the Jeep pulled into the tiny village. Several small houses, built of tin, stood side by side. Two dogs with their ribs poking out immediately ran up to them, sniffing in hopes of food. Frantically, Bendi searched among the river rafters' smiling faces for Digger. He wasn't there. Her heart sank.

Manuel was surrounded near the Jeep by local villagers, *Ticos*, who'd come out to shake his hand. Bendi caught his eye as he excused himself to find Danny and Francisco. She trailed along behind Manuel filled with a growing sense of panic.

"Have you seen Mr. Taylor?" Manuel asked Francisco, whom he'd found lugging equipment toward the three Jeeps that had arrived about 20 minutes earlier.

"No, he never showed up, but we want to go and help look for him." Francisco set down the paddles he was loading and looked curiously at Bendi, standing shyly just behind Manuel.

"No. You guys need some rest," Manuel ordered.

"That is all we have been doing for the last two days, Manuel," Danny interjected. He'd come up just in time to catch the last of Francisco's sentence. "We feel responsible. We want to go."

"Besides, we are the best river guides that you have," Francisco added with pride.

Bendi stepped forward, clearing her throat.

"This is Miss Porcelli, Jonathan Taylor's, I mean Digger's girl-friend," Manuel introduced her reluctantly. He turned to Bendi. "These are the guides who were with Digger."

"How do you do," she nodded to them, then turned back to Manuel. "I don't want to seem rude, but how soon are we leaving? When are we going to look for Digger?"

"Yes, Manuel, he has been missing a long time now," Francisco chimed in.

Manuel shot him a warning look, and then issued his order. "We will head out as soon as the other rafters load their equipment." He strode off to help, leaving Bendi and the two river guides to stand and look at each other uncomfortably.

"Nice to meet you, too," Danny offered awkwardly. "We, um, we wish you good luck in finding your boyfriend." He flashed a look at Francisco and the two of them nodded politely to Bendi, then hurried off in Manuel's wake before she could ask any questions.

Exasperated, Bendi looked around for Ortega. She found him a few yards away, handing a smiling *Tico* woman fifty *colones* for a papaya cut into quarters. He gestured for Bendi to join him at a crude table and offered her some of the juicy fruit.

She took a piece halfheartedly. "Please talk to me, Ortega. I don't want to think about what might have happened to Digger—and no one here seems to be in any hurry to find him. So, please tell me more about the stone spheres."

He gazed at her kindly, as if to say he understood. "Well, if you want to know. First of all, as I told you yesterday, they really are a mystery. But let me try and stick with the facts—today," Ortega added with a little laugh, "but just today.

"Remember the W's that I talked about? Who, what, where, when, why, and how? Well, let us look at the when. The stone spheres were first discovered by archaeologists Verneas and Rivet back in the early '20's. Then in the '40's, work by Stone, Lothorp, and Mason stirred up a renewed interest. They began to map out the different sites where the spheres were located. Later, a Brazilian named Ivar Zapp came out with a *different* theory. He believed that Costa Rica was the center of civilization thousands of years ago—a part of the mythical Atlantis—and that the spheres were used as inter-oceanic navigation. The alignment of several groups of spheres interestingly point to the sacred sites around the world. Now, Licda Quintanilla has written several articles on the subject of the spheres. Anyway she believes, like many others, that the stone spheres could have been made in the first century, but more likely around 500 A.D. Then she believes the sphere-making flourished between 1000 and 1500 A.D."

"Why did they stop making them?" Bendi asked.

"Well, everyone agrees it had to do with the decline of the Aztec, Incan, and Mayan cultures, which directly related to the arrival of the Spanish Conquistadors. The Spaniards basically wiped out the Meso-American culture. Other factors also affected the decline of those cultures, but still, the Conquistadors and Christianity were the major contributors to one of the swiftest, most devastating declines of any culture in the history of... I am sorry. I will get back to the point.

"Now with the 'where.' There have been a few scattered findings of the stone spheres, from Vera Cruz and the Yucatan in Mexico, all the way down to Buenos Aires in Argentina. All of those spheres were of the smaller circumference, so I do not believe that they were made at those different sites but were probably traded and then transported by boat. By far, the majority of the stone spheres have been found around the lower Terraba River and the mouth of the Diqui River. That is, in southwestern Costa Rica, close to the Pacific Ocean.

"When we have found them, they have been on tops of mounds, placed in graves, or hidden within homes. Of course, the homes are not standing anymore, just the slightest hint of the walls remain."

"But how were they made?" Bendi interjected.

"Let me return to some of the details that we do know. Most of the spheres were made from granite, but a few were made from lava and also from *coquin*a, a limestone that is the result of shell deposits millions of years ago. Fire was probably used to aid in the initial roughing and shaping." Ortega gestured with his hands. "Stone tools were used in chiseling, pecking, and smoothing the surface. Last year I came across a stone sphere of a quality that was beyond any that I have seen previously. There was hardly any spalling."

A pig snorted directly behind Bendi and she jumped. She threw a hand over her chest, then realized what the intruder wanted. She reached over for one of the papaya skins and tossed it several feet away for the pig to feed on. Laughing at herself, as the pig waddled over to its reward, Bendi turned her attention back to Ortega. "What do you mean spalling?"

"Spalling is like chipping or splintering," Ortega explained as several chickens clucked their way over to join the feast. "The original blocks had to be cut from beds of granite. As you saw at the *Museo Nacional*, the spheres range in diameter from one foot to seven feet— which means the larger spheres had to be made from granite blocks weighing almost thirty tons. To produce such a megalithic structure would take many men, and much time, resources, and talent.

"How the larger ones were transported is one of the many mysteries of these spheres. It is hard to believe that any Pre-Columbian civilization could have transported them. Some of the spheres have been found fifty miles away from the source of the rock. The large sphere that you saw at the *Museo* was discovered in the lower Terraba region; that meant it had to be transported twenty miles upstream on the Terraba River, then another ten miles on smaller streams, and then over another fifteen miles through dense jungle. Remember, all of that from the perspective that the Meso-American culture did not use the wheel for transportation."

"Is there any idea about why they were made?" Bendi asked.

"Much of the significance of an archeological find is based upon its location within the home or community, also its alignment with other, similar objects. When the United Fruit Company came here in the early 1900s to harvest pineapple and sugar cane, they cut and burned down parts of the rainforest. Some of the spheres were damaged and many had been taken from their original locations and placed in yards, gardens, and museums. Some were even split wide open, because of a rumor that there was gold inside. I believe that story was resurrected from the early belief of the Conquistadors. So you can see, by the time archaeologists arrived, much evidence had been destroyed.

"We have discovered other sites, though, that have been intact. There have been cases where groups of stone spheres were found. Some formed triangles and others lined up in straight lines, aligning with particular stars or constellations. That is why people believe they were of astronomical importance and therefore of ritual significance. We have found several located in grave sites, which also suggests some type of ritual.

"Archaeological finds have led me to believe that the stone spheres represent the sun. Obviously, the sun is light that gives warmth and life to everything. Many cultures throughout history worshipped the sun as a god. But the traditional scientific viewpoint does not believe that is the case at hand, with the stone spheres, because all Meso-American cultures represented the sun by a disc, not a sphere.

"I believe that the original makers of the spheres were in some ways more advanced, more self-actualized than other cultures. They used the spheres as a symbol of a symbol. The spheres were a symbol of the light of the sun, which to them was a physical symbol of the light of gods, or the light of the Divine or the light within—the soul."

"How did you come up with that?"

"My thesis project"—Ortega sucked in his belly self-consciously— "many years ago was to study the various legends of the indigenous tribes in Central and South America. My hope was to unravel any commonalties between these supposedly isolated peoples. Well, I discovered several, but the one that excited me the most was a common thread found within many of their stories or myths. It was about a mysterious crystal, in the shape of a sphere, that the gods sent here. According to the legends, the gods wanted to remind us that they were always present and within all things.

"Somehow the custodians of this crystal had turned it into a sphere of stone which would only be revealed at the proper time and to the proper person. Actually, the word crystal used by many of those tribes is best translated as our word, light. So I believe there is some kind of connection between the stone spheres and this metaphorical crystal or light."

Dogs barked and chickens clucked as Manuel started across the road towards Bendi and Ortega. Behind him, Bendi could see Danny and Francisco tightening a kayak to the top of a Jeep. Two others, filled with weary rafters, sped off down the dirt road.

Ortega looked up, then raised his voice. "Speaking of meaning, others feel *las esferas de piedra* had to do with social status. You know, the bigger the balls, the more important you are," he laughed heartily.

Manuel looked at Ortega with disgust.

"I am sorry, Miss Porcelli," Ortega apologized. "It's an on-going joke among the gentler sex in my profession. It is about how so much of our history seems to be formed by the male ego, or should I say, the male—"

"Ortega," Manuel interrupted sharply.

"It's all right, Manuel," Bendi reassured him. "I need a little levity right now."

"We should be going," Manuel said in a commanding tone. "We are already very late because of the earlier traffic. Danny and Francisco will accompany us." He jerked his head for them to follow him back to his Jeep.

As they drove away, several of the villagers waved them on with big, bright smiles. Bendi realized that everyone in this country seemed happy, whether they lived in busy San José or a tiny, impoverished village in the middle of the jungle. What really makes people happy, she wondered, money, modern conveniences, cars? These people had little or none of that, but they still appeared to be happy. Then she answered her own internal monologue: What they did have was family, the sky, the rainforest, and each other.

Birds chattered as the two Jeeps woke up the local animal population. As ever, the road was windy and bumpy. Bendi's arms grew sore from holding onto the Jeep's side handle. Many times they had to forge streams where the water rose halfway up the doors. A couple of hours had passed since their last stop and they still had not seen any people or villages. The jungle became thicker as the Jeep brushed aside dangling branches and hanging vines. It was more difficult to see the Río Pacuare as the river played hide-and-seek with Bendi.

Finally, Manuel pointed at two ruts in the road that traveled toward the river. "That is where the rafters and Mr. Taylor camped on their last night in the jungle. We should be at the final take-out point in about an hour."

Before every turn, Bendi's stomach tightened with anticipation, hoping to see Digger standing by the side of the road. After every turn, she felt deep disappointment. Her mind raced to the end of the road. What if he wasn't there at the take-out? That could mean that he was injured somewhere along the river, or worse yet, that he had drowned. She quietly held in her sobs as the Jeep bounced through the rough terrain.

Now the road tightly hugged a wall of rock on one side and a steep ravine on the other. Turning a corner, Manuel slammed on his brakes. Danny and Francisco's Jeep behind them slid sideways, nearly hitting them and ending up inches away from the edge of the ravine. First Manuel and then the rest of them piled out to stare at a small landslide blocking their way. Three-foot-deep rocks and dirt covered the road ahead for a distance of about twenty feet. Bendi peered carefully over the edge; she could see where the landslide had continued all the way to the edge of the river.

"We have to go back," Manuel announced.

"No!" Bendi interjected. "We can walk over this and hike to the end of the road."

"You are right," Manuel turned to look at her. "But that would take too long. We could never make it back before dark. And believe me, the last place you want to be is in the jungle at night."

"So what are you going to do?" she asked.

"I am going to call the local authorities and tell them of our situation. They will send some help to clear this road. Danny is going to drive you and Ortega back to San José, then Francisco and I will raft down the river tomorrow and look for your friend."

"I'm going with you," Bendi said stubbornly.

"Miss Porcelli, let us do our job. We will let you know the minute we know anything."

She transferred all the energy from her sadness and fear into standing her ground. With arms crossed firmly, she looked intently into Manuel's eyes. This was different for her. Usually she acquiesced to people in authority, but a previously-unknown sense of power welled up inside of her. There was also something else. She felt, at least in this moment, sure about herself, about her needing to be there, about her dreams.

"You will just be in the way, Miss Porcelli," Manuel added, exasperated.

"I know that you believe that, but I can help you in some way. I can't explain it, I just know it! I'm going, that's all there is to it!"

Manuel looked to Ortega, who raised his eyebrows and shrugged his shoulders.

"Okay, okay," Manuel sighed with resignation. "I guess a few more eyes couldn't hurt, but you'd better be prepared to get wet," he warned.

"Thank you," she said to Manuel and then turned to Ortega, "And thank you. I appreciated your company."

"What do you mean appreciated? I am going with you," he said resolutely. "I believe you when you say that you can help the search in some way. Remember our conversation yesterday? I also believe that somehow you can help me with my work."

"I know you have not whitewater-rafted before," Manuel said to Bendi, "but have you, Ortega?"

"*Sí*, I have many times, here in Costa Rica and also the Amazon."

"*Gracias a Dios* for small favors." Manuel jokingly made the sign of the cross over his chest.

They backed up the Jeeps and turned around at the first clearing. Turning off at the two ruts in the road, they drove into the abandoned rafting camp. There, securely tied, was the raft left by Digger's rafting group when they decided to hike out to the village. Danny and Francisco unloaded their gear and set up several tents, as Manuel radioed the local authorities about the landslide. He wasn't sure of the protocol, but he asked them to inform the American Embassy about the missing man.

Bendi walked to the river's edge, where Ortega joined her. The water swiftly swept by as they stood listening to the dull roar of the downstream rapids. Somehow, standing on ground where Digger had stayed gave Bendi a small amount of relief.

* * * *

Vines hung like heavy ropes twisting down from high above. A shaft of sunlight penetrated through the thick jungle and lit up several towering hibiscus plants; their purple-trumpeted flowers glistened with moisture. Digger had lost track of how long they'd been walking through the rainforest. He had no idea how Angélica knew which way to go since there were no trails, not even a slightly worn path. She could have been leading him in circles and he wouldn't have known the difference. He just followed her every move. Throughout the day Angélica continued her relentless barrage of questions but Digger refused to answer them. He was frightened. Frightened about what was going to happen to him. Could Angélica's tribe help him get back to civilization? Even if he did manage to get back, how could he undo the mess he'd created back in the States? Besides all of that, he really didn't feel like himself. Maybe this is what people feel like when they're in shock. Maybe, he thought, but it was more than that. The sensation of falling into the darkness, which he'd experienced while holding onto the round boulder in the raging river, still lingered in his belly.

Digger heard a rustling of bushes off to his left. He turned to see the commotion when a pauraque, a type of whippoorwill with coloring that looked like dead leaves, flew from its nest on the ground. A grayish peccary sniffled its way through the dampened rainforest floor. The strange pig-like animal glanced up at Digger and then disappeared into some underbrush.

"Let us stop here," Angélica said. She knelt before a plant that had huge arrowhead leaves. Digging into the ground, she pulled up several elephant ear roots. She brushed the dirt off and handed one to Digger.

"Are there any special eating instructions?" he asked sarcastically.

"No, but it is always a good rule to eat slowly."

Still a little tender from the previous night's experience, his stomach growled with anticipation. Biting into the starchy, potato-like root, he expected an earthy taste but was surprised by the rich, nutty flavor. He ate slowly.

Angélica shoved a bamboo shoot into the trunk of a tree that had orange-reddish roots protruding from the ground. A white, latex-like liquid dripped out.

"Here, drink some of this," she ordered.

Digger did as he was told. When they finished eating and drinking, Angélica, without a word, disappeared into the rainforest. Digger quickly stood up and followed her. Their journey through the jungle had varied from struggling through almost impassable undergrowth to enjoying patches of open space. But the rainforest was always filled with surprises—from gorgeous bromeliads to ugly peccaries.

A couple of times he'd asked Angélica if they were lost. She just gave him a look that shouted, "You've got to be kidding." Another time she'd actually answered him: "The only one lost here is you." He tried not to worry about it and just trusted that she knew the way.

After walking slightly uphill for quite some time, a wall of rock with every kind of plant growing from its crevices flanked them on their right. A little winded, Digger asked if he could take a break.

Without answering him, Angélica walked over to a pair of huge, umbrella-like palm trees that hugged the wall. Pushing the fronds apart, she stepped through and seemingly disappeared into the granite wall. Digger at first heard a rustling of leaves and then nothing. He had no idea what she was doing. Maybe, he thought, she's looking for something else to eat. When she didn't return, he followed her steps and walked into a clump of hanging moss. Brushing it aside, he saw Angélica standing in sunlight at the end of a narrow split in the wall of rock. She had somehow discarded her bathing suit and was now wearing a loincloth that covered her front and back; tied together on the sides with strings. Another string around her neck held up the same material, which was fashioned into a bare-midriff halter top.

Digger tried not to stare at her as he walked through the natural passageway. When he stepped into the light, the sky was cloudless and bright blue as it hung over a multitude of shades of green, two hundred feet beneath them. It had been days since Digger had seen the whole sky.

The sight was breathtaking—he was looking down at what must have been a centuries-old crater, several miles in circumference. At the bottom was a rolling green forest gently held by sloping walls of rock, laden with lush green vegetation. Off to the far right, the east, he saw a waterfall that spewed out of the middle of one sloping wall. The water cascaded and tumbled into a stream that ran through the middle of the bowl-shaped valley. The stream fed into a pond on the opposite side of the crater, to the west.

Rapidly dipping down into the hidden jungle to the left of where Digger stood was a narrow path that clung to the rocky cliff beneath him. The trail seemed to disappear before it reached the pond and stream, but then he could see it continuing on the other side, ascending a small hill buttressed against the slanted western crater wall. On top of the hill was a cleared area that looked like a miniature quarry. He could see sections of the sloping rock wall that looked as if they had been chipped out.

Squinting from the sunlight reflecting off the pond, Digger thought he saw several large colored balls scattered on top of the little hill.

Chapter 9

"Would it not be more confusing to you ...
if you called yourself a name that you are no longer?
Something that you were in the past?"

The last few minutes felt surreal to Digger. First he'd been at the shaded ground level of a dense rainforest. Then he'd slipped through a crack in a wall of rock, and now he could feel the full force of the sun on his face and see the expansiveness of a wide-open, blue sky. As he looked down, he saw another thick jungle, far beneath him. Like jewels scattered among the predominantly green trees were bright vermilion poró, purple jacaranda, and florescent yellow corteza.

Angélica motioned and Digger carefully followed her down the narrow and steep path which sloped into the previously hidden jungle. One slip, he thought, and I won't have to worry about getting back to San José.

Soon the narrow trail leveled out onto a narrow shelf. While Angélica kept moving ahead, he stopped for a moment to survey their surroundings. On his left was the crumbling crater wall which restrained the advances of the jungle; below him the ground sloped down to the pond fed by the stream. And several hundred feet beyond the stream, he could see steps leading up the hill to the small quarry. From this vantage point, foliage blocked any view of the strange, colored spheres he thought he'd seen from above the crater.

Far off to his right were plots of farmland; from this distance, the only crop that looked familiar was corn. Nearby he could see patches of open land, with various styles and sizes of dwellings nestled beside the stream. All the homes seemed to be built on circular mounds, with thatched roofs, and they were connected by cobblestone paths. Some had stone walls and others were built with wooden posts and shoots of bamboo tied together. From the look of things, he estimated that as many as a couple hundred people could be living within this village. They were still pretty far away, but the women he could see were all dressed like

Angélica, while the few men that he could make out were wearing loin cloths. The villagers haven't noticed us yet, he thought. Or maybe they have and just don't care. He hurried on down the trail to catch up with Angélica.

Suddenly, a tree on their right swayed as a young girl jumped down from her lookout. She ran up to Digger and stood before him, gazing intently into his eyes. In front of her chest, she cupped her hands as if holding a delicate butterfly. Then she moved them to his chest, before pulling her cupped hands back till they were halfway between the two of them. Her palms opened up and faced the sky, as her arms spread wide.

Digger surmised that she must have been around eight or nine years old. As her bright blue eyes continued to look at him unwaveringly, he began to feel uneasy. She didn't avert her stare as she turned her palms and pushed downwards.

"She wants you to bend down," Angélica said.

"What do I say?" Digger felt uncomfortable; he hadn't been around children very much.

"Whatever you want," Angélica answered .

Digger put his hand out. The young girl momentarily looked at Digger's outstretched hand, then returned her gaze to his eyes. He felt as if she were looking for something. Then the girl threw her arms around his waist. She backed off and in broken English said, "My name is Vawaha." Glancing over at Angélica, she then awkwardly stuck her hand out towards Digger.

Charmed, Digger moved his hand to hers and gave a slight shake. She giggled.

"My name is Digger," he said formally.

"Is that your chosen name?" the little girl asked.

"Well ..." He looked over at Angélica for help. She looked back at him blankly, as if to say "you are on your own." He scrunched up his eyebrows at her and turned back to Vawaha. "It's a nickname," he smiled.

Vawaha looked confused and cocked her head.

He tried again. "My parents named me Jonathan. So, yeah, I guess you could say that Digger is my 'chosen' name."

Apparently satisfied, the girl grabbed his hand and started leading him down the path. Digger kept up with her reluctantly. From behind, he could hear Angélica's taunting, "I guess you made a friend. It must be all your charm—or maybe your ease of conversation!"

"Very funny," Digger responded as he struggled to match Vawaha's energetic pace.

As they drew closer to the village, he noticed that tens of humming-birds and electric-blue, morpho butterflies were fluttering everywhere.

Finally, they reached the bottom of the hill, where a group of people had already gathered, lined up reception-style.

"Where's the cake?" he joked. "This could take a long, long time," he added, surveying the number of tribe members who'd come out to greet them.

As he stood uncomfortably between Angélica and Vawaha, each one stepped before him, gazed into his eyes, and then cupped their hands. They went through the same motions that Vawaha had performed, including finishing up by giving him a hug.

In between two of the greeters, Digger turned to Angélica. "Friendly tribe of yours," he said nervously. The length of time of each hug had moved into the uncomfortable zone for Digger. It went beyond the "quick hold and release" that had always been easy. His mind instantly started its chatter: Why is she or he holding me this long? Is this sexual? Do I want this hug to continue? Do I want it to stop? What should I do in return?

He remembered his first real hug; it had been a total shock. He was seventeen years old and was dating an older woman–of eighteen. On their third date, she gave him a genuine, heart-felt hug. It was more than the obligatory squeezes that Digger had previously called hugs. That embrace from his girlfriend felt great, but also scary. In those few seconds, he felt a rush of information and feelings. There he stood with his arms at his side, not knowing what to do. He instantly knew that, because he did not know what to do, there was something very unhealthy about the situation. The stark realization was that he couldn't remember ever being hugged like that.

That first experience of a true hug was a sharing that seemed even more intimate than a kiss. The kiss was from passion, but the hug was from someplace different, someplace deeper.

He brought his attention back to the present to see that Vawaha had grabbed an older man from the crowd and was now leading him toward Digger. The man appeared to be in his late sixties, with receding white hair and a long scar on his right forearm. He greeted Digger in the same way as the others. But from this man's brown eyes, Digger felt a peace and calmness emanating.

"His name is Digger," Vawaha blurted out. Angélica smiled as she pulled back the young girl's long, shiny-black hair.

He gently touched Vawaha's head, "I know, my child," he said in broken English. To Digger he added, "My name is Mashuba." He then took a step toward Angélica. After completing the typical greeting, he said, "I am glad that your journey was safe and successful."

"What do you mean successful?" Digger cut in. "We nearly got killed and I'm still in the jungle!" He started to relate the events of their trip.

"You are here, are you not?" Mashuba interrupted as he gave him an orange, fleshy fruit. "That is successful." Then the old man raised his hand and the crowd stepped back respectfully. He said to Digger, Angélica, and Vawaha, "Let us walk."

Digger looked around as they walked toward the center of the clearing. Outside one of the homes was a rimless, tripod grinding stone with carvings of animals. Several storage jars stood outside one of the stone homes. Off to his right, a worn-out path traced around a strangler fig. Its twisted vine encircled the trunk and branches of a huge ceiba tree. Beyond the clearing, he could see the plots of crops more clearly now. Some of them were filled with tall vegetation, but one of the plots featured smaller plants and it was being tended by several people who were on their hands and knees. He tried to see the waterfall in the distance but his view was blocked by the lush jungle. Looking across the shallow, babbling stream, which was about twenty yards wide, he saw the cobblestone path that led to the hill.

"That is where the Keepers of Wisdom work," Vawaha pointed.

"Oh yeah?" Digger replied. "And what do the Keepers of Wisdom work on? Can they help me get back to San José?"

"I will answer many of your questions later," Mashuba interjected. The old man nodded toward a group of women and children standing near the stream, staring at Digger, but keeping a respectful distance. At Mashuba's nod, the children ran over noisily and pulled at Digger, dragging him back to where the women were waiting. Digger looked helplessly back toward Angélica and Mashuba, but they seemed unconcerned, engrossed in their own conversation. Meanwhile, the women had one by one begun giving Digger their formal greeting.

He was still wearing his blue swimming trunks, sandals, and T-shirt with the big-webbed frog's feet clinging to an oar. As he ate the delicious fruit they offered, he tried not to squirm in discomfort while they touched different articles of his clothing, feeling the fabric. From their reaction, it seemed as if they'd never seen anything like it. It was hard for him to believe that they'd never seen a T-shirt before, but who knows? He had read about some tribe in the Amazon that had never been touched by the modern world. He also remembered that Danny and Francisco had talked about parts of this region that had never been explored.

As he listened to their chattering, their speech sounded like a mixture of different native tongues, something he'd never heard before. At least some of them spoke English, but he also heard several different dialects of Spanish. Ever since Bendi had received her bilingual teaching degree, she'd been teaching him Spanish. Given his present circumstances, he was glad he'd paid attention.

What had happened to Vawaha? He looked around for the girl but couldn't see her anywhere. Then she surprised him by appearing, as if from nowhere, just behind his left shoulder, grinning up at him. He opened his mouth to say something to her, but just then a woman reached out and tapped the frog on his shirt.

She quickly recoiled, as if expecting that it might jump from her touch.

"T-shirt," Digger said to them all in English.

They all laughed and took turns touching the imaginary frog. Digger noticed that most of the villagers in sight were women and children. He wondered if the men were out hunting or doing whatever males of indigenous tribes do.

A young boy tugged on his shirt and then handed him a palm-sized, ornate, clay object with several small holes in it. As Digger turned the artifact in his hands, he noticed that, depending on his viewpoint, the object looked like a toucan, or the head of a pig, or the head of an elephant. He recognized it as an ocarina, but when he blew into the mouthpiece, he could only make one trembling high pitched tone. Digger handed the object back to the young boy who proceeded to play it better than any of the studio musicians Digger had worked with in L.A . Several other children with similar ocarinas joined in the whistle symphony.

By now many more of the villagers had paraded by to catch a glimpse of the stranger. Several of them came up to him, made their greeting, and gave their names, while a few stood back with scowls and simply observed. "My name is Digger," he said to the woman standing before him who'd just offered hers. She began to speak in a tongue he couldn't understand. When he shrugged his shoulders, she tried Spanish. He still didn't get it.

Vawaha came to his rescue. "She is asking the same question I did. Is Digger your chosen name?"

Digger nodded his head to the woman and then asked Vawaha, "What do you mean, 'your chosen name'?"

Vawaha, excited to have Digger's attention, answered quickly, "At birth, we each were given several names. In the past, our family name was the one we kept throughout our life, the one that we were recognized by. It was usually that of the father's family, but in some tribes one was given a *Naal*, the mother's family name. Over generations, our family names have built a history. Others would respond to you based on their perception of that name, and you, in return, would respond to their behavior."

Digger thought about his own name, Jonathan Taylor. He remembered the razzing that went on at family gatherings. "He has the

Donovan"—the *Naal*, his mother's maiden name—"nose." "Digger has the Taylor intelligence." "But he has his mom's love of music." "He has his father's temperament." Based on all the relatives' names, the bantering would go on about all their different characteristics, from physical to emotional, from idiosyncrasies to personality, from possibilities to limitations. This discussion of inherited traits would be part of the regular course of events at all the family get-togethers.

Vawaha continued, "Then our parents gave us a name for our individuality. If they saw us as a bird, or hoped for us to carry on the noble characteristics of that animal, that is what they would call us. If they saw us as the sky, or a fish, or a monkey, that would be what they would call us, and then tell all others. By that name given to us, we would declare ourselves to the world, and by that name we would respond."

Digger almost missed what she was saying, he was so amazed by the adult quality Vawaha's speech had taken on. But he was also fascinated by what she was explaining. She was on to something.

"This naming ceremony was well-meaning," the little girl was saying. "It was what our parents wanted for us, but even so, it was for themselves. The name was what they liked and what they wanted. In truth, it was from their perspective—their hopes, and their beliefs. But here within the tribe, we can choose our own name."

"How and when do you decide?" Digger asked.

"One decides after... I am not sure what you call it—when you are no longer a child, when your body and mind have developed."

"An adult," Digger suggested.

"Yes, that is it," the girl nodded eagerly. "To answer your other question—how—you choose the sound of you." Two birds chattered amongst the trees. "Do you hear? They call for each other. They know each other's sound and they carry it within themselves."

Disappointed by his lack of attention, the others had drifted slowly away. Now Vawaha walked over toward a hollowed-out log and motioned for Digger to sit on it. When he did, she took his hand and placed it over his chest. Then she picked up a solid chunk of broken tree limb. She lifted it high and, just missing his head, brought it down hard on the log. Once over the initial fear that he was about to be clobbered, he felt the impact of the contact.

He realized Vawaha meant much more when she used the word "sound." She meant the feel—the resonance. Digger replayed the moment. The reverberation had started in his buttocks and moved up to resonate within his chest and his hand, which Vawaha had placed there. For him it was the sound of a low C played on the piano. He told her of his new understanding.

"It can be even more." She narrowly missed his head as she struck the log again. "What did you hear before I struck the log?"

"The sound of the branch whizzing by my ear."

"So if you had to put those sounds together to make a word, what would it be?"

He thought for a moment, then said, "Whooooshwaampp!" The few who'd stuck around to watch laughed at the name. Digger smiled at them. "So if I thought—I don't, but if I thought that sound resonated with who I truly was, I could give myself that name. And everyone, when they saw me, would say," Digger waved his hand in the air, "Hola, Whooooshwaampp!" They all laughed again.

"What you would do is"—she cupped Digger's hands in front of his chest—"gather the sound of your name, Whooooshwaampp, and then from your heart, you would share it with the other person." She brought his cupped hands towards her. "Then you would free that vibration by bringing your hands halfway between us"—she demonstrated again— "and then, opening your palms up, you would let your name ride the wind of spirit!"

"So what name do you want to be called when you grow up?" Digger asked.

"It is Vawaha. The Keepers of Wisdom have allowed the children to choose their names early, before we reach what you call adult."

"Why?" he asked.

Vawaha shrugged her shoulders. "I do not know why, but I am glad that they have."

"So how did you choose your name?"

"One day I climbed high on the rocks." She pointed to the quarry on top of the hill across the stream. "I had been sitting there for a long time, wishing I could fly. I wanted to know what it felt like to be a bird, to go high in the sky, to see all the jungle beneath me. I wanted to ride the wind.

"After a while, a hawk landed on the next boulder. I kept perfectly still because I did not want to frighten him. As we looked at each other, I gave him our greeting in my mind. When he flew by me, I actually heard his wings flap and in that moment I felt my name. It was his last flap before the jungle exhaled him into the wind." With eyes closed, a peaceful smile upon her face, she breathed, "Vaaawaaahaaaa."

Digger had always felt uneasy around children. He never knew what to say or how to act. But this child was different somehow. Who is this little girl? he wondered. Not like any child, or even adult that I know!

"So tell me of your chosen name," Vawaha urged him. "Dehh, ggaa, eerr." The children nearby laughed as Vawaha broke his name down. As if chanting, they intoned, "Deeeehhh!"

Digger was amazed; it sounded like a tree full of the twelve-year cicadas rubbing their legs together.

Then two young boys got on their haunches and hopped around like frogs croaking "Ggaa!" while Vawaha growled "Errrr!" They were all quite amused with the sound of his name.

"What does it mean?" Vawaha asked again, and then answered her own question. "Dehh, ggaa, eerr. Let me guess. If I had to go with the creature sounds, I would say you are one who hibernates but when you awaken, you fill the jungle with your song. You do not crawl or go slowly but jump over obstacles. And you do so with the fierceness of a beast." She stood back with crossed arms and looked proud of herself.

"Well, Vawaha, that's very interesting," he said. "I'll have to think about that one. But if I have to go by your definition of a chosen name, I don't believe Digger would apply."

"Why not?" she asked.

"Because I did not really choose it. My nickname, as we call it, was kind of handed down to me by my friends. I just accepted it."

"Why did they give you that name?"

"Where I come from, names are not given for their sound or their feel. My name was given to me for a couple of reasons." He explained to Vawaha the same thing he'd told Angélica about his digging, his searching. Then he explained about his love of softball, picking up the broken limb and what looked like a small pine cone. Digging his sandals into the dirt, he threw the pine cone up, hitting it with the broken limb. The seed catapulted through the air and landed in the middle of the stream. The children all laughed and clapped as they watched him running in a circle, touching imaginary bases.

"You will have to teach us that game," Vawaha shouted, now sounding more like a child again.

"Sure," he caught his breath as he circled back around to her. "Can you ever change your name?" he asked.

"*Sí*, if later on in your life your name does not match who you are, of course you can. And you should," she said matter-of-factly.

Digger thought about all the different stages that had occurred in his life. He laughed to himself about all his possible names: from being the fearful boy, "Ahhnnooo!" to the searching adult, "Whhooaa," from the musician "Laladumdum," to the ball player, "Hitit," from the lonely man (the sound of nothingness played loudly in his head) to... He stopped for a moment.

Wouldn't it be confusing to everyone to be changing your name all the time?"

"Would it not be more confusing to you—" it was Angélica who was suddenly standing behind him, speaking in a whisper and reaching around him to touch the center of his chest—"if you called yourself a name that you are no longer? Something that you were in the past? Or worse yet, Digger, a name that another has given to you?"

He turned to face her, surprised by her sudden appearance, and stammered a bit. Vawaha giggled.

"Now you are speechless again," Angélica said. "I must bring out the silence in you. Or maybe the children bring out your words."

As Digger scowled at her, he saw Mashuba walking toward them in his slow and purposeful way. Digger was glad to see the old man; he'd gotten the impression he was some kind of leader here and maybe he would be Digger's ticket home.

As soon as Mashuba was close enough to hear, Digger began, "I don't mean to be rude, but, how the he...ck can I get back to where I'm suppose to be? I need to get back to the river, to civilization. I need to let people know that I'm all right. They've probably sent out search parties for us by now. But they won't be looking for us this far from the river. They might think we're dead. Can you help me?"

"That is not an easy question to answer," Mashuba replied. His soft eyes searched into Digger's. "I will tell you that your concerns and safety are very important to me, to all of us—more than you can ever know. But first we need your help."

"You need *my* help? I don't understand. What can I do for you?"

Chapter 10

*"Your intuition
knows order in the confusion of chaos,
smells fairness amidst the stench of prejudice,
hears compassion through the dissonance of hate,
and sees light in the darkness of the jungle."*

Digger felt unsettled as his mind raced. This seemed like a very nice place but still he needed to get back to San José. Who were these people anyway? A nine-year-old girl who wasn't a child, a Costa Rican Gandhi, and a strange but beautiful woman who seemed to enjoy making him feel uncomfortable. They were all okay but this wasn't his home; besides, why in the world would they need him? *He* was the one lost. He was the one who needed *their* help.

He turned to Mashuba again, insisting, "Explain to me how *I* can possibly help *you*. I'm confused."

"Let us go across the stream," the old man motioned to Angélica and Digger.

"Can I come with you? *Por favor*, please?" Vawaha looked at Angélica with pleading eyes.

"I do not know," Angélica turned questioningly to Mashuba. With a smile, he tilted his head and then gave a slight nod, as they set off through the village toward the bubbling water that swiftly glided over rocks and small boulders.

"Thank you! Thank you!" Vawaha called as she ran ahead of the slow-moving adults.

Digger was growing impatient for an answer and was about to ask again when Mashuba finally began to speak.

"Everything in the jungle has its place, its function. Everything is interconnected." Mashuba stopped, bent over, and picked up a handful of the rainforest floor. Angélica and Digger looked at several insects which moved amongst the dirt and dead leaves.

"All that is within the jungle is dependent upon everything else,"

Mashuba said. "No event ever occurs that does not effect every creature, plant, insect, or rock–from creating life to giving food, from providing shelter to offering companionship. There is even that which brings death so that new life may begin."

"What does this have to do with me? With what I have to do?" Digger asked impatiently.

"No *thing*, no *one* can exist in this place without receiving something. Also without giving something." Mashuba carefully placed the debris back onto the ground and continued, "With all of this receiving and giving, you might say that there are millions of relationships that are interacting in every moment. It is the same for you now with us–within the jungle. For it is your destiny–"

"Hey!" Vawaha yelled as she ran back to the lagging adults and took Digger by the hand.

"I will explain a little more when we reach the quarry," Mashuba sighed. Vawaha walked beside Digger for a moment, then tugged on his T-shirt. "Ask Mashuba how he got his name."

"Ahh, the little one must have been talking with you about chosen names," Mashuba chuckled. "Well, mine comes from the water of the fall and the stream." He pointed upstream, in the direction of the waterfall that cascaded into the leafy jungle below.

Vawaha couldn't contain herself. "He can be as still as the deep part of a stream, but when it is time, he has much power, as the fall of water!" she blurted.

"Before the water reaches the fall, Maaaa"—Mashuba's vocal cords resonated—"Shhuuubb"—his hands tumbled downwards and then smoothly motioned downstream—"Aahhh!"

Digger replayed Mashuba's name in his head. "I'm sorry. I don't get the connection between the sound of your name and the sound of the stream."

With a confident look Mashuba turned slowly to Digger. "You do not have to." He pointed to himself. "It is *myyy* name."

Hopping onto rocks and boulders, Vawaha made a game of crossing over the stream. "So what's the 'chosen' name of your tribe?" Digger asked.

"The answer is a difficult one," Mashuba replied. "Not only because of its name, but because it is not a tribe in the sense that I think you mean."

"Well, do you have a name, any name that you go by?"

"*Los Otros!*" Vawaha yelled from the opposite shoreline.

"That is what some call us and how many here refer to themselves," Mashuba agreed.

"I know in English that means 'The Others.' But why a name like that?"

"It is difficult to explain, but in essence we do not call ourselves by any name. For there is no such name that exists that can describe who we are, because we are constantly changing. It is difficult enough to try and give your own self a name. For you are much more than the symbol of your name, are you not?

As he turned around to nod at Mashuba, Digger began to slip off a mossy rock. Angélica reached out and steadied him. Vawaha waited impatiently on the other side. Finally, they all made it across and began the trek up the cobblestone path, which stretched several hundred feet before it became the steps leading up the hill to the quarry.

Digger didn't say anything about it, but he was glad he was finally going to find out what it was he'd seen there, from a distance, when he was standing above the rim of the crater. Instead, he asked, "Why couldn't the tribe give themselves a name by a common feeling or vibration? Like you do with your own names?"

"Using sound is just one way to name your self. That is how Vawaha and I have chosen our names," Mashuba answered. "But others, like Angélica, use different names that might resonate with touch, sight, an emotion, a concept, your life purpose, or anything, really. So if we were to give our tribe a name, it could go on forever and no one would ever be able to remember it. We could be called the MashubaVawahaDigger-TalltreeScentofflowerSweetLeapingfrog—"

"I get it. I get it," Digger interjected.

"—PeaceFlowingSSSSSSWhoosh Tribe," the old man finished. "And know this: that would only be the name of the tribe *for now*. Next week, the name of the tribe would be different, for we are always changing, always evolving. Some would leave, others might come, but we all would have interacted with nature, each other, and therefore, in some way we would be different. We could be different by tomorrow, by tonight, by the next moment.

"When you try to name something as wondrous, as flowing and interchangeable as a group of people, it is quite impossible. Words can be cages. Like the people who capture the flying creatures and keep them caged within the cities."

As if on cue, a burst of color flew by them and landed on a nearby tree. The bird, with its ruby-red chest and an avocado seed in its beak, was a foot long but also had a two-foot, emerald tail that extended gracefully beyond its body. It was the most beautiful winged creature Digger had ever seen.

"That bird is not its name," Mashuba nodded toward the magnificent display of feathers. "It is much more. But for now and forever more, it will be remembered as the quetzal because it reminds people of the great leader, Quetzalcoatl, who wore its feathers as part of his headdress. It is lucky for the bird that it knows only the cages of man and not the cages of his language. For if it did, it is possible that after some time, the bird would believe it is its name and that it should be kept in a cage for others to see. Then it would never leave the 'comforts' of that imprisonment. Never remember that it can fly. Never remember that it can return to its home in the jungle."

Mashuba stopped walking a moment as a breeze rustled through the trees, loosening leaves from their hold. It was as if he were the director and with a silent cue, the jungle had become alive. The loud roar of several howler monkeys echoed through the rainforest as a pair of yellow-throated toucans flew overhead. Their red-tipped, lime-green, orange, and blue bills were the same size as their bodies. Vawaha chased after the rainbow-hued creatures.

Until the conversation came to a halt, Digger had hardly noticed any of the beauty before him. Now he watched as the colorful birds flew to a nearby branch and dined on fresh figs. He noticed Mashuba slowly inhaling, as if he were filling his lungs with the colors and sounds of the rainforest. Then after a slow exhale, the elder continued to walk in his slow, methodical way.

"Is this where they met and stayed?" Digger asked.

"No," Angélica, who'd been following along silently, finally spoke up. "We did not have any so-called place or village. *Los Otros* can be found anywhere, whether they are an individual or a group, in the cities or high up in the mountains. But when they did gather in the jungle, it was always in a different place. The location would change as the jungle called to them to experience its many wonders."

"How did people know where to find you if you kept moving around?"

"They just did," she shrugged.

"What do you mean, 'they just did'? Did you leave a map or directions in a secret place?"

"No, we did not have to. All those who seek *Los Otros* eventually find us, so there is no need for maps or directions. The birds do not have maps; the monkeys do not get directions; the fish need no highway." Angélica gave him her look.

"But they do call for each other; they make sounds, or leave scents behind," Digger argued.

"Yes, that is true, but there is also something else that occurs," Mashuba interrupted their banter. "There are triggers, so to speak. The triggers are usually very subtle road signs. In your culture, it could be a passage from a book or a scene from a movie or a certain shape or number. When you see, feel, hear, or sense those triggers it awakens within you a sense of knowing, a sense of direction."

"Are you talking about intuition?" Digger asked, as he took the first of the hill's steps. Vawaha, long ago frustrated by all their talk, had disappeared ahead of them again. Like her, he was becoming impatient to get to the top.

"You might call it intuition, but let me explain some things first," Mashuba equivocated. "There are different aspects to who we are. At the core is our spirit—with the body, emotions, and intellect woven through. For the body, it is the eye that recognizes light and the ear that recognizes sound. With that recognition, the physical then knows a sense of direction, provides itself nourishment, creates safety, or makes itself strong. For the spirit, the 'eye' or 'ear' is called *intuition*, and that intuition recognizes those usually-invisible road signs. Your intuition knows order in the confusion of chaos, smells fairness amidst the stench of prejudice, hears compassion through the dissonance of hate, and sees light in the darkness of the jungle. With that recognition, the spirit then knows a sense of direction, provides itself nourishment, creates safety, or makes itself strong. As much as we develop our physicalness through our senses, we need to develop our spirit through our intuition."

"That recognition, that intuition might have happened to me but only a couple times," Digger admitted. "Nothing I can really count on."

"It is the only thing to count on," Mashuba said firmly. "Besides, you use it more than you think, especially in your music. Do not blame yourself too much for not recognizing it, for you have not been taught. But the remembrance is in here." Mashuba touched Digger's chest. "You know what to do."

"So the ones who have intuition find you," Digger said.

"Maybe. Maybe not. Because it is not only the ones who have intuition, but the ones who then try it out. The ones who find us have put into action that unclear, hazy feeling that is sometimes layered with the ooze of logic or the muck of ego or the sap of conformity. The path is not a straight one, nor should it be. They must not fear the jungle, but know that the jungle will provide for them. For as their path winds like a snake through the underbrush, so their lives will touch all the events that will lead them to where they need to go."

Digger heard Vawaha hurrying to greet them as they finally reached the last of the steps. She grabbed his hand again and pointed proudly to the quarry behind her. "This is where the Keepers of Wisdom work."

Digger's eyes widened as several brightly-colored stone spheres covered with etched symbols came into view. Each sphere looked as if it had been meticulously painted with a dazzling array of colors that seemed to make them come alive. Many of the symbols appeared to be geometric shapes: circles, four-, six-, and eight-pointed stars, and all the different types of triangles. Next to many of the geometric shapes were patterns of dots and lines that looked like Morse code. Other symbols were vaguely similar to Chinese, Japanese, Hebrew, or Arabic writing— or Egyptian hieroglyphics. But the more he stared at them, the more he realized that these symbols were not any of the above. They were like nothing he had ever seen before.

Realizing he had not breathed since he first caught sight of the intriguing sculptures, he quickly inhaled. Letting out a long breath, he forced himself to slowly scan the scene before him. Ranging in size from one to seven feet in diameter were ten colored balls of stone lying scattered over the unevenly terraced hilltop. Several small trees and bushes had taken hold within cracks on this rocky surface. Digger noticed a hundred-foot-wide section of the granite wall had been chiseled out, leaving piles of rocks strewn about.

Vawaha ran up to one of the giant, round objects and placed her hands about six inches above it. She closed her eyes and soon looked as if she'd gone into a trance-like state.

Kneeling next to a two-foot sphere to get a closer look, Digger found himself mesmerized by the colors and symbols, none of which made any sense to him. All he could do was stare at them.

Angélica walked over, knelt next to him, and placed her hands on his temples, turning his head to face hers. Her green eyes eased softly into his sight. "As confusing as it might be, this is what you are looking for. This can help you get back home. But we need you to accomplish something here first. We will not survive—in fact, *you* will not survive if you fail. The implications go way beyond what you can see and touch."

Digger was thoroughly confused. He had no idea what she was talking about. "What is it that I need to do?" he mumbled, highly conscious of the soft coolness of her fingers on his temples.

"We need you to imprint one of the stone spheres," Mashuba offered serenely as Angélica continued to gaze into Digger's eyes. Digger couldn't quite bring himself to look away and up at Mashuba, who was now standing behind Angélica.

"What do you mean, 'imprint'?" he asked, still slightly dazed by, first the spheres themselves, and now, Angélica's closeness.

She finally dropped her hands to her knees. "That is the difficult part," she sighed. "We cannot tell you. To be more precise, we do not know exactly what it is that you will do, or rather, *how* you will do it."

"Only you know," Mashuba added. "But we can tell you that it has something to do with interacting with a sphere of your choosing."

Angélica smiled compassionately at his confusion and rose to her feet. "Think of it as having a relationship—with the sphere."

"And now, before darkness falls, we will leave you here to think over what we've told you," Mashuba announced. Before Digger could protest, the elder had gestured to Vawaha and the three of them began to descend the hill, leaving Digger alone in this strange place, with the radiantly decorated stone sculptures.

Bewildered for a moment, Digger sat with his mouth gaping, trying to think what he should do or say. When the words finally reached his lips they echoed off the crater wall but the trio had already disappeared down the path. "Relationship? With a rock?"

His attention was distracted again by the sphere he'd been scrutinizing when Angélica had placed her fingers on his temples

He was awed by its intricate design and brilliant colors as his eyes strained to pick out the detail in the starlit evening. But when had the sun set? How long ago had Mashuba, Angélica, and Vawaha left him alone?

Chapter 11

"… the masses were never told that the power, the sphere, is within…"

Bendi awoke as several howler monkeys bellowed out their ferocious roars. She rubbed her eyes and felt surprisingly rested; it was the first time in several days that she'd slept more than three hours. She quickly got dressed and stepped outside the tent to see the river guides, Danny and Francisco, preparing the raft and kayak. Overhead, the gentle but raucous howler monkeys sat with their legs hanging over branches while they lazily chewed leaves. She just shook her head at them.

After a quick breakfast, Bendi and the others put on their life-jackets and scarred black helmets and set out on the river. In the raft, Bendi sat behind Danny on one side, while Manuel sat behind Ortega on the other side. Francisco paddled the kayak downstream to survey the river.

"I need every one of you to paddle," Manuel ordered sternly. "It will take work to get through the rapids. Miss Porcelli, do everything exactly as Danny does. We all need to be in unison. I do not want to be looking for another person on this river. *Entendido!*"

Bendi loved to be near the water, but being in waves—nevermind whitewater—was scary. Even though she felt intimidated by the river, she had to restrain herself from responding to Manuel's macho attitude.

"Focus on paddling during the rapids but otherwise keep a sharp eye out along the riverbanks for anything, anything at all," Manuel said sharply.

In front of them, bubbling whitewater covered the entire width of the river. Bendi tightened the straps on her life-jacket.

"Three forward strokes! Let us try and keep to the left of that big boulder. Everyone seems to wrap around it. Believe me, we do not want that to happen to us. Back left! Hard right!"

The raft bounced hard through the rapids. Bendi could hardly keep her eyes open as water splashed from all sides. Bouncing off the large boulder, they rushed on through several more yards of whitewater. At the end of the rapids, Francisco glided to shore to wait for them. When he saw that they'd made it safely through, he paddled along the shallows of the riverbank, checking out both sides. He was looking carefully for any debris or sign of Digger.

"Stop!" Manuel called out. The rafters stopped paddling so they could scan both sides of the river. The banks were strewn with dead bushes, tree limbs, and boulders. Francisco yelled over to Manuel, "Nothing!" and then paddled further downstream.

Ortega turned back to comfort Bendi, "Do not worry; we will find him."

"Pay attention to Francisco," Manuel ordered.

They watched up ahead as the kayak swiftly bounced over five, partly-submerged boulders all lined up in a row, ten feet ahead of each other. It formed a cascading staircase with tons of churning water pouring down it. Through the bubbling water, the kayak disappeared and reappeared several times as Francisco paddled furiously—and then shot out into calm waters. He held up his paddle in both hands to signal that he was 'okay.'

As they began their own bouncing trip down the watery staircase, Manuel yelled, "Paddle! Paddle!" Bendi's knuckles turned white as she dug her paddle into the river. Every time the bow of the raft dipped down, a wall of water slapped them hard, totally drenching everyone. She stopped paddling momentarily as Danny bounced high off the side of the raft. With one hand he quickly grabbed the safety line. "Paddle!" Manuel screamed.

She didn't like rollercoaster rides and this was surely ten times scarier. Again the bow crashed hard into a wall of water. Then as quickly as the ride had begun, it was over. Her heart was still pounding as the river slowly pulled them along.

"Good job, everyone," Manuel congratulated them. "Shortly up ahead we have a set of rapids, then Caliente Falls, and then more rapids. You need to do everything I say. Okay?"

Francisco paddled hard to get close to the raft. "The river must have flooded out recently because there is something new up ahead. There is a hole right before the two boulders!"

"Great," Manuel said.

"What's a hole?" Bendi asked anxiously.

Danny turned around. "It's where there's a drop-off after a big boulder. The water flows over the boulder and digs into the river bottom, creating a hole. If you fall in, it takes time before you come up to the surface. It's like being in a washing machine. Make sure you hold on."

Bendi could see the percolating river straight ahead. The deafening sound of the rapids nearly drowned out her next question, "What is Caliente Falls?"

"Just a little drop of about six or seven feet!" Manuel roared back. "To ensure success, we need to be heading straight, directly after the hole, so we can slip in between two boulders. That will put us straight before we go over the falls. Here we go!" He started barking out orders: "Right!... Back left!... Stop!... Forward!"

When the raft approached the hole, the bow bent over the boulder. Ortega bounced backwards and then slipped off into the water. Manuel reached over the side and grabbed onto his arm. "Hurry! Help me get him into the raft!" he yelled to Danny.

Danny dropped his paddle and grabbed both sides of Ortega's life jacket. With one swift movement, he pulled the hefty archeologist back in.

"Left hard, right back!" Manuel bellowed. They quickly returned to their positions. "Forward! Hard! Hard!"

Bendi stared at the two boulders, and a chill went down her spine. She was scared, but she was also feeling something else that she couldn't quite define. The raft slipped in between the two obstacles. In the next moment, Bendi could only see air as they were spit out over the falls. All their bodies slammed forward as the raft hit the water and then bounced wildly from side to side.

"Paddle! Paddle!" Manuel yelled, as the raft bounced hard off a boulder. "Hard left—now forward!" He continued shouting orders until they were safely through the rapids.

"Good work, everyone," Manuel smiled slightly.

Bendi looked over at him. She knew he was troubled about Digger's disappearance, but etched into his face she saw satisfaction, excitement—and yes, even fun.

If she had to be honest with herself, she'd felt those same things—to a degree. What was it? Why was it? Then she realized that it wasn't so much that they'd conquered the river; it was that they'd survived it. They were alive. Through skill or luck or both, they'd made it through. There were still more rapids to survive, but at least they'd had the opportunity—some might say privilege—to be there.

Digger had always tried to explain to her about playing ball. All he wanted was the chance to play in the championship game, he'd told her. You honed your skills and practiced and played the whole season to have a shot at that, he said. Winning was fun, but all he truly wanted was the opportunity to play, the opportunity to test out all that he'd learned. That was the thrill.

Manuel stopped his smile when he saw Bendi looking at him. He quickly turned to look further downstream, toward Dos Montañas Pass. Leaning forward, he strained his eyes at the sheer granite walls. "Back left. Hard right. Let us get over to the shoreline and take a small break."

Danny jumped out of the raft and held onto the bow line. They jumped out as Francisco paddled over. "Why are we stopping?" he asked.

"I want you to go down and check out the Pass," Manuel ordered. "Something doesn't look right. I do not want any surprises. Bendi, you and Ortega check the riverbank upstream. Danny and I will walk a little ways and check the conditions of the river."

As birds chattered above them, Ortega and Bendi walked slowly upriver, looking for any signs of Digger or the raft.

"Did you know that there are over 250 different species of birds in these rainforests?" Not bothering to wait for an answer, Ortega continued, "Did you know that Costa Rica comprises less than one-tenth of one percent of the earth's land mass, yet it holds ten percent of all its known species?"

"I didn't know that. Ortega, yesterday you never finished talking about why you thought the stone spheres represented the sun."

Ortega stopped walking and smiled broadly, happy to oblige anyone who wanted to talk about his favorite subject. "If you remember, my thesis was based on finding a commonality among the legends of various indigenous tribes. Well, not only did I discover a story about the stones spheres, but there seemed to be one about its makers—a mysterious tribe of Outcasts. Just recently, everything seems to have fallen into place to support my theories. I discovered some petroglyphs that seem to suggest what I have proposed, that the sphere represents the sun, which represents the light within."

Bendi motioned him to keep walking and searching, as he continued excitedly, "The largest of Costa Rica's archaeological sites is at Guayabo, on the slopes of Turrialba. It is not far from here; in fact, we passed it on our way here. It was a very old city which thrived somewhere between 1000 B.C. and 1500 A.D. For the last fifteen years of digging, the most interesting archeological finds at Guayabo have been remnants of streets, aqueducts, causeways, pottery, and metalworking. But a couple of years back, we discovered a clay jar with red-and-black drawings that depict several of the stone spheres. In the picture, one sphere is located among a group of people, then another one is high in the sky, like the sun. But the most interesting part is that inside every person depicted in the painting is a smaller sphere. I believe that corroborates my story about the sphere being a representation of the soul, the light within."

"Don't any other cultures believe that?" Bendi asked.

"Some, but the basis of many religions around the world and throughout our history is based on the Divine or God being outside of us. That is, of course, unless you personally were part of the bloodline of the gods—like a king or pharaoh. Then the power, the gods' lifeline, would reside in you. So the masses were never told that the power, the sphere, is within themselves, otherwise they would not need any divine rulers, would they? "

Ortega took a breath. "I am sorry I babble on. It is hard for me to hold back. I will try to keep on the point." He continued, "Needless to say, this painting that was discovered will cause much controversy and as many opinions as there are species of birds, no?"

Bendi smiled and asked, "So what about this mysterious tribe? Did they make all these spheres?"

"No, not all of them, only a small portion. All the hundreds of others I believe were just copies. In the legends they talk about a meeting place 'in the middle of the cradle.' I believe that is right here in Costa Rica. The three great Meso-American civilizations were the Incas from South America, the Aztecs from Mexico, and the Mayas from the Yucatan down to Honduras. Costa Rica was the crossroads between all of them, literally in the middle of those great cultures. According to the legend, these Outcasts recorded information on twelve spheres that are secretly hidden somewhere in the middle of the cradle."

"We found something!" they heard Manuel yell from downriver. Quickly, Bendi and Ortega ran along the shore toward the sound of his voice.

Danny and Ortega were hunched over the ground near where Manuel was standing.

"What is it?" Bendi asked hopefully.

"What do you think, Professor?" Manuel asked Ortega.

Ortega examined the ground. "Well, it is most definitely the charred remains of a recent fire. Whether or not it was Digger's, we do not know. Are there any people who live out here?" he asked as he meticulously eyed the surrounding area.

"No, at least none that we know of," Manuel replied. "The closest people are from the village where we picked up the rafters."

Ortega examined a low-lying branch that hung over a long, flat boulder and then looked at the surrounding ground. "Did any of you walk over here?" They all shook their heads. "Do not move. Stay where you are. There is a faint footprint here from a sandal. It is not very clear, much has been washed away, probably from the rains. Also, this branch has a fresh cut and looks as if someone tied a rope around it." Ortega walked back to the charred area of the fire remains. He looked carefully around everyone's feet.

"What are you looking for?" Manuel asked.

"The owner of this footprint." He pointed to the small imprint of a bare foot between Manuel and Bendi. "Danny is the only one who is not

wearing sandals and his foot is much bigger than this print." The archeologist squeezed the tip of his chin for a moment, and then confidently
added, "Yes, I would say that if Digger was here, he had company."

"Was he kidnapped?" Bendi asked frantically. "I have heard of
tourists being kidnapped by rebels from Nicaragua!"

"Calm down, Miss Porcelli," Manuel said. "That is just media-hype.
Yes, it has happened but it is still very rare and then only on our northern
border. We are at least one hundred and fifty kilometers from there. I do
not know what happened, but if it was Digger who built this fire, then
something must have happened for him to camp out here, only a little
way from where he started." He noticed the worried look on Bendi's
face and added, "But if it was him, he was still alive. Don't worry, Miss
Porcelli, we will find him. Let us continue."

As they walked back to the raft, Bendi noticed that Ortega fell
behind, in line with Manuel. She glanced back to see them whispering.
Straining to hear without letting on, she caught only a few words: "... by
the boulder... big cat prints... much bigger than a margate... maybe...
jaguar." Then she heard Manuel shush Ortega. She pretended not to
notice.

When they reached the raft, Francisco paddled up. "You were right.
There was something different. The earthquake must have loosened parts
of Dos Montañas Pass. Sections of the granite wall have fallen into the
river. It looks like boulders are scattered throughout the pass. It will be
tricky, but I think we'll get through okay."

Danny and Manuel pushed the raft carrying Bendi and Ortega into
the water, hopping in and letting the river slowly pull them downstream.
As they approached the pass, with its twenty-story cliffs, sounds of the
rapids echoed back to them of the impending danger. Bendi again felt
uneasy and fidgety and sensed that it wasn't so much from the rapids,
but something else. She continued to paddle and directed her gaze back
to the shoreline. It looked as if a tributary of the Río Pacuare veered to
the left. When they drew closer, she could see a small stream there, with
fallen trees and bent-over bushes. "Shouldn't we get out here and look?"
she suggested.

"That is just an old riverbed," Manuel answered. "The Río Pacuare
has not run through there for hundreds of years."

"But look at the trees and bushes," she insisted.

Manuel ignored her and focused his attention back on the entrance to
Dos Montañas Pass. She glared at him until he told them all, "Keep your
eyes on the shore; if you see anything, let me know."

Bendi wasn't satisfied, but she kept silent. She looked as far as she
could see down the ancient riverbed. Feeling that something was important about this place, she glanced upwards from the river floor to the top

of the valley. Off in the distance, a feline figure standing on one of the rocky bluffs stared back at her.

"What's that?" she pointed.

Ortega and Danny turned to see. The figure slipped behind some tall trees in the foreground.

"What?" Ortega asked

"I saw something big and black on that bluff over there." She pointed again. "It was like a big cat, maybe a leopard."

"There are no leopards in Costa Rica," Manuel said dryly. He stared meaningfully at Ortega, as if to say, *Keep silent.*

"I didn't say anything!" Ortega blurted out.

"Say anything about what?" Bendi was not going to be put off so easily.

Manuel grunted, "Ortega thought he saw some tracks of a jaguar, but it was probably just a big oscelot. Bendi, you would never see a jaguar out in the open, especially in daylight. And if you did, it would have had been orange with black spots. No one has seen a black jaguar in these parts for decades." He added gruffly, "Now let us keep our eyes on the river."

Bendi kept looking for the animal as they approached Dos Montañas Pass. Just before the raft entered the lengthy, narrow waterway, Bendi could have sworn she saw the black feline staring back at her from between the trees.

Inside the stony passage, Bendi noticed small branches and big splinters of what looked like a eucalyptus tree, stuck in several cracks about fifteen feet above the waterline. The water must have reached that high once, she thought. Now the river funneled furiously through the pass, tossing their raft between the canyon walls. Up ahead, Francisco's kayak bounced off one of the walls and turned upside down. As Bendi watched in horror, he quickly flipped himself back up, spitting out water and gasping for air.

Manuel's orders echoed off the canyon walls as they tried to avoid the boulders strewn in pinball fashion through the narrow pass. As the raft dipped and turned, water engulfed them from all sides. Again Bendi was reminded of a rollercoaster but with no guarantee that the vehicle would still be upright at the end of the ride. As they shot out of the narrow pass, they all heaved a sigh of relief.

Manuel didn't let up. "Hard left! Back right." He guided them toward a patch of calm water near the shore.

Bendi tried to catch her breath as she turned back to look at the scarred walls of Dos Montañas Pass. She found it hard to believe what she'd just been through.

"The earthquake and rains did some damage," Francisco called over as he glided up next to them. "The river is totally changed here and also probably further down. Did you see the debris, five meters over our heads back at the entrance?"

"Digger would have had lots of trouble navigating through all of this," Danny agreed.

Bendi's heart sunk deeper into her chest.

After a short break they shot through several more rapids and then the river became smooth as glass as it narrowed even more. They paddled slowly in silence, until they approached a huge sign that read:

Wild River Excursions
Final Destination

Hope you enjoyed rafting the most remote and dangerous river in Central America!

Two jeeps waited for them next to the sign.

"What now?" Bendi asked.

"We will get more help and go down again tomorrow," Manuel said solemnly. "This time we will have searchers work both sides of the river. We will see if there are any signs of him trying to walk out of here. You can go back—"

"I'm going with you," Bendi quickly interrupted.

"Me, too," Ortega concurred.

* * * *

For Digger it had been a restless night, one of those sleeps where he didn't remember being awake but didn't remember sleeping, either. He was seemingly in both worlds at the same time. The major contributor to his restlessness was his growing frustration. He needed to get back to civilization, to San José, to the United States. Why wouldn't *Los Otros* help him? And what was this *thing* he had to do? Imprint with a stone sphere! Have a relationship with the rock!

After Digger had found his way down from the quarry in the dark, he finally caught up with Mashuba, but the old man hadn't been any clearer. He simply ushered Digger into a hut and said he'd see him in the morning.

Now, opening his eyes, he was startled to see Vawaha standing a foot away, looking directly at him. "Good morning," she smiled.

He carefully maneuvered out of the hammock. Even though he hadn't had a great sleep, the hammock had been surprisingly comfortable. He stretched his back and scanned the small, barren, bamboo dwelling.

Vawaha cupped her hands, extended them to him, and then completed the *Los Otros* greeting. This girl is relentless, Digger thought, but he responded by doing the same.

Then he asked, "Why do you look at me so intensely?"

"That is what we do. We believe that the opening to the spirit is through the eyes. So if you want to truly know someone, you need to look into their eyes," Vawaha said.

"*Pura vida,*" Angélica called from the open doorway. She exchanged the *Los Otros* greeting with Vawaha and Digger. "How was your sleep?" she finally asked Digger as she looked into his eyes.

He shrugged his shoulders.

"That is expected. You are sleeping in a new place and on a new bed." She pointed to his hammock with a smile and then turned to Vawaha, "Do you mind if I talk with Digger alone?"

"But I want to stay with him." Vawaha grabbed Digger's hand.

Angélica bent down and looked into the girl's eyes. "You can come by a little later. *Por favor.*"

"Okay," she relented.

"I'll see you later, " Digger called after her as she slipped out the door.

Vawaha smiled back at Digger and then trotted off toward a group of children.

"Let us go back to the spheres," Angélica suggested.

"And then what? What do you want me to do? I"—Digger pointed to himself—"want to go back to San José—now. It's nice here, but I don't understand why you can't take me back. People are worried about me… or at least I hope so. There are things I need to do, my music, my—"

"Nothing is ever more important than what is before you at this moment," Angélica said.

"And this moment I have to go back to San José," Digger insisted.

"Then go back. No one is stopping you, Jonathan Taylor—Digger. Go back. By the way, did we not go through this before?"

"You know I can't go back by myself. I don't even know where I am. I need your help."

"First of all, you *can* go back by yourself, but you don't know that you can do it. Whether you make it alive or not is another question. Secondly, you are correct that you do not know where you are. Thirdly, again you are correct because you most certainly need my help, our help. I am also telling you that we need your help. It is more important than you realize. Focus on now, what is before you, your present task at hand, so to speak." She turned and left the hut.

Digger reluctantly followed Angélica, crossing the stream behind her as she delicately stepped upon the rocks and boulders. "What is more important than I realize?" he called after her. "You can't tell me what that task even is!" he whined.

"You know what it is—to imprint on a stone sphere. You just have to discover how to do it," she reminded him.

"Why do I have to do this?"

"Enough of the questions, Digger." She sounded annoyed. "Is asking questions what you always do when you are unsure, when you don't know what to do next?"

Within in his own mind, Digger heard the clank of a metal door shut.

Angélica's voice grew louder as she continued, "Sometimes knowing the why is not important. You just have to do it. Even when you do not know what to do. I know that is confusing but..."

All it took was a voice, usually his mother's, to reach a certain decibel before the programmed door shut automatically; then it became quieter for him. It wasn't as obtrusive or as annoying when the door was shut. For protection, he'd developed this technique during his adolescence. But now, in his adult life, most of his relationships had suffered from this device. His ex-wife had been a master at detecting the shutting of his door. She would yell at him, "You're not only locking out the bad stuff, but also the good stuff!"

Though she would rarely yell, Bendi was even better at it. She could tell the moment before the metal door slammed. He felt a pang of hurt in his chest and wondered what she was doing right now.

"... do something, anything differently," Angélica was saying. As she reached the other side of the river, she came to a halt. Digger almost bumped into her. "I heard that back there."

"You heard what?" he asked.

"You know what I mean. Is this another way you do things, closing up, keeping silent?"

Digger walked around her and didn't answer. They climbed the steps toward the top of the hill. As they rose above the rainforest canopy, the view was stupendous. Huge, billowy clouds drifted swiftly over the green lush valley.

Angélica let out a noisy breath. "Okay, okay ask away; at least questions are better than silence."

Digger didn't respond, standing in silence among the stone spheres. The scene was surrealistic, with the out-of-this-world appearance of the spheres silhouetted by the natural beauty of the jungle. He had been so preoccupied about this notion of "imprinting" one of them and about getting back home that he had completely forgotten about how beautiful and mysterious the spheres were.

Chapter 12

"I'm not really sure about anything."
"That is a wonderful place to be."

Several small iron pots lay near a fire ring at one side of the quarry. Digger watched as an elderly woman crouched beside the pots dipping a short, thin piece of frond into a mortar filled with purple dye. Around the bowl were several plants and a stone muller—a pestle with a frog motif.

"She uses those pots to melt down gold, silver, iron, and copper, and then very carefully outlines some of the designs." Angélica explained. "The plants are used to make the dye to color the stone spheres."

"It's beautiful. The color is almost iridescent," Digger marveled.

The woman turned her wrinkled face toward Digger and smiled. She stood up and gave him the *Los Otros* greeting and then looked into his eyes for a moment. Without saying a word she went back to her task.

The sphere she was working on had already been painted with several shades of yellow and orange. It looked like a geometry lesson gone wild: lines, angles, dots, circles, triangles of all kinds—isosceles, right angle, equilateral, and acute. They intersected one another at different points around the sphere.

Taking a closer look, Digger inspected what looked like ancient symbols.

"That is a language that would be similar to Egyptian hieroglyphics," Angélica told him.

"What does it mean?"

"Well, you know how in Japanese writings one symbol means more than any English word could describe? Like the English word for wind could describe a meteorological event, while the symbol of wind in Japanese could mean the relationship between sky and earth, the eternal aspects of change in our lives, the idea of acceptance, and so on."

A scene from Digger's mother's wake flashed within him. He and his brother were standing by the open casket. Their aunt walked up to give them her condolences. She knew their mom better than anyone else, and so she also knew what her two nephews had experienced growing up. She said, "You boys have been through a lot." His brother Jeff responded with a simple, "Yeah." With just that one word, Digger knew what his brother meant. In an instant, the scenes of the previous forty years had moved through him—some good, some bad, some angry, and a lot that were confusing and frustrating.

Digger reflected. That one word, *yeah*, was filled with thoughts, information, hopes, fears, expectations, and the full range of emotions. What ancient symbol would that one word be? What would it look like if he were to see it etched on some primitive stone carving?

"*Mira, aquí,*" Angélica called as she walked nonchalantly toward another sphere. "Look here."

Digger shook his head—a gesture most people make unconsciously to rid themselves of unwanted memories. He turned to follow Angélica, looking out over the jungle as he walked. A thin mist hung over the rainforest canopy. Several miles away, on the opposite crater wall, he could see the waterfall; centuries ago, a small river had tunneled a hole through the foliage-laden wall.

It's like being on another planet, he mused as he watched the glimmering water disappearing into the mist. "You live in a beautiful place," he told Angélica as he turned back to the sphere she'd wanted him to see. "How many spheres are there?"

"Well, there are a total of twelve being worked on," she answered. "But hundreds have been made over generations. They are not all ours." She sat down on a huge, "ordinary" boulder and Digger joined her.

Behind them, Digger heard some trees rustling. He turned around and looked down the steps to catch sight of a group of white-faced monkeys, playfully swinging in an old oak tree.

"What do you mean not yours?" he asked, as he turned back to face Angélica. He tried not to notice how the early morning light reflected off her smooth skin.

"It began well over a millennium ago. The early *Los Otros* began chiseling out spheres, which looked like granite balls with no paint or symbols. The other tribes heard of the power of the stone spheres and tried to copy what we had done. So they merely cut out the spheres from blocks of granite and then believed that they had the power. Many of their chieftains kept several in their villages. Some kept them in their homes, and some were buried with them. But they did not understand."

"Understand what?" Digger asked.

"Understand the true significance of the sphere."

"Which is what?"

"Which you have to discover... do not get mad at me," Angélica added hastily, with a laugh. "They did not understand that the mysteries and the power came, not only from the form, though the sphere in and of itself has much power, but also from the intention and energy that was put into them. There is a relationship, a sharing that occurs between the creator, the rock, and the one who observes. Like an artist—a painting is more than just colors, brush strokes, and form; the creation is a physical, emotional, intellectual, and spiritual expression. The spheres that you see here are special—there are no others like these, and no one has ever seen them but the people who are here in this village. The Keepers of Wisdom, which is what we call our Teachers, have gathered here to create these beautiful sculptures."

"So who are these Keepers of Wisdom?" Digger asked. "Is she one?" He pointed to the woman who was coloring one of the spheres.

"No, she is an apprentice. The Keepers of Wisdom could be said to be sculptors, historians, painters, healers, orators, scientists, philosophers, and musicians. They are our "Wise Ones." At every point in time and in every culture, there is at least one Wise One. Each Keeper of Wisdom is in a high but varied state of awareness of Universal Knowledge. They have gathered here from the many different cultures to share with us their Knowledge. And in their gathering, their combined states of awareness paints a complete picture. This picture—Knowledge—contains the Truth of All That IS, and much more importantly, it contains the how; the Knowledge of how to live, how to discover who we truly are, how to find our way Home."

"Then tell me, how can I meet any of the Keepers of Wisdom? Maybe they can help me with this 'imprinting' business." Digger's tone was giving away his skepticism, but Angélica ignored it.

"They are around, at least for a little while," she replied smoothly. "When you are ready, one or more will appear."

"I'm ready, I'm ready."

"When you are *truly* ready," she emphasized.

"Well, how come I've never met any Keepers of Wisdom before this? How do I know that they really exist?" Digger demanded.

"Trust me, they are always around. Some have been very noticeable and are worshipped by others who have built religions around them; some are more quiet and can only be found in the most remote places. And some are camouflaged by the cities that they live in or the jobs that they have or do not have.

"So did *they* imprint with the stone spheres?" he asked.

"Yes, most definitely!"

"Okay, then tell me what you mean by imprint"— Digger thought he had her cornered now—"because when I think of 'imprinting,' I think of what happens when a baby duck opens its eyes for the first time and sees its mother."

"*Imprint* is the only word in your language that comes close to describing the meaning," Angélica said. "But to use your definition, you must realize how very important imprinting is to the duckling; it is needed to survive, it is the first step, it leads to a new life. Putting yourself into the duckling's perspective, you have just left the egg and are now in a 'new world.' You need to be nurtured, guided, and loved.

"But the process of imprinting enables the duckling to remember so much more than just surviving. The truth of it is that the duckling already knows within itself what it needs to survive, what it needs to evolve, what it needs to be the best possible duck."

Angélica stopped talking for a moment and walked over to a place where the ground was muddy from a trickle of water dripping out of a crevice in the moss-laden wall. She lightly placed her bare foot into the damp ground. Then she slowly raised her muddy foot, leaving a perfect imprint. She looked up at him expectantly, then continued, "The word imprinting also means much more. It is something like that," she motioned toward the footprint, "except much more gentle. Imagine that you can *imprint* all of you—all the different aspects of who you are: physical, emotional, intellectual, and spiritual. You would basically leave behind all that is you. What you take with you, is still all of you, but much more..." Angélica agilely lifted her foot and bent her leg, showing Digger her muddy sole "... because it is also all that you have touched."

"Deeggrrr," Vawaha yelled, as she came running up the steps. She ran over and gave him a hug. "What are you doing?"

"Angélica is telling me about the stone spheres," he smiled at the precocious youngster.

Vawaha ran over to the largest spherical structure, which was almost twice as tall as she. Digger and Angélica followed.

"What do they all mean?" he asked Angélica, while Vawaha placed her hands inches from the colorful sculpture.

"Each sphere has a central message," Angélica replied. "There are spheres for governing, traveling, education, spirituality, healing, relationships,—"

"This is the Communication sphere," Vawaha interjected.

"So tell me all about it," Digger said as he crouched down to her level. He'd never had children of his own; in fact, he never really gave it much thought. He liked children, yet he wouldn't go out of his way to be with them. But with Vawaha he was beginning to feel more and more comfortable.

Vawaha's demeanor transformed into teacher mode; she stood up straight and spoke precisely: "This is one of the most important spheres. These symbols"— she pointed to several circles and triangles that had code-like markings next to them—"represent the many different ways people communicate."

"Language is very important to us," Angélica added. "One of our biggest activities of the day is to learn and teach about the many languages. I have been the one who has gone to the big city of San José and learned English. Others have learned *Español* from visitors to our land. We all have come from many different villages and taught each other our own languages and customs. It is with great pride that we do so."

"It's great that you learn all the languages, but why spend so much of your time doing it?" Digger wanted to know.

"We spend our time because of what happens to our minds, or should I say, it is what does not happen to our minds. What did it take for you to learn Spanish?"

"Well, the best way to learn it is to immerse yourself in the culture," he answered, "but I didn't go to Mexico or Spain. I learned it from my girlfriend, Bendi. It took learning a whole new vocabulary, lots of practice, and learning to change around the order of the language. Like to put the adjective after the noun: in English we say blue shoes, in *Español* it is shoes of blue, *zapatos azules*. Linguistically speaking, it does make more sense."

"So to learn Spanish well, you had to let go of your way of speaking, no?" Angélica arched an eyebrow at him. "Learning a new language forces you to think differently. For instance, English is a very difficult language, but so is your way of life. A language usually reflects the beliefs of its people. In your language and most others, it is said that a man *is* white, a city *is* beautiful, a job *is* boring. The *is* makes everything so definite, so limiting. But each one of those things is actually much more than your sentence describes. Besides, no one *is* ever this or that; one *is* always becoming. But there is nothing in your language that allows you to speak or think in such ways."

A few birds began to chatter loudly and like a ripple in the water, others joined in the conversation. Angélica laughed at their timely demonstration and continued, "Anyway, learning new languages forces you to let go of your own way of thinking and pushes you to think like another. That is wonderful practice for everything else you do in your life."

In his peripheral vision, Digger suddenly caught sight of a dark, crawling creature the size of a big cat. He leaped off the boulder he'd been sitting on. While Angélica and Vawaha laughed with great glee, he turned apprehensively to see what it was. An armadillo scrutinized him and then waddled back down the hill. He realized that the boundaries for his perceived safety were quite different in the jungle from being in San Diego.

"I didn't know you had armadillos here. I've only seen them in Texas," Digger said, trying to sound calm and feeling silly about his fear of the benign creature.

At that moment, a butterfly fluttered between them and Vawaha chased after it.

"Who is that little girl?" Digger shook his head. "She is not like any child I've ever met."

"She came to us two years ago," Angélica answered quietly, watching Vawaha careen joyfully around the quarry.

"Where are her parents?"

"All we know is that her father went deep into the jungle one day and never returned. She felt her mother did not look hard enough for him. So when Vawaha searched, she became lost. But then she found us. She says she misses her parents but she is much happier here with us."

Digger found this story hard to swallow. "She made it through the jungle alone? By herself?

"To some, I am sure it is hard to believe a child or anyone could find their way within the rainforest. That is because many people have lost the qualities that could assist them on their journeys. Those qualities were suffocated when they became adults. But Vawaha still has them, and they are finely tuned."

"Look who I found dancing with the winged ones!" Mashuba took Vawaha off his muscular shoulders and gently set her back on the ground.

"I was telling Digger about the spheres," Vawaha chirped to Mashuba.

"By all means, continue!" Mashuba turned to Digger and bowed while he cupped his hands. The huge granite ball stood before them, with every color of the rainbow fluidly painted onto its etched surface.

"Here!" Vawaha pointed to a circle on the stone sphere. It was outlined mostly in a beading of gold but was completed in a thin line of silver. "Everything in the jungle is joined, like a circle," Vawaha explained, happy and proud to perform her teaching duties. "So our communication has to do the same. Everything we communicate by our thoughts, our feelings, our words, or our actions goes out into the jungle and somehow comes back to us like a circle—no matter what our language or culture."

"I understand," Digger said.

Mashuba spoke up. "Realize that there is a difference between understanding, and *knowing*. *Understanding*"—he pointed to his head—"is a process of the mind. But when you truly *know* something, anything, it is found in your heart, your soul. That knowing shapes the reality of your present and drives the direction of your next action. Think back on many of yours and others' conversations. Was the communication truly happening for the purpose of knowingness, or did it have some other purpose? Perhaps the need for regurgitation of thoughts and emotions, or a singular appreciation for the sound of your own voice, or a chance to try and prove that you are right in the other's eye?" He winked at Digger.

High above the hill, a hawk circled and screeched. Vawaha turned and looked upward as the hawk dove into the clearing of the quarry and settled on one of the spheres, just a few paces from the little girl. As the four of them stood motionless to watch, tiny droplets of water dripped off the hawk's sharp beak. Digger glanced back at Vawaha and was surprised to see tears beading up in her eyes. Then, with a loud shriek, the hawk flapped its wings and flew off, high above the jungle.

"That is a sign of their coming!" Vawaha cried out to the adults. "They will be here soon. Very soon!" She looked urgently at Mashuba.

"You know, Vawaha, signs can have many interpretations. In other tribes, tears of the hawk mean new birth," Angélica suggested gently.

"It can be both," Mashuba added solemnly.

Vawaha cried, running toward the path.

"I will go with her," Angélica said, as she ran to catch up with Vawaha, who was already halfway down the hill.

"What was all that about?" Digger wondered aloud.

"Nothing you have to worry about," Mashuba intoned.

Digger glanced questioningly at Mashuba but then turned to look at the display of spheres. "This is all too much. How will I ever understand... I mean, *know* how to imprint one of these things? To be honest, I'm not really sure about anything."

"That is a wonderful place to be," Mashuba smiled.

"What do you mean a wonderful place to be? It's confusing and frustrating!"

"Just know that is where you want to be—for now."

"I suppose *that* will help me imprint on the sphere?" Digger asked sarcastically.

"Yes, it can," the old man replied seriously. "It is a great beginning."

Chapter 13

"Most tribal cultures believe in a never-ending spirit,
what we might call a soul,
that travels and inhabits different places and times."

The sun glistened off the rainforest canopy beneath the hill, catching Digger's eye for a moment. Then he turned back to the colorful spheres, struck again by the bizarre quality of the situation he was in. He gave up asking questions, as Mashuba stood silently by, just watching him. Instead, Digger focused his attention on one particular four-foot sphere. He circled around it.

"That is what you might call the History Sphere, " Mashuba offered, his dark, sinewy body moving toward Digger.

"What does this mean?" Digger was gazing at one of the designs. He was mesmerized by the intricacies of this art, which was not only painted but also etched to different depths.

"Do you really want to know?" Mashuba asked.

"Of course I do; that's why I asked the question." Digger was puzzled by the peaceful man's response.

"Interesting that you picked this design out of the many that are here. For this circle that you have been looking at is a story of Earth. It has been told that human civilizations have come and gone three times before now. And—"

"Wait a minute," Digger interjected. "Are you telling me that our civilization dates further back than 8,000 years?"

"Oh, I am sorry. I didn't realize that you believed everything in your history books." Mashuba's lips gave way to an unpretentious smile. "To continue. All the symbols that are attached to the lower circle are the representation of the total sum of the history of those previous civilizations.

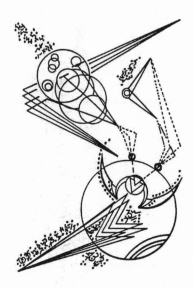

"Now imagine your Bible, the works of Shakespeare, all the thoughts of your philosophers, the history of your art and music and politics, the history of your warring civilizations, everything from every perspective in every language from every point of what you believe to be your history, all of that is said by this." Mashuba pointed to the symbols that were within the circle and nestled into the four arrows.

"Everything that has ever been written or known about man in this present civilization is contained in those symbols?" Digger exclaimed incredulously.

"No. Most of those designs represent the various possibilities for the future, the so-called potential of the human race. All that of which I spoke is in just this *one* symbol." Mashuba pointed to what looked like a sloppy numeral three."

"I'd say I'd find that's hard to believe," Digger responded.

"Really?" Mashuba countered, "I do not understand your computer world, but is it now not possible for a tiny little piece of mineral to hold unbelievable amounts of information?"

"Yeah, but I need the computer to relay the information. I can't read the chip by looking at it."

"Digger, do not be so limiting. Think bigger, feel bigger, allow bigger, *be* bigger! You are the computer! And a lot more."

Digger didn't know how to respond. He had no way of knowing if what the old man had told him was true or not. He decided to ask another question, "Whose symbols are these?" Digger pointed to the ones that were just outside the circle but underneath the four lines.

"That is the history of visitors from other places, they have been called everything; including gods, Star Teachers, aliens, and angels. These visitors could also be said to be Keepers of Wisdom but whose homes are..." Mashuba pointed up toward the sky then back toward the symbols underneath the four lines. "These markings tell the story of how and why they came."

"Where do these 'gods' reside–on Mount Olympus?" Digger joked.

"That is not far from the truth. Many of these visitors that I speak of are found in your myths, Bibles, and legends. But they have actually come from other places."

"Okay, I'm not going to argue with you..." Digger shook his head and thought, this old guy can believe what he wants. I'm in the middle of an isolated rainforest and these people probably believe in many things that modern civilization has debunked. "Let me ask you, though, why were they here?"

Mashuba motioned Digger to follow him over to one of the few trees that had been able to grow on the rocky hilltop. The elder grabbed one of the lianas that hung down from a branch and placed the vine in front of Digger's face. Meticulously, Mashuba picked at the tiny fibrous strands of the vine as he spoke, "Each one of these strands could be said to be the essence of this vine. Our bodies have similar structures."

"Oh, you mean like DNA?" Digger asked.

Mashuba looked quizzically back at him.

"Nevermind," Digger added, "Go on."

Mashuba continued picking at the fibers. "I can also tell you the core of this vine, this tree, indeed the jungle, is much more than you can see or touch. And so it is for you—for me. We not only have a physical body but also a spirit body. And this spirit body also has strands—fibers of 'light' that contain the essence of your soul.

"Some of these beings, or Star Teachers, spend much time trying to ignite that spark in our 'light' strands, or as you call it, DNA. Having that spark ignite helps us remember that the other aspects of us, the physical, emotional, and intellectual, are not truly us. Feeling that spark reminds us that we are all made of a beautiful light, the light of our spirit that is intrinsically connected to the light of the Divine."

So much for thinking this old man primitive! DNA? Aliens? What next? But Digger simply asked, "How do they do that?"

"They do it in many ways, some are invisible and communicate with us through thought or emotion or intuition. But others are visible and visit us every once in a while."

"You mean some of them are here walking around our cities and farmlands—talking to us?"

"A few. But others have allowed their soul to actually become human, like what you call reincarnation. When they do this it is like having amnesia. It is then a long process of moving through generations, eventually evolving an awareness of their past and their purpose." Digger felt Mashuba's stare sink deep within him. It felt unsettling yet comfortable. Mashuba continued, "Once these souls become aware, they begin to remind others of this light, of this connection to all spirits.

"A handful of these beings create 'triggers' to help us find our way back Home. Birds who fly thousands of miles to nest in the same exact spot every year are guided by unknown triggers, whether they are visual cues from the stars, or patterns of wind, or various pulls from the magnetic earth. So each soul can recognize visible and invisible triggers which stimulate a sense of knowing that goes beyond logic and helps them remember what nourishes them, what shelters them, and also what lights the path of their journey."

Mashuba let go of the vine and lightly brushed his hands. "I need to speak at a gathering in the village. I will talk with you later."

"Wait—I have just a couple more questions. If we have all these 'good' gods, or Star Teachers as you elude to them, why is our planet such a mess?"

Mashuba paused on his way to the steps. "First of all, this is what you would call a jungle of *choice*. Anyone is free to choose whatever direction they wish. Next, all things being in balance, there are the opposites to the Star Teachers. They are also visitors, but we call them Fear Walkers. They have established many different kinds of triggers which feed their ways, ways of survival, pain, and isolation."

Digger couldn't hold back anymore; he had to say something. "Mashuba, all the things that you've told me are kind of hard to believe."

"Whether you believe as we do or not does not change the truth." Mashuba placed a hand on Digger's shoulder. "The past drives much of our present and therefore our future. Know the past and what part it has played or is playing, no matter how hurtful, or secret, or bizarre, or forgotten. Remember that you cannot change those things that are unconscious or hidden. But once the light, your deep and expanded awareness, shines on your past, you can see it for what it is; you can learn and then change your perspective of it, let go of what you do not need, and keep that which you desire for your present, for your future.

"Now," Mashuba turned toward the path again, "I must go. Please take your time with the spheres and enjoy yourself."

Digger looked over every sphere and tried to make sense of all the designs; hoping that he could discover a way to "imprint" himself with them—on them? For them? To them? He sighed. But he came up with nothing.

As he continued analyzing the spheres throughout the day, Mashuba's final words to him about the past kept replaying in his head. He couldn't shake the strange feeling that he had lost something. His experience here with the stone spheres, like the previous day, had somehow 'triggered"—as Mashuba would have said—faint memories of the forgotten symbol. It was like absently standing in front of an open refrigerator; just a moment before, you were perfectly clear about what you wanted but now the memory was temporarily lost. You secretly hoped that if you gazed long enough at the various items the lost memory would come back to you.

A slight drizzle began to fall. Digger tilted his head back and let the refreshing rain splash onto him. He rubbed his hands over his face and arms and took a deep breath. Realizing that he was famished, and also very wet, he decided to return to the village. He'd only moved ten feet when he stopped and turned around. The design that Mashuba had explained, that one on the Sphere of History that was supposed to represent the Earth, was just one of many that adorned the massive stone sphere. It struck him suddenly: If just that one design is of Earth, what do all the other circles and symbols represent? Mashuba's words echoed in his head. "Do you really want to know?"

* * * *

The foliage seemed to grab Bendi's feet as she walked along the jungle trail. Although exhausted, she felt a need to find the bubbles. Eventually she arrived at a small trickling stream and decided to follow it. Walking for a while she came upon the stone spheres again. This time a black jaguar sat on top of one of them. After staring at her with its bottomless black eyes for a moment, the feline disappeared as it slipped behind the brightly-colored object.

When Bendi moved cautiously closer to locate the missing jaguar she noticed that next to a smaller sphere lay a limp body. She knew it was Digger. She hurried to him, turning his body over. His forehead and arm were covered with dried blood. As fear pulsed through her veins, she reluctantly put her ear to his chest, heaving a sigh of relief when she heard his shallow breathing. Then a dark shadow appeared next to her and she could feel a hot, moist breath burning the side of her face. It was the black jaguar again, staring into her. She let out a silent scream.

Bendi bolted upright in her sleeping bag, breathing hard and heavy from fear of the black feline. But her fright, frustration, and despair were slightly overshadowed by a sense of hope—hope that her dream was somehow based on reality, that Digger was still alive. The rest of the night she couldn't sleep. She lay there immobile until the jungle began to stir.

Finally, dawn broke the darkness and Bendi dressed quickly to go out and try to start the propane stove. A few minutes later, Ortega opened the flap of his tent, rubbing his eyes.

"*Venga aquí,*" Bendi said in a loud whisper.

Slowly Ortega pulled himself out of the tent. Sleepily, he helped her as she fumbled with the propane.

Anxiously, Bendi related her dream as she put coffee on the stove. "So what do you think?" she asked excitedly when she'd finished.

"The most intelligent, powerful, and mysterious creature of the jungle is the jaguar," Ortega began in his thoughtful way, sorting through a box of pots and pans for a couple of cups. "The name itself means 'one who kills with one leap.' Maybe you dreamed about the jaguar because you thought that you saw one yesterday. But many of the indigenous tribes of South America believe the jaguar is the symbol of the *sukai*, or what you might call a shaman. Shamans have been known to do many things, from miraculously healing people to killing them in bizarre and tormented ways. Who knows? Maybe one is trying to communicate with you—or maybe even trying to protect Digger."

By now, the others had risen and Bendi and Ortega were interrupted by breakfast preparations, chatter over plans for the day's search, and clean-up tasks. As soon as they finished, several Jeeps with trailers of new search equipment from Wild River Excursions pulled into the camp. With the new arrivals, the search team consisted of about fifteen people. Under Manuel's direction, they quickly outfitted and dragged to the river's edge three additional rafts and one more kayak to prowl the river for signs of Digger.

Manuel also ordered several of his people to stay behind and set up a radio for communications. "This will be our base camp," he announced. He directed them to unload the coolers of food and camping gear they'd brought, and to set up the additional tents. "When you are done, drive down to the take-out point and pick us up. Be very careful because the road is treacherous, especially where the landslide occurred." To the others, he added, "I want the rest of you to slowly sweep the river like we did yesterday, with one kayaker and two rafts on each side of the river. But this time, I want at least one team on each side to walk along the shores wherever possible. If any of you find anything at all—call it in."

Soon Bendi's wet, bumpy adventure on the Río Pacuare began again, but as the sun rose in the sky, so did her hopes. Manuel, Ortega, Danny, and she led the search on the right side of the river. They received their first baptism of water when they shot through the first set of rapids. All the rescuers kept eyes busy, scanning river and land.

After shooting over the "hole" where Ortega had fallen out of the raft the day before, and then plummeting down Caliente Falls, all the teams immediately beached their rafts and kayaks. The rescuers walked back upstream along the shoreline, looking again for clues. The teams across the river from Bendi's called out when they found the charred fire remains Manuel had found the day before. Manuel called back to explain, and urged them on.

The teams searched for about an hour—with no luck. As Bendi's group walked back to the raft, she could see Dos Montañas Pass off in the distance. An uneasy feeling came over her again.

As they paddled slowly through the calm waters approaching the entrance to the Pass, Bendi turned to her left, hoping to see the jaguar. She tapped Ortega, who was sitting in front of her, on the shoulder and pointed down the ancient waterway.

"Here's where I saw the jaguar last time," she said quietly, so the others wouldn't hear. "It didn't hit me till now, but this could be the stream that I dreamed about last night." She turned to Manuel, "Don't you think we should get out and search that old riverbed?"

"If teams on that side of the river see anything, they will let us know."

"I think *we* should check it out. I have a strong feeling that Digger could be down there somewhere."

"Our job is to run the river on this side; let the others do their job on their shore, Miss Porcelli. Don't let your imagination run away with you."

Manuel's tone and words echoed those of her skeptical friends and family when she was younger, always telling her she imagined too much. Her soul then felt all the muted torment of holding back those insights; those lost moments of truth, those lost moments of herself.

She looked up once again and saw a black silhouette standing on top of the rocky bluff. The raft was just passing the old riverbed and ready to take on the rapids of Dos Montañas Pass when, in one swift movement, Bendi dove into the water.

"Back left. Right forward. Hard!" Manuel shouted.

Bendi swam furiously as the river pulled her toward the dangerous rapids. Her body slammed into a rock and she lost her breath momentarily. Struggling to reach shore, she finally made it to shallower water. She fought to stand up as the strong current tried to sweep her feet from underneath her.

The raft landed a little further downstream. Manuel was upset. The last thing he needed was a *loca* woman on his hands. As they walked towards Bendi, Ortega tried to explain to Manuel about her dreams.

"There it is," she pointed.

The three men turned to look off in the distance, where a black spot rested on top of a steep cliff. Manuel grabbed a pair of binoculars from Danny.

"*Dios mío!* It is a jaguar." He turned to Bendi. "But you cannot expect us to follow your interpretations of your dreams."

Ortega looked at Bendi apologetically. "I only just told him some parts of your dreams."

She ignored the blushing archeologist to focus on Manuel. "Maybe I can't expect you to act on my dreams. But I'm pleading with you to let *me* check it out. Just for a little while."

"You cannot go off on your own," Manuel insisted. "It is dangerous. Rescue plans need to be followed. I have done this before; please let me do my job."

Ortega had walked a short distance away and now he called, "Come—over here!"

He was on his knees, pointing to a fault-line in the earth that transversed the old river bed: the entrance to the river way had sharply dropped three feet

"I am no geologist, but this looks as if it just happened," Ortega said.

Bendi turned around and walked in the direction of the jaguar as the three men stared at the aftermath of the geological event.

"Look at this!" Bendi exclaimed. A little further downstream she stood four feet higher on top of another fault-line.

Manuel, Danny, and Ortega quickly trotted over. Danny then climbed up and excitedly said, "And the whole riverbed is soaked. That means the river could have moved through here."

"Look at all the growth that has been damaged," Ortega added and then he knelt down inspecting the freshly cut slice of earth. After a moment of silence he said enthusiastically, "Listen to me and tell me if any of this makes sense."

Ortega continued, "We all saw the landslides in Dos Montañas canyon. What if they temporarily dammed up the Río Pacuare? The same tremor that caused the landslide probably caused the fault-line and dropped the entrance of the old riverbed over there, where we were just standing. The river, now backed up, had nowhere to go, except to follow the path of least resistance. Naturally, the river ran wild through this old riverbed, causing the fallen trees and all the destruction you see along here."

"Then Digger would have had no choice the following day," Danny interjected. "The river would have swept him down this way!"

"There are always after-shocks following an earthquake," Ortega added, hiking his Khaki shorts back up to his belly as he stood up again. "Some can be almost as powerful as the initial tremor. Let us say that at some time after Digger went through here, another after-shock occurred and does two things: First, it raises this fault line here, *aquí*, cutting off the flow of Río Pacuare, thus dramatically shoving the river back towards Dos Montañas Pass. Secondly, the after-shock loosens up the temporary dam and after a little time, the river finally pushes through the debris and continues on its merry way through the Pass." Ortega stood silently, admiring his own hypothesis.

"You have come up with some crazy ideas, Ortega," Manuel shook his head skeptically. "That is a lot of maybes. A lot of coincidences that all had to occur."

"You have run the river for many years," the archeologist countered. "You know that between land, sky, and river, many unusual things can occur."

Bendi finally spoke up. "We came across nothing on our first trip down the river. Forget my dreams—now, even if it is remote, at least you have a reason to look further ahead, *verdad?*"

Seeing that he wasn't going to get anywhere by disagreeing, Manuel gave in. "*Bueno*, okay. I will go along with you, Miss Porcelli—for now."

He took Danny's walkie-talkie and relayed a message to the other teams that he, Danny, Ortega, and Miss Porcelli were going to search a short distance up the old riverbed. He instructed them to continue their search downstream as planned.

From the raft, Danny retrieved a backpack with food and water. The narrow ancient riverbed varied from ten to thirty yards wide; Manuel and Bendi focused their search on one side, while Ortega and Danny combed the other. The jaguar was nowhere in sight.

After several miles, Danny exclaimed, "Wooh! A major strainer."

Straight ahead was a huge ceiba tree lying across most of the riverbed. Its tentacled branches had been stripped by the force of the river.

"What's a strainer?" Bendi asked.

"It's about the most dangerous aspect of river rafting," Danny replied. "The tree and its branches act as a strainer and catch everything the river funnels through it. So if you get too close, it can puncture the raft. But if you happened to fall in, you can be pinned into the branches by the force of the water and easily drown."

As they approached the fallen tree, they noticed bushes, a small tree, and some wilted sugar cane draping on the barren branches.

"What is that?" Manuel said pointing to a tan plastic piece entangled within the branches.

They all stared in silence at the piece of equipment, as if it would tell them a story—a story of what had happened to its owner, a story of adventure, and hopefully a happy ending. But all that stared back at them was a splintered piece of a paddle blade with "Wild River Excursions" stamped on it.

"Base camp, can you read me?" Static was the only answer to Manuel's bark into the walkie-talkie. "Anyone, can you read me?" Still no answer.

"There is too much interference here. Danny, leave the backpack and work your way back to the raft; try to get hold of the others." Manuel handed him the walkie-talkie. "See if they have come up with anything, and tell them what we have found. If they get to the take-out point and still have not found anything, tell all the teams to meet us here as soon as possible, and to bring their camping supplies, and let us hope they get here before it is too dark. You should also radio the *policías* and tell them what we have found," he added. "See if they can give us any help. That jaguar is pretty daring to be out in the middle of the day. I would feel a lot better with some fire power."

Danny left Manuel, Bendi, and Ortega sitting on the fallen ceiba tree, eating sandwiches.

Bendi was too excited to eat much. She watched a flock of tiny chlorophonias fly out of the jungle, their bright blue, green, and yellow feathers dotting the sky. They landed on a nearby tree to eat the berries off huge mistletoe clusters draping off the tree's branches. The deep barking of a howler monkey echoed through her bones. "Are there any indigenous people here in Costa Rica, like maybe descendants of those people you called the Outcasts?" Bendi asked Ortega.

"What Outcasts?" Manuel interrupted.

"Ortega was telling me about a mysterious tribe that lived here in this region hundreds of years ago. And that possibly they had something to do with the stone spheres," Bendi answered.

"Where did you get that kind of information, Ortega?"

"From the legends that I have gathered of several tribes indigenous to South America," Ortega replied placidly.

"Miss Porcelli, there is no mysterious tribe," Manuel huffed. "Anyone who knows Costa Rican history knows of the *Chorotegas*. They originated in southern Mexico and settled in the Nicoya Peninsula, on the western side of Costa Rica, in the 14th century. Their name means 'Fleeing People.' Your friend is mixing up stories between his imaginary 'Outcasts' and the Fleeing People."

"I know very well about the *Chorotegas*, Manuel. What I speak of is not the same. The Chorotegas were like the Mayas and the Aztecs, who were very militaristic, had slaves, and maintained a rigid class system. This other tribe, the Outcasts, were very different. They were peaceful, and the whole purpose of their existence was to get away from the likes of the Chorotegas and the Mayas."

"Is there anything written about this story?" Manuel asked.

"You know that the Church and the Spanish obliterated almost every recorded piece of our Meso-American history and culture. Besides, according to the stories I have heard, the rulers of the Aztecs, Incas, and Mayas supposedly decreed to have any mention of the Outcast tribe erased. So all records of this tribe were destroyed before the Conquistadors arrived."

"How convenient for you," Manuel said sarcastically.

Undaunted, Ortega added, "Besides, just because it is not written down somewhere does not mean it is not possible."

Bendi listened to them argue. She could tell that Ortega was used to debating his views. He obviously felt strongly about his beliefs and even stronger about his right to speak them. At the same time there was a calmness in his voice. She asked, "So do you believe that such a tribe still exists?"

"First of all, anything is possible. It all depends on how you interpret the stories I have heard—literally, metaphorically, or both. One perspective would be that there are still descendants of the original tribe alive somewhere in the rainforests of what would now be Nicaragua and Costa Rica. In fact, this very part of Costa Rica that we are now entering has never, ever been fully explored. So who knows?"

"You know there are no indigenous tribes left in this region!" Manuel exclaimed indignantly.

"I do and I don't. I do know that no one has ever found any yet. But recently in South America, a tribe called the *Kogi* were discovered. They had been thought to be an almost mythical people who escaped the Spanish Conquistadors by living high in the mountains of the Amazon rainforest. No one had seen them in over four centuries, that is, until last year. So who knows?

"But another perspective, Miss Porcelli, would be that the Outcasts' spirits are the only thing that still inhabits the rainforests. Most of the tribal cultures believe in a never-ending spirit, what we might call a soul, that travels and inhabits different places and times."

"Or another theory," Manuel interrupted, "is that some people get paid to just think of any wild or crazy story, and then spend their life trying to prove it."

"And that is another possibility," Ortega agreed without the slightest hint of irritation.

Manuel grunted and stood up from the ceiba.

"There he is again!" Bendi's voice quivered with excitement as she pointed toward a rocky bluff they could see through the trees.

Ortega got to his feet. and Manuel looked up to see the black jaguar standing on a rocky bluff off in the distance. At its base, two hundred feet below the majestic animal, they could see what looked like an opening, maybe to a cavern, about fifteen feet wide. Bendi and Ortega glanced at one another and immediately began walking toward it.

"Hey!" Danny yelled from a distance. Bendi and Ortega halted for a moment as Danny appeared, slightly out of breath. "The other teams came up with nothing. But they won't be able to make it until the morning. What do you want to do?"

"We had better head back to where we left the raft," Manuel decided. "Our supplies are there and we can set up camp before it gets too dark. We do not want to be someone else's dinner tonight, *verdad*?" He looked pointedly at Ortega, then Bendi.

Reluctantly, Bendi and Ortega turned around and headed back to the raft with Danny and Manuel. But before they left the clearing, Bendi took one last, longing look toward the bluff. The cat was gone.

She'd been trying not to think about Digger's condition or where he might be. Ortega's stories helped. Now she asked him, "So do you really believe that there is a connection between the Outcasts and the stone spheres?"

"Yes, I do," Ortega answered as he worked his way through the jungle overgrowth. In fact, we are finding corroborating evidence in the Yucatan—at the recently discovered ruins of Cobá."

Bendi stopped in her tracks. "Ortega, I don't understand all the things that are happening but somehow this is way beyond coincidence. Digger and I were at Cobá." She told Ortega about their trip and Digger's experiences; of seeing a blue spiral painted on top of the pyramid, of being inside the vestibule, of his sense of falling. The archeologist stopped walking for a moment and just nodded, thinking. He looked as if he'd traveled to another place... another time.

Chapter 14

*"Ask the right question and you will eliminate much of your doubt.
Answer the right question and you will never feel doubt again."*

Throughout the night, Digger hadn't been able to shake the feeling that someone was watching him from a distance; someone tall, someone different, someone familiar. Since the faintest hint of dawn, he'd been sitting on a comfortable tree stump with a view of the plots of crops. The sound of drums from the tribe's festivities the night before still played within his head. The members of *Los Otros* had tried to get him to partake in their ceremony but he'd refused. He loved listening to the music and the drumming, but to get out there and dance would have been too embarrassing.

Digger noticed an old woman near the center of the village who was beating agave plants with a stone mallet. After several blows, she would spread the pulpy fibers apart and beat them some more before weaving a string of vine between them. Digger realized she was making the clothes that many of *Los Otros* wore.

At his feet, several small, round, mysterious shells zig-zagged slowly over the ground. One of them shook and then cracked, a tiny appendage protruding from the opening. Within a few moments, the mystery was solved: a half-inch-long, marooned-colored beetle broke though the shell and scampered under the protection of some fallen leaves. Soon there were more escapees.

As he sat, Digger's thoughts and feelings kaleidoscoped within him: he felt lonely and cut off from all that was familiar and also struggled to grasp this concept of 'imprinting' a stone sphere, which he didn't have a clue how to do. He tried to figure out his difficulties with Bendi, with his mother, with his life. But no matter how much he thought he'd dealt with those issues, he still found himself returning to the same old painful place.

Another shell cracked, and one more beetle scampered under the fallen leaves. Curious, he picked up the newly opened shell and broke it between his fingers, exposing a brown, mushy substance. Digger leaned over to examine the pile of shells. Picking up several more, he noticed that they all had a hole from a previous escape. He broke them open and found that, unlike the first shell, these were empty.

Just then a sparkle of light from a nearby bush caught Digger's eye. He scanned the general area for the aberration and saw, stretched between the gangly, leafy branches, a magnificent, dewy spider web that was glittering with scattered rays of sunshine. Trembling in the light breezes, the intricate architecture spanned at least five feet. Digger leaned over to take a closer look and to his amazement, a camouflaged, greenish-brown spider was making repairs to its home. As he watched, it crawled to the ground, passed the pile of empty shells, and moved toward the newly-abandoned one. The spider dragged the empty shell to the pile of others, then slowly returned to its home.

Before he could wonder over this strange ritual, Digger was interrupted by some noise coming from the garden plots. From where he sat, the garden area appeared to cover several acres; it was filled with many different varieties of flowers, vegetables, and fruits. His attention was drawn to the plot closest to him, where several children and adults were tending smaller plants. With a serious look on his face, one young boy was pulling gently on one of the saplings. An older woman several feet away leaned toward the boy, as if to tell him something, but then drew back. She returned to her own task, but kept an eye on him. Meanwhile, the youngster kept tugging and pulling on different parts of the little tree.

Digger could see another child creating a mound of dirt, and almost completely burying a flowering plant, until only the flower itself was sticking out of the ground. Several adults nearby who were tilling rows of dirt completely ignored her. Elsewhere, other children and adults planted seeds. Digger noticed that each of the children was planting differently: one would leave the seed exposed, another would cover it with dirt, while yet another poured on lots of water, which would surely wash the seed away, he thought. Apparently, there was no supervision from the adults. How could such a beautiful garden grow with such haphazard gardening methods?

Baffled, he turned back to another puzzle: the beetles at his feet. Now a baby beetle had moved closer to Digger and toward one of the recently-hatched shells. It climbed inside, and after a couple of minutes, came out again and ran back to the cover of the fallen leaves. A larger, adult-sized beetle then scampered toward the pile of empty shells and with some effort, squeezed its way back into one. The shell tumbled and skidded back and forth over the ground. Immediately, the camouflage-colored spider in the bush left its home and raced to the mobilized shell, dragging the unfortunate adult beetle quickly back to the shimmering web, where it proceeded to weave its new treasure into a silvery ball for a future meal.

"*Regressar* beetle." Digger flinched. He turned to see a youthful, hand-holding couple and an elderly woman standing behind him.

"I am sorry, we did not mean to startle you," the man said in broken English, Spanish, and a native tongue that Digger was beginning to decipher more easily.

"That's okay. I just didn't hear you come up behind me," Digger said. "My name is Digger." He cupped his hands to extend a *Los Otros* greeting.

After the ritual was completed, the man smiled, "We know who you are. My name is Chucan. This is Seentar, what you would call my wife."

"And my name is Darant," the older woman added.

"You were saying, about the *regressar* beetle?" Digger asked, motioning for them to sit near him.

"Yes, that is one of the names that is given this odd little creature," Chucan nodded as the three of them settled onto nearby rocks that looked almost as if they'd been placed in a circle for this exact purpose. And maybe they were, Digger suddenly realized. This jungle village was certainly full of stranger things... the beetles, for instance.

"What does that name mean?" he asked Chucan. "I've been watching their behavior for some time and I don't understand what's going on. And now that spider over there has entered the scene."

"It is 'the beetle that returns,'" the old woman, Darant, explained. "Have you seen the little babies?"

Digger nodded and explained what he'd witnessed.

"When the beetle is being hatched," Darant continued, "it moves around in its shell, trying to find a way out. When it finally pokes through, it quickly gets out and finds protection. But the young beetle still does not yet know that it can find its own nourishment, so it returns to feed off its unused food supply within the shell—that brownish material you found in the first shell. By the time the baby beetle runs out of food from its shell, it has learned how to get nourished elsewhere."

"What about the bigger beetle I saw going back to the empty shell? The one the spider captured?"

"Ah," she smiled a toothy grin. "Even though they get food elsewhere, many times the older beetles behave as they did when they were younger."

"No one really knows why," Chucan piped up. "It is what you might call a, uhhh... hobbit?" Chucan raised his eyebrows.

Digger suppressed a chuckle. "I think what you mean is *habit*. Well, what about the spider's behavior?"

"The spider builds its web near the beetles' nest," Seentar, a lovely young woman with long, braided hair, spoke for the first time. "It is so well disguised that the beetle does not know that a spider is even in the area. Piling up the recently hatched shells, the spider then waits for an adult beetle to return. When that happens, when the beetle goes back into a shell and repeats its youthful behavior, the movement catches the attention of the spider. Being in the shell, the beetle never knows that the spider is even coming—until it is too late." She looked up at her husband with a meaningful twinkle. "Immediately, the spider weaves the shell into its web, where it injects the beetle with some fluid that paralyzes it. Then as the spider needs nourishment, it feeds on the numbed victim."

"Oh now, isn't that just like living back in the States," Digger grimaced. "Let me change the subject." He gestured toward the garden fields. "The whole time I've been here, I've seen lots of women and some children, but hardly any men. Except for you, Chucan—and Mashuba, of course. Why is that?"

Before Chucan could speak, Darant cut him off with a hearty laugh, "Well, I do not think that many men can find this place! It is not on any map. If they cannot use this," she pointed to her head, "they are lost—which is most of the time!" She jabbed Chucan gently in the ribs with her wrinkled elbow. He just shook his head at her; obviously, there was much affection between them.

Was she his mother-in-law? Or his mother? He didn't feel comfortable to ask, so instead Digger asked the old woman, "And why did you come here?"

"I came because my husband could not give me what I wanted." Her tone had changed to utmost seriousness. "He did not understand me. It was not until later that I realized I did not understand myself. I had tried to talk with him, but by then it was no use. He would just rant and rave about all the things that a woman was supposed to be—and how I was not like that. Well, I heard about *Los Otros* and eventually left to find them. I have been here for many years."

"We came here," Seentar interrupted, as she squeezed her husband's hand, "because our families, my tribe, would not let us be together. You see, in our village it is told to us who we should marry. The decision is made by our families or by our leaders."

"When I was young, I was orphaned from my tribe by a battle," Chucan continued the story. "I traveled for many days before I came upon Seentar's tribe. After many years, they eventually accepted me, but not when it came to marriage. It was not proper, the gods would not approve, they said. According to them, the gods would have done harm to them if they would allow such a thing. Seentar and I do not believe the gods would do anything at all to those who follow their heart." He looked lovingly at his wife.

"The heart," Seentar said quietly, "does not have eyes or a mind or a sense of time. It does not recognize another heart by its color, beliefs, or age. It does not know what territories the other heart has lived in, or what leaders or religions it holds to be true. The heart does not know of past deeds or future hopes; it can only live in the present."

As if on cue, from the gardens came the lilting song of a young girl who was singing softly to a tree no taller than her own height. They all turned to listen. The unrecognizable words counterpointed the twirps, cheeps, and throaty calls of the jungle birds.

When the young girl had stopped singing, Chucan said quietly, "All things have heart. The tree does not care if a man or child sings to it. An ocean does not care if an animal or human feels its waiting liquid embrace." A scorpion scooted across one of the boulders in front of them. "The scorpion does not care if you are a wise old sage or a greedy leader. The rocks do not care about your past concerns or your future dreams. All that they want, all that they need is the sharing of your heart."

Digger was struck by the similarity in their speech to things Angélica had said while they were in the jungle, or on the river. He was quiet for a moment. Then he asked, "Do you know why I am here?"

"To help us," offered Chucan.

"Do you know what I'm supposed to help you with?"

"No, not the particulars," Darant interjected, "nor is it important for us to know. But we are all here to help each other, in many ways. That is the destiny of each of us."

The young girl began singing in the garden again and Digger turned to listen. When her song ended, he asked, "What are they growing down there?"

"Many things," Seentar smiled broadly. "Minds, behaviors, beliefs. Oh, and also vegetables, flowers, trees, and herbs."

Digger laughed. She definitely reminded him of Angélica—where was she, anyway? She would have loved this: he was going to take the bait. "What do you mean, 'behaviors, minds, and beliefs?'"

"It is like what you might call a school. The children and the newcomers assist the Keepers of the Garden to tend the fields. But in the beginning, their task is to do it on their own, with no instruction. They can do anything that they wish to their designated part of the garden. Their only purpose is to try and assist the plants in growing. So, some sing to their plants, some plant seeds below the surface, while others plant them on top, some help support the plants by tying them to twigs, and others might do nothing at all. All that is requested is that their intent be always clear, 'to assist the plants to grow.' At the end of each day, they get together with the Keepers of the Garden and discuss each others' techniques and results.

"It is not so much *what* they learn, but *how* they learn that makes a difference. Beliefs are hatched out of 'whats,' while behaviors are hatched out of 'hows.' The whats can and will always change but if you know the hows—how to think, how to behave, how to act, how to love, you will be led to the edge of the heavens!"

Vawaha suddenly appeared out of nowhere, as was her habit, running up to Digger and giving him one of her exuberant hugs. He could get used to this, he mused, surprised at his own reaction. "Where have you been?" she bubbled over. "I have been looking for you all morning!"

"I've been right here, finding out more about your village and the *regressar* beetle. Also contemplating on what I'm supposed to be doing. Maybe I should be thinking about *how* I'm supposed to be doing," Digger added playfully, with a twinkle in Seentar's direction.

Vawaha looked at Seentar for a second, but decided to ignore Digger's teasing. "What are you going to do today?" she demanded to know.

"I have to discover a way to do this so-called *imprinting* on a sphere. Unless you can tell me how"—he tugged playfully on a lock of her hair—"I thought I'd find out more about all of you. What do you like about being here?"

"Everything is so exciting and new. It is fun. I can ask all kinds of questions and everybody wants to help me understand and really know things."

"That is definitely true," Chucan nodded. "When we first truly became aware of *Los Otros'* way, we could not talk to enough people, listen to enough stories, try enough things. Everyone was so interesting. Everyone had different experiences."

"I found it difficult to go to sleep at night," Seentar agreed. "Several of us would talk around the fire for hours sharing our stories. There was always something to learn."

"It is the thirst for growth," Darant told them. "This thirst is like the body of a young child; it grows very fast. But that of which we speak is a hundred times more. I remember in the beginning, when I first became aware that there were really people who felt like I did, I could not get enough. It is still exciting now, but in the beginning everything seemed new and magical. A whole new world opened up; new ways of looking at yourself and others, different ways of doing things. There was no guilt about any of this. All of it fed my heart and my spirit."

Seentar reached for Chucan's hand. "There was a wonderful sense of community in my old village, but all I got was ridicule when we went against the wishes of the elders. But here, even if people do not agree with what you say, they still support your thoughts or feelings. They do not try to silence you, or worse, *kill* you."

Darant added, "It is very difficult to be experiencing all of this excitement and be with others who do not see it your way. For me, it was very lonely." The old woman's eyes took on a distant haziness. "First, I felt disconnected with those around me, whom I had felt very comfortable with before: my family, friends, children, and even my husband. They did not seem to understand what had happened to me. In the beginning they said it was 'just a phase,' but as they saw me talking more about it, they became frightened. Then they judged me, and sometimes very harshly. Later they rejected me. Before that happened, I stopped sharing my ideas and insights for I saw that it was painful for them—but also for me." She came back to the present, taking in the three adults and Vawaha. "Now I see that they just did not understand me. I discovered that once I experienced that beginning part, that growth part, I could not be silent; it was too painful. In fact, it was more painful to hold back than to speak out. So I had to find others who shared my pain and my excitement."

"But it is still painful!" Seentar burst out. "Because I want my father and my mother to understand me. I still feel the eyes of my parents burning my skin. They feel they have been betrayed by me. But I have not betrayed them!" Chucan squeezed her hand tightly, and Digger could see what strength the two of them drew from one another. He felt a twinge of envy, then quickly pushed it aside.

"There are so many self-doubts," Darant nodded in understanding. "I have enough doubts about myself when I follow all the familiar 'rules.' And then when I step outside that imaginary boundary into the unknown, I constantly question myself. That is a time when I came up with the best question I could ever ask: 'Who am I?'"

Darant then looked deep into Digger's eyes. "Ask the right question and you will eliminate much of your doubt. Answer the right question and you will never feel doubt again."

She then spoke directly to Seentar, "Most young souls define who they are by what is outside of them, what is around them, who their family is, what tribe they belong to, how much they have accumulated, what village they live in, what ceremonies they perform. But the truth is that we are all of spirit. If you are wondering where all of your doubts come from, it is most likely that you are trying to fit into someone else's view of who you should be."

"Speaking of someone else," Digger interjected. "Vawaha, why were you so upset yesterday when you saw the hawk? You said *they* were coming. Who are—"

Suddenly a commotion down by the river caught their attention. A group of people appeared, carrying a still body on a makeshift stretcher toward the center of the village.

Digger couldn't see who it was, but Vawaha leaped up from the tree stump. "Tomanja!" she cried, and ran down the hill toward the stricken body.

Chapter 15

"Around the time of what you call death arrives the greatest opportunity to learn—for everyone."

Digger was out of breath by the time he caught up with Vawaha. Angélica and Mashuba were already there, examining the weathered body of the elderly woman. She could barely move, but when Vawaha appeared, she reached out her arms feebly. They hugged for some time, as tears ran down both their cheeks.

"Why are you here?" Vawaha kept asking the old woman, who was at first too overcome with emotion to reply. Vawaha looked up at the adults. "This is my grandmother, Tomanja," she explained.

Finally, Tomanja weakly began to tell her granddaughter about her journey, talking while the others carried her stretcher to a cool shelter near the center of the village, setting it down gently. "I heard talk of our rulers helping some foreign people to find *Los Otros*. I knew you were alive. I wanted to warn you and bring you back." She raised herself up in earnestness, grasping her granddaughter's arm. "I saw them in the jungle, but I do not believe they saw me. I heard them speaking about the power of the stone spheres and that they will kill all who get in the way of their finding them." Gasping for breath, she sank back down on the stretcher.

Angélica handed Vawaha a gourd of water and the girl pressed it to her grandmother's lips. The elderly woman sipped slowly and then closed her eyes; her breath was short and labored.

"Please help her!" Vawaha pleaded with Mashuba.

"I am sorry; there is nothing that I can do," he said sympathetically.

"Then send for the *sukai*, the medicine man! He can help!" Vawaha demanded.

"I am sorry, but he is on another journey."

"But you know where he is! You can find him and tell him to come back and help my grandmother," Vawaha pleaded.

"He is needed where he is," Mashuba said gently. The elder

crouched down to Vawaha's eye-level and said quietly, "Be with her now, for every moment is precious."

Digger watched as Vawaha looked into her grandmother's eyes, which had opened again, fluttering in uncertainty. Vawaha's own eyes filled with tears that streamed down her face as she stroked her grandmother's hair.

"You can't find this guy, this shaman?" Digger asked.

"He is gone," Mashuba answered. "In truth the *sukai* is attempting to help you in your return. Do not ask me how; you will not understand—at this time."

"Well then, is there anything I can do?" Digger asked solemnly.

"No, it is her chosen time. It is time for her spirit to pass through," Angélica answered.

"What do you mean 'chosen time'? No one chooses to die!" Digger hissed in anger.

"You can believe that if you choose," Angélica replied calmly. "But we are not the puppets of the gods. We believe that our own spirit chooses when to enter a body and when to leave it."

"I'm not even going to go there with you, Angélica," he responded tersely.

"You should listen to Angélica, for she speaks the truth," Mashuba counseled.

Two women and a man carrying baskets appeared in the doorway of the shelter. Draped in a light, red-and-black fabric, they also wore necklaces that were strung with various semi-precious stones. Vawaha and the others silently stepped to the side to allow the three entrance. They stood around Tomanja, who now lay on a bamboo bed and, in unison, greeted her *Los Otros*-style. Then the two women sat gracefully on either side of Tomanja, while the man knelt at her feet. They emptied the baskets they'd brought and placed the contents carefully on the ground. Digger watched as one of the women mixed powder and water in a mortar, and then gently put the potion to the dying woman's lips. The other woman softly sang a soothing melody, as the man gently massaged fragrant oils into the old woman's worn feet.

"Who are they?" Digger whispered to Angélica.

"They are the Keepers of the Gate," she answered softly.

"What do they do?"

"They help the person's spirit to pass through. Their job is most revered by members of *Los Otros*. The Keepers of the Gate help ease the pain and fear by comforting the body, mind, and heart, and by making connection with the spirit," she whispered. "They will stay with Vawaha's grandmother until she passes through."

"That is not their only job," Mashuba interjected quietly. "They also give comfort and insight to the family, friends, and other caregivers. All are deeply affected by this momentous event. We believe that this life is filled with possibilities and learnings. Learnings to remember who we already are. Around the time of what you call death arrives the greatest opportunity to learn and to grow—for everyone."

Digger looked at all the paraphernalia strewn around the dying woman. Some things don't change, he thought.

Digger grabbed all of his mother's medication and personal belongings that were sitting around the hospital room and placed them in her suitcase. After he'd flown out to Phoenix, the doctors told him that his mother would need twenty-four hour care and that he should think about putting her into a nursing home.

Mrs. Taylor had pleaded with Digger to take her back home. He talked with his brother, Jeff, and they discussed all the possibilities. The rollercoaster ride had definitely begun. It would be easier on them if they would place her in a nursing home; she had been a difficult enough lady to be with when she was healthy, but when she was sick, it was almost impossible. Yet they knew their mother's greatest fear was to be left in a nursing home, like her parents so many years ago; their mother had made them promise they would never do that to her. Then there was the reality of being with their mother on a daily basis, which they hadn't done for well over twenty years. How would they deal with the practicality of getting on with their lives while living the day-to-day encounters with someone dying of lung and breast cancer? But lastly, their mother needed them now, maybe for the first time in her life. Despite all the things that she had said and done, she was still their mother and they loved her—as much as they could.

Digger and Jeff talked about their guilt for even having this discussion. Shouldn't their response have been an immediate, "Of course we will take care of you; you are our mother"? That's what "good" sons would have done. The reality was that they cringed at having to go over to her house on holidays, so why would they want to go through this ordeal? They had put their shields up most of the time because they never really knew when they would get stung. Yet at times she was a woman who was very giving, at least to her friends, toward whom she could be charming, witty, and somewhat loving. Family was a different matter. After Digger or Jeff opened up—it could be the next moment, or the next day, or sometimes even the next week—but eventually, when the distance would lessen between her and them, the stinger would do its deed.

This deathly illness of their mom's, in just a short time, had triggered all those feelings which had been carefully stored away for so many years. They had been hidden away by polite phone conversations and dutiful appointments on holidays and birthdays. Unconscious decisions of protection for emotional survival, made by resolute young boys, were now in jeopardy for the two, semi-conscious, injured adults.

Digger hired an air ambulance and flew his mother back to her home in Palm Springs. Jeff and he decided to hire a caretaker and then take turns in commuting from San Diego. On that first day, Digger picked up the doctor's prescriptions—thirteen in all. As he inquired about their purpose, he discovered she really only needed six of them for her illness; the rest were to counterbalance the negative side-effects of the original medications.

A hospital bed was rolled into his mother's bedroom, along with an oxygen tank and mask. He sat there at her dining room table, stacking morphine patches and filling pill boxes with a rainbow of medications.

As the Keeper of the Gate's haunting song wafted through the open-sided hut, Digger kept staring at all the paraphernalia surrounding Tomanja. He finally roused himself enough to ask Mashuba if it would be okay to stay with Vawaha.

Mashuba nodded, "We will see you this evening, then," and he took Angélica by the arm and led her from the shelter.

Digger moved closer to Vawaha and placed his hand on her shoulder. She turned around and smiled, and then introduced Digger to her grandmother, who blinked up at him feebly. He then quietly stepped back to let the two of them have their time together. Sitting down next to a pole, he leaned back to watch as Vawaha gently placed a moistened leaf between her grandmother's lips. A horrible gurgly cough spewed forth from Tomanja.

His mother had difficulty talking between her shortened breaths, so Digger had placed a small bell by her bedside. In the beginning it wasn't so bad but it ended up being a curse. His brother and he made a game of it to see how many times she would ring the bell in a given hour; the record was eighteen times. The requests varied from changing the TV channel, even though she had a remote control (to be honest, though, she couldn't work it even before she was sick) to getting more water, answering questions about her medications, giving her more morphine, and many times, complying with her request for a cigarette.

A repeated scene in his mother's bedroom was the most ludicrous, masochistic scene—one only a Stephen King could have visualized. Digger wished he could kidnap the CEOs of the tobacco companies, right before the eyes of the politicians in D.C, where they were claiming that nicotine is not addictive. He would have dragged them to his mother's bedroom and made them witness the scenario.

His mother would ring the bell because she couldn't breathe. Her lungs, filled with phlegm, brought torment with each breath. Turning the oxygen valve on, Digger would place the mask over her face. After several minutes, she'd want it off. Then the bell would ring again. This time she would demand to smoke a cigarette. The doctors had said to let her smoke if she wanted to. At first, Digger wouldn't allow it—but that always ended up with his mother throwing a tantrum like a little child. The point of fact was that she was going to die anyway, why not let her have the things she wanted? So Digger would light up a cigarette and place it in her mouth. She could only take a few painful puffs before she began to hack and cough up brown mucous. He would again place the oxygen mask on her face.

This scenario repeated continuously for the first three months. It was only when she couldn't even lift her head that she stopped asking for the cigarettes.

Digger knew that children take on many of the characteristics of their parents, even though the child swears they won't be like that. But there are other characteristics that are never repeated. Even though his mother and father had been incessant smokers, Jeff and he had never smoked a cigarette in their lives. It wasn't that he hadn't incurred other bad habits, but smoking wasn't one of them.

Steamy swirls of smoke filled the hut as one of the women Keepers of the Gate placed herbs in a pot of boiling water. With a feather in her hand, she stroked the healing vapor toward Tomanja's face.

"Will that help her?" Vawaha asked.

"It will ease her pain but it will not cure her. Did your grandmother not have this ailment for some time?" the woman asked.

Vawaha nodded.

"We will do what we can to make her journey comfortable. Is there anything that we can do for you?"

Vawaha shook her head. Digger saw how Vawaha looked at her grandmother: with sadness and grief, but also with much love. He hoped that's what his mother saw in his eyes, but he doubted it. He'd cared for his mother and loved her as much as he could, as much as she would let him, but he knew there could have been so much more. He still felt tremendous guilt for not loving his mother enough. Though he had no idea how much love was enough, he felt it should have been more. A "good" son would have loved his mother more.

He listened as Vawaha and her grandmother talked, when she was awake and able to utter a few words. Only catching a few words here and there, it sounded to him as if they were reminiscing about old times.

Off in the distance, he heard drumming—and someone playing a flute. It was a sad tune but also one of lightness; that was one of the rare, magical qualities of a flute.

The soft piano music of David Lanz played in the background as Jeff and Digger interviewed yet another caretaker. Generally, there was an understandably high burnout rate with caregivers but their mom had really put those people to the test. Digger truly believed that when each caregiver worked with his mother, they came to a crossroads in their career. They either decided that this was the profession they were truly meant for, or they came to the realization that no matter how much money (which was not much) or personal satisfaction they received, it would never be enough. Digger and Jeff had already been through four caregivers in two months.

His brother and he were thankful for these helpers, who gave so much of themselves and often took the brunt of their mother's anger. They also received help from a hospice nurse who would come to the house three times a week to check on their mother's condition. The hospice worker was extremely understanding and supportive; it was a relief to hear her walking up the sidewalk. She understood what they were going through more than anyone else possibly could.

After thirty minutes of interviewing, they hired the new caregiver on the spot, but she couldn't start until the following day, so both Jeff and he decided to stay.

Starting early that morning, the pain had been unusually bad for their mom. Digger had given her extra morphine, which eventually made her a little delirious, but it seemed to control her pain. Now, hearing his mother's gurgly cough shortly after the new caregiver had left, he went to her room to check on her. She was in a deep sleep. He slipped one of his CDs into the stereo and walked back out to the living room to talk with his brother.

A scream from the bedroom caused them both to jump out of their seats. They rushed to their mother's room. Her eyes were half shut but she was talking loudly to some imaginary person in the corner. Her speech was mostly mumbled, mixed in with the clarity of a few words, "doctor Macu…" "shit" … "cancer" … "You can't get me down…" Digger went to her side to ask if she was all right. She didn't respond. Meanwhile, Jeff scanned the room just to be sure that there wasn't really anybody there. Their mother continued with her muttered dialogue, interspersed with pangs of voiced pain. As quickly as the episode began, it ended with her falling back into a deep sleep.

A couple of hours later they heard clapping. Again they went to check, this time to see their mom with a broad smile upon her face. She cheered some imaginary person with garbled words. "That's my son!" was the only recognizable phrase. Digger shook his mother hard. Her head dipped and eyes opened.

"I'm hungry. I want some food," she said angrily.

"Mom, what have you been talking about?" he asked her.

"I haven't been saying anything," she wheezed. "Where's my food?"

Jeff made a sandwich, poured a glass of juice, and tried to feed her, but all she took was a couple of bites and a sip. Digger then gave her the medications. She fell right back to sleep.

Later in the afternoon they heard their mother crying. They found her with her eyes closed, but tears were falling onto the pillow. Her arm stroked the blanket next to her.

"Are you all right, Mom?" Digger asked. No response. "Mom, are you all right? Are you in pain?"

"Why did you leave me?" Their mother continued, "The boys are out of the house. Now there's no one at home," she cried softly into the pillow.

"She's talking about Dad!" Jeff whispered in surprise.

"But he died more than ten years ago," Digger replied. The realization crept softly into his consciousness that his mother was going through different episodes in her life. She was replaying them backwards in time. He told his brother what he thought.

"That must mean the first time she screamed was when she found out she had the cancer," Jeff said. "She yelled out her doctor's name, Dr. Macuso. That must have been the conversation she was having with him."

"The happiest I'd ever seen her was when she came to the opening of the Warner Bros. film, my first film score. She clapped and clapped to where it was almost embarrassing," Digger added.

They turned to look at their mother as they heard her slow, labored breathing. She was fast asleep and hopefully out of pain; they both quietly hoped, not only the physical, but also the mental and emotional.

While watching the Cubs playing the Dodgers on TV, they heard their mother scream at the top of her injured lungs. They bolted into her room again, this time to the words, "Pick it up!"

"Pick up what, Mom?" Jeff asked.

"Pick it up!" she screamed with her eyes wide open.

"Okay, now what do you want us to do with it?" Digger bent over and picked up an imaginary object. He and his brother decided to play along with this unknown drama.

"Take it with us to the hospital!" she yelled.

Jeff pointed his index finger at Digger. "Remember?"

It all came back to him. They were very young and had just returned from the Ice Capades when Digger shut the car door on his brother's finger. Their parents had to search for the finger before they took him to the hospital. The doctors sewed it back on, but at times when his mother wanted to make Digger feel guilty, she would point at Jeff's scarred finger. "See? That is what happens when you don't listen to me. I told you to be careful!"

Now they both smiled uncomfortably at each other for a moment as the recognition of their mother's unfolding scenario sunk in.

After they'd slept for a couple of hours that night, they again heard their mother cry out in pain. Digger turned on the light in her room to see his mother clutching her stomach. "Are you all right, Mom?" he asked again.

The only response was groaning.

"Why is she clutching her stomach?" Jeff, who'd also hurried into the room, asked Digger. "The pain has always been in her chest."

"I don't know why, but I think you should call for help."

Jeff agreed, and went to the other room to call the hospice.

As Digger stood watching helplessly, his mother continued to groan and exhale quick, short, raspy breaths. Then with one loud scream, she opened her eyes and looked down at her feet. "What is it?" she cried.

Jeff ran back to the doorway. Digger, on the opposite side of the room, stood with eyes wide at this strange behavior.

Their mother asked again, exhaustedly, "What is it?"

"I don't know what you're talking about, Mom. What is what?" Digger replied.

An unheard voice must have answered their mother's question because now she said, "A baby? A baby boy? But I never wanted a child! I don't want this child."

Jeff and Digger were stunned by her words. All they could do was stare at the imaginary baby at her feet. Totally unaware of the painful secret that she had unleashed upon her sons, their mother grumbled a few more words, turned over, and went back to sleep.

Neither of them moved. Eventually they looked at each other, not knowing what to say, not knowing which of them she had referred to. But they knew the reality of the situation was that it didn't make a difference. Those until-now-unspoken words said volumes about their mother's behavior. Memories of a frustrated, unhappy housewife and mother flew back in their faces; the screaming at the slightest noise or untidy mess, the ever-present feeling that whatever they did was never good enough. Digger thought to himself, this revelation is the kind of stuff that could send a person to a psychiatrist for the next twenty years.

He felt hurt, betrayed, and angry, but those feelings were minor compared to another one that began to overwhelm him. The strange thing was, that overwhelming emotion felt good, whatever it was. His mind tried to tell him he was wrong, he couldn't be feeling good; he'd just discovered that his mother never wanted children, that she never wanted him. But the stark reality was that her words were a confirmation of the truth—the truth he already knew.

A thick, musty smell infused his nostrils as deep within him a heavy wooden door quickly opened. He let out a big sigh. He knew as an adult that children always think it's their fault when their parents are upset. He had gone over his childhood a hundred times and each time swept out a little more of the mess—of the guilt. But not until that moment, when he heard his mother's words, did he realize he had been fooling himself. He could have sworn nothing was left in that cold, barren room—that it wasn't his fault. But in that room, unbeknownst to his conscious self, was the guilt that somehow he was to blame for his mother's unhappiness. Now his mother's unwitting words had opened that door and vaporized all that had been held within.

As Digger stood there staring at his brother and listening to their mother's labored breath, he realized the name of that overwhelming emotion—that flower which felt so good amongst the thorns—it was RELIEF. He took another long, deep sigh and went to speak what he had felt in his heart. But before the words reached his lips, Jeff echoed them back: "I thought it was always me!"

Vawaha's grandmother coughed and Digger moved to stretch his back; it was sore from leaning up against the pole. He watched as Vawaha gently placed a cool cloth upon her grandmother's forehead. The Keepers of the Gate were still seated around the elderly woman.

"How is she doing?" Digger asked Vawaha.

The young girl turned and forced a smile, but said nothing.

"Are you all right?"

Vawaha nodded and finally said, "You go to the ceremony tonight. I will be all right."

He wanted to respect her wishes, so he agreed. "But I'll check with you later."

"Thank you for staying with me," Vawaha called as he took his leave.

Tired from sitting all afternoon, and a little drained by his memories, Digger walked slowly to where *Los Otros* held their fire ceremonies. He found Mashuba and Angélica, and told them what he knew about the old woman's condition and Vawaha's vigil.

During the day, *Los Otros* all wore similar attire and appeared to be very calm and peaceful. But here around the fire, the people were draped in a multitude of colorful costumes and headdresses, and they were definitely in a festive mood. But Digger just stared absently at the festivities, lost in his thoughts.

Angélica pulled gently on his arm, "Let us dance."

"No thanks. I don't feel like dancing," he said, barely looking at her.

Normally, Digger would have been fascinated by *Los Otros'* music. There were eight drummers pounding on drums of several sizes, from bongo-width to arm's length. Each drummer played a unique beat that somehow seemed always to fit perfectly with the overall rhythm. The music he'd heard them play so far would be hard to classify—something like an eclectic composite of African, Peruvian, Native American, Aboriginal, Mexican, and more. Rattles made from gourds and various styles of flutes complemented the intriguing sound.

"But you did not dance last night," Angélica insisted. "You just sat there and let us have all the fun!" The music became louder as the drummers pounded harder on the skins, while the rhythm grew more complicated.

Digger had always felt self-conscious about dancing when he didn't know the steps. And from what he'd seen the previous night, it all looked ridiculously complex. Besides, as true as that was for him, the day's events hadn't exactly left him with an inclination for festivities. He begged off again, and Angélica quickly disappeared. He was a little surprised by her reaction, but was too tired to think about it. Instead, he turned to Mashuba. All he really wanted right now was to go home. Maybe the old man would finally offer some tangible help… maybe he'd take pity on him…

"Mashuba, I still don't have a clue on how to imprint the stone spheres, and I need to get back home. People must be worried about me. And I have work to do. But today, I didn't even have a chance to spend any time at all with the spheres," Digger added apologetically.

Mashuba turned slowly to Digger and, with a half-smile and calm voice, replied, "The answer to your question is not always where you think it should be."

Frustrated again, Digger sat there sulking for the rest of the night, letting the music gently weave in and out of his body.

He wasn't sure if it was the exotic rhythm, or being around Tomanja and Vawaha, or recollecting scenes with his mother, or "D—All of the above," but something began to happen to him. It was like a thread in a garment that began to unravel, and there was no way he could ever put it back the way it was. His fear was that it would continue to unwind and eventually leave him naked—a nakedness that he had never seen or felt, a nakedness that would reveal his loneliness.

Chapter 16

*"Everyone and everything comes before you to assist you on your path.
Nature and all of its creatures are wonderful messengers."*

Rafts filled with soaked archaeology students and *policías* arrived at the entrance to the ancient riverbed. It was early in the morning, but Bendi had already been up and anxious to get going. Manuel explained to the newcomers the situation with Digger, what they had found, and how they'd seen the jaguar. As the new teams labored to set up their camping gear, Ortega and Bendi headed down the old riverbed; neither one of them felt like waiting for the others.

"Have you had any more dreams?" asked Ortega.

"Just one. I was in a dark jungle and heard bushes rumbling about. Whatever it was, it moved slowly and sounded like it was dragging something heavy. Then, the rainforest lit up with a bright light but it wasn't the sun; it was much brighter and bigger. All I know is that I felt good about the light being there. What do you think it all means?"

"Who knows? Maybe nothing. But let us keep our eyes and minds open, anyway."

As they walked around the "strainer," the fallen ceiba tree where they'd stopped searching before, Bendi noticed a large black tarantula being chewed on by a strange-looking animal. It had a long nose and tail, with sharp teeth and raccoon-like paws.

"What is that?" Bendi exclaimed.

"Coati. They forage around for fruits and, as you can see, insects."

Bendi and Ortega watched quietly as the coati finished its meal. When the animal heard the rumblings of the approaching searchers, it quickly disappeared into the dense jungle.

Suddenly Bendi felt drawn to look further down the old waterway, where the rocky bluff stood high above the cavern opening. There again perched the mysterious cat. She called the others' attention to it and they all stood gaping at the proud feline, who was standing unafraid, peering down at all of them with a look of superiority. The *policías* nervously removed the rifles from their shoulders. Then the jaguar turned slowly away from them and disappeared over the top of the hill.

The jungle became quiet for a moment, then without a word—even from Manuel—the searchers moved in unison through the ancient waterway and toward the rocky bluff. All Bendi could hear was the constant knocking of a busy woodpecker, and the pounding of her heart. A pair of brightly-colored toucans flew across her path as they reached the base of the steep slope where the cavern yawned wide.

It looked as if there had been an explosion between land and water. Huge shards of shale were strewn in front of the opening, along with rocks, boulders, and fallen trees. The mighty river had left its mark as it was violently turned in its course by the rocky wall.

Bendi and Ortega were the first to scramble over the debris for a look inside the fifteen-foot opening. For different reasons, their hearts raced as they saw a large stone sphere in the shadow of the cavern. Ortega ran over to inspect it immediately. But all of Bendi's hopes were hanging on the possibility that her dreams might somehow be connected to this physical world; that Digger would be lying there behind the stone sphere, that his weathered body would still be alive. As she stepped further into the dim enclosure, which was about ten feet high, her eyes swept around the stony cavern in an eager search for him, but as soon as they adjusted to the darkness she saw only rocks and pebbles, with a few bushes and driftwood stacked in the far corner. Her shoulders drooped as she walked dejectedly outside where the sun had peeked into the narrow opening created by the abandoned riverway.

Something mystical about the scene before her re-awakened her interest. Visions of her earlier dreams superimposed themselves onto this present reality as she caught her first sight of what lay beyond the rocky bluff and its gaping cavern.

"Unbelievable!" Ortega gasped as he came up behind Bendi. Manuel's searchers had poured into the cavern behind them, poking around in the debris for clues, so Ortega had escaped to get some air. Now they both stared at several spheres of varying sizes scattered down the old riverbed. They'd all been too distracted by the jaguar and the cavern to notice these magnificent specimens before. As Bendi and Ortega stood in awe, the early morning sun threw elongated shadows of the spheres toward them.

Then Bendi stepped quietly in among the stone balls, which ranged in diameter from two to five feet. She felt a definite energy emanating from the granite spheres; she couldn't explain it, but it was there.

Ortega, meanwhile, had shouted over to his students. As they flooded out of the cavern each of them stopped in their tracks. They were struck silent, gazing in reverence at the scene. Then the spell was broken and the students, with Manuel's search teams close behind, rushed down the riverbed for a closer look at the ancient relics.

After a few minutes, one of Manuel's searchers called out, "*Venga aquí!*" He was standing beside one of the larger stones. At the top, a handful of granite had been chipped out. A few inches below that, dried bloodstains were clearly visible in the morning light.

Bendi squeezed her way through the crowd to inspect the grayish granite sphere. Softly, she reached out her fingers to touch the cool stone. She knew Digger had been here.

Manuel barked several orders. The search teams split up checking the immediate area and also further downstream. Ortega, his students, and Bendi stayed behind amidst the spheres.

"This is my dream, Ortega!" Bendi whispered excitedly when she was finally able to pull him aside from his eager inspection of the archeological jackpot. "The jungle, the stream, the trail, the spheres, the cat that eventually turned into a jaguar, everything—except that Digger isn't here! These spheres, even though they are not colored, are the clue. I can feel it."

"I know, I can feel it also," Ortega agreed sympathetically. "Let us continue to examine them to see if we can find any more clues."

As Manuel walked back toward them, Ortega took a few steps to meet him. "Can I make a call on your radio? I need to call the *Museo* and the *Universidad de Costa Rica* for help with all of this." His wide gesture took in the surrealistic scene.

"We do not need any more people," Manuel answered firmly. "This is not an archaeological dig; it is a search party."

"That is precisely why you need my help," the archeologist insisted. "That is what I do. Search. Search for clues. I piece together fragmented bits of objects and information and then hopefully come up with answers. I believe, along with Bendi, that these spheres can lead us to Mr. Taylor. I told you about her dreams." He motioned again toward the riverbed. "Look. All the things that she dreamt have come true. Except for the body, supposedly Digger's. My people can search for clues among the spheres, while you search other areas."

Bendi kept her silence while Manuel paused to consider Ortega's words. Then he clicked on his walkie-talkie. "Has anyone seen anything, anything at all?" All the responses were the same: "*Nada.*" He turned to the professor and asked, "How many people could you bring?"

"Six, maybe even ten," Ortega answered quickly.

"Okay—but remember, they are to be looking for clues about Jonathan Taylor, not your magical stones," Manuel warned.

"Of course," Ortega replied.

Bendi felt a flood of emotion pass over her—relief, gratitude, hope, and... and something else she couldn't quite grasp. But whatever it was it felt genuine; genuine in a way that didn't have to do with Digger, it had to do with her, only her.

* * * *

Digger felt someone breathing on his back, but he couldn't see who; his vision was fuzzy and his thoughts dazed. Then sharp teeth punctured his right shoulder and he tried to scream, but nothing came out of his mouth. Realizing that his throat was parched, he tried to swallow. It didn't help. Now, as his blurry vision turned to darkness, the hot breath condensed on his neck, and he felt himself being dragged along the ground.

His next sensation was of being in a hollow, confusion and claustrophobia slowly rising to a panic within him. The only things he was sure about were that his body was shivering, that he had a fever, and that his head was pounding. As he struggled to get free, a black shadow held him down.

As Digger tossed in the hammock, still semi-conscious, he thought he heard Angélica's voice off in the distance saying, "We have to help him; he cannot have much more time..." Then he heard Mashuba, "You *did* help him, by bringing him here. But now it is up to him." Digger struggled against the black shadow, but he still couldn't open his eyes or move his limbs. The voices continued, Mashuba's loudest, "As far as our present situation is concerned, it is already set in motion. I do not think there is much we can change. *They* will be here soon enough. We have to hope that he imprints one of the stone spheres, and quickly..." Digger exerted all his strength against the darkness holding him in sleep until, finally, he was able to wrench his eyes open. As his blurred vision cleared, he saw Angélica standing over him, looking worried. A movement near the door caught his attention; he could barely make out the silhouetted forms of Vawaha and Mashuba before they slipped outside.

Digger jerked and then sat up straight. "What a nightmare! I thought I heard you talking." He swung his feet onto the ground. "What are you doing here?" He smacked his lips several times. "I'm thirsty."

"Let us go down to the river," Angélica suggested.

They spent some time by the stream, where Digger kept drinking and splashing water over his body. He didn't feel well. The only way he could describe it was that he felt nauseous, light-headed, and "spacey."

Further upstream at the side of the hill, a group of white-faced monkeys were making lots of noise as they played in the pond. The birds gossiped high in the trees, spreading word of the day's events. Digger sat on a half-submerged boulder in the river, hands resting on his lap as the frolicking stream cooled his feet. He thought about home. *Los Otros* would help him, they said, if only he managed to "imprint a sphere." Give me a break. What kind of ridiculous proposition had he gotten himself tangled up in? That was the most ludicrous thing he could think of right now—this notion of interacting with a *rock*!

Angélica, thank goodness, was leaving him pretty much alone. She hardly said a word as she watched him splashing in the water, but every once in a while, he thought he caught a worried look passing over her face. Once, he almost asked her a question—but then he remembered how skillful she was at making him talk about things he didn't want to talk about and thought better of it.

Finally, feeling a little better and also a little restless, he suggested wryly, "Let's go up to the stone spheres. Maybe I'll get hit by a bolt of lightning and..."

"Look!" Angélica interrupted, pointing at a dragonfly circling over Digger's head.

Its wings, stretching over half a foot, were transparent—with golden tips. Digger kept perfectly still as the insect performed a dazzling show before his eyes. The dragonfly then swerved in front of his face and landed on his hand.

At first he was afraid to say or do anything—he didn't know if dragonflies could bite. But after a few seconds, he calmed down. He was amazed by this immense, beautiful insect sitting on his hand. After a few minutes, it took off and flew in a seemingly haphazard way around the stream.

"That was incredible!" Digger exclaimed.

"It must have had a message for you," Angélica smiled enigmatically.

"What do you mean, a message?"

"Everyone and everything comes before you to assist you on your path. Nature and all of its creatures are wonderful messengers."

"So what does it mean when a dragonfly lands on you?" he asked skeptically.

"Each culture has its own interpretation, but amazingly enough, they tend to be very similar. Dragonfly is about illusion, about our unconscious acceptance of the physical world as our only reality."

The creature suddenly flew back to Digger and hovered a couple of feet in front of his face. As several shafts of light pierced through the jungle canopy, one of them struck the dragonfly, illuminating the otherworldly iridescence of its wings.

"It is magical," Angélica said. "Does not that rainbow radiance remind you of a different place and time? Dragonfly can stimulate the memories of our origin. With that stimulation comes the inevitable aspect of change."

As the dragonfly flitted away, Digger glanced over at Angélica and was struck by the way the same shafts of light were causing her long, dark hair to glisten with its own radiance. She smiled at him and a small dimple appeared on her cheek. He'd never noticed it before.

Now the dragonfly reappeared and rested again on Digger's hand. "I have never seen one land on anyone before! So it must really be talking to you," Angélica noted.

This time, Digger tried to clear his mind and open up to any messages that came his way. He felt a little silly, and nothing came to him—but he was still filled with awe about literally being touched by this creature when a blue, orange, and yellow parrot made a dive bomb from a nearby tree. The dragonfly quickly flew off into the thick of the jungle.

As they left the stream to walk up the hill to the quarry, Digger kept thinking his problem was that he just hadn't asked Angélica, or Mashuba, the right questions. He wanted to ask her how they built the stone spheres. How did they make them so perfectly round? And did they ever transport them out of the crater? But for every question that came to him, its importance suddenly disappeared.

Just before they reached the top, Digger turned around to take in the breathtaking view of emerald crater walls around them and puffy clouds barely overhead, skimming the canopy. In the distance, he saw the waterfall spilling down the aging crater wall, feeding the stream that eventually fed the pond beneath them. He inhaled as if to take in all this beauty before turning to finish the climb. Angélica, who was already waiting for him at the top, beamed down at him with pride, probably because she noticed him appreciating her home, he thought, a little embarrassed.

Once he reached the quarry, he moved directly into the center of the giant works of art. He gazed at them all in turn and felt—something—something he couldn't explain. Again, the History sphere caught his attention. Angélica followed him as he walked over to it, peering at the design he'd studied before. Digger found the four reversed arrows that intersected the bottom circle. Within the circle was a half-moon shape. "This reminds me a little of a pendulum. What does it mean?" he pointed.

"It represents how we live. Many believe that life and all of its intricacies are either this *or* that. The truth is that life, including thoughts and emotions, is this *and* that."

The white-faced monkeys, dripping wet from their romp in the pond, noisily climbed several lianas to the top of a tree below the quarry's edge. Angélica pointed down toward the mischievous creatures. "Like the monkeys that play on the vines, the journey is in the swinging."

Digger smiled at Angélica's comment but within he felt a deep uncomfortableness with the swinging. His swinging between ideas about how to 'imprint' a sphere, and how to get back home. His swinging with the myriad of emotions related to his mother, to Bendi, to Angé... he stuffed it all inside and turned his attention back to the sphere.

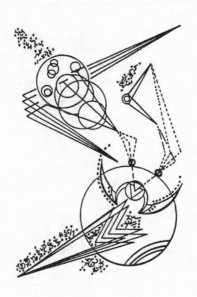

"What about these dots along the edge of the pendulum?" he asked.

"The easiest way to explain that is to say it is like the Asian 'yin' and 'yang.' What you call your female and male aspects."

"But there are more dots on the left side than the right. Why is that?"

"That is the female side. We believe it is easier to move toward the path of spirit and away from the illusion of self by using more of the feminine aspect."

"I don't get it."

A small puddle of water lay to their left. Angélica picked up a stone and placed it two feet away from the puddle. Then she picked up a stick and drew a circle around the puddle and the stone, and set the stick down between the puddle and the stone so that all three were lined up—puddle, stick, and stone.

"Imagine that we are made up of all these parts, but our basic nature is that of air—spirit. The stone is our physical self and the stick is our intellectual self." She brushed the puddle of water with her fingers. "This is our emotional self. Our life's journey is to move more with spirit," she opened up her arms above the circle. "Remember, we are all of these, but in different proportions. Most men rely on these for their journey." She picked up the rock and the stick. "But most women rely on water, emotions. Let me tell you that it is easier to move into air by being water."

She dropped the stone and the stick into the water. "Which of these will first become air? All it takes is a little light from the sun to know your answer."

"Are you saying it is easier to be spiritual if you are a woman?" Digger asked, eyebrows arching.

"Remember," she grinned, "each person has both male and female aspects and that includes equal amounts of emotion. But to answer your question, in one way of perceiving, yes it is easier. Because the very nature of having a woman's body, nevermind your cultural teachings, makes it easier to have emotion flow. That is one of the reasons you see more women and children than men in our village. It is easier to find *Los Otros* with your emotions than with your mind or body.

"Think of moving through life as a river-rafting experience. The raft is your body and your mind plans and navigates. But the river, representing your emotions, is what actually propels you. You need all three in balance—mind, body, and emotion—to make your journey. But if you spend more time on the strengthening of your raft or the planning of your trip than being on the river, your journey might take longer and also be more difficult."

Digger just stood there. That thread, the one he'd noticed unraveling earlier, had just unraveled a little more, exposing more of his emotions, exposing more of his "stuff." He didn't know what to say.

Angélica waited out his silence for a moment, then continued more gently, "All I am telling you, Digger, is that those who have lots of practice on the river, those who just allow the river to flow and do not fight it, or try to hold it back, have an easier time of it. Sometimes the ride is scary, sometimes it is life-threatening, but there are many, many times that are peaceful and serene. It is all part of the journey."

Chapter 17

"It is a fierce battle that occurs in silence in every moment. Do not be fooled by the silence."

Angélica and Digger walked silently back down to the stream.

Digger stopped and drank water while Angélica waited for him. Looking up toward the garden plot, he noticed the same young boy and older woman he'd watched working the land yesterday. This time the boy was tugging and pulling on the plants. He pulled hard on one until, roots and all, it came out of the ground. Again, the woman started to say something, and then stopped. She turned back to her own tasks, all the while keeping an eye on the boy.

"That's an interesting way to learn," Digger observed, "but it's hell on those plants!"

"The same could be said about your relationships," Angélica bantered.

"Hey—that's not nice! Maybe a little true, but still not nice."

"I am sorry, but that is the situation that brought you here, correct?"

"*Mot, mot*" sounded above them as a purple-crowned bird voiced his opinion.

"Maybe," Digger replied defensively and changed the subject quickly, "I still don't understand why you or someone can't take me back? Certainly there has to be a search team looking for us. Besides all our talk has been about me. What about you? What kind of a river guide lives deep in the jungle, far away from the river? Where did you grow up? And what kind of relationship 'stuff' do you have?"

"First, if I told you why you just can't walk back to San Jose, you wouldn't understand—not now anyway. And your questions about me? Well, all I can say is that before you can truly get to *know* about me, you've got to *know* more about yourself. You have to trust me on all of this, Digger."

As she spoke, he looked into her eyes. His frustration eased when he realized with surprise that he did trust her—more than anyone else he'd known.

Mashuba had apparently walked up behind them and listened quietly to their conversation for a moment, because he added with a chuckle, "At times, Digger, you are like a *carnon*."

"What's a *carnon*?" Digger asked.

Mashuba gently rummaged through a bush that was next to him. He pointed at a five-inch centipede that clung to a half-eaten leaf. "Here. A *carnon* is a creature of the jungle that carries with it all that it has touched."

Digger looked down at the strange-looking animal and chuckled. The creature was covered with hundreds of tiny hairs that acted like Velcro. Attached to the insect were mementos—pollen, debris, and dirt—of every place it had been. "Oh, you mean like carrying baggage!" As Digger spoke, several golden-tipped dragonflies appeared, hovering above Mashuba's head.

"People who move through this world like a *carnon*," the old man continued, unperturbed by the flying-visitors, "just try to survive. The paradox is that by attempting to control the present with the ways of the past, they will only ensure a future of extinction."

"Or this beautiful creature comes along"—Angélica pointed smilingly, as several more dragonflies flew over their heads—"and reminds us of the illusion of this world, and to be aware of the arrival of change!"

Digger watched as the magical insects played above the boulders and stream. He stayed perfectly still as one of the insects rested for a moment on his shoulder before it flew off to a bush.

"Let us go down to the strangler-fig tree," Mashuba suggested. The three of them then walked through the center of the village.

Digger noticed one of the golden-tipped dragonflies circling near the spider-webbed bush where the regressar beetle shells were piled. The spider was sitting complacently on its home, devouring its latest paralyzed victim. Descending quickly on the spider, the dragonfly suddenly transformed this predator into nourishment. *Nobody's safe from change*, Digger thought wryly.

Finally, the trio stood upon a worn path circling around a strange-looking plant on the outskirts of the village. A "strangler fig," Mashuba had called it. Digger was struck first by the way its wiry, twisting limbs had completely enfolded the tall, thick trunk of a ceiba tree. He'd seen several of these during his trip, and the guides had explained how the outer, vine-like fig tree uses the inner tree for support to grow on, eventually killing its host. Thirty feet up, the fig branched out and crawled over three long limbs that reached out horizontally from the tree. Typically the fig dropped only a few vines to the ground where they rooted into the soil. But this strangler fig in front of him was unique. It had dropped numerous dangling vines which had become so dense as they plunged toward the soil, that they now formed three textured walls of living wood. The effect of the strange growth was that it made three separate, triangular compartments surrounding the main trunk.

"Do you know what this is?" Mashuba asked Digger.

"Yes. The river guides told us about them."

"The jungle needs light to survive," the old man began, "so every plant struggles to find the sun's nourishment. The real battle for light takes place at the top of the rainforest. It is a fierce battle that occurs in silence, in every moment. Do not be fooled by the silence."

Mashuba looked meaningfully at Digger. He then pointed to the ground with all of its dead leaves and branches. "But it begins here, where we stand. Down here is the death of the past but it is also the nourishment for all that surrounds us. You need to have a strong foundation or you will never make it to the top."

"But the strangler fig doesn't have a strong foundation, yet it makes it to the top by using another tree," Digger countered.

"You are correct. I should have been more precise. I should have said that you might make it to the top, but you cannot stay there for any length of time. Because the strangler fig spent more of its time attaching, rather than going within and driving its roots deep into the ground, it will more quickly deteriorate. Mashuba gently brushed the debris on the rainforest floor with his foot and eyed Digger as if taking his measure, then went on, "We call this tree *Gutubo*." It had a very majestic sound when Mashuba pronounced it, Digger thought, although he'd never heard of anyone naming a tree before.

The old man began to move slowly, admiringly around the ceiba, while Digger and Angélica followed so they could hear his richly intoned, rhythmic speech. "The legend of this mighty tree tells a story we all need to remember. When the host tree was just a sapling, it was very aware of all the other plants and animals. It spent much time in sending its roots deep into the earth and soaking up nutrients wherever it could.

"The young tree learned how to move its way to the light by knowing itself, its potential, and its relationship with all that was around. It took many years and much struggle before it finally reached the canopy of the jungle, where the light is at its strongest. Then, for many years, the mighty tree stood tall amongst all the others, spreading its branches and giving life. Its awareness was focused mostly on the future, to see where it could spread more of its branches. It had been so long since the tree was a sapling that it forgot about its roots at the floor of the jungle.

"A strangler fig sprouted on one of it's branches. And like all living things, it wanted the light. But this plant did not want to spend any time in developing strong roots and did not look within to discover how it might reach the light. The strangler fig only uses, while giving nothing back—nothing but death.

"Slowly, the fig covered the trunk and limbs. Only when the fig had almost reached the top did the mighty tree become alarmed. But soon Gutubo talked itself into complacency. 'I do not remember this plant covering me. But it must have been on me a long time to grow so tall! Still, nothing about me has changed, so what is the harm?' the tree thought to itself. So Gutubo ignored the fig and continued its day-to-day business of providing shelter and food for the many birds and insects.

"The fig continued to cover the tree, and now hanging from Gutubo's limbs, it sent its long root-vines down into the ground. Over many, many years, in slow and subtle ways, the mighty Gutubo forgot what it had once looked like. It forgot about its strong trunk, about its reaching limbs and grounding roots. It began to think it was the strangler fig, and relied more and more upon the strangler fig's roots. Eventually, in the silence of the jungle, Gutubo was slowly strangled and began to die.

"Gutubo is now rotting," Mashuba concluded, showing them a crumbling patch just visible through an opening in the dense fig-covering. "Soon, all that will be left is the surrounding strangler fig—with an empty core. But sooner than the fig realizes, it, too, will crumple back to the forest floor. For its roots do not travel deep.

"You see," he turned to Digger, "this plant needs others to cling to. It is nothing without the mighty tree, Gutubo! It forgets that its strength comes from its strong host. And after Gutubo's death and the next great storm appears, or the one after that, the strangler fig will fall to the rain-forest floor and also die."

Digger gazed in awe at the drama unfolding before him—the killer fig, with its intricate, tangling vines, embracing the dying, hollow center of its once-strong host. Just at that moment, he was distracted by several low-vibrational 'flits' over his head. He turned to see blurred wings, long black beaks, and bright purples and reds illuminating the tiny bodies of several hummingbirds. In the next instant, they flew over to various flowering bromeliads that adorned the dying Gutubo. An unexpected smile came to Digger's face.

Angélica finally spoke up. "Gutubo is the 'tree of many eyes,'" she told him. "It helps us to see and think differently. We use it as a tool to help us solve problems."

"I have no idea what you're talking about." He turned from the jewel-like birds and bromeliads to give her a puzzled look.

She blushed, to Digger's surprise. But before he had time to wonder why she'd been acting strangely of late, she went on—not in her usual tone of bold self-confidence, but this time almost apologetically. I'll never understand women, he thought with a sigh.

"Many of our difficulties with others," she was saying, "whether they be with individuals or tribes, usually come from our personal beliefs about what is 'right' and what is 'wrong.' When there is disagreement, usually both parties feel they are right. The same is true when an individual is what you maybe call 'stuck'—is that the word? That person in some way, conscious or not, feels or acts as if their way, their perspective, is the *only* way. Remember the design we talked about, with the pendulum? Many people find themselves on opposite sides of that pendulum." Now her cheeks were flaming again, but she went on resolutely, sneaking a nervous glance at Mashuba, whose face was as unreadable as a freshly-carved stone sphere, Digger observed. What's going on here?

"The reality," Angélica said, for about the hundredth time since he'd met her, "is that the jungle does not know right from wrong; it only knows that there are unlimited ways of doing and being. It allows for an infinite variety of species to live within it and allows those species to adapt and change. We as humans bring the jungle to a different level. We have the capability of being conscious about our place within it. And because we have that higher consciousness, we have the mental and emotional capability, in the present, to know our past and change it, so that we can have a different tomorrow. We use Gutubo, this living structure, as a symbol of a way to remember to do that."

"I'm not sure I understand what you're saying. What does this tree have to do with anything?" Digger responded.

"You can see how the vines have formed what looks like three separate rooms? Let us say that you are having an argument with someone and you want to come to some resolution. First, we go and stand in this room and state our position—totally from our perspective." She probably wasn't kidding, he thought; he could see that many feet had worn a solid path around and in and out of the three "compartments" surrounding Gutubo.

"When you feel that you are complete, you move to the next room— the swing of the pendulum! From that position, you must state things from the other person's point of view. This is a big challenge to see how far you can stretch yourself. We do not have to agree with anything that comes out of our mouths; we just have to see things through the other person's eyes."

"That's not easy!" Digger interjected. "It could take a long time for that to happen…"

"Of course it could," Angélica interrupted. "But the level of difficulty is proportionate. How do you like that word?" she grinned, pleased with herself. "I just learned that one a little while ago, on my last trip to San José. Anyway, the level of difficulty is proportionate to how strongly you feel you are right. So, many people stay in that room for a long time—hours, months, years, or lifetimes—however long it takes to see through the other person's eyes!"

Mashuba's calm voice interrupted. "To assist you in that room, as Angélica calls it, with the opposing perspective, you must detach, reduce your ego, and be objective; plus, you need a strong sense of yourself. A strong sense of yourself allows you to look at the other's point of view and still feel good about yourself."

Angélica nodded in hearty agreement.

"This is starting to sound like my old psychology classes," Digger joked.

"Sorry," Angélica blushed again, but she wasn't going to let this drop, he could tell. By now, he'd figured out she was up to something, and it probably had to do with her ideas about his relationships, and she'd probably enlisted Mashuba in all this. What had she told him? Now it was Digger's turn to feel embarrassed.

"Depending on the person and the issue," she went on, "you may need to come back to this room many times. But once you have accomplished seeing through the other perspective, you can then go to the third room. There, you state all other possible points of view: tribal, religious, spiritual, inter-dimensional, and so on. Again, you do not have to attach yourself to any of those views; you just have to see and possibly even feel them—if only for a moment. When we feel completion of this, we then walk around the tree and allow our minds to be blank. We allow all the perspectives that we have gathered from all the rooms to move across and within our mind. Then we choose the one that brings us closer to a state of balance—the one that feeds our spirit." She beamed in triumph, as if she'd just finished circling Gutubo herself—she had, in a sense; she'd walked in and out of each compartment as she described how *Los Otros* used the tree.

"This tree," Mashuba added, "is used for healing everything, from a child angry at her parents, to a village angry at another. We also use it to help ourselves in matters of the heart—or let go of old ideas and beliefs that no longer serve our 'chosen' name—who we are now."

"Try it?" Angélica pushed Digger gently toward the tree. Mashuba frowned at her.

Digger had known this was coming. So this is what she's been working up to all this time—his true confessions! And she was going to be on hand to listen in! No way! He refused to move.

"Go ahead," she urged.

"Angélica," Mashuba said sternly. "It is a private time."

"Yes," Digger piped up gratefully, "private." He glared at her. "Besides, I don't know what you want me to do."

"What do you feel you should do?" Mashuba asked.

"This is probably not what you're after, but I really feel I should be with Vawaha right now. To see if she is all right." He looked at Angélica, expecting her to throw more words at him. But she didn't. She simply stood there with her long black hair falling down over her crossed arms, looking serene and... disappointed. He felt a pang he hadn't expected when he saw that look.

Mashuba just nodded his head gravely.

Digger took the cue and fled the scene. Even a dying grandmother was going to be better than this kind of pressure, he thought as he hurried toward the shelter where Vawaha was sitting watch with Tomanja.

* * * *

The roar of the river and the muffled rumblings of boulders being pushed sluggishly through Dos Montañas Pass echoed back as the searchers returned to their campsite at day's end. They'd combed through every inch of the site near the cavern, where they'd found the old riverbed to be filled with the magnificent round stones earlier that morning—but no more clues had come to light.

Now Bendi, morosely chewing her dinner, looked up as a multitude of birds called to one another through the slowly darkening rainforest. She turned to gaze up the river, toward Caliente Falls and its rapids.

"Water scares me," she said aloud, to no one in particular among the group eating by the camp stove. "I don't understand the fascination Digger has with it."

"Given the present circumstances, I don't mean to be out of place," Manuel replied, "but the river *is* beautiful. In fact, it is much more than that. It is alive and has its own personality. The river talks to you, if you are open enough to listen. Maybe your friend Digger had the ability to listen. I know you are worried," he added more gently, "but we have found some clues. That is a good sign. Plus, we will soon have more help."

Bendi didn't respond. Her insides were tied up in knots and she suddenly lost her appetite. As she internally reviewed all the facts, the situation appeared bleak—but something inside of her told her she was closer than ever. She gently rubbed her stomach and decided to change the subject.

"Ortega, yesterday you said you disagreed with many of the other archaeologists about the stone spheres. What makes you different from the others?"

"After the previous curator at the museum died," he explained, "my appointment as his replacement was extremely controversial among my colleagues. That is when many of them became very vocal."

Manuel rolled his eyes, but Danny and Francisco scooted closer to listen in.

"It would have to do with perspective," Ortega continued. "The only way I believe that I can explain it would be to say that I am an archaeologist with spirit—a student of anthroposophy."

"What is anthroposophy?" Francisco asked.

"It is a way of looking at the world with spiritual eyes. The term actually began at the beginning of the century with a Dr. Rudolf Steiner from Austria. He believed, as I do, that Spirit needs to be considered in all areas, from medicine to education, from politics to sociology, and from anthropology to archaeology. There was also a famous French theologian and writer by the name of Teilhard de Chardin who said, 'We are spiritual beings having a physical experience.' Many people believe and act as if they are only physical. If they do happen to believe in a spiritual perspective, many still have the tendency to act as if they are 'physical trying to have a spiritual experience.' That same perspective is then instilled into any role that individual plays; whether as a carpenter, a politician, a parent, a lover, or an archaeologist."

Manuel shifted noisily, making faces of extreme boredom. "Go on," Bendi urged.

Ortega smiled gratefully at her. "Most archaeologists rarely begin their journey of inquiry from the spiritual perspective. First of all, most people have confused religion and spirituality. You can find both together, but not always. One can believe in a religion and still not be spiritual, and also one can be spiritual without being in a religion. So I am different in my basic perspective of life and our world. I believe that some of the greatest mysteries of our earth are still mysteries because we try to solve them from the illusionary belief that we are physical beings first. Therefore, all the clues we look for are, of course, in the physical world.

"For example, the huge statues on Easter island, the menhirs of England, the stelae of the Mayans or Incas, and our own Stone Spheres are still mysteries—perhaps because we have only looked for clues within the physical realm."

"What are you talking about, Ortega?" Manuel finally challenged him.

"If you are only looking at the physical realm, you would spend much energy investigating the size of the spheres, or their alignment, or their markings. I am not saying we should not look at those characteristics, but again, those are only *physical*. From the stories I have heard, it was not gold that was inside the spheres, or any 'thing,' for that matter. It was *energy*." Ortega's eyes lit up when he said the word. Bendi had the feeling he truly enjoyed startling his listeners—whether a group gathered around a campfire or a conference filled with his peers. No wonder they thought he was trouble! she smiled to herself. She rather liked this part of his personality.

"Remember when I told you that for my thesis I studied with the indigenous tribes of South America? Well, according to their legends, the Outcasts put demons or great spirits into the stone. The elders of the tribes I studied with believe special people can access the information, powers, and healing from the spheres. I tend to agree with them! I believe that with all these structures—especially the spheres—certain information or energy, or whatever you would like to call it, was placed into them. They are only waiting for the right person, or persons, to come along who can receive this information."

"And you probably think you are that special person!" Manuel scoffed at him. "If I can use an American expression, 'That is the biggest amount of bull I have ever heard!' Sending energy into rocks and then receiving it. That is nonsense."

"Not really." Ortega remained unflustered. "Do you have any *niños,* Manuel?"

"I have three," he answered cautiously.

"Well, when you pick up one of your children in your arms and hug him, what do you think you get from that?"

"That he loves me, and cares for me, and I somehow feel better afterwards," he said proudly. "What does this have to do with your rocks?"

Ortega ignored the remark and pressed further, "And when your wife softly touches you, what do you get?"

"Hey—none of your business!" he flushed. Bendi pretended not to notice, while Danny and Francisco guffawed.

"A sense of love and caring, right?" Ortega grinned. "So without words, in both instances they gave and you received some emotion, some information, and some healing—for that is what love conveys. If you were to then bump into a friend, that friend might feel—receive—that you were somehow different, a little more happy, or contented, or maybe even a bit, a very little bit more loving toward them. So in a way you were a receptacle for that invisible energy, that emotion, that love, no?"

"But rocks do not talk," Manuel argued, still fuming over his humiliation.

"But everything is energy, so rocks can *receive* energy from you and *give* energy to you—just like everything else does! Would you agree that if you were to sit on a rock, you would give the energy of heat from your body to that rock? And that I could then sit on that rock and receive your warmth?" Ortega sat back expectantly, knowing he'd won.

"I suppose, " Manuel had to admit.

"Well," Ortega rejoined briskly, "emotions are energy, also—and so are thoughts. So why can they not be stored or transferred from a rock just like the heat from your body?"

"Well, I have never heard a rock talk to me," Manuel said defensively.

"Your friend did not hear your words but he still received that energy from you. Besides, you cannot tell me that when you go rafting, the river does not move you! Or that you do not feel 'energy' from the river." Manuel was silent. "The river has stored much information, and even feelings, from all that it has had contact with—the earth, the heavens, and we humans. And if you are really in tune with the river, you can pick up on that, no? Earlier you mentioned about the river being alive, having a personality, and yes, even talking to you."

"That was different," Manuel protested.

"It is? How so?" Ortega grinned.

"I cannot waste my time on such nonsense!" Manuel sputtered and stood up abruptly. "I have to prepare some things for tomorrow. Be ready for an early start," he barked at them and then strode off to his tent.

Ortega chuckled, while Danny and Francisco slapped their knees in glee and shook his hand. Ortega simply bowed his head in mock modesty, but Bendi noticed a special gleam in his eye when he looked back up. She hadn't said so, but she believed every word of what he'd said.

Chapter 18

"May we continue this dance of life throughout lifetimes,
so that we may know each other more deeply.
Through that knowing we shall experience the grace of body,
the peace of mind, the love of heart, and the embodiment of spirit.
By that knowing, we shall be One with the Divine."

Digger knew that Mashuba and Angélica wanted him to journey around Gutubo. But he didn't want to do it—not yet. He could feel their disappointment, especially Angélica's.

He'd told the truth about wanting to be with Vawaha, but he couldn't deny that he was also running from the pressure he'd felt from Angélica. His mother had always pushed him, and his habitual reaction was to run the other way—if not physically, then mentally and or emotionally. Now guilt slashed another cut on the skin of his consciousness.

As he walked toward the hut sheltering Tomanja and Vawaha, he tried to distance himself from this masochistic emotion by replaying in his mind the story of Gutubo—the "tree of many eyes."

When he reached the bamboo dwelling, he stood outside for a moment, watching the Keepers of the Gate. One of the women was tending the exhausted grandmother, while another ground plants in a bowl. The man was talking quietly with Vawaha, his hand lying gently on her shoulder.

As Digger moved closer, he could hear Tomanja's breathing—a gurgly noise of internal drowning and then that terrible stench—it was all too familiar. He'd smelled that odor when his dad had died. And that same foulness had oozed from his mother, days before she passed away; it was the scent of death.

"How is your grandmother doing?" Digger knew the answer, but he asked the obvious anyway.

"Not well," Vawaha answered, trying to hold back a whimper. "I know she will 'pass through' soon. At least then all her physical pain will be gone. Then she will be like my hawk and dance with the wind!

But I will miss her." She couldn't hold back the tears at that thought and began to cry.

Digger put his arms around her; he didn't know what else to do or what to say. No one ever does, he thought. Words are necessary at times, but for *real* moments, moments with any amount of depth and feeling, they seemed superficial. Even though hugging was not comfortable for him, he felt that much more could be communicated by a touch—or a sound. That's why he loved his music; he felt he could communicate a whole passage from any book by playing a few notes with a couple of chords.

Still, he knew his piano was his voice, but also his crutch. His eighty-eight keys never talked back to him; they never pushed him, never asked him for anything, never did anything that he didn't want them to do. As painful as it was to admit, it was true: his relationship with the piano had also alienated him from women, from Bendi, at times even from himself.

Tomanja tried to speak. Vawaha turned from Digger to sit next to her grandmother, while the man braced her up so that she could talk easier. Coughing several times, she spit out green phlegm. Smiling, she was now able to talk a little bit easier, and began to reminisce with Vawaha about their times together.

Digger stepped back and settled down on a bamboo mat. As Vawaha and Tomanja conversed, he held back his tears as he gazed at the expressions on their faces. No, it was more than that, he thought; it isn't just the look, it's the feeling between them; the feeling of love they share. He actually felt embarrassed being there; it was a little like being a voyeur, being privy to such a moment.

That exchange of love was what he'd wanted with his mother. There were moments during those last few months when he'd actually felt a deep love for her; but they always seemed to be punctured by moments of guilt. Sometimes that would be induced by his mother reciting old phrases he'd heard over and over again when he was boy: "You should obey your mother." "If you loved me..." And when he got older: "What will people think if you don't come over for Thanksgiving?" Then there were the—consciously denied—self-recriminations regurgitated by his own mind: "Good sons don't do that to their mother." "If I do that, or don't do this, she won't love me."

Now the dull, tumorous ache of the belief that he was never good enough resonated within him. He'd learned how to handle part of that pain, the belief that his *mother* never thought he was good enough. But the most tormenting aspect of that ache was created long ago, in some forgotten childhood moment when he'd begun to accept that belief as his own.

Having all those deeply felt emotions brought to the surface so easily by a saying or a look was usually more than he could bear. Now here he was in the present, physically several thousand miles away, but still emotionally back in Palm Springs, a few weeks ago.

He looked again at Vawaha and Tomanja. Even though sadness and grief played between them, their love by far played the loudest. Regardless of the situation, he wanted what they had. As he hazily viewed the scene before him, Digger's mind wandered backward in time...

At the hospice, his brother and he had met with the social worker. "Your mother is a very bright woman," she'd said. "And quite a handful." They'd nodded their heads and smiled. "She is also very scared and knows the end is near. Would you like to all meet together tomorrow? This would be your chance to say anything and everything to her. It would be a wonderful opportunity to bring all of your issues to closure. Not only yours, but hers, too."

Jeff and he readily agreed, and silently hoped for the impossible.

When the social worker arrived the next day, their mother was feeling the best she'd felt in weeks. Sitting up in bed, she smiled as they all came into her bedroom.

"Do you remember why we are meeting today, Mrs. Taylor?" the social worker began.

"Yes, to talk about things, " his mother answered.

"Who'd like to begin?" the woman asked.

As Digger stared at his mother's frail body that day, he'd felt sorry for her. During the past few months, he'd witnessed close up the havoc that cancer had wreaked on her body. Although she was seventy-two, she had been a beautiful woman, her high cheekbones and striking features still turning a head or two. But within a few short months, the disease turned her into a shell of skin and bones. The sight of her sunken face and the sound of her labored breathing would leave an indelible imprint on him for years to come.

Despite the social worker's upbeat opening, they'd all sat there silently. Where do you begin? Digger thought. For years, he'd tried to talk with her, but it was of no use. Maybe this time would be different because she knew she was going to die soon. Maybe she would open up; what could she lose? The silence was still prevalent as the social worker looked in turn at each of them.

"Well, I guess I'll be first," Jeff finally offered. "What was it like growing up with Grandpa and Nanny?"

"What kind of a question is that?" his mother asked.

"You've never really talked about your childhood to us. What was it like?" his brother repeated.

"I don't know what you mean. I've told you everything about my childhood," she answered.

"No, you haven't," his brother rebutted.

"What is it that you really want to know?" the social worker hinted gently.

"Okay, how did you like being a parent, being our parent?" Jeff tried.

"What kind of a question is that?" his mother replied again, obviously annoyed.

"It's a simple question," Jeff returned with exasperation. "Were you happy as a parent? Did you enjoy being a mother?"

"Of course I did!" she said loudly. "I loved you boys. I did everything for the both of you." Her voice was rising.

Both Jeff and he had chuckled nervously under their breath.

"What's so funny? You think an old lady dying is funny?" their mother responded.

"No, I don't," Digger said. "But what *is* funny, is you telling us in an angry voice that you enjoyed being our mother! Mom, we just would like to know why you were so unhappy as an adult, why you were always yelling and screaming at us. It seems you were always on a short fuse. We couldn't have been that bad as kids. What was your childhood like? What was it like for you to grow up? Mom, both of us love you. Don't shut us out; talk to us. These are normal questions that normal families ask. But we've never discussed them."

"I've told you everything, and as far as my voice, that's just the way I talk. I'm an Irish Catholic mother and that's how we all talk." As she spoke to Digger her voice became louder, "Why did you quit your job in Chicago to be a bum in Florida and then end up being a waiter in San Diego? Why don't you tell me why you got divorced? No one in our family has ever gotten divorced!"

"Everything seems to be going quite well," his brother said sarcastically.

Digger had hardly heard her last few words; the steel door had slammed shut. The social worker then tried to establish commonality by changing the topic to times they'd shared together which were positive. Most of that conversation revolved around vacations at Shawano Lake in Wisconsin.

Then the silence returned. Finally, Jeff and he had looked at each other—and confronted her. They told her about the episode they'd witnessed a couple of weeks previously, when she'd gone back in time to the moment of giving birth, and then shouted that she didn't want a child.

She just sat there stone-faced as she listened to her sons' story.

"Mrs. Taylor, what do you think about what your sons have just said?" the social worker probed.

"Nothing. It was just the ramblings of an old lady who was on lots of pain medication. I can't be held responsible for dreams or any such things," she stated.

"Mrs. Taylor, is there anything that you would like to say to your boys?"

"There's nothing to say that hasn't already been said," their mother said matter-of-factly.

"Is there anything you would like to say to them, to bring to closure before..." the woman hesitated a moment, "before you move on."

"I don't know what you want me to say."

"Well, do you love your sons?" the social worker asked.

"Of course I do," his mother had answered, looking at the social worker.

"When was the most powerful moment that you felt love for them?"

"Well," she said, as she gave the slightest glance at his brother, "I loved him the most when he took care of his grandmother, my mother, who had advanced Alzheimer's disease. He was seventeen and I was in the hospital so I couldn't take care of her. He stayed home from school and did everything for her, from feeding to bathing her after she had made a mess in the bed."

"Can you tell him that?" the woman urged.

"He knows that I loved him for that," she responded, again looking only at the social worker.

"But can you look at him and tell him?"

His mother looked straight ahead.

"How about Digger?"

"Well, his music. He plays beautiful music. That's what I love him for," she answered, again refusing to look at him.

He saw the tears welled up in his brother's eyes as he closed his own.

"Can you tell him that to his face?" the social worker tried again, pushing gently.

"He heard me—besides, he knows it; I don't have to tell him," she answered nonchalantly.

"Mrs. Taylor, you know that you probably have less than a week to live." She nodded. "Before you die, wouldn't you want to tell your boys to their faces that you love them?"

"They know that I love them," she insisted, staring directly at the social worker.

"All I'm asking you is," the woman's voice remained soft yet firm, "would you turn your head several inches and look at your boys and tell them to their faces what you're telling me?"

"They already know," she answered and then coughed several times. "I'm not feeling well. I would like you all to leave."

Digger's stomach had squeezed into his throat as the runaway emotional rollercoaster plummeted violently. The ride took him places he didn't think existed, places of resentment, anger, love, compassion, newly-found connections, old wounds...

His mother had lain there scared, emaciated, and lonely. The irony was that he felt all of that about himself.

As he listened to her wheezing and coughing, he felt a sadness; a deep sadness that came from the realization that his mother's cancer was not what was killing her.

Later, after he'd driven back to San Diego, he described the session to Bendi. He remembered lying next to her that night in bed, in a partial fetal position. She'd caressed him and told him that she loved him. But her words came from far off in the distance, and he barely felt her touch. The boyhood-constructed steel door had been shut tight.

Mashuba and Angélica startled Digger as they sat down on either side of him.

"Where were you?" Angélica asked as she lightly touched his hand.

"A long way off." He looked into her eyes and added, "But trying to be right here."

Vawaha stood at her grandmother's feet as the old woman's chest heaved upwards toward the sky. Her lungs let out a long, gurgly sound. Several moments passed in silence.

Tomanja was desperately attempting to continue her life, painfully sucking in more air. Her body had been successfully going through this process for decades. So why wouldn't things work like they used to? Her body was confused; it did not know any other way but to try and hold on.

It was the next long, gurgly sigh that pushed a well-hidden button within Digger and a gate quickly opened—the gate that had locked up all his experiences with death. It was impossible to let out just one idea, one experience, one memory, or one emotion, without letting them all out. So a stampede occurred within Digger: the imminent loss of this woman whom he didn't even know, the grief for his new friend Vawaha, the frustration of what he believed to be the senseless death of his father, the tragic loss of a friend who was hit by a speeding train, the sadness and guilt associated with his own mother's death, the frightening death of a classmate as the young teenager collapsed next to him in gym class; his own youthful confusion over the wakes and funerals of his grandparents. The memories of a lifetime.

He'd never talked about death in school or on the streets of South

Chicago. Sure, people died—they died from many different causes—but to actually talk about death and all of its effects on you personally, was taboo. He'd held back so many emotions, and each was multi-faceted...

The elderly woman's body continued, despite the pain it was causing; even though there was no more hope, even though it was time to let go. The body pushed on with another labored breath, then...

Silence.

But within Digger, the stampede continued as his fears grabbed him by the throat. What if he lost someone close to him? What about when he died? What kind of dying would he have to endure? What is after death—Hell, Heaven, something beyond his comprehension, or worse— nothingness?

Too much. Overload. With the fervor of a madman, he wrestled internally with all of these thoughts and emotions and tried to drag them behind the gate. But his effort was futile.

Now the Keepers of the Gate were focusing a couple of feet above Tomanja's body, slowly circling the woman with loving smiles.

Her lungs stretched for air, one last time. And then with a short exhale and slight twitch, her body gave up—and rested—finally.

A gust of wind blew over the canopy of the rainforest. Digger could hear the leaves break from their branches and land softly on the thatched roof. He saw tears drop off Vawaha's cheeks. Before he even knew of his own, he tasted the saltiness on his lips.

Vawaha remained standing over her grandmother's body. As she spoke in her own language, Angélica translated for Digger, drawing her face close to his to whisper softly in his ear, "May we continue this dance of life throughout lifetimes, so that we may know each other more deeply. Through that knowing, we shall experience the grace of body, the peace of mind, the love of heart, and the embodiment of Spirit. By that knowing, we shall be One with the Divine."

He couldn't figure out how word spread so quickly through the village, but now the sound of an ancient bass instrument began to reverberate softly through the jungle. The same three low notes were repeated, with the second note higher and third note lower than the first. Duummm, Dum, Dumm. A flute joined in, weaving a haunting melody.

The Keepers reverently covered the body with a white, gauzy material and placed twelve, wild pink orchids on top. Angélica, Mashuba, and Digger approached Vawaha, exchanging only the silence of hugs.

Two drums now accompanied the other instruments.

Vawaha looked into each of their eyes for a moment and then walked out of the hut with the Keepers of the Gate.

"Where are they going?" Digger asked.

"To be with her," Angélica replied solemnly. "They will find some place to Vawaha's liking and then they will be *with* her. If she has questions, they will try and answer them; if she just wants to be heard they will listen; if she wants silence, they will be quiet. At some point in time, they will be with her to review the richness of this event."

"What do you mean, *richness*?" he wondered.

"That of death and dying. We believe that the purpose of the various events in our lives is to illuminate our way back Home, to what you might call God or the Divine. The events surrounding one's physical death are rich experiences; ones in which there is much to learn, not only for the one who is 'passing through,' but for all those who are touched by it. In fact, that is the last and most wondrous gift that the dying give to us"—she smiled with that radiant glow she always seemed to express when trying to explain something to him—"the gift of light for our present journey. It is up to us to find that light, that gem amidst the jungle!"

"I'm sorry," he apologized. He meant it sincerely. He was too confused to think or talk, or to find something positive in all this; the stampede of emotions was still going on within him. "I need to take a break from all of this," he tried to explain to her—and to Mashuba, who had been standing quietly near, like the pillar of strength he always seemed to be.

"Meet us at the ceremony tonight," the elder said. "Please."

Digger nodded absently before escaping to the fresh air outside the hut.

The music continued to drift through the jungle's corridors; its rhythm pulled Digger aimlessly through the village. He didn't know how long he'd been walking, but night had fallen by the time he noticed he was sitting on a boulder next to the stream.

He looked upstream and then up into the sky, where a corridor of lights twinkled. In the next moment, a shooting star streaked across the backbone of the Milky Way. Its stay was short, but the flickering light gave a brilliance—for those who cared to watch—that always made an impact. That star's impact might have been felt by the beauty of its trail, or the wonder of its origin, or the love of its light, or the deep felt connection of its placement in the heavens. But no matter where in the sky you saw it or how short its duration, it always made an impact.

That was when it hit him. His viscera twitched as his body began to shake. The weight of all his gathered and unreleased emotions drove him to the ground. He sobbed; the deep-down, can't-get-your-breath, nose-dripping, gut-wrenching kind of sob. It was like a volcano that for years had been boiling deep within—first exploding through the surface, and then continuing a long, steady flow.

Tears falling from his cheeks splashed onto the pebbles and slowly fed the stream. He wasn't sure who he was crying for—Tomanja, his mother, Vawaha—or was it for himself? He knelt on the ground weeping for some time.

The whole reason for this trip had been to get away from this demon he'd been living with for the last five months. The pain, he thought, wasn't about his mother's actual death. In truth, that was a godsend for his mom, and also for his brother and himself. No—most of his pain came from all the related issues that had surfaced: childhood issues, old issues, hidden issues, the I-already-thought-I'd-dealt-with-this-issue issue.

Then there was his response; no, his *reaction* to it all: reverting back to his old self, holding things in, shutting Bendi out, running away to Costa Rica to leave it all behind. Somewhere within himself he'd known better; he'd known that it was all locked inside and that he could never truly run away. But he'd tried to do it anyway.

Slowly getting up off his rock-indented knees, he took a long, deep breath. Carefully and a little shakily stepping across the stream, he felt almost pulled up the hill to the quarry. When he reached the top, the moon, almost full, cast shadows from the stone spheres. He gazed at them, all spread out, and one particular sphere drew his attention. He walked over to the seven-foot gold-and-purple sculpture, with its finely-etched geometric shapes. His vision became blurry, so he closed his eyes.

Not knowing why, he slowly outstretched his hands in front of him. He felt a little tingling, as if thousands of tiny fingers were gently massaging his limbs. He also noticed a gentle resistance the closer he moved his hands toward the stone sphere. At one point, his hands could move no further and he thought he'd touched the mysterious object.

When he opened his eyes, he was shocked; his hands were still a foot and a half away from the sphere! "Hey—what's happening?" he exclaimed aloud.

"No questions."

He jumped at the sound of Angélica's voice directly behind him.

"Don't scare me like that! Where did you come from? I didn't see you anywhere."

"Forget all that. Bring your attention back to what you what you were just doing," she urged him. "You were feeling the sphere's energy. Just let go, and continue."

He could see she was dead serious. So he took another deep breath and repeated what he'd done before—with the same results. Baffled, he started to walk counterclockwise around the sphere, still feeling its energy. With his next step, he was driven backwards a couple of feet.

Tentatively, he took another step and found himself pushed a little further away. He turned to Angélica and started to ask a question. The look she gave him clearly communicated, "Be quiet and just continue." The next couple of steps brought him back to the same distance from the sphere he'd been when he started. He continued his counterclockwise motion, when all of a sudden he found himself pulled into the stone sphere. His body pressed firmly against the cold granite. He quickly pulled himself off.

"You are a surprise, Digger," Angélica laughed. "Just when I thought there was no hope for you, just when things should get harder, you somehow turn it around!"

"What just happened?" he was still staring wide-eyed at the huge purple-and-gold stone.

"Everything and nothing," she replied enigmatically.

Chapter 19

"Many veils camouflage our spirit
and many layers of knowingness surround the challenges in our lives.
We need to experience these challenges in various ways and many times
so that we may bare our multi-faceted spirit.
You do yourself an injustice, if you expect anything less."

Digger studied the sphere, as if searching for the trick of a magician. He jumped back when momentarily, reflecting the light of the moon, two large, fierce, black-and-white-speckled eyeballs glared up at him. An Io moth flapped its wings several more times before it flew off, lost to the darkness.

Regaining his composure, Digger turned to Angélica and asked, "Did I imprint with the stone sphere?"

"When you imprint, you will not have to ask the question, you will just know. So what do you know?"

"I felt more like the stone sphere imprinted with me, than I did with it!"

"That is probably true."

"First, I felt the sphere to be larger than it looked. Then as I walked around it, the sphere was like a magnet; pushing me away. Then exactly halfway around, it pulled me in! What *is* this thing?"

"It is the Traveling sphere; it is about how we move through our universe, whether it be through space, through time, or in the moment," Angélica explained calmly, her eyes glittering in the moonlight (only hers were real, unlike the Io moth's false patterns). "You just experienced one of the most profound lessons. If you lived like you acted in the last few moments, you would be one of the most enlightened beings on this earth," she said with a soft chuckle.

"What are you talking about?" He didn't like being laughed at.

"Do not go backwards on me, Digger." She was suddenly serious. "Do not always be so quick when one gives you information to immediately ask a question. Stop, think, but most importantly *feel*. You just told me you felt a magnetic pull and push. What you did correctly was to allow yourself to feel the pulse of the universe, and you traveled along accordingly. You did not resist until the end, when you pulled yourself off the sphere!" She seemed genuinely pleased with him, and that, he liked. He listened more attentively as she continued, "The universe is constantly pushing and pulling, like the opposite ends of the pendulum, back and forth. If you do not resist, there is no resistance. Life is simple. But the pain in our lives occurs when we push instead of being pulled, or when we pull rather than being pushed."

"So the spheres are just representations of the universe," Digger concluded. "Really, of ourselves." He stopped for a moment and thought. "Okay—of *me*." Angélica smiled broadly and nodded. "But how can I *imprint* with *me*?"

"There you go asking questions again! Just know that you are much further along toward accomplishing your goal than you were several moments ago," she said with a sigh.

Digger thought of the weeks' happenings and felt the questions immediately beginning to back up in his mind: What is the purpose of the Traveling sphere? How was he going to imprint with a sphere when he didn't even know what that meant? And how would *Los Otros* help him get home?… He did everything in his power not to open his mouth with another question.

"Let us go back down; the ceremony for Tomanja will begin soon," Angélica suggested, as if she knew the struggle going on inside him.

He was grateful for the diversion. Okay, he thought. Maybe all her ideas aren't so bad.

In silence, they walked back down the steps toward the village. Digger's critical self had by now changed the awe of his experience with the Traveling sphere into a belief that he did not know anything. He felt stupid about not knowing how to imprint a sphere: stupid about falling into old patterns, stupid about always getting himself into jams, stupid about not "getting" life. He just wasn't good enough.

When they came near the stream, several bats swooped over them. Digger instinctively put up his arms to protect his head as the bats circled around.

"Be open!" Angélica quickly urged.

"Be open to what? I'm just protecting myse—" Digger felt the wings of one of the bats hit his head.

In that moment, time seemed to stop as the events of the last several months flashed instantaneously before him. In that moment, he had an "ah-ha" awareness about learning. He realized, not in any logical sense but in a deep, knowing sense, that learning is rarely a process of the light turning on and something becoming instantly and completely known. He now knew, on a deeper level, that the truer aspects of his existence were much richer and therefore needed time, experience, remembrance, and action. The essence of anything is rarely found on the surface but is discovered through the process of continuous unfoldment; the action of peeling away the layers, feeling each layer, remembering all the lessons of the previous layers, and then bringing that awareness to the present.

A deeper layer of a previously known concept now peeled away, and left him with the knowingness that he couldn't escape his mother's death and all that clung to it. Also, that physical distance means absolutely nothing when it comes to matters of the mind, heart, and soul.

Yet another layer of the same concept peeled back, revealing to him that he truly takes with him all of his experiences, thoughts, emotions, hopes, dreams, and fears—even when it came time for him to "pass through."

"Are you all right?" Angélica sounded concerned.

He'd been standing still, staring off blankly, and now he blinked at her in the moonlight. "I'll meet up with you later," was all he could say as he headed straight for the strangler fig.

As shadows played among the gnarled vines, he watched shapes and forms flowing over Gutubo. The strangler fig and Gutubo's trunk appeared as a metamorphic totem pole: it was like repeating or staring at a word; the longer he looked at the once-familiar form, the more it transformed into something unfamiliar and strange. He blinked several times and then stood in the "compartment" formed by two of Gutubo's limbs that were draped with living fig roots. He closed his eyes.

Taking a deep breath and gathering his courage, he stated out loud all of his thoughts, feelings, and beliefs about his relationship with his mother.

The moment those previously unheard words escaped from his lips, they scattered towards the freedom of the night. Some were coated with years of compliance; some no longer rang true in his heart. Some tore at his throat before they materialized in the humid jungle; some felt quite silly; and some echoed another person's voice.

The indignant tone in his voice had been whiny at first, but soon turned to frustration. In the beginning, he didn't recognize the emotion. But as he continued speaking from his perspective, the sound of his voice transformed from aggravation to anger, to rage. It was then that he recognized this voice: it was that of a child's, a young Jonathan. It frightened him.

He backed out of Gutubo's arms and rubbed his throat. He looked around apprehensively to see if anybody had been witness to his private confession. Not wanting to deal further with his latest self-exposé, he quickly trekked toward the center of the village where *Los Otros* had gathered.

Digger decided to first observe from a distance before he plunged himself into yet another strange new experience. Fortunately, no one had noticed his approach, so he could watch safely for a little while before deciding how far he wanted to involve himself.

From where he stood on the outskirts of *Los Otros'* circle, he could see Vawaha sitting between Mashuba and Angélica. One of the Keepers of the Gate came toward her, placing in front of the young girl a necklace that her grandmother had worn, then stepped back to join the other Keepers, all of whom were completely nude, their bodies covered with painted designs that looked like the symbols on the spheres. Now the music, which had been thrumming continuously, stopped for a brief moment as several *Los Otros* carried strands of coconut shells forward to place them over the necks of the Keepers of the Gate.

Within the circle, the body of Tomanja lay on top of a bamboo mat with poles on either side, the twelve pink orchids still decorating the center of her white shroud. The Keepers of the Gate poured oils over the shrouded form and then lifted the mat onto the fire. As tall flames shot up towards the heavens, a heavy, sweet fragrance permeated the village. The music had begun again, and now several drummers performed, accompanied by tribal members playing clappers, flutes, and rattles with an unnerving dissonant sound.

The Keepers, laden with the heavy coconut shells, crawled around the ground, periodically crying aloud. Several times they broke out in tantrum-like squeals and screams. The discordant melodies and rhythms continued until the Keepers stood up. A young boy ran into the circle and cut off several of the coconut shells from their necks. The music segued to a less dissonant melody, with more recognizable patterns within the drumming. The Keepers now danced around the fire in clumsy fashion.

As the dance progressed, more young boys ran out to cut shells off the Keepers of the Gate and the dancing became more fluid. A low reverberating tone emanated from a long hollow bamboo shoot that Chucan played. Several flutes now joined the emerging melody. Eventually, only a few shells remained on each of the dancers as they jumped effortlessly over the fire. One woman Keeper lay down before Vawaha, as the other two removed the last of her shells from her neck. She then jumped up and swiftly moved in and out of the circle, looking into the eyes of the gathered *Los Otros* in turn. Returning to Vawaha she held the girl's hands for a moment. Then gently letting them go, she danced with the lightness of a prima ballerina. A man threw powder into the fire's belly and it burst into a massive ball of flame. As the musicians returned to the earlier, haunting song Digger had heard them playing off and on throughout the day, the other two Keepers gradually slowed and halted their dance. Without anyone noticing, the female dancer had disappeared into the darkness of the jungle.

As Digger stood watching, he wondered what it might mean to be one of *Los Otros*, having a sense of previously unfelt power, believing in himself, conscious that every decision was truly a choice, knowing that the events in his life were not just accidents and that he was truly the creator of his existence...

He had to admit that even though he might not be a full-fledged *Otros*, his experiences during the last several hours had created a small shift within him. Slightly edging beyond the belief that he was only physical, he'd just begun to know deeply that Spirit is a true realm. With that glimpse of awareness came another avalanche of questions: What do all of the spiritual realms look and feel like? What are their purposes? What is the meaning of our physical world? What about humankind's past history? What about the beginning of planet earth and our so-called "human" race? Where did the journey of spirit begin, and where is it taking the human race—where had it taken him? What part did he really play in all of this? If and when he found that out, was he even capable or worthy of the task?

With all of these questions, the sense of God became magnified in his mind beyond the previously unthinkable. There was so much more out there than he'd ever believed before! A part of him felt that the grander he saw things, the smaller he was.

Digger turned suddenly as he felt Vawaha standing next to him. He picked her up in his arms and held her tightly.

"What is going to happen? What are we going to do?" she asked.

"I don't know, Vawaha. I don't know," he answered, not really knowing what she was asking. Did she know all the things that he was thinking, that he was feeling? Or was she just talking about herself? Or was she worried about the fate of *Los Otros*—or all of the above?

* *.* *

Amidst the diffused morning-light, Bendi stood ankle deep in the Río Pacuare as she gazed downriver at the steep granite walls of Dos Montañas Pass. She heard the sounds of human voices intermingled with the rivers' rumblings. Turning around she noticed the new search teams paddling toward her. Beaching their rafts and kayaks at the entrance to the ancient riverbed a television crew from San José and the archaeological teams from the *Museo Nacional* unloaded their equipment. A little while later more *policías* arrived, along with a half-dozen reporters from various Costa Rican news agencies, including a reporter from the *Tico Times*—an English-language Costa Rican newspaper. After setting up camp the newcomers made their way down the ancient riverbed, where they milled around the newly discovered stone spheres in amazement.

Bendi was flustered by all the commotion, but also thankful. The more people and media, the better chance of finding Digger.

Ortega was beaming as he spoke to the reporters about *las esferas de piedra,*—the Stone Spheres—the upcoming archeological conference, and especially his theories. When his staff and students were finished unloading their equipment by the cavern, he instructed them to begin work. "That is where I believe the stone spheres were stored before the earthquake. The flooding river probably washed away anything of use, but check carefully anyway. Remember, we are primarily looking for clues about the missing river rafter, Mr. Taylor. If you find anything at all, let me know right away."

A few members of the rescue party went off to search the nearby hills, while Manuel instructed the others to hike further down the ancient riverbed. As Bendi spoke with several reporters, she felt as if someone were looking at her from the jungle surrounding them. She looked to either side—and could see no one. But when she looked up toward the rocky bluff, she spotted the black jaguar sitting on its haunches, looking down at her. She could swear he was staring at and through her. Surprisingly, it didn't scare her. In fact, the mighty animal's stare went straight to her heart. And it felt good.

Excusing herself from the questioning reporters, she slipped out of their sight. Even though climbing and heights in general usually frightened her, she began the trek up the hillside toward the rocky bluff. Periodically, as she came to small clearings which allowed a better view, she caught glimpses of the black feline. At times her hike up the slope was dream-like, as if the animal were drawing her to it. Then at other times she wrestled with her primal fear and couldn't believe she was actually moving *toward* the predator.

Out of breath when she reached halfway on the sloping hill, Bendi carelessly pushed aside a prickly bush. She suppressed a scream. Curled up on her path was a large, well-camouflaged snake with half of a rodent sticking out of its mouth. The fer-de-lance, the deadliest snake in Central America, slowly swallowed the furry mammal. As she watched the victim's tail disappear, she stepped cautiously backwards, realizing she'd better be more alert. She checked her steps around fallen, rotting trees and placed her hands only where she'd first taken care to inspect for unsavory creatures.

When she finally reached the top of the rocky bluff, she quickly scanned the area for the jaguar but didn't see him anywhere. Thankful for a level surface, she bent over to rest her hands on her knees and gasped to catch her breath. The steep ascent, the sun, the humidity, and the anticipation of coming face-to-face with the mysterious feline had her heart pumping wildly. When she stood up, she noticed the shadows entangled among a pile of boulders near the edge of the bluff. Wasn't that where the jaguar had been sitting all those times?

She edged over to peer down the several hundred feet to the ancient waterway below. She couldn't see the cavern, which must have been directly below her at ground level, but she did see bug-sized people moving in and around the scattered spheres.

The view was stupendous from here. She let her vision follow the narrow riverbed back to their campsite, where the real Río Pacuare veered off on its normal, raging course and disappeared into Dos Montañas Pass. For a moment, she turned to look behind her, where miles more jungle sloped gently up and away from her. Then as she turned back to the view, her body trembled as a jolt of fight-or-flight response kicked in—there on the pile of boulders perched the fierce-looking jaguar. She was only about thirty feet from him, frozen to the spot as they stared at each other. But the longer she looked into the animal's eyes, the less fear she felt. In fact, she felt oddly as if they both had similar concerns. Was that possible?

Tentatively, she moved closer, still staring into the wild creature's eyes. She was possessed by a feeling that, somehow, this animal knew about Digger and his whereabouts.

"Yes, I do!" a voice rang out.

Bendi shook her head. *Did the jaguar just speak to me?* The large predator continued to stare into her eyes. She realized that she'd actually heard the statement in her head. The cat sat down on its haunches and licked his leg.

"Did you just speak to me?" Bendi felt silly asking her question aloud, as if talking to her long-lost house pet. She moved to within ten feet of the jaguar.

"Yes!" came the reply.

It wasn't like actually hearing words; it was more like a sense of knowing. The jaguar continued to lick himself as the sun glistened off his whiskers, which were as long as her forearm.

"Now is not the time."

"What do you mean, *now is not the time*? I want to know where Digger is!" she said softly.

Her logical mind couldn't believe she was having a conversation with a jaguar. It all seemed so surreal, like in her "flying" dreams. In those nighttime escapades, the experience of her body flying wherever she directed seemed so natural; it was an integral part of who she was.

Of course, she could fly. There was no surprise involved at all, just the sense of pure enjoyment. Only when she awoke did it seem unbelievable.

"Not now," the unspoken message sunk into her consciousness.

Before Bendi could ask her question again, the hairs on the jaguar's back stood on end. The feline's muscles tensed and its tail snapped back and forth. Glancing quickly to the valley below, the jaguar leaped toward Bendi.

Night suddenly descended upon her as a blackness covered her vision. Two quick shots rang in her ear as bullets ricocheted into the jaguar's shadow and off one of the boulders. Light re-appeared instantly as the huge cat leaped easily over her, disappearing into the jungle.

"*Paren*! Stop!" Bendi screamed down into the valley.

"Are you all right, Miss Porcelli?" Manuel yelled.

"I'm fine. Don't shoot anymore! I'm fine."

"What are you doing up there alone? Get down *pápido*." Manuel turned to the *policía* at his side who had fired the shots. "*Ella está muy loco,*" he said, pointing to his head.

Turning around, Bendi searched for the jaguar. She listened for any noises but heard none. Dejectedly, she hiked down the hill. The further she descended, the angrier she became. It wouldn't make sense to those men, because they thought she was in danger, but she had almost gotten an answer about Digger's whereabouts. She would never be able to make them understand what had happened. But it was real to her, just as real as her dreams had been, just as real as the ground beneath her feet.

Two *policías* met her halfway down and escorted her back to the riverbed. They admonished her in Spanish, which she feigned not knowing. At first, she felt like a prisoner as she walked between the two armed officers. Then she felt as if she were a little girl being punished—believing that she had done something wrong.

Then the voice of the jaguar replayed in her head and momentarily neutralized her guilt. In the next moment, she felt an irrepressible sense of power. But she questioned the ownership of that feeling. Did the power stem from her encounter with the wild animal? Or was it the jaguar's power? Or was it her own power—the result of acting on her intuitive insights and having them come true?

When she reached the riverbed Manuel lectured her. She stood there and took it all in. If she tried to explain, he would surely have thought she was crazy. Finally, Manuel finished his rampaging monologue with a question, "What were you thinking?"

"I wasn't thinking. That was the whole point," Bendi answered defiantly, scowling back at him.

"Ahhh," Manuel grunted. Shaking his head, he changed the subject, and none too gently, "The scouting team discovered another paddle a short way down the riverbed. And several more kilometers further down they found the raft, ripped to shreds. Sorry, there are still no signs of Mr. Taylor."

Bendi refused to be discouraged. "I feel that Digger is here, in this area," she said emphatically.

"You are probably right, given the fact of the bloodstains on that sphere," Ortega interrupted as he hurried breathlessly toward them. "Are you okay, Bendi?" She nodded to him, as he stepped between Manuel and her. Ortega caught his breath and continued, "And I found more. This time it was in the cavern, in two different places. One bloodstain was on a wall and the other on a rock hanging from the ceiling."

"How could there be blood on the ceiling of the cavern? It must be over three meters up!" Manuel questioned.

"From the waterline still visible in the cavern and the surrounding area, we can see the river must have at least been one to two meters deep during the flood, and as you said the top of the cavern is no more than three meters high from the riverbed floor. Conceivably, the raft could have funneled into the cavern, knocking him into the rocks."

"Miss Porcelli." Manuel took a deep breath. Combing his black hair with his hand, he said in a more considerate tone than he'd taken before, "I know I do not have to spell it out. The facts do not look good, in fact, they look very bad. The raft probably flipped as it came out of the cavern. Somehow Mr. Taylor was able to grab onto one of the spheres, but eventually he grew tired. And the river washed him downstream. Even if he did survive, the jungle sometimes has a very quick way of disposing of the injured."

"Digger cut his head," Bendi insisted, ignoring Manuel's bleak statements. "There was blood on his head and his arm—in my dreams." After she explained to Manuel in detail all the dreams she'd had, beginning in San Diego, she summarized, "Colored balls that turned into stone spheres, a stream that led to a cavern, the black cat that turned into a jaguar, the dried bloodstains, *and* the body that was still breathing. All but the last segment has come true—that's why I feel, I *know* he is still alive!" Her eyes began to mist over. "I know the jaguar and the stone spheres have something to do with his whereabouts, in this area."

"I am sorry, Miss Porcelli. It has been almost a week," Manuel said.

Bendi tried to speak, but Manuel interjected, "Today the teams will finish their search downstream and then... I will center the search in this area, for one more day."

"*Gracias, muchas gracias,*" Bendi said with grateful relief.

"But if we do not find Mr. Taylor by late tomorrow afternoon..." Manuel's shoulders slumped a bit and his voice became weary, "I am sorry. I will have to call off the search."

Ortega put a comforting arm around her shoulder and walked slowly with her toward the cavern. "Are you okay?

"*Sí*, I am all right."

While the professor consulted with his student workers, Bendi took time to reflect about her bizarre exchange with the jaguar. He talked to me, but not with a voice or words; somehow he entered my head. I know that he knows where Digger is. But what did he mean about now not being the time? Now is not the time for what? To find Digger? If not now, when... in an hour, a day, a week? Digger needs me! I feel he is somewhere close. Very close. I'm sure of it.

Bendi looked down the riverbed and watched Ortega's people move in and around the stone spheres. Manuel barked instructions over the walkie-talkie. She glanced up toward the area of her encounter with the black jaguar and felt her legs still shaking from the vigorous climb. Several dragonflies danced in the air above her head—just out of reach.

Chapter 20

*"... miracles are beyond your experience
because you believe they are only reserved for the gods."*

Darkness surrounded Digger as he drifted in and out of wakefulness. He could hear the bellows of a howler monkey burst into his head, reminding him of how he'd been awakened every morning of his childhood by his hollering mother.

With his eyes still closed, he took a big breath and tried to relax. Out of the darkness came a vision of a stone sphere—one he hadn't seen before. It was painted impressionistically, in bright purples, pinks, oranges, and reds. The geometric shapes covering the three-foot sphere were more flowing than on the others; rather than triangles and squares, the shapes were more like circles, half-moons, and wavy lines. His body vibrated as waves of energy flooded into him, bringing feelings of total peace and acceptance.

Now his body began to shake violently from side to side.

His eyes popped open to see Vawaha trying to shake him awake.

"Are you all right?" she questioned him urgently.

"Yeah, I am," he mumbled groggily. "How are *you* doing?"

"I am all right, too. I miss my grandmother, but in my heart I know that she is in the Light. Is that not where we all want to be?"

Digger nodded and then fumbled out of the hammock. Squatting down to her level, he gave Vawaha a hug. "I need to go back to the spheres," he told the girl. "Do you want to come along?" She smiled happily and let her head fall on his shoulder for a moment.

Strolling through the village in the morning sunlight, they stopped at the stream, where they drank water and plucked mangos that dripped fresh juice down their arms as they ate them. His headache began to subside, but his stomach cramped a little. Also, a dull pain had begun to pierce his right shoulder. The last few days I've been a wreck, he thought. In fact, how long have I been in the rainforest—nine, ten days? Five days with Angélica, maybe? It all seemed like a blur. The only thing that had any clarity was that he needed to go back to the spheres.

"Can we go to my magical place first?" Vawaha looked up at him with pleading eyes.

"Sure, but how about later? Right now, I really think I need to see the spheres."

"But I want to take you to my special place now," she whined, with a touch of sadness.

Digger looked up toward the quarry and then back at Vawaha. He took a deep breath and smiled. "Sure. Where is this place?"

"It's a secret; follow me!"

With neither of them saying a word, Digger followed her as she frolicked her way upstream, toward the opposite crater wall, gleefully kicking and playing in the water. Mimicking her behavior he'd become lost in the moment, as the sights, sounds, and feel of the jungle flowed through him.

Soon he could hear the pounding of the nearby waterfall echoing towards them. Vawaha scampered effortlessly across some slippery rocks to the other side of the stream and he tried to follow, using a maze of hip-high boulders to steady himself. He was looking over at her, to see where he should be heading, when his hand reached out for another stony ledge to brace himself—

"Do not move!" Vawaha yelled. "Do not move anything!"

He quickly looked down and saw that his palm was about six inches from the poised stinger of a deadly scorpion, nervously awaiting his soft flesh. He promptly recoiled his arm—with a sigh of relief.

"You have to pay attention to everything you are doing," admonished the young girl as she splashed back to take his hand and lead him across.

"Thanks," he flushed. "I'll try."

He followed her through the jungle for another several hundred yards, until finally they arrived at the waterfall. Digger gazed upwards. The sky-reaching walls were covered with green, lush vegetation—gripping vines, colorful bromeliads, and several types of moss which clung to the cracks, while tons of water slammed before him, causing a cooling mist to rise. The sun shone down upon them and made a futile effort to evaporate the moisture on his skin.

Unable to be heard through the roar, Vawaha tapped him on the shoulder and pointed. Hanging there above them, one end touching the waterfall and the other in mid-air, was a magnificent rainbow, each color clear and luminescent. They watched in silence as the rainbow gradually melted into the mist.

He suddenly felt Vawaha vanish from his side and turned to see her following a rocky trail near the base of the waterfall. When she disappeared around a sharp turn, he quickly followed her.

The sight that opened up to him was like a story book picture: Vawaha, with a big grin on her face, was swimming in a small pool of water formed by a basin etched into the side of the crater wall. Smooth, long boulders surrounded the hidden pool. He couldn't resist; Digger jumped in and felt the instant coolness of the deep pond. In this granite enclave, the deafening sound of the waterfall was diminished to a comforting rustle of water on rock.

"This is my magical place," Vawaha explained excitedly. "I come here a lot. Do you like it?"

He couldn't imagine liking it more; but in response he just chased her around the pool, laughing and frolicking like a six-year-old, until they were both too tired to swim any more.

As they pulled themselves out of the water onto a sun-warmed shelf, a shaft of light streaked down towards the pond and sparkled across its rippled surface. Digger settled quietly on a smooth rock facing the pond, with a view spreading off toward the rainforest, while Vawaha climbed onto a small ledge behind him. He didn't feel like talking or even asking questions as a sense of peace swelled within him, and he was glad Vawaha didn't break the silence. As he closed his eyes and listened to the sounds of the rainforest come alive, he understood why she liked this place so much. He could hear the faint, splashing sound of the waterfall and his mind set it to music. Usually, in San Diego, he only received his inspiration at night, sitting at the end of the Mission Bay jetty. But now the jungle was alive with orchestration. Why hadn't he heard it before?

In his mind, a piano repeated an arpeggio, mimicking the sound of the waterfall. In a flowing melody, several flutes trilled high notes as birds sang in the trees. A soft rumbling of a cymbal imitated some unknown creature moving through the leaf-strewn floor of the rainforest. As the symphonic background of the jungle played, the violins in his mind rose to a crescendo.

He didn't know how long he'd been sitting there, but when he finally opened his eyes, an orange, blue, and yellow macaw was perched on a boulder in front of him, staring quietly back at him. He didn't want to scare it away—or lose his mental clarity of sound—so without turning his head, he slowly moved his eyes around to soak in all the richness of the jungle. He squinted in wonder at the thousand diamond sparkles dancing erratically across the still pond. How can nature arouse such awe in its simplicity?

Then something floating about in the water startled him. He squinted harder to discern its form, but it had vanished. Taking a breath, he returned to his enjoyment of the surface sparkles. Again, the unrecognizable form darted just beneath the water. He couldn't believe his eyes—

the sunlit sparkles seemed to have penetrated the surface and were now contouring the perfect shape of an underwater butterfly! The only difference was the finger-sized thickness of its body. What the heck is that? he wondered. Instantly, the object disappeared. He shook his head and blinked a few times. The sun and water must have tricked him. He turned around to see the biggest grin yet on Vawaha's face. He quickly turned back to the water.

Did he really see something? 'Let go,' he heard mentally, and 'expect.' Expect what? 'Just expect there to be anything, everything.' You're imagining things, Digger. 'There are worse things to imagine,' his other inner voice argued.

He took a few more deep breaths and focused back on the diamond sparkles. Like the automatic focus on a camera, images flashed into clarity as a dozen, water-sparkled, iridescent butterflies crystallized before his eyes. The winged creatures drifted with a slow, fluent movement. Most of them glided on top of the pond, but several undulated a few inches below the surface.

Digger sat there wide-eyed. He turned back to Vawaha, who giggled girlishly.

"You know about all of this?"

She nodded, her hand covering her gleeful mouth.

He turned again to stare at the pond. This can't be happening. Immediately, the scene before him changed back to ordinary, erratic sparkles of sunlight on water. He closed his eyes and took several breaths to clear his mind of ordinary "logic" and doubts. When he opened them, the mystical forms floated before him once again. Every time that his so-called logical mind wanted to disbelieve, he canceled that thought and replaced it with an expectation of *more*, an expectation of *different*, an expectation of *beauty*—and the winged fairy creatures reappeared.

He soon lost track of time as his private showing of nature's secrets unfolded before him. He felt like a child again, believing that there is truly magic in this world.

"Maybe we should get back to the spheres?" Vawaha interrupted cheerfully. "I wanted you to see—but I shouldn't keep you from what you have to do to help *Los Otros*."

Reluctantly, Digger nodded. She was right, but he didn't want to leave. He stood up and took one last look at the magical pond. As he started to walk back toward the deafening waterfall, he joked with Vawaha, "Who knows? Maybe one day I'll actually see someone walk on water!"

Behind him, a small, green, basilisk lizard jumped off a shoreline rock and, virtually airborne, scampered across the top of the water.

Digger turned at the sound, but only in time to see the reptile leap to safety on the other shore.

When they reached the stream crossing, Digger waded in pensively, paying little attention to where or how he was traveling. He splashed down the middle of the shallow waterway, busy staring in awe at every bird, insect, and tree that came into his view, quietly wondering if there were another world inside of them that he hadn't noticed before. Vawaha, several yards away, had stopped to steal up on an unsuspecting fish. Playfully, he kicked the water and scared both her and the fish.

"Hey!" she yelled, and then splashed him back.

"What *were* those things I saw back there, those reflections?" he finally asked as he caught up with the girl.

"We call them *Shashunas*, but I think in your language they would be called water fairies," she said coyly.

"Water fairies. I was afraid you might say something like that," he sighed.

"It does not make a difference what you call them: Shashunas, Star Teachers, or Wooosshhwaaamps. You give them any name you wish, but they are what they are," she shrugged in childish simplicity.

They walked back toward the village giggling and talking about his experience. Vawaha told him there was much more to see at her secret pond. She made him promise to visit it again.

With lightened steps, they ascended the steep incline to the quarry. Mashuba and Angélica were standing among the spheres, looking out over the jungle. Uncharacteristically, Digger couldn't wait to tell them about his experience at the pond and barely gave the greeting before he launched into his tale.

Mashuba nodded seriously, but Angélica just kept smiling at Digger as he gibbered on about the magical happenings. "There is hope for you yet," she teased, "—and for us," she added more seriously.

"But I've never seen anything like that before, and I've been in nature hundreds of times. In fact, I don't personally know of anybody else who has seen anything like it!"

"So it must not exist then," Mashuba said facetiously.

When Digger turned to answer him, he was suddenly struck by the sight of a new sphere partially hidden behind the elder. He forgot all about the water fairies. "This is it!" he exclaimed as he pushed passed Mashuba to stand beside the waist-high sphere. "This is exactly what I saw in my dream this morning! I know this sphere wasn't here before. Where did you find it?" Digger bent to inspect the brightly-colored globe with its flowing, painted lines and shapes.

"It has been in my hut," Mashuba answered mildly.

"But how did you get it up these steps?" Digger scanned the area for any mechanical aids that might have been used and saw none. "It must weigh at least several tons!"

"It is not as heavy as you believe," Mashuba teased, puffing his chest and flexing his arm muscles.

Just to be sure, Digger tried to move the sphere but as he expected, it wouldn't budge. "Really, how did you bring it up here?"

"It was easy," Angélica smirked.

"Yeah, right," he answered sarcastically.

"There are many different ways to move and be moved within this dimension," Mashuba stated calmly. "And there are many different dimensions within dimensions. That means that your potential and the limits that you have placed on yourself and your world are very different than you think. Your difficulty is that you tend to think you are three-dimensional when you are at least ten. Just because you are not aware of those other dimensions does not mean that they do not exist."

Digger groaned. Not another lecture. What now?

Mashuba, responding to his grimace, persisted, "Within your dreaming dimension, can you not fly over valleys and forests and move through walls and mountains, all in a moment's time?"

Well, he had a point there, Digger thought. But before he could say anything, Mashuba went on, "That dimension is still present in this waking moment, along with all the other dimensions. It is just up to your awareness, your consciousness, to decide on which dimension you will focus. Most humans choose to focus on the third."

"I'm not sure I understand. It's hard to believe that other dimensions exist, much less focus on them!"

"You mean in addition to your ability to see Shashunas?" Mashuba quipped.

"Okay, okay. Humor my Western-thinking, three-dimensional-logic embracing, doubting mind and give me another example," Digger countered.

Several insects scurried for protection as the wise man crouched, smoothing out a small area on the quarry floor. He tapped his finger into the loose soil, motioning Digger to bend and see—a slight indentation had been left behind. "One-dimension would be just a point in space," Mashuba explained. "Two-dimension has sides—a place to move left, right, forward, or back." He drew several smooth lines on the surface of the dirt. "Now all the 'beings' who live in this two-dimensional world are aware of points and of lines, but they have never known of a three-dimensional being. They cannot even conceive of its existence. You who believe you are just a three-dimensional being—composed of points, lines, *and* depth—come along and place your finger on their two-dimensional world." Mashuba took Digger's hand and placed a finger on one of the lines. "Now to those two-dimensional beings, you magically appeared out of nowhere. You came into view as this unexplainable *thing*, known as a finger to you." Mashuba removed Digger's finger from the line and showed him the several fine particles of dirt that were attached. He then moved Digger's finger further down the line and gently scraped it while continuing, "The two-dimensional beings are amazed and perplexed. I can hear them calling out, 'This *thing* has just appeared and disappeared into nothingness. And also several huge particles of our world have disappeared and then magically re-appeared in another place. It is a miracle!'"

Vawaha giggled. She grabbed Angélica's arm and pulled her down to huddle across from the men. Mashuba continued, "They have no language to explain this mysterious event. Even if they did try to explain it, their understanding would be shallow, because they could only describe the experience in two-dimensional language. Besides, they would probably think that the tip of your finger was the whole experience. But you, being conscious of more than two dimensions, know there is infinitely more to the universe than that part of your body.

"Their astonishment over your finger is the same as it is for you when fourth- and fifth-dimensional events occur in your supposed three-dimensional reality. You are completely amazed when all of a sudden you see a golden halo behind someone's head, or have a near-death experience, or hear of someone who walked on water, or listen to someone's account of their out-of-body experience, or see Shashunas. Because it goes beyond your imposed, three-dimensional limits of reality, you claim that it never happened. Or that it was a miracle. And miracles are beyond your experience, because you believe that they are only reserved for the gods." Mashuba stood up, brushing the dirt off his hands.

Angélica smiled at Digger across the two-dimensional world between them, while Mashuba added, "Believe me when I tell you that your knowingness of multi-dimensionality is far short of even seeing the tip of a finger! Yet on that two-dimensional world, your finger would probably be considered a god, though you would laugh at those 'line beings' for thinking so foolishly. But when multi-dimensional events happen in your perceived three-dimensional world, many try to define them exactly that way."

Digger, still crouching beside Mashuba's drawings, realized that the elder had not answered his question about how the sphere was moved—or had he? He suddenly felt overwhelmed as the lectures and encounters of all his days with *Los Otros* collapsed in upon him. He brushed the dirt off his knees as he and Angélica stood up at the same time, gazing at each other—she was looking expectant; he just felt tired. Vawaha was still staring at the lines and points in the dust.

Mashuba put a comforting arm on Digger's shoulders. "The past, present, and future also play into these dimensions. All at the same time. All in this present moment. And I see that you are filled with my words, but before I finish let me say that, for now, what you need to realize is that you are a part of all these dimensions and more. All that inhibits you from experiencing them is your perception of who you think you are."

Digger looked blankly at the wise man.

"You are the sphere within spheres," Mashuba went on, "the one point, the drawn line, the placed finger, the infant in your mother's womb, the fearful little boy, the loving adult, the Keeper of Sound, the one who flies high and looks down upon yourself, and the mysterious *thing* that magically transports huge particles of earth from one point to another. Know that you are also the accumulation of all your previous journeys into this physical world and all other worlds; you are the spirit that is all-powerful and already knows how to get Home."

Vawaha smiled admiringly at Mashuba, while Digger stood there, trying to take in all that had just been said to him. "What you're asking is difficult. I was never taught to think like this. I wasn't even taught how to ask these kinds of questions."

"You can handle it, Digger," Angélica teased, knocking lightly on his head.

Mashuba frowned at her and said to Digger, "Your only task at hand is to move through all that has just been stated. To feel and sense the spheres within the spheres. To allow help from the dimensions that are beyond your mind's grasp."

"I don't see how that will help me imprint one of the stone spheres; that is what you want, isn't it? That's why you're telling me all this?" Digger asked bluntly.

"There you go again," Angélica scolded, "setting a limit, confining a belief before you have had time to digest what has just been said!"

"Okay, okay. I'll shut up," he said, a little irritated by her pushiness. Why was she so concerned about him, anyway? She'd been pushing him since the day they met, that morning when her voice called him awake... a rustling noise interrupted his reverie. A huge iguana scurrying across the ground had stopped in front of him and was now rhythmically bobbing its head. He caught a smile on Mashuba's face, but before he could ask what was so funny, Digger suddenly felt a tug on his left side. The manifested dream-sphere was pulling him like a giant magnet—just like the Travel sphere had done yesterday. Without saying a word, he remembered what he'd learned and allowed himself to be enticed by this resplendent piece of decorated rock. Lightly touching the sphere, he felt a tingling move rapidly through his fingers and up his arm. "What do they call this one, anyway?" he asked Mashuba.

"It is the stone sphere that is at the core of our world, the universe, really," Angélica interjected. "Try and do the same thing that you did earlier at the pool," she challenged him.

Agreeably, Digger stepped back and cleared his mind of any preconceptions about this sculpture. He blurred his eyesight to focus softly on the object. Then, as his eyes adjusted, hundreds of sparkling lights filled his vision.

"I'm seeing lights that appear to be swimming in mid-air," he marveled.

"Oh, those!" Angélica replied. "Some call those air fairies; others call them the life of the universe, or in your Asian cultures, *chi*. It is good, though, that you can see them. It means that you are moving through one of the veils of dimensions." Mashuba grunted his agreement. "Now move beyond them," she urged.

Digger tried to do as she instructed. After a few moments, he noticed that beyond the sphere a bright, greenish hue flowed over the rainforest canopy. Even the natural rock formations around the quarry were outlined with a faint yellowish glow. Then he saw a pink ball of energy behind the stone sphere. He could actually feel it. Then it hit him.

"This is about... this is a Love sphere!" he blurted. As he continued to look at the sphere with its shadow of pink, he saw wavy lines of energy—like from a heated highway. When he looked closer, he could actually see the energy moving counterclockwise around the stone sphere. He sat down in front of it and moved his hands over the stone. He felt silly, like a gypsy hovering over a crystal ball. Let it go, his other thoughts commanded. Hundreds of soft prickly sensations touched his fingers and moved up his arms into different parts of his body.

Suddenly, this moment, suffused in the pink light, reminded him— like a déjà vu experience—of the night of his first Hollywood audition, of the dream-like meditation he'd experienced before taking the stage. Until now he hadn't been able to remember much detail; he'd just known it was wonderful, transcending, and very significant to his life. Now he flashed back on a similar pink glow, a beautiful woman... but he couldn't remember who she was. He did remember the feeling, though, and it was tremendously uplifting—like now. For a moment, the vision of a tall, powerful man flashed before his eyes, but it quickly dissipated.

As he continued to sit before the sphere, hundreds of flashes of individual moments flowed through him. The images moved too fast for any recognition, but the emotion of love was clearly identifiable: from compassion to friendship, acceptance to joy, empathy to passion.

Digger slowly stood up and faced his friends. "What I'm feeling are the imprints of others, aren't I?"

They all three smiled and nodded at his inquiry. He then noticed a bright violet light around Vawaha, a luminescent green around Angélica, and an iridescent white and purple around Mashuba. He stared with delight. "Now I'm seeing colors around you guys! That's pretty cool."

"You are now at least at the beginning of seeing the spheres within spheres," Mashuba reassured him.

"Do all the spheres have the capability of doing what I've just experienced?"

"Remember, everything is energy, and all energy is interconnected," the elder replied. "The rock at some level absorbs and interacts with all other energies, whether they be physical, emotional, intellectual, or spiritual. But the rock does not decipher what energy it takes in; it only soaks in what is around it. So that is why it is very important that one be focused and balanced when transmitting, or *imprinting,* energy to these spheres. The clearer you are, the clearer it may be for all those who wish to receive from this stone what you have imprinted."

Digger was surprised. "So you're saying that the meanings of these spheres come, not only from the inscriptions, symbols, and colors, but from what the spheres have absorbed?"

"Is that different from anything or anyone else on this planet?" Mashuba queried.

"Remember—it is only in your relationship that such an exchange can occur," Angélica interjected softly.

"But how many people would try to have a relationship with a rock to find answers?"

"And how many people really find *the* answers, *the* truth, they are looking for?" Mashuba retorted.

"True, but that's because it's much easier to look at the exterior, the symbols." Digger added defensively, "I've been taught to do that."

"Even though that might be true, you and others can no longer use that as an excuse. Your spirit knows better. It knows that to find the truth it has to get to the heart of the matter, so to speak. In every moment of your life, your spirit yearns to slip through the illusionary surface of all things and create a compassionate, accepting, and loving relationship. It is the only way in which you can bring light to your darkness." Mashuba then added with a lower voice that resonated into Digger's gut, "It is the only way for this planet to survive."

Chapter 21

"... the wind never stays on anything or in anyone,
for it is always in motion, never to be held,
never to be kept—only to be shared."

Waves of humidity wafted up the hill as the mid-afternoon sun shone brightly on Digger and the stone spheres. Not only the heat but also the constant barrage of new information was making him feel uncomfortable. He wanted the protection of the shaded jungle. Moving toward the steps and wiping the perspiration off of his brow, he said "I'd like to go back to the stream to cool off."

"Spoken like a true Keeper of Wisdom," Mashuba smiled. "One who is in the moment, has clear intentions, and is in action." Vawaha and Angélica cupped their hands in a sign of acknowledgement, *Los Otros* style.

"Thank you," Digger answered awkwardly, not sure if they were serious or joking. Embarrassed, he headed down the hill and the others followed.

After drinking from the stream again, he felt the need to return to Gutubo, so he politely excused himself. As he started down the path, he could hear Angélica and Vawaha move to follow, but Mashuba muttered something to them that he couldn't hear; when he turned to look back, they were nowhere to be seen.

Walking under the protection of the jungle canopy brought him relief from the hot sun, yet the humidity still stifled his breathing. He nodded as he passed several of *Los Otros* on his way through the village to the "tree of many eyes." When he reached Gutubo, he just stared at the strange tree's draped-vine compartments for a while. Finally, he drifted over to the section where he'd spouted all of his "I'm right" perspectives concerning his mother. The angry voice of young Jonathan began to reverberate within him again, so he quickly moved to the next section, where he was supposed to speak things from her viewpoint.

Just as he was about to give it a try, a mother arrived with her young son. He was embarrassed about being with Gutubo, as if he'd been caught coming out of a therapist's office or a confessional. He wondered if they'd heard him.

Slowly, the woman led her son around the worn-out circular path, explaining simply what he was expected to do. Then she gently ushered him to the "I'm right" section, where the child began immediately to cry and yell. It sounded to Digger as if he'd caught on to the idea pretty quickly.

Disturbed by the noise, Digger kept his silence as the mother led her son toward him. She exchanged the *Los Otros* greeting with him, saying, "My name is Winauka. I hope we did not disturb you?" in the usual mixture of broken English, Spanish, and indigenous dialect.

"No problem."

"Can I help you with anything?"

The young boy was doing as Digger had been, just standing there, looking blankly at the remnants of Gutubo.

"I don't know," Digger replied. "I think your son and I might be having the same problem. It is very difficult to speak from the other person's perspective."

The son was pouting now, standing with his arms folded.

"My son is very angry with me," Winauka explained sadly. "I left his father several years ago. He now blames me for much."

"I've never had children, but I can imagine that it would be very difficult to explain to him what your reasons might have been," Digger empathized.

"Many of *Los Otros* left their families and villages because what they did or felt or thought was not 'acceptable.' Some were outcasts for wanting to create different styles of pottery, some for playing different types of sounds, some for painting different symbols, some for speaking different thoughts and concepts, some for believing in different gods, some for loving different people. In my tribe, it was unforgivable for any wife to leave her husband, especially a wife with a son! Such a crime was punishable by death.

"But my son is more important to me than anything," Winauka explained, a pained look crossing her face. "I could not stay there and have his father teach our son about fighting, about hating other tribes just because they worshipped other gods, or had different *sukais*, or painted their faces with different colors.

"Our tribe had been fighting for many generations. I could not bear to have my son continue in that way. So I crept away one night with my son and spent several weeks traveling the jungle before I found *Los Otros*. Now I am attempting to teach my son a new way; where he can be the 'All That Is Possible' and still allow others the same. It is much easier to do that here in this village."

Digger listened with interest to the woman's story, noticing how much her soft-hearted voice contrasted with the fire of conviction in her eyes. She continued, "Many hold their life as being this or that, left or right, up or down, good or evil, wrong or right. But the spirit and heart do not know the concept of my or your tribes' 'wrongs' or 'rights.' My son blames me for everything; he believes that I have done something 'wrong' for leaving the village and his father. So for him to be successful with this section of Gutubo, he must be able to let go of being 'right' long enough to see and hear another way."

Digger sighed and looked down at the silent little boy. "It must take a lot of practice to allow yourself to see from the other person's point of view. Right now, I'm having difficulty with that myself."

"If I may make a suggestion: imagine yourself as a tree, looking down at the situation you are having difficulty with. What would this old tree say about your situation?" Winauka asked him.

At that moment, a strong gust of wind swept over the canopy and whispered down through the strangler fig's limbs, gently cooling their faces. "Feel the wind, for it is full of wisdom," Winauka suggested. "For ages, it has moved through the hearts and spirits of all who have graced this planet. It has traveled to all the lands and waters. But the wind never stays *on* anything or *in* anyone, for it is always in motion, never to be held, never to be kept—only to be shared." Her voice grew soft and wispy, "To share, you must let go and allow your branches to part. By doing so, if you listen carefully, you will hear all that the wind has gathered: thoughts, pains, knowledge, fears, loves, hopes, insights, and dreams. And in the letting go shall you be touched by those experiences. Again, not to hold them to be true or false, but to share for a moment—a brief moment—the soul of another."

Winauka glanced down at her son and gently brushed his hair before looking back at Digger and continuing, "Each journey around Gutubo takes one to their past. Many believe that what composes the past are the events; the time I left my husband, when I gave birth to my son, when I was beaten by my father. But my true past is composed of the emotions and beliefs that are contained within those times. So even though the events of my life will always stay the same, my past will change as my perception changes. That is what Gutubo is all about.

"Remember, each time you complete the circle, you are renewed and shed another layer. You then walk with a lighter step, see with younger eyes, listen for the first time, and touch with a child's fascination. Eventually you become a child who knows, not of the past or the future, but only of what is before him in the present, in the moment."

Smiling, she leaned down to her still-pouting son and took his hand.

The little boy broke free of his mother's grip to chase several blue Morpho butterflies down the path. The mother sighed after him, smiled patiently, and then set off to follow, after nodding an encouraging good-bye to Digger.

Alone now, he allowed the meaning of Winauka's words to seep into his consciousness: wind and wisdom, right and wrong, past and present.

Right! Wrong! He thought about life with his mother. Of course, I'm right! was his knee-jerk response—as an adult he'd never thought other-wise. He couldn't forgive his mother for some of the thoughtless and emotionally cruel things she did to him. He'd wanted her to admit that *she* was wrong, in some way that would legitimize his anger. But the reality was that his mother had never apologized for any of her actions. If they were in an argument or even a discussion and Digger dared to state an opinion that was different from hers, she never said, "Well, I could be wrong," or "You might be right." In fact, she'd never, in his recollection, ever said, "Well, Jonathan, let me think about it." She was always right and that was that. So why argue? Why discuss anything? Why even talk?

He sadly admitted to himself that he held everything inside. It took much less energy that way—or so he had believed. If he kept quiet, there was never any hope or expectation or disappointment to confront. He knew how everything would go. His mother would yell or scream for a while, he would keep quiet, eventually she would stop, and then he would go off to play ball.

How could he ever see his mother's point of view? The answer was loud and clear in his head, "You can't! At least not coming from the right/wrong perspective."

He thought of what Winauka had said about being a tree and turned to look up at a towering hardwood tirra with its yellow-tipped crown. This is silly, he thought, but then again he'd just seen water fairies. Anyway, nothing else was working.

He moved closer to Gutubo and stood within the section of walled-vines. Okay, he said to himself, I'm a tree and looking down at my life. Taking several deep breaths, he focused softly on the living-wood sculpture in front of him. As before, the longer he looked, the more the twisted shapes appeared to move and change form. A startling vision of his mother's emaciated body came into view. He shook that sight and replaced it with the way he'd seen her most of his life—as a beautiful woman.

Before he realized it, his consciousness had subtly changed. He was not himself looking down at his mom, but more himself looking and feeling through his mom. At the time it didn't matter that this didn't make sense; he just went with the moment.

Digger felt his mother's love for his gentle father turn to anger as he drank—alone—in the darkness. He sensed her intelligence, and also her disdain for her husband because he'd only had a high-school education. She wanted intellectual stimulation and felt she'd married beneath herself. Digger felt her frustration to be with someone who didn't know all the things that she knew. Who didn't know the difference between Sartre and Descartes, who couldn't explain the economic conditions that brought on World War I, who didn't have a rudimentary knowledge of the life and death of stars.

Suddenly the angry Jonathon slipped back in. *That didn't give her the right to treat us with ridicule and superiority!* Let it go, Digger, he told himself. He took another deep breath.

Again, through his mother's eyes, he saw himself at his college graduation and felt her contentment and pride. Even though it didn't come through her words, he felt her internal determination, as she'd always prodded him to be anything he wanted. Encouragement washed through his mother as she pushed him to try different studies in college, different jobs after he graduated, and different places to travel.

A smile came to his—really her face as he saw himself, little Jonathan, practicing the piano. He heard his dissonant attempts to play chords.

Like a jolt, Digger felt her resentment over being a mother; she thought it held her back. She'd wanted to accomplish so much in her life and had tried so hard to be a career woman. But it was an uphill battle because that wasn't acceptable in the 50s or 60s. For centuries, society had silently ordered mothers to stay home with their children. He felt her frustration and didn't know what to do with all of it. Then he felt the regurgitation of her words—the screaming and yelling at her sons and husband.

The wind rustled again through the jungle. But little Jonathan wanted to be heard over the wind—he wanted to ring out from the pulpit and preach his hurts so that he could feel righteous in the wrongs that had been done to him!

It was a struggle, but Digger let the voice of the wind speak louder. He took another deep breath and allowed the rigid branches of his ego to let go and sway a little further. That permitted him to feel his mother's unseen childhood pains; those hurts that continued into her adult- and parenthood; those hurts that were beyond his knowing; those hurts that had no name but felt raw to the touch. He felt her confusion at having an education but not all the wisdom, at knowing the "right" words but not having the "right" experiences, at being a parent but not wanting to be, at feeling scraps of love but not knowing how to ask for more.

Time seemed to stand still as the entwined trunk of Gutubo and the gnarled fig's branches gave way to a vision which slowly unfolded before him: snow-covered ground sparkling with moonlight. Digger stared into the emptiness of that lonely, crisp, and still evening. A shiver moved through him when he realized that he was staring at his mother's love. A love represented by the stark beauty of that cold night scene. A love filled by many moments of silence. A love layered over by her mind, and therefore unspoken from her lips.

He then saw the two of them standing in the frigid night; their joined warm, bitter tears falling onto the frozen snow. The pristine crystal flakes melted to form a trickle of water, then a narrow peaceful stream, then a raging river, until finally they created a foamy cauldron of white rapids that blurred his vision.

Eventually the river calmed again to a quiet stream. Different scenes now layered onto that vision and he felt his mother's heart tingle as she peeked into his boyhood room, her gentle rocking as she held his small, curled body, her pain as she patched his bruises, her sense of pride as he played the piano for her friends, her regrets as her sharp tongue lashed out, her sadness as she held back her internal, private promises to speak—finally speak—her fears, her hopes, and her love.

Now that he'd felt many of his mother's unheard voices, he recognized some of his own. Those unexpressed silent voices echoed a potpourri of pain and comfort, hurt and compassion, fear and love. Yet now there was no mistaking their origin, their innocence. It had been hard work all his life, fending off those childlike voices that wanted to be heard. Young Jonathan had, not only one voice, but many that had been masked by the "logic" of the adult—Digger.

Another layer peeled, leaving not an understanding but a deeper knowingness: As hurtful as it might be to have those voices heard, it was a hundred times more painful to hold them back. Those voices spoke of a childhood past and Digger was no longer sure that he could silence them one moment longer!

Wwuuuuupp! Wwuuupp! The loud, high-pitched cry startled Digger back to his surroundings. Several spider monkeys were calling to each other noisily as they dangled from branches. Using their agile, skinny limbs and tails, they moved swiftly from tree to tree. One jumped fearlessly more than thirty feet, deftly grabbing a hanging vine to stop his momentum.

Digger took a step back from Gutubo and sat down on a fallen log. As the hidden sun drew closer to the horizon, he could see patches of a bright, reddish-pink sky. He continued to sit on the decaying trunk well into the early evening, as the sights and feelings of his latest experience sifted through him.

A slow, methodic beating of the drums brought Digger back to the moment. He stood up and shook out the stiffness in his joints. Slowly, he walked toward the final section of the strangler fig. A full moon had risen and now cast an eerie, dim blanket of shady light upon Gutubo. He tried to focus but in his peripheral vision, the distant fire danced from side to side, drawing his attention with its mystique of celebration. As he turned toward the enchanting flames, he noticed in the far distance several shadowy figures, one of which had the shape of a jaguar. Strange, Digger thought. The flowing specters were walking up the steps toward the quarry.

Maybe they're the Keepers of Wisdom, he thought excitedly. If I can catch up with them, maybe they can tell me how to imprint one of the spheres and finally get home!

As he started off briskly toward the hill, the jungle grew darker as several clouds blocked the light of the moon. Clambering up the darkened steps he wondered, who are the Keepers of Wisdom and what are they up to here in the dark of night? He tripped over an exposed root and found himself sprawled on the ground.

Lying there for a moment, waiting for the pain in his shin to subside, he noticed two green, glowing dots poking out of the darkness, inches from his face. He stared at the strange-looking apparitions and tried to figure out what they were. Muffled voices echoed down from the hilltop and he thought he heard Angélica saying, "Is someone following us?"

He looked up to see a tall well-built man standing at the top of the steps. "No, I do not see anyone," a faintly recognizable voice answered.

Maybe he shouldn't have come, Digger thought. If the Keepers of Wisdom wanted to speak with him, they would have made a point of contacting him.

As the two glowing green dots moved, Digger held back a scream— he suddenly saw that they were the eyes of a six-inch spider. He carefully crawled away from it and then gave a sigh of relief. Maybe he should go back down; he'd had enough excitement for one day. In the next moment his hair stood on end. Instinctively, he dug his nails into the ground as an invisible force tried to drag him up the hill. But before a sound could leave his throat, the unseen force stopped. What the hell was that? He tried to catch his breath. Lying there motionless, he listened to the distant drumming interspersed with the croaking of several nearby frogs.

He had to find out what was going on, so he quietly and nervously got to his feet and continued his trek up to the quarry in careful silence. The hidden moon made it difficult to see, so when he reached the top, he crouched low and squinted through the darkness. "How could that be?" he exclaimed, leaping up. He circled the quarry, walking in and around the darkened spheres. No one was there.

* * * *

The vibrant hues of the Costa Rican rainforest had given way to the shadows of the night, as the last of the search teams returned to camp. Bendi and Ortega were eating their dinner, when Manuel walked over to them.

"The teams downriver ran into a dead end," he explained. "The old riverbed eventually became overrun by the jungle; apparently the river just flooded out into the lowlands. The water was only a half-meter deep, like a marsh. As far as they could, the teams went into the brush but all they found was a broken paddle; nothing else." He shrugged, offering Bendi a look of sympathy. "As I said before, tomorrow will be the last day of the search. But as you requested, Miss Porcelli, we will maximize our efforts in this area." He added gently, "I hope your dreams and your jaguar lead us to your Mr. Taylor."

Bendi didn't respond. She finished her meal in silence, cleaning her utensils in a puddle left behind by the once raging river. She tried to imagine it, tried to picture Digger paddling down it... but no vision came.

Later, after they'd all retired to their tents, Bendi was sitting quietly in hers, unable to sleep, just thinking. She heard a shuffling step outside.

"Are you all right?" Ortega called softly. "I saw your light..."

She popped her head outside, glad for the interruption of her troubling thoughts. "I can't sleep. I'm too nervous about tomorrow," she confessed.

"Let me take your mind away from all of that," Ortega suggested. "Want to go for a walk?"

"A walk? Now? It's pitch black out there. Besides, isn't it dangerous to be in the jungle at night?"

"The jungle is safe and dangerous, in the day or in the night. Anyway, I think you might like it," Ortega hinted playfully.

Well, he hadn't given her any reason so far not to trust him; she had come to enjoy his stories and his company. They'd kept her spirits up through much of the strain of the past few days. Why not? she decided.

A beam of light from the professor's flashlight was the only thing that guided them. The chirps and bleats of crickets and frogs blanketed the pitch-black jungle. Ortega shined his light at the base of a huge tree. He bent down and, with a stick, gently shoved aside some underbrush.

"There, do you see that?" he asked.

"No," Bendi said, and she leaned further over. Then she saw a tiny red-and-black frog, no bigger than a nickel. "It's beautiful!" She reached down to touch it.

Ortega quickly grabbed her arm and pulled it back. "It is beautiful, rare, and deadly. This tiny frog is covered with poison. The tribes of South America would rub their spears and arrows against the skin. If only your fingertip gently brushed the back of this frog, you would be dead in a matter of minutes."

Bendi quickly stood up and took a step back. Ortega, still crouching, told her sadly, "This species has dwindled down to just a few sightings a year. This could be the last red dart frog that any human eyes ever see! I know it is redundant to say this, but as each species becomes extinct, we lose a part of ourselves, a part of our humanity." With his stick, he gently replaced the underbrush.

They'd walked a little further when he motioned Bendi to stop again. Her heart began to race as she heard snuffing and snorting. Then it became a crunching and tearing. The darkness seemed to magnify every sound and transform the shadows into monster beings.

Ortega quickly pointed the beam of light at a low-lying branch. She felt foolish as she saw the beady eyes of a small, furry, brown animal with a long, dangling tail. It was busy chewing some smaller mammal, using its strong claws and powerful jaws to portion out its meal. Startled by the light, the creature jumped off the branch and into the safety of the darkness.

"That was a kinkajou," her night-guide proclaimed.

"You think all of this is fun?" she asked sarcastically.

"Fun and magical!" He turned off the flashlight.

It took a minute before Bendi's eyes adjusted. At first, she thought they were playing tricks, like after having your picture taken. Then hundreds of tiny, cool, green lights danced in her vision—fireflies and click beetles signaling each other, Ortega explained. She stood motionless, mesmerized by the scene. It was enchanting.

"Look over here," Ortega whispered loudly.

She knew he was only a few feet away, but she still couldn't see him. Turning in the direction of his voice she saw the dark shadow of a thick, tall tree. Studded and glowing upon this shadow were green iridescent blobs. The moment felt unreal, as if she'd stepped into a Spielberg movie. "Those are mushrooms," Ortega quietly answered her unspoken question.

A tightness in her chest reminded her that she had forgotten to breathe. Slowly inhaling, she smelled the exotic fragrance of an unknown orchid. Ortega then took her by the hand and led her several yards, into a small clearing. She gasped, believing that not only the rain-forest, but the whole sky was filled with thousands of fireflies. It took her a few minutes to realize that all the sparkling lights in the velvet darkness above her were really the backbone of the Milky Way.

There was no way to express what she beheld in that moment. She couldn't speak, knowing that any words spilling from her lips would diminish the experience. Nature is truly magical, she thought. Anything seems possible here!

Somehow the experience helped her believe that Digger could still be alive. There was hope. As long as there was mystery and magic, there was hope.

"Orion's belt," Ortega pointed to the heavens.

"I know," Bendi answered. "And the Seven Sisters, just off to the right." She pointed to the clump of stars known as the Pleiades.

"I remember what you said about that being Digger's favorite star cluster. And also about his experiences at the Mayan city of Cobá. Did you know that the Pleiades played a big part in many different cultures, including the Meso-American cultures of the Aztecs, Incas, and especially the Mayas? Earlier this year, I was at the Aztec ruins in Teotihuacan. It was a remarkable ancient city in central Mexico that would have rivaled Egypt in its prime! In fact, that city had more than two hundred thousand inhabitants when it was thriving. Teotihuacan was also a major trade center and even had ethnic neighborhoods. Several years ago, paintings of the spheres were discovered in a secret chamber in the Pyramid of the Sun in Teotihuacan. They were similar to the ones we recently found close by in Guayabo, except that they had figures of Star Brothers next to them."

"Star Brothers? Who are they?" Bendi thought she could see a glint of a grin on Ortega's night-shrouded face.

"That is how I refer to them. It is the name given to them by many Native American tribes. When you hear people talk about the possibility of intelligent beings from other planets visiting this world, they speak as if it were a phenomenon that just started in the late 1940s. I told you that I studied among many of the indigenous tribes of South America. They all have stories, dating back centuries, that tell of being visited by Star Brothers. Many cultures believe that we have been or still are being visited by beings from other places. There are several theories that suggest they helped in building our pyramids and other massive stone sculptures. So why not help with the stone spheres?"

Bendi found this idea intriguing. She shivered involuntarily, although the humid night certainly wasn't cold.

"The ancient city of Palenqué, in southern Mexico, is a sacred site of the Mayas," The professor went on. "And the alignment of all its temples mirrors the heavenly relationship between the Pleiades and Earth. In fact, Teotihuacan supposedly was built on a grid in honor of the Pleiades. Karl Taube, an archaeologist, discovered that, at the city's east axis, on the day that the sun passes directly overhead in the spring, about May 18, the revered Pleiades star cluster makes its first annual pre-dawn appearance. And it is exactly on the west axis that the Pleiades sets."

Ortega's quiet voice began to blend into the rhythmic song of the crickets and tree frogs and Bendi felt both dazzled by the stars above, and mesmerized by the professor's words. But her mind was racing to keep up with the magnitude of their implications.

"The Mayas also had a connection to our Star Brothers. Their cosmology is an ancient star system that integrates the cycles of Earth and the Pleiades. Our 365-day Gregorian calendar is only three-dimensional, and is based on the cycle of Earth relative to the sun. But the Mayan 260-day calendar is very intricate and multi-dimensional, based not only on space and cycles, but also on time."

"Do you believe all that you are saying?" Bendi wondered.

"Being an archaeologist, I have to believe there are treasures beyond our wildest imaginations that will reveal our origins to us. A book called *Forbidden Archaeology*, which is over fifteen hundred pages, systematically and painstakingly lists and documents such unpopular findings termed 'out of context'—findings that do not fit into any of our presently-held theories or postulations. For instance, it reveals evidence that several pyramids in Egypt and Central America are over 50,000 years old. But those findings do not fit into the so-called accepted theory that our civilization has only existed for 8,000 years."

"Wow," Bendi gasped. "That's quite a lot of time to fill in; I mean, if that's true, what happened during those missing 42,000 years?"

"I do not pretend to know all about these matters, yet I do know that I do not know—everything. But please do not tell anyone I said that!" Ortega chuckled. "What puzzles me, though, is how people can be so closed-minded about themselves, about others, about the universe." He looked up into the brilliant heavens. "But it is in these moments that I remember why. It is because they have lost sight. Most people live in the cities, under roofs, so they do not look up anymore. They do not make the effort to surround themselves with nature, with the darkness, with the infinite. Without that reminder, it is easy to forget about the wonder, the mystery, the limitlessness of the universe! Just look at what is before us. As I look up into the night sky, I know there is so much more that we do not know."

Bendi heard them before she actually saw the blotches of darkness swoop over her, circling before they disappeared into the night. "What was that?" she cried, flailing her arms above her head.

"Bats," Ortega replied matter-of-factly.

"I hate them!" she exclaimed.

"Bats circling over you is actually a good sign, or good medicine, as a *sukai* would say."

"What do you mean, *good medicine*?" she retorted. "It didn't feel good to me!"

"According to Meso-American belief, bat symbolizes rebirth. To be reborn, you have to die—symbolically. The Mayas believed that to evolve, you have to let go of your past, the past being the personas of whom you have believed yourself to be, including all your old beliefs, perceptions, and roles that you have played. Bat medicine was also used more recently by North American shamans to help them move through that symbolic death. One of the final steps of their ritual was to be buried for one day in a coffin, with only a thin bamboo shoot sticking out of the ground to breathe through.

"Even on Fiji's Turtle Island, prospective shamans would be completely buried, except for their faces, which were covered by a thin piece of cloth. They called this the Night of Fear, because they would be in total darkness and have to listen to foraging creatures on the ground. All their fears, real and imagined, would quickly surface so that they could be known. And once known, allowed to die." Bendi shuddered at the thought. "The bats visited you tonight," Ortega suggested gently. "That is an honor, if you believe in such things. It could mean that you need to die symbolically, for some reason; that your fears need to die, that you need to let go of parts of your old self—perhaps that you need to grow in new ways?"

She could feel him smiling at her encouragingly, but she kept silent and allowed his words to be engulfed by the dense rainforest. Bats and aliens—what could she say to that? What a combo! Staring out into the darkness she watched the dance of green lights... for a moment, her sense of hope wavered as she remembered the purpose of those glimmering green firefly lights—to attract a mate.

She felt a deepening sensation of discomfort over her emotional tether to Digger, yet her heart ached with his absence. She longed for his kiss, his touch, even the sound of his music, which had sometimes filled her with a strange kind of emptiness. Had she actually felt insecure because of his relationship with his music? She wondered, thinking back to the time when she'd wrapped her bare body around his while he was trying to play the piano—wanting to get inside him and feel what it was that he felt... because she felt... lonely... angry... sad...

Each click of a cricket shifted her to a different emotion. Each flash of a firefly's faint glow was a reminder of her search for love... from Digger... from her father...

Bendi felt the jarring shock of the now-conscious connection between the two most prominent men in her life. Why hadn't she ever realized it before? She'd tried so hard to give both of them all her love but they just never seemed to be around to receive it.

She looked up at the stars again. How could I have tried to fill so vast a thing as another person's soul? Especially when my own has been so empty?

As she tilted her head back towards the jeweled sky, her old thoughts and emotions seemed insignificant and petty. She willed them away—and in their place a new sense of awe and childlike wonder overtook her. Maybe Ortega was right about the Star Brothers. So much space out there.

Immediately she changed that thought: So much space *within me*. Maybe there *was* something to this "bat medicine." What needs to die? What do I need to let go of? What needs to grow?

Chapter 22

"... we are all on the same journey, a journey of heart, a journey of spirit."

Digger knew he'd seen several people and what he thought to be a large feline walking up the hill to the quarry just a moment before he got there. And he could have sworn that he'd heard Angélica's voice. Where had they gone? As the thumping of percussion from the festivities below rolled through the jungle and bounced off the quarry walls, making it sound as if there were a hundred drummers, he wandered among the moonlit spheres. The hilltop was empty of people and animals.

Confused, he hiked slowly back down the hill, guided by the raging ceremonial flames. As he carefully approached the center of the village, he noticed that *Los Otros* were dressed in uniquely colorful tunics. When he moved closer he saw the young couple Chucan and Seentar sitting near the fire, cuddling, and next to them—predictably—was the older woman, Darant. She waved him over eagerly. As he approached, she smiled warmly, motioned him to sit down, and offered him a basket of fruit. The rest of the tribe, it appeared, was dancing joyously around the fire.

Well, it probably won't hurt to sit and watch, he thought. He chose a freshly-picked mango from the basket, thanked Darant with a grateful look, and settled somewhat reluctantly between the old woman and Seentar. Chucan nodded at him from Seentar's left and grinned, while Seentar merely greeted him with smiling eyes. No way will they get me involved, he thought, immediately wary of their motives.

It was a festive scene with many of the dancing *Los Otros* wearing intricately woven headbands while others were adorned with beautiful feathered headdresses. After a while, he noticed a pattern; it seemed anyone could join in the dance—or they could just sit and watch. That put him more at ease. Some of *Los Otros* danced by themselves, others danced in couples or groups. Although all were dancing in sync with the rhythm, they each danced their own style. The result was an almost chaotic pattern of movement, but with complete harmony created by the beat. "I really enjoy your music," he called to Seentar and Chucan above the music, as a tremor emanating from the drums passed through the ground and up into his body.

Darant, who was sitting on his other side, leaned over with her toothy grin to shout in his ear, "There is a rhythm in the jungle, but not all can hear it. That pulse can be felt in all things. *Los Otros* feels that vibration. And I believe that our rhythm will soon be yours," Darant nodded in time to the beat.

"There you are!" Vawaha exclaimed as she ran up to Digger, looking all grown up in her misty blue and deep purple tunic with several multi-colored feathers tied to her long hair. She clutched at Digger's hands, pulling him to his feet. "I have been looking for you! And so has Mashuba! You must come now!"

Before she could drag him off to the other side of the circle where Mashuba was sitting, Digger managed to say goodbye and thank his friends for their company. They just laughed at Vawaha's enthusiasm as she pulled him away.

No sooner had she gotten him halfway toward Mashuba than the music transformed to a slower rhythm and the little girl began slowly twirling around, her arms cascading in the air like a young ballerina. She stopped dancing for a moment and tried to pull Digger with her into the inner circle of dancers.

"Sorry, not now," he refused stubbornly, "maybe later." He was comfortable dancing with Bendi, when he knew the steps, but dancing *Los Otros*-style was clearly different—too many variations! And which was the right way? If he tried this, he'd definitely look the fool.

Vawaha pouted for a few seconds, but then some other children danced by and she quickly became caught up in their enthusiasm and danced away, leaving Digger to find his own way through the twirling bodies.

"You're looking mighty dapper," Digger chuckled as he plopped down next to Mashuba who was wearing an all white tunic with a rain-bow of colors circling his chest.

"I will take that as an honor," the elder said with a wry smile. "So, have you learned anything new today?"

"Everything has been very enlightening—and puzzling," Digger responded. He thought of his magical encounter with the Shashunas earlier that morning, then the conversations about dimensions within dimensions, experiencing the imprints of others with the Love sphere, his sessions within Gutubo's arms, the mystery of the invisible force that tried to pull him up the hill—and the disappearance of all the people he'd seen climbing to the quarry, just moments before he got there. "Yes, very confusing in an enlightening sort of way," he grinned good-naturedly.

Mashuba nodded with a knowing smile. "It is wonderful to have you join us for the ceremony," he said sincerely.

"It feels pretty good to be here," Digger had to admit. He meant it. Despite the unanswered questions, the frustrations, the days with no apparent progress toward getting back to where he'd begun (did he even want to go back? he wondered briefly—then quickly cancelled the thought) despite all his confusion, *Los Otros* now felt to him like long-lost friends. He felt comfortable, challenged, but also accepted for who he was here, and... and *loved*, was the only word he could think of—truly loved. The heat from the fire warmed his skin as he thought about this wonderful village and its people.

But those newly-felt emotions shoved him to the opposite side of the pendulum, which brought a pain—a pain of discomfort and disconnection from all the people he'd shut out of his life: his friends, his family, and Bendi.

"Mashuba," he began, hopeful that the old man could enlighten him on this, "it seems that after I understand something important, or learn more about myself, the opposite happens—I feel more out of balance."

"That is a healthy way to explain it. I mean about balance," Mashuba said over the music, which had grown softer now. "It is the 'Ogoranno'—one of the ways of learning." The old man got slowly to his feet, reflections of the fire dancing amongst his white hairs. "Stand up," he commanded. Digger complied, baffled. "Now bend your right leg and place your heel high on the inside of your left thigh, balancing only on your left leg."

Digger tried to do as he was told, but fell out of the difficult pose several times. "This is harder than trying to pass a DUI test," he joked.

"Keep your focus," Mashuba instructed firmly.

After a few moments of struggle, he finally exclaimed, "I'm doing it!"

"I can see that; now close your eyes."

At first, it was difficult to keep his balance because there was nothing to focus on, but he soon found his equilibrium. An unsettling sensation quickly overtook him, that even though he was in balance, his body felt like it was swaying several feet. He opened his eyes to get an idea of how much he was *really* swaying—but to his amazement, his body was barely moving. "With my eyes shut, I felt like I was more out of balance than I really was," he said in wonder.

"But you were not, were you?" the old man twinkled. "When you went within, you had a heightened sense of balance which made you more aware. So the slightest movement away from equilibrium was also heightened. That is Ogoranno. You have actually made progress, but because of your heightened awareness, it *seems* that you are further away. Do it again. Close your eyes."

Digger struck the stork-like pose again. He wondered if by now the entire tribe was staring at him and he peeked open one eye to look. No, they were too busy dancing, he discovered. He quickly closed his eyes again and focused on his balance.

"Now think of a vine that is pulling you straight up from the top of your head."

He tried it—and instantly felt stronger and more balanced.

"With each new learning comes growth. Now raise your hands above your head," Mashuba commanded.

Again, he felt as if he were wildly swaying.

"But sometimes it feels as if you are going backwards—more out of balance," Mashuba said. "Know that you are not; it just feels that way to your mind. You are just learning to do more. The more you feel—know—of balance, the more you are aware when you are not in balance."

After a few moments, Digger regained his stability.

"Okay, now bring your leg down. What you just experienced, Ogoranno, also holds true for the emotional, mental, and spiritual aspects of yourself. Now try balancing on your right leg and again, keep your eyes shut."

"This side is easier to do than the other."

"It is the same for all. As you move through life, there are sides of yourself that will attain balance easier than other sides of yourself."

He opened his eyes to see Mashuba standing several feet in front of him in the same pose. They stared at each other for a few moments. Then Mashuba began to rock from side to side. Immediately, Digger started to lose his balance.

"Do not look at me. Focus on an immovable object," Mashuba commanded as he continued to sway. Digger tried to focus on a boulder a short distance away, but was distracted by Mashuba's wobbling.

"See how easy it is to get out of balance? The events of your life will always be changing, swaying from here to there, lifting you up and then bringing you down. You need to go within to find that immovable force. For your spirit is always strong, stable, and steadfast. Spirit focus can provide balance for you."

Digger barely held his balance as Mashuba continued to wobble. Finally, the sound of clapping behind him was too much added distraction and Digger fell out of his pose.

Angélica suddenly appeared, emerging from the darkened jungle wearing a thin delicate skirt that began at her waist and ended just above her feet. Swirling teal-colored lines, that looked like Milky Way constellations, decorated the peach colored material. Loosely draping the top half of her trim body was a sleeveless blouse that ended two inches above her navel.

"What happened?" she chided Digger with amusement. "You were doing so well."

Digger didn't answer and just looked at her. She was beautiful!

Angélica then looked at Mashuba for a moment before asking Digger, "Would you like to dance?"

Even though he wanted to be near her, dancing was not what he would have chosen. He resisted at first, but then, seeing it was the only way, reluctantly acquiesced. Clumsily, he moved about, trying to imitate Angélica's moves.

This is ridiculous, he thought. I can't do this. I don't know what I'm doing. People must think that I look really stupid! He looked around at the other dancers; they seemed lost in their own movements. Then he looked at those who weren't dancing but sitting in the circle. Some were busy talking, some were looking at the fire, and some were smiling as their gazes traveled among the dancers. But no one was paying attention to him. No one was pointing and saying, "Look at the new guy! He dances funny—it's obvious he doesn't know what he's doing."

Angélica must have sensed his apprehensiveness because she immediately danced closer to him. He could actually feel her breath as she said, "Remember, you are a Keeper of Sound; so use your mind—not to be critical of yourself, but to create space for the music to have a relationship with your body. Shut out the illusion of sight, close your eyes, and feel the music. Your body already knows how to dance; you just have to get out of the way." He could see that she was definitely practicing what she preached. For a moment, he forgot himself as he appreciated her fluid gracefulness.

Being a pianist, he'd always *felt* music, but he'd only allowed his fingers to dance. Being Digger, he'd never fully allowed his body to move with a sound. Now he tried harder, still moving awkwardly at first, but as the music picked up with a newly infectious beat, he gradually loosened up. As his inhibitions slowly began to fade, the rhythm pulled at his body while his legs moved more freely than ever before.

This isn't me, his critical mind argued. I can't move like this.

Immediately, his dancing became erratic and clumsy. This was a drastic change of sensation and he felt uncomfortable as his self-doubting mind struggled to regain its control over him and restrict his motions. He had to rid himself of this overworked organ; with a purposeful and powerful gesture, he put both hands on his temples and then flung them symbolically toward the fire. He envisioned his nagging self-criticism burning up and transforming into minute embers that slowly drifted up towards the stars. That transformation from thought to fire to air created the space in him to dance once again—joyously.

As the tempo increased, Digger totally let go. The rhythm pulsed through his body as he moved wildly to the passionate music. His buddies from Chicago had thought he'd gone "Californian" when he moved to San Diego—but if they could see him now, they would lock him up and throw away the key. He didn't care, though. He let himself become lost. Lost in the music. Lost in the jungle. Lost in time.

The music then segued to a slower, more sensuous beat, with flutes delivering their melodious embellishments. He opened his eyes again to see Angélica dancing passionately around him to the soft, intricate beating of drums. "Close them," she whispered.

That was the last thing he wanted to do. He wanted to gaze into her eyes. He wanted to watch her move.

But when he did as she asked, he could feel the reverberation of the drums lift his feet and gently place them back down as his body turned slowly in broad circles. The music played in his viscera and resonated in his bones. Blood rushed through his body as his hips began to sway gently. Then his shoulders followed. As he accepted the rhythm, he danced like a sensuous woman.

Angélica brushed by him and his eyelids popped open as he felt the touch of her flesh. Immediately he was blinded by the raging flames of the fire just a few feet in front of him. When he turned around, he was startled to find himself standing face-to-face with Angélica. He didn't know what to say or do. Nervously, he blurted the first thing that came to his mind, "I... I... ahhh, thought I heard you and others at the quarry earlier. But when I got to the top, you were gone." He instantly felt stupid. Not that he didn't want to know, but because that was not at all what he wanted to ask.

Angélica's eyes strained slightly in the firelight, as if measuring how much to tell him. His heart jumped when she lightly touched him and led him through the groups of dancing *Los Otros* to a quiet area just outside the ring of people. She stopped and turned to him, standing between him, with the dark jungle at his back, and the brilliant bonfire before him, so that he saw a halo of flames dancing around her head like a nighttime volcanic eruption.

The music stopped and the rainforest became instantly quiet as Angélica grinned. Even though it was quite impossible, he could swear that he could actually *hear* her smile. That sound was intriguing, inviting, and totally harmonious with the jungle.

He jumped as Vawaha's loud voice cut in, "You keep leaving me!" The little girl appeared from the edge of the circle, hurrying over to his side. He ignored her, his eyes never leaving Angélica's melodic smile.

"You didn't answer my question. Were you at the quarry or not?"

Vawaha strained on Digger's arm. "You don't want to miss this," she insisted.

He could swear Angélica's smile became a touch more enigmatic. "I was there," she laughed, as Vawaha pulled Digger away from her.

"I don't understand—I didn't see you there," Digger shouted back at her as Vawaha pulled him along and a group of *Los Otros* walked between them.

"Remember," Angélica called back, "the meaning of my name? I am a traveler. A traveler between the tick and the tock!"

He lost sight of her completely as the crowd closed in around him. He thought affectionately, chuckling to himself, this woman is traveling, all right—traveling in circles around me.

Vawaha had dragged him to the far side of the fire, where most of *Los Otros* had now gathered. He finally looked down at her as she pulled on his arm, jumping up and down. He smiled at the girl and asked indulgently, "Okay, what's going to happen?"

"You will see," she responded gleefully.

Now *Los Otros* began arranging themselves, cross-legged, in a broad circle around the bonfire. Vawaha led him to a spot and pulled him down next to her. He looked around, but couldn't find Angélica's face anywhere among the crowd, or even Mashuba's. It was so dark just beyond the circle of firelight, he reasoned; she could still be here, but hidden in the outer shadows of the crowded circle. He wanted to get up and go look for her, but he didn't want to hurt Vawaha's feelings, and whatever he was supposed to watch was beginning...

A woman lightly brushed the taut skins of a high-pitched drum, creating a hypnotic beat, as a young girl ran out and placed a mask by the fire. From where he sat, Digger could see one of the musicians, holding a pan flute arrangement of four reeds tied together with vine. The man stepped forward a little from the circle and began to play a lively melody.

"This is different," Vawaha explained eagerly. "I have been waiting for this new ceremony."

"Really? Why?" He looked down at Vawaha's long black hair.

"Ceremonies are just symbols," she shrugged simply. "Mashuba says that ceremonies put into physical form the stories of our minds, hearts, and most importantly our spirits. They are ways for us to honor, to celebrate, to give thanks, to remind, to guide us to the 'All That Is Unseen.'"

He didn't want to disillusion her, but he thought to himself that, as far as his own life, he'd found that most any kind of ceremony meant nothing. Even in the business world there were rituals—certain unspoken ways, unwritten rules. But for him, it showed up most clearly in religions, like having Latin read and sung at church when he was a boy, or having to go to confession, or abstaining from his favorite things during Lent.

The flute player stopped suddenly and the ground beneath Digger quivered lightly with a new sound, a low rumbling like an Australian didjeridoo, apparently emanating from a long, thick, hollow, bamboo stalk in the hands of another musician. As a second young woman ran toward the fire and placed another mask at its edge, Digger made a mental note of this musical effect. He wondered if he could corner some of the musicians later, maybe convince them to let him try some of their instruments. Meanwhile, his mind catalogued the rhythm for future reference—that is, if he ever got home again, ever went back to composing again...

"Mashuba says ceremonies are very useful and can be joyous," Vawaha interrupted his reverie. "But he says we get into trouble with them because many began centuries ago. Since they are rooted in the past, they can lose their meaning when they are not relevant to us and our lives now. Mashuba believes that our stories are always changing, so why shouldn't our ceremonies?" She looked up at Digger with radiant eyes. "It does seem lazy and silly not to create new ones, doesn't it? And besides—it's more fun this way!"

Digger nodded and smiled down at her. While she'd been talking, new instruments were played in turn, and each time, a new mask had been placed by the fire. Some looked like ferocious animals, others were feathered like birds. He even saw some that looked like giant insects, with only a few that appeared human. "Exactly what is this ceremony supposed to represent?" he asked.

"One of the laws of the jungle," Vawaha muttered, her attention captivated by the movement in front of them.

"Which law?" he persisted.

Oh, you know—our connection," she said with a little irritation. She looked up at him as if he were just too dense. "With the rainforest, with the heavens, with each other..."

"Ah," he nodded, pretending complete understanding. "And do you have any other ceremonies?"

"Twelve altogether. And each year *Los Otros* changes a different one. Of course, they all have a specific purpose and meaning. This one is about connection."

A very unexpected sound came to Digger's ears—faintly similar to rock and roll. He raised his eyebrows as Vawaha looked at him with a big grin, watching him closely. "Angélica tried to show them a little of your music. Did she do well?"

"Sounds good," he lied good-humoredly. Actually, it sounded completely out-of-sync with this place and he had to suppress a laugh. She would try something like that, wouldn't she? he thought fondly.

When a complete circle of masks had finally been placed around the fire, the music stopped. All around him, people stood up and walked forward to inspect the ornate disguises. Following their lead, Digger went to view the mask that had been presented with the rock-and-roll beat. The human face looked lifeless compared to the others.

"Why does this one look different?" he asked Vawaha, who had stayed at his side.

"Angélica said it would represent your culture best this way, and she told the carvers exactly how to make it," she explained innocently. "Do you like it?"

Before he could answer, the musicians struck up again with flutes, rattles, shakers, and drums, shaping their tones into an enchanting melody. He merely smiled, surveying the festive crowd. If only home were like this, he thought—and in some ways, he had come to feel very at home here—a home where his "family" was supportive and encouraging, a home where his spirit was ignited, a home where he was truly accepted. He still wanted to go back to San Diego, knew he must because that was where he belonged—but he also wanted to take as much as he could of *Los Otros* back with him. Much more than just their music. He looked around again for Angélica, hoping to see her among the glowing, happy faces pressed around him, but when he turned, a woman pushed one of the masks into his hands. All around him, people were tying the elaborate carvings on their faces eagerly, clamoring for their favorites.

He looked down at the one in his hands. It was an exaggerated caricature of a human face, more like an alien than anyone he'd ever known. Well, what the heck, he thought, I've already tried dancing. What can be so hard about this? He tied the strings behind his head, adjusting the wooden mask so he could see more clearly.

An alligator-masked man was demonstrating a series of dance steps and the others were mimicking his movements. Digger chuckled to himself—a jungle version of country-and-western line dancing? He found a place in line and after a few more minutes of instruction, followed the masked *Los Otros* as they formed two concentric circles around the fire. The inside circle faced out, as the outside circle faced in. He imitated the others and danced the simple movements they'd just been taught. This is easy, he thought, shuffling his feet slightly and moving his hands and arms in graceful, broad circles.

The big drum stopped suddenly and so did the dance. The inner circle moved one person. Then the music and movement began again. It reminded Digger of games he played on the playground in elementary school—except that across from him was a long-nosed anteater and a moment ago he'd been dancing with some kind of green praying mantis.

In the beginning, Digger focused on his partners' masks. From ornate birds to fearsome jaguars, from beautiful orchids to ghoulish faces, the disguises took on life as they moved amidst the shadowy firelight on the edge of the jungle. He was surprised by his gut reactions to the dancing forms—fear, wonder, panic, joy, scared, and loving. But after a while, he discovered that nothing else seemed nearly as important as the eyes that stared back at him from behind the facade; not the shape of the dancing body, not gender, not the mask itself, no matter how intricate. All he could see was the eyes. All he could hear was the rhythm. And all he could sense was the connection.

To his amazement, Digger felt a bond with every person he encountered. With that connection of eyes alone, there seemed to be an exchange of unconscious awareness, a feeling of peace, a feeling of acceptance. Whenever the drummers stopped pounding, he felt a sense of sorrow and loss and didn't want the person in front of him to leave. He wanted to grasp their arm, remove their mask, and sit them down to share stories, find out all about them, and maybe discover the source of the unique kinship he felt with them. But as the music began again and the next person stood before him, he was quickly swept away with a renewed sense of discovery and connection.

Yet even without words, Digger began to receive impressions about whoever was before him. He felt as if he could sense their joys, their losses, their excitement, their searching, their hopes. Within this overwhelming experience of discovery, he detected one amazing common thread: each and every person was the same—not because of skin color, religion, country, or any other physical illusion, but because what flowed from behind their masks was always pure spirit.

Suddenly "spirit" was no longer a belief drilled into him in catechism class, or any philosophical, ethereal concept. It was actually a concrete sensation, an energy that he recognized in others for the first time—and now began to feel stirring within himself.

Within those rivers of spirit flowing in him and through the eyes of the others, Digger identified two seemingly distinct and opposed currents: First was the flow of pain; that even though life molded unique individual experiences, all people shared some form of suffering. But the second, ever-present current was that of love—the love that each person had for themselves, the love that overflowed to whomever or whatever was near them.

And in that realization came a sense of relief, a lifting of the steel door, a deeper connection with himself, a camaraderie of shared pain that stretched over genders, ages, classes, religions, cultures, and continents, a knowingness that we are all interconnected whether we be a musician or a computer programmer, an attorney or a tribesman, a waitress or a CEO, a parent or a child. Digger felt comfort with the knowledge that we are all on the same journey, a journey of heart, a journey of spirit.

The drumming stopped momentarily and the next person moved stealthily in front of him. As the music began again, this person's eyes peeked out lovingly from behind electric-blue butterfly wings. A rush of energy pulsated up and down his body as their gazes locked. Warmth filled his chest and he felt totally accepted by this person. With grace, and in an identical, purposeful way, they mirrored each other's movements as he felt her sparkling green eyes sinking to the very core of his being. She was able to do that, not only because of who she was, but also because he allowed her. He flashed back to that moment—so long ago—when he'd grasped her life jacket and tried to pull her from the raging river. In that brief instant, a bond had been forged between them—a bond that felt stronger than one built over lifetimes.

The drums resonated in Digger's solar plexus as their eyes continued to search, to discover, to communicate, to probe. He wanted to stop the dance and hold her, cradle her in his arms and make wild passionate love with her. But mesmerized, their bodies continued to undulate to the trance-like rhythm in the prescribed steps until, unknowingly, they gradually drifted away from the circle. In unison they stopped.

As Digger slowly took off his mask, that internal thread within him unraveled some more. He felt exposed and vulnerable to this woman. But in that nakedness he could hear the rhythm of the jungle, feel the heat from her body, see the love in her heart, and knew the spirit in her eyes.

As Angélica removed her gleaming butterfly mask, their joined gaze sifted deep inside their souls. And in that exchange, they knew each felt exactly the same. Without touching, they touched as few couples ever do.

Digger fully realized now the thin veil that had separated them over the last week—the thin veil of denial; the denial of their feelings, the denial of their love, the denial of the unconscious, intrinsic, connection between them—the denial that even beyond the passion, the love, something different, something more, something unfinished had not even begun.

"I can't believe that…" Digger began.

"Me either," Angelica responded.

"Are you feeling the same as…"

"Yes," she whispered softly.

The pain of not touching her was finally more than he could bear and he reached out to take both her hands tenderly in his; the sensation was electrifying. She smiled up at him as she softly pressed his palms in return. Slowly, they eased into each other as their lips drew closer...

Dipping abruptly beneath their arms and squeezing between them, Vawaha blurted, "Mashuba wants to meet with you *now*, Digger." She inserted a determined hand between theirs and pulled Digger away, back toward the fire...

Chapter 23

*"The only time that you can see your shadow
is when you have turned away from the light."*

Angélica's look of shocked disappointment followed Digger as Vawaha dragged him through the crowd of *Los Otros* toward a waiting Mashuba. Digger had thought Vawaha made it up, that the elder didn't really need to see him now, but the old man was standing impatiently when they arrived. "We must go to the quarry now," he said with typical firmness of purpose. He was definitely accustomed to leading, and to being obeyed, Digger mused.

"But—right now?" he questioned, glancing over his shoulder at Angélica, who was making her way towards them.

"Can it not wait until later, Mashuba?" she pleaded as she stepped close to Digger, slipping her fingers quietly between his, out of sight of the others.

"No, it cannot." He fixed her with a stern look.

Vawaha piped up, "But I want him to stay and dance with me! Do not go with them," she pleaded with Digger, looking up at him with her intense blue eyes. "Don't leave me again!"

"No, Vawaha," Mashuba firmly admonished the little girl—but with a level of understanding he hadn't displayed for Digger and Angélica. "Digger and I must take care of important matters now."

Large crocodile tears streamed down her face, as she stared at Digger again. "At least let me come with you," she begged.

"Just Digger and me," Mashuba reiterated. He glanced at Angélica and then squatted down close to Vawaha's face. "We will all get together in the morning," he assured her gently.

"No!" the little girl shouted, glaring boldly at Mashuba. She turned and threw her arms around Digger's waist. "You cannot leave me again."

Digger felt her small body shake as she sobbed. Crouching down, he squeezed her gently. "Vawaha, why are you so upset? I'm only going with Mashuba for a little while. I will return. Believe me." He quickly glanced up at Angélica. "I'm not planning to leave—just yet."

As Digger stood up, Angélica reached out brown, slender fingers to touch his arm lightly. Mashuba gave him a firm nudge forward.

As they crossed the stream, Digger looked back to see the silhouette of Angélica holding Vawaha in her arms.

"Where is your focus?" Mashuba asked.

"I don't know, that's my problem. I feel like I'm in a whirlwind."

"Is that so bad?" the elder inquired.

He sighed loudly. "I know—you'll probably tell me that's how life is supposed to be—'constantly changing,' or something like that. But this is all new for me. For a week I've been living in a totally strange environment, with unusual people, seeing and experiencing life in a new light, listening to you tell me about everything from strangler figs to multi-dimensions! I came here, I think, because I needed quiet time to think some things over—like my mother's death. But instead I get lost on a river, pummeled by earthquakes and water and Angélica's endless questions, then kidnapped by strangers who tell me they're going to hold me hostage until I 'imprint' on one of their very weird stone spheres! And oh-by-the-way, these spheres do strange things to anyone who stands too close to them!" He was warming up, relieved to finally express some frustration over the whole scene. "I came here to figure out why my relationships with women are so messed up—and now I've got two total strangers pulling at me, trying to..." he sighed again, looking back toward the now-distant fire, thinking how one of those "strangers" was more familiar to him than any woman had ever been—in fact, she was right this moment consuming his brain in a kind of inner fire. "Mashuba," he finally admitted, "I'm not sure now if I even want to go back home!"

The old man just nodded knowingly, and urged Digger to continue his climb up the steps. The full moon was enormous now, as it was about to descend to the edge of the crater wall above the stone spheres. The luminescent orb illuminated their steps, casting their shadows far behind them toward the village, which was still emanating a lively music that floated up the hill with the two men.

Digger sighed deeply again. "Even though life appears to be laid-back here, it's not. Things seem to progress rather quickly and now my own life seems to be moving at light speed."

"It is not only you who are feeling that way, but many people," Mashuba responded. "Spirit is becoming bolder. By that I mean the spirit that resides in everyone is demanding to live its truth, now. So we *are* moving, as you put it, at light speed. This must be, so that we, human-kind, can travel to the next path on our journey. For we are now standing at the crossroads of history. Which path will you choose? The decision is momentous for you, for us, for all."

"Well, I'm not sure about other people's paths, but I'm having a hard time keeping up with my own."

"Remember what I said about being in balance? About Ogoranno? In these present times, life and its events—the form—will be constantly changing, so you need to focus on that immovable force I told you about. Or to say it in another way, to commit to and with your spirit." Mashuba raised his hands, "Enough of this lecturing."

"Shit!" Digger exclaimed involuntarily as he tripped over a rock and fell down to his knees.

"Are you all right?"

"Fine," Digger grumbled, brushing himself off. Embarrassed, he tried to change the subject. "It seems like I've been here forever." He pushed ahead on the path, taking the lead from Mashuba as if to prove how fast things were moving for him.

"Time is no different than anything else; it is illusionary in this universe," Mashuba, who couldn't seem to resist an opportunity to teach again, volunteered. "Its meaning is all relative to where you are. And where you are, is fluctuating in many dimensions. But when you are in the moment, you are blended with all aspects of yourself. In that state, there is no position to be relative to; you are here and there, past and future, in awareness of all."

Digger turned around to respond, as he continued to walk, "Are you saying there is no past or future?" His foot caught on a stone step and he sprawled to the ground again, his knee landing on a small rock. "Damn it!" he blurted as sharp pain shot through his leg. Lying face down in the soil, he spit out dirt but it still coated his moist lips.

Mashuba caught up and stood at his side, but didn't offer to help him up. "Why do you do that all the time?"

"Do what?" Digger growled, more embarrassed than ever.

"Do what you were just doing. Attempting to walk forward while you were looking back. You do it all the time. You have done it for most of your life, haven't you? And the result is always the same." He shook his head sadly, then turned abruptly around and started to walk back down the hill.

"Hey," Digger shouted after him. "Where are you going? Why did you drag me up here if you were just going to leave me? Is it because I fell down?"

Mashuba kept walking, with his back turned. "I will see you later," he replied nonchalantly. "You do not need me anymore."

Digger was stunned—both by Mashuba's mysterious actions and his own clumsiness. What had he meant about doing the same thing all his life? He stood up slowly. The edge of the quarry was just a step or two away. He turned back for a moment to watch his friend descend the hill, walking out of Digger's shadow. Looking down at the village reminded him of Angélica. He wanted to go back to her. But suddenly the pull of the spheres was stronger. An inexplicable sensation came over him that he needed to be among them—now.

The gigantic full moon now perched atop the crater wall, bathing all that was within its sight in a cool light. It almost looked touchable as it hovered above the silhouettes of the huge round stones. Digger turned slowly and surveyed the moonlit landscape. A faint sparkling of light from the distant waterfall shimmered across the moon-shadowed canopy. Even though he couldn't see a cloud, Digger felt the presence of an impending storm somewhere over the horizon.

Nervously, he walked back and forth amongst the shadows of the spheres. Imprint, imprint, what the hell do I have to do to imprint a sphere?

Perched high on a ledge of the crater wall, a hooting owl called to him, its big, blinking eyes adjusting to the various shades of the moonlit jungle. Breathing deeply, Digger thought of Mashuba's advice and imagined the moonlight washing away all his concerns—all but the present moment. A little twitch fluttered in his right shoulder. He turned slowly in that direction, moving his body away from the moon a few soft steps. Did *he* actually turn his body, or was it turned? Immediately, he "bumped into" a soft, pillowy, *invisible* wall. The twitch began again, and again his body turned. This time he walked toward the light of the moon as something gently guided him. He thought about resisting, but was too exhausted—mentally and physically. The truth was, whatever was happening felt good. He reasoned there was some purpose for this maneuver, he just had to figure out what.

Again he hit the invisible wall. And again, the twitch and gentle turn, as he moved through his and the spheres' shadows. He took another step before the invisible wall gently rejected his body. The twitch in his shoulder, the gentle turn, and again he stepped into his own shadow. But this time he became totally engrossed in what lay before him. His shadow, so clearly defined by the full moon, captivated him with a child's new-found fascination. He played with it for a while; his shadow did everything he did; it had no choice. It cannot exist without me, he thought. The shadow is an aspect of me—but it is *not* me.

Like the haphazard placement of a piece in one of his life's puzzles, whose picture and shape had been forgotten, the moment froze and a simple truth swept through him with the force of a tsunami:

The only time you can see your shadow

is when you have turned away from the light.

Concepts, questions, emotions, and insights quickly tumbled through his mind and permeated every cell of his body, a jumble of thoughts it might take him weeks—maybe a lifetime to unravel:

My shadow is a reflection of me,

of my past, of old ways of thinking, feeling, and being.

My forward momentum in life has always been thwarted

because I reacted to life's situations in my old ways.

Most of my pains have been caused because I was looking back!

I've had many shadows, one of which is the angry boy,

young Jonathan.

The shadows of that hurt and mistrustful little boy have interfered

in my relationships with women; never letting them in,

always making me run away.

How long have I been walking in my shadow

or in the shadows of others?

My shadow is searching for love,

but as with all shadows, it has no capacity to hold it.

I am not only looking at my shadow.

I am looking at the shadow of human civilization.

No time left for me to be in the shadow!

Otherwise, like Gutubo, I will lose myself!

There is neither good nor bad within shadows. As in this jungle, all

people, all things, and all events are here to learn from,

to remember, to remember about the light.

I need to make a commitment to walk toward that light.

All of this ran through his mind in a moment. The clarity astonished him. How could he receive so much information in such a short amount of time and yet totally *know* it? His own voice answered, but not from his head. It answered from somewhere near his heart, "Because you already knew it. In truth, there really is no learning, there is merely remembering, remembering of the *real* you; the spirit you, which is always present within the *layered* you called Digger."

Now he moved quickly toward the Love sphere, with all of its flowing designs drenched in silver light. Sitting down in front of it, he said aloud, "Okay—I'm open to whatever is supposed to happen."

Several bats swooped down out of the night and he put his hands up in an instinctively protective response. As they made passes over his head, he thought of what Angélica had said about the messages animals can bring. He didn't have any idea about the message of bats, but it couldn't be good! Immediately he stopped himself, and changed that thought. Just because I don't like bats doesn't mean their message has to be bad. The night creatures then flew off, crossing the moon's path.

Digger brought his attention back to the multi-colored sphere. Taking several deep breaths, he said, "I am ready to imprint—Wait. Cancel that statement."

He thought, I could be *ready* my whole life, but never really do it. I could say *I will* and because *will* is in the future, it could never happen. Only this moment exists. For all of eternity, there will be only this moment. He took another breath and said with a conviction that resounded in his gut, "I *am* imprinting."

As he sat staring at the sphere, the events that had brought him to this moment began to flow into his mind. But as he became entangled in remembrances, each one propelled him further away from the present moment. Every time he became aware of the intrusion, he willed it away, let it go, and returned his focus to his breathing—now, here.

A blanket of darkness smothered the jungle as the moon sank behind the crater walls. For hours, it seemed, nothing happened. Slowly, his thoughts gave way to the silence, interrupted only by the hoots of the bright-eyed owl—a creature who had the ability to see clearly through the deceptive shadows of the night.

He kept his gaze focused hazily on the sphere. When a pink aura popped up behind it, just as it had before, Digger smiled to himself. Intuitively, he knelt down and draped himself over the round object. He sensed the smoothness of its shape as the cool granite soothed his face, arms, and belly. Sinking into the stone as if it were a huge pillow, he soon felt invigorated by a solidness that stretched him deep into the earth.

He also felt an urge to be above the sphere and stood up, opening his stance and arms. Still sensing that depth of solidness he stretched equally as far into the sky.

The thread that had been unraveling within him now completed its task, stripping him of his masks, of his voices, leaving only his bared soul. Like a submissive wolf lying on his back, exposing his genitals to the lead of the pack, panic and vulnerability overcame him as the soft underbelly of his very being was exposed.

His reaction to his whole life had been to protect—protect and build walls. Standing in this vulnerable position, before this unrevealed mystery, fear retracted his groin and left him with a cold, queasy, sickening feeling of expectation.

The energy of the mysterious sculpture moved powerfully up his legs and into his viscera. Instead of the punctures of cold, hard teeth, he felt the soft, warm caress of the wind. The breeze swirled around and enveloped him. Then abruptly it stopped. And waited.

An awareness hit him hard: that it was easier for him to receive— from Bendi, from his audiences, from his family—even though that receiving could only be through a small opening in his steel door. But what about the act of *giving*? Giving with intention, with focus, with commitment, with love? That had been nearly impossible for him to do, crouched as he was behind his protective enclosure. Someone would have to come very close to his walls in order for him to reach through that tiny opening and give them something—anything.

But he quickly remembered Ogoranno. Was he really that far out of balance with his giving or did it just seem that way because he was now more aware? Besides, was it that he didn't give enough or was it that he didn't give in the way or depth that people expected of him, like his mother, like Bendi?

In an instant he reviewed his life, Gutubo style, and discovered that it was all true; at times he didn't give enough, at times he didn't give at all, and yet at other times he did, in fact, he gave in ways he never fully realized. But in this present moment he actually needed to give, not only because the sphere asked it of him, but also because he had much to give.

How could he do that? What part of him was great at giving? Instantly he heard the melody. *Of course, my music!*

Exposing himself even further, he took another breath and stretched to grasp the highest limbs of the trees, allowing himself to sway in the wind, open and vulnerable.

As if a symphony of musicians played within him, he gave of his music. That song sprang from his throat, permeating the rainforest with the sound of his voice. It radiated from his pores like a thousand sweet-smelling orchids replenishing the jungle with their fragrance. Within that music he then gave of his excitements, his talents, his strengths, his private hopes, and his aspirations.

The sphere gladly accepted this offering. But it wanted more. More of what? He felt dizzy as he looked out into the darkened void of the jungle. Focus, Mashuba had said, on an immovable force, something that is always there, something that doesn't move while the world around constantly changes, something that will drown out the yelling, something that can raise the heavy, steel doors a little more, something that can reach out through the darkness and touch me.

Then he remembered the common thread that flowed from behind *Los Otros'* ceremonial masks; it was spirit. His only choice was to go inside. Deep, deep within. And so he told himself, "I *am* going within. I *am* within. I *am* finding the…" The dizziness stopped as a bluish-white light flashed in the distance. Then the light became a laser beam, extending from deep in the forest all the way into his chest. That ray of light effortlessly moved him several feet away from the sphere.

Digger used the light—the light that he now knew was his—and searched within himself for the darkened corners, the dank, secret passageways, the blocked, hidden rooms that concealed all of his regrets, all of his faults, all of his fears. That light easily maneuvered through his convoluted maze and bathed each discovery with compassion.

As he gave himself his own love, sharp pains exploded in his intestines while a cold sweat formed on his brow. Bile seeped upwards into his throat and he knew this experience was far worse than his physical episode with the berries. But instead of his bowels eliminating and his stomach regurgitating, it was his mind, heart, and spirit that gushed. Instead of the giving of his rank excrement or his acidic, undigested food, he gave of his putrid, unhealthy thoughts, of his vile emotions, and of his adopted, soul-destructive beliefs. He gave of his fears of being without: without his mother's love, without purpose, without society's approval, without his father's companionship, without his music. He gave of his disappointments, of his perceived short-comings, of his negative attitudes, of his cancerous concept of not being good enough, and then, with one agonizing, pregnant push, he gave of his hurt little boy.

The release of his self-imposed heaviness left him with a refreshing lightness. As agonizing as that purging experience was, he now felt cleansed, released, free. The beam of light now transformed into a delicate, yet powerful, pinkish beacon as it eased him back in front of the Love sphere.

His vision now filled, as the day before, with the moments of others and he knew again that he was sensing the imprints that had been left with this stone sphere. But compared to his life back in San Diego, the people, their clothes, and their languages seemed to be from faraway places and from the distant past. At first he felt uncomfortable, as if he were looking through someone's private diary or photo album, but even more so, because he could see, hear, and feel exactly what they were feeling. Each imprint brought a brief moment of sharing that was beyond any of his previous experiences. The clarity was magnified a hundred times more than the other day; it was because of his new lightness of soul, he thought. I'm more receptive to their imprints because I'm more receptive of me, of my essence.

The visions changed. As if his life were composed of millions of individual threads, he saw himself as a beautiful tapestry. All of his memories—sights, sounds, thoughts, and emotions—wove seamlessly through this artful piece of work. He then recognized hundreds of moments of his life. As each scene flashed, a pressure-felt thump imploded into his chest and he knew that, at last, he was imprinting!

Some scenes were of loving times and others of challenging times. They all quickly rifled through his own private viewing room: playing piano at his first recital, his mother comforting him when he bruised his leg, calling Bendi to ask for that first date, fishing at sunrise on Lake Shawano, looking into Angélica's eyes, looking over his mother's dying body. He tried harder to bring that particular snapshot into clarity, but it was just out of focus. More snapshots came: of his dad tucking him in at bedtime, of diving in Key West and seeing the wonders of a coral reef, of playing ball on Sunday afternoons, of fighting with Bendi before he left for Costa Rica, of his parents' pride at his college graduation, of hearing his mother's sarcasm when he first saw her in the hospital, of playing passionately at his first Hollywood audition.

Each scene was intrinsically connected to every other scene. There was no real separation between people or places, emotions or thoughts, dreams or nightmares, hopes or failures. Somehow the realization of that deep connection gave him a recognition that he'd been around for a long, long time. And with that knowingness of longevity, came an indescribable wisdom that somehow his life, this crazy world, and human civilization all made sense, all had a deep purpose.

As his moments continued to imprint upon the sphere, he had a profound awareness that each imprint, whether it was of him or others, by water or by desert, of loving times or hurtful times, that each of those moments were about spirit trying to emerge, spirit trying to embrace all that fell into its sight, spirit, with only the slightest hint of light, trying to allow love to burgeon.

As the imprints kept flashing before and within him, he felt an uneasiness that he couldn't shake. He sensed there was something incomplete about his imprints as compared to the imprints of others. It felt insignificant within the scope of everything that he was experiencing, yet at the same time it was important. Something was missing.

The scenes before him started to dissolve as he tried to discover what that difference was. Before he knew it, his doubting mind had kicked into full gear, trying to find a "logical" answer. The imprinting faded away.

"Damn it, Digger!" he cursed aloud. "Now is not the time to be logical or rational. Just feel!" He knelt in the blackness as a cool breeze swept over the crater wall and dipped down to lightly brush every hair on his body. He could barely see the sphere in front of him, but the sweet smell of night-blooming jasmine overpowered his worrisome thoughts and feelings. He focused back on his breathing, back to deep inside himself, back to his love.

With his next breath, the tiny silica particles that physically formed the granite sphere sparkled magically in the dark night. Each glittering silica molecule ignited the one next to it. Soon, all he could see was one shimmering ball of light. His body began to float and, turning backwards, entered the sphere. He wasn't afraid, and with dream-like confidence, he allowed himself to experience this new journey. His shadow was thrown long into the darkness of the jungle. But as he moved closer to the middle of the sphere, it grew smaller and smaller. Still suspended, he stopped floating and knew that he'd reached the center. All he could see was light beneath him, on top of him, all around him. Nothing else, not even the slightest hint of a shadow remained. In this place, he had the most amazing sensation of peace and unconditional love. Every cell within his body felt delicious, as the rarely-felt love sank into his very core. He hoped that he could remain this way forever.

Forever—his mind tried to grab hold of that concept, which was beyond holding. His doubting mind then quickly found a place within him that did not believe he could have such a thing as unconditional love. It was the same illusionary place that told Digger he wasn't good enough, that he didn't deserve to feel that love for a day, let alone *forever*.

In the next instant, his own fear quickly brought his body out of the sphere of light. His shadow grew in size until he felt himself kneeling on the ground again.

Without even reprimanding himself for letting his self-criticism interfere again, he took another breath and immediately restored his internal focus. A gust of wind moved among the spheres and Digger could hear music. At first he thought the heavenly sound was coming from the sleeping village far below. But to his surprise, he quickly realized the music was emanating from the spheres themselves as the ageless zephyr played amongst them. He recognized the individual notes of leaves, bushes, and plants as the trees and crater walls played powerful chords resonating deep within the earth. The rhythm of the stream, pond, and waterfall underscored the melodies of each of the jungle's creatures. It was an incredible musical composition possessing beauty and rawness, sweetness and harshness, gentleness and power.

He soon noticed that one of the wavy designs on the Love sphere was pulsating and transforming back and forth, from two-dimensional to three-dimensional. He widened his gaze to take in the whole sphere and discovered that all the geometric shapes were doing the same thing! With each beat of this mysterious music, the symbols were coming to life.

As he focused on the gyrating symbols, the sphere began to spin. Rapidly turning in a counterclockwise direction, the vibrant colors melded into each other. With each revolution, like with each trip around Gutubo, the Love sphere became renewed. Digger wobbled and grew extremely dizzy as his body began to spin simultaneously with the sphere. Everything before him became a blur. He feared he would be flung out into the darkness, into the void, and there would be nothing out there for him to focus on, nothing out there for him to hold onto, nothing out there, but him.

As the spinning continued, he still heard and felt the music of the spheres. With the experienced ear of a musician, he heard the unified beat of each of his cells. That beat was connected to the pulsation of his mind. That pulsation in his mind played to the throbbing of his heart. That throbbing in his heart reverberated to the rhythm of earth. With that euphoric, intrinsic connection, he felt a vastness of universes within himself. And finally, the centrifugal force threw each one of the sphere's three-dimensional, sacred symbols into the darkened jungle.

All the parts of his past that had previously crowded his limited self now appeared to be smaller. All the boundaries of body, limits of mind, and restrictions of emotion began to recede. All the debris that had clogged his darkened hallways and rooms shrank. All because there was so much more room to *be.*

Like the sphere, he whirled through space and time, letting go of symbols that he'd drawn: of family, jobs, degrees, trophies, education, intellect, physicality. He let go of the colors that he'd childishly painted: of his emotions, his personalities, his relationships, his characteristics, and his music. He let go of the painstaking inscriptions that he had knowingly and unknowingly etched into stone that formed his beliefs, his judgments, his biases, and his perceptions. All of it now spun off him.

This dance with the Infinite continued until there was nothing left. Nothing left but his spirit. Nothing left but the Light.

Gradually, the spinning came to a halt and darkness slowly returned. Digger felt the coolness of earth pressed against his skin; somehow he'd been thrown to the ground. Sitting back on his knees, he stared at the Love sphere, not surprised to see that the once-colorfully decorated sphere was now just a gray, plain ball of granite. He could swear it was staring back at him. That's when it hit him. It was so simple!

The truth was that there was no difference between that sphere or his mother, the trees or the birds, Vawaha or Bendi, his music or the river, the stars or the earth, Angélica or himself. To "imprint," all he'd done was move through illusion, through form, to connect—soul to soul—and allow the river of Spirit to flow effortlessly through him with its current of love. For *everything* is spirit. Everything is LIGHT.

The tops of the trees began to swirl furiously. A high-pitched sound filled his head. Then the hairs on his body stood on end as the air became filled with static electricity. He covered his eyes as several rows of bright white lights blinded him. Between fingers, he could see each row spinning in an opposite direction from the ones next to it. This light clearly came from outside himself, not from within. Pressure squeezed his body as if he'd just dived two hundred feet beneath the ocean. Even shielded by his hands, his eyes still hurt from the light.

The next thing Digger recognized was the dampness of the ground. The air was perfectly still. The silence of the rainforest was deafening. He jumped nervously when the hoot of the owl penetrated the tranquility.

He picked himself up, rubbed his eyes, and then squinted into the night. What had just happened? He'd been floating within a light. Imprinting. Spinning with the Love sphere. And... he looked around but there were no signs of the mysterious lights, only the faintest hint of approaching dawn.

He was overcome by a desire to find Angélica. He longed to tell her of his accomplishment—although he had no idea how his imprinting on the stone sphere would help *Los Otros*. But he was happy in some way, in any way to give back to them a little of what he had received.

As his eyes adjusted, he was dumfounded by the disappearance of all the spheres! He squinted, and in his line of vision appeared the silhouette of a man sitting cross-legged on a boulder, with a small sphere in his lap. Without fear, without any apprehension, he walked toward this man. This man who had been his friend in forgotten lifetimes. This man from a faraway place. This Teacher.

Chapter 24

"For this Earth is a newborn within this galaxy.
This galaxy is an infant within the universe.
And this universe is a child within all universes."

Bendi reached out in the bitter darkness and felt a cold, moist wall of rock. A mildewy odor permeated the gloom, as if wet clothes had been stashed in a dank corner. She realized she was on her knees when her head bounced off a ceiling of stone. She choked as a meaty, primal, hot breath scorched her face. Two yellow eyes with bottomless centers blinked open. Her scream was silent as she cowered against the damp wall.

"The time is now," was the message of the hypnotic eyes. Her tension eased a little when she realized that it was her jaguar. But her heart still raced, not only from fear, but also from expectation.

"Time for what?" she sent back telepathically.

"Time for action. What is your intent?" the piercing eyes retorted.

"My intent. My intent is to find Digger," she explained. "Where is he?"

"He has been many, many places," came the answer.

"But where is he now?"

"Here. He has been here all the time. But after you find him, then what?" the big cat responded.

She became aware that she was dreaming, but she was still confused. Where was *here*? What did intent have to do with anything?

"Everything!" was the response to her thoughts. "Everything in the jungle. Intent distinguishes you from the animals, the plants, the rocks, and from every other being. Intent creates the direction toward which you move. With the intent of living your soul's purpose you will find..."

"Wake up," Ortega whispered loudly outside her tent.

Still in darkness, Bendi's eyes popped open.

"You want to get an early start, don't you? This will be the last day of the search, unless we come up with something," Ortega urged her awake.

Clouds had descended and now silently touched the ancient water-way. As Bendi and Ortega settled on a boulder a short time later, a fine, misty drizzle fell upon them. Over coffee and sweet bread, Bendi explained to Ortega her latest dream.

"It very well could be that a *sukai*—" the archeologist suggested as Bendi gave him a quizzical look. "Remember, I told you that is what the Mayas called their shamans. This *sukai* could be playing the role of the jaguar and delivering messages to you in dream-time. I have experienced many strange things on my travels, and have heard of even more bizarre happenings. Many of those inexplicable events were attributed to a shaman. He seems to be giving you clues. Could the place you dreamed about have been a small cave or hollow?"

"Possibly," Bendi said eagerly.

"Well, I did overhear a rescuer mention about some dens and small caves he discovered further downstream. Let us at least begin there," the professor suggested.

* * * *

Dark, heavy clouds filled the motionless sky as Digger approached the stranger in the quarry, which was now empty of spheres. Dawn was just beginning to pierce the night's blanket. Purposefully, he blinked his eyes in the gloom, trying to get a better look at the stately man sitting before him.

"Hi! I'm Digger," he cupped his hands in greeting. "Have we met before?"

There was no response. Maybe he doesn't understand English. As Digger drew closer, he saw that there was a small sphere in the man's lap which was colored in radiant shades of green and violet. He felt as drawn to it as he did to the man

"*Hola me llamo,* Digger."

"I know very well who you are," the man responded in perfect English.

Digger knew that voice. It was familiar, but he couldn't place it. He watched intensely as the huge man lifted the heavy, soccer-ball sized sphere with ease and placed it atop a nearby boulder. Then dipping a leaf into a bowl, he brushed clear liquid onto the sphere. After several strokes, he unfolded himself from his lotus position and slid down the smooth rock to stand before Digger.

Unlike most of *Los Otros*, he was well over six feet tall, broad-shouldered—and more than a little intimidating. He could have played line backer for the Chicago Bears, Digger thought.

"How are you doing, Jonathan?" he said in a surprisingly casual tone.

Digger could barely see the man's face in the dim light. "Do I know you?"

"My name is Zorinthalian."

A tingling sensation moved through Digger's body. The name triggered a memory, something about that audition night, long ago in Los Angeles, that meditation he never could fully remember. He'd always felt like he visited somewhere that night, in his meditative state. And now he felt that this imposing figure was from that mystical place.

"Yes, you do know me from that place—and many others."

"Uhhhh..." Digger stammered. He just read my thoughts!

The man smiled a broad, playful grin.

"Really, who are you? And where have all the spheres gone? And how did you move them? And when did you move them? And why are you here?" As Digger heard the questions gushing from his mouth, he was actually afraid this "Zorinthalian" might answer—instinctively fearing the man's words could somehow forever shatter his own fragile, glass ego.

"I am helping out," Zorinthalian replied matter-of-factly. "Work needed to be done at this time. You have just imprinted with one of them, so you know some of its effects. I told *Los Otros* that I knew you could do it," he grinned.

"Wait a minute. Are you saying you knew that I was coming here? But all of this was an accident! Having a fight with Bendi, leaving San Diego and coming to Costa Rica, signing up for a river-rafting trip, the raft tipping over, ending up with *Los Otros*... It was all by accident!"

"You know better, Jonathan," Zorinthalian chided. "There are no accidents. Remember that you create everything in your life."

"I know, I know, I've been told that. But still... this is all confusing," he sighed, looking around for mechanical aids or some other evidence of how the spheres might have been moved.

"If you think it is confusing now, just you wait," Zorinthalian teased. He turned around and grabbed the small but heavy sphere; the clear liquid had already hardened into a strong resin-like coating. "This is what I am finishing up, the Heavens sphere."

"I haven't seen that one around." Digger felt a compulsion to touch the small sphere. He studied the intricate lines and thousands of miniscule dots that were engraved into its violet and green surface. None of it looked familiar, yet he had the strongest feeling of déjà vu. "May I touch it?"

"Of course." Zorinthalian handed him the round rock.

Digger's biceps quickly tightened as he grasped the heavy but intriguing sphere. What was so familiar about it? He turned it over in his hands, looking for clues; it was as if he'd written a memo to himself but had forgotten the message—and where he'd put it.

"What is it?" Zorinthalian looked intently at Digger.

"Nothing."

"Tell me," Zorinthalian commanded softly.

"Well, I don't know what to say. I believe that it has something to do with a meditation experience I had several years ago. Something, well, *many* things, that I'm supposed to remember. I feel like you were there— wherever there was. But there's also a key, some kind of symbol that, if I see it, is supposed to help me remember. Trouble is, I don't even know what the symbol looks like. I just have this vague memory that it's sup- posed to exist." He sighed again heavily. "When I first saw the spheres, it triggered this same strange yearning in me. Now as I see you, and also touch this particular sphere, the feeling is a hundred times stronger. I'm frustrated! I feel like it's all here before me, but I just can't see it!"

"Yet," Zorinthalian added compassionately.

"Can you tell me what I'm looking for?" he asked eagerly, as he set the weighty sphere back down on the boulder.

"Sure," the man answered confidently.

Digger waited for him to elaborate, but Zorinthalian just gazed back at him. Digger encouraged irritably, "We-ell..."

"Well, me telling you is not going to bring your memory back. You need to experience it. And like all of the events of your life, you will do so at the right time and in the right place." Zorinthalian chuckled, then added, "Don't give me that long face of yours, Jonathan—it will happen soon enough."

"Well, can you tell me anything? How about this sphere?" Digger begged in frustration.

"This is what might be called a map," the tall man offered.

"A map of what? All I see are tiny little holes and a few thin lines."

"A map of the heavens, of course. That's why they call it the Heavens sphere."

"*You're* the Star Teacher *Los Otros* has been talking about?" Digger's eyes opened wide with amazement.

Zorinthalian nodded, crossing his arms.

Digger's excitement soon turned to bewilderment as the implications of the Star Teacher's presence sunk in. "All of this is like a dream. It's all so confusing."

"Do you remember what you need to do when things are confusing and spinning around?"

Digger just stood there, not answering, feeling overwhelmed.

"I need you to remember," Zorinthalian urged. "*Los Otros* needs you to remember. Everyone needs you to remember!"

"Remember what?" Digger grumbled.

Zorinthalian lightly slapped Digger's arm. It startled him and his eyes widened with shock. What kind of Teacher is this?

"Remember how not to become dizzy," Zorinthalian began reciting. "Remember to look for an immovable force. Remember *Los Otros* and who they truly are and what they stand for. Remember all that you learned here at this village. Remember what is of your past and does not serve your present. The spheres will help you remember.

"And soon there will be Teachers who can help you—some of whom are Keepers of Wisdom. But there are also others, like myself, who can assist you." He looked straight into Digger's eyes. "But in order to survive, you and everyone else needs to *remember*!"

"Believe me, I'm not going to forget any of this. So it's not going to be a problem," Digger said, rubbing his arm resentfully.

Zorinthalian shook his head sympathetically. "Everyone forgets when they come to the physical world. It is understandable, so that is why we created these triggers, which stimulate you to remember. You, as a human race, have temporarily forgotten your past, your connection to everything and everyone on this planet, your connection to the..." Zorinthalian pointed up to the early morning sky. He reached over and placed his hand on the Heavens sphere. "Our people actually created this sphere, when they first came."

"You're getting far out here, Zorinthalian," Digger said with disbelief.

"Yes, and no. Yes, it is far out from your present way of thinking— of being. But no, it is not far out in the reality and vastness of this universe. Now, I'm sure Mashuba gave you his..." with a stone face, Zorinthalian continued in a deep, rhythmic tone, "'dimensions within dimensions' speech."

Digger laughed.

The Star Teacher amiably slapped him on the back and led him over to the lush, vegetation-covered wall. Attached to one of the cracks was a beautiful bromeliad, with its green, succulent leaves and roots dangling in the air.

Digger saw that the bromeliad was partially filled with water and that within it, plant debris was dissolving and decaying. He looked closer and saw snails, wiggling mosquito larvae, and even a few tadpoles.

"Inside there is a universe of its own, so to speak," Zorinthalian stated. "Everything here is living, digesting, excreting, interacting, reproducing, and dying. It is a nutritious mix that feeds the plant.

"Let us say that this plant, the bromeliad, is Earth and the tadpoles are humans. The tadpoles believe they are separate from the rest of the jungle. They say they can prove it. 'Look, we are the only creatures in the water of this bromeliad—oh, except for those slow snails and lowly larvae. Our world is surrounded by air, with nothing else around us except for that piece of rock. But as you can plainly see, that rock has no life.'

"From deep inside the watery plant, the tadpoles can barely see any other bromeliads, nevermind see life within any other beautiful plants. So they proclaim that they are the only living beings in this jungle. And because of that belief, they do not care to explore how they even arrived at their present location within that plant.

"Now you and I, standing here amidst this luscious rainforest, know all of that not to be true. We have been to other parts of the jungle. We have seen other life, with its unique diversity abounding in every corner. We know that these particular tadpoles have only been around for a fraction of a moment within the life of a jungle.

"Those tadpoles do not even realize that they will become wondrous, curious, hopping frogs, who will not only inhabitant the world of water but who will also experience and thrive in the dimensions of air and land. But we were here long ago—at least relative to the tadpoles' time reference—when the first frogs left their offspring within the watery confines of this plant.

"Those original frogs, so to speak, have long since traveled to other parts of the rainforest. But now as the heavens and the earth are in a unique alignment, it is time for them to return. In this reunion, the tadpoles have an opportunity to understand and eventually know their history, their purpose, and their possible futures. All of this can become known to those tadpoles who are curious and adventurous—those tadpoles who care to move beyond their world and see the beauty of the jungle, feel its rhythm, and know its beginnings." Zorinthalian turned to Digger in the early morning light and added quietly, "For if you took a moment from your busy life to look upwards and behold the heavens, you would be able to see your sun as just one of many. If you could extend even further, you would see your Milky Way as just one light. If you could stretch yourself far beyond your self-proclaimed boundaries, the boundaries of your supposed past, you could see this universe as just one sphere of light. Then you would know your journey. Then you would know from whence you came. Then you would know the connection of all.

"For this Earth is a newborn within this galaxy. This galaxy is an infant within the universe. And this universe is a child within all universes."

Digger sat down on a rock and dropped his head into his hands. He was definitely on overload. "I can't take all of this in."

"You can't? That is odd, because it is who you are. It is who I am. It is who we all are." Zorinthalian continued playfully, mocking him, "Oh, you must be speaking about the self-created, limiting boundaries of your mind. Well, then you are absolutely correct. It is true. You cannot take it all in." His arms opened wide to the jungle. "But what about your spirit? You can take everything that has happened to you in your life, in the jungle, this night, and hold it within your spirit. And *still* have enough room to hold several more universes!

"This is a crucial time in your human history," the Star Teacher continued, seriously now. "The earth, the rivers, and the heavens are in a unique alignment, thus creating a place where each is blending into all; when commonalty between worlds, cultures, religions, governments, and businesses can be felt, when, in this moment, the past, present and future can be seen, when from somewhere far beyond, the sweet music of our common destiny can be heard."

Lightning flashed off in the distance, lighting up the waking village below. Several seconds later a thunderous clap rolled over the jungle canopy.

"There is no time for sitting on the fence anymore." Zorinthalian's voice deepened with import. "The road is divided but your path is clear. It is in this moment, that you have to make a decision, that you have to be clear on your intent. Will you move toward the light? Or will you move away from it?"

Digger looked up quizzically at the Teacher. "I'm not sure what you're asking of me. I'm not sure what you want me to do."

"I've already told you. Remember!" The tall man gasped suddenly, turned for a moment, then turned back and said urgently, "It is time for you to go now. I need to finish with the sphere."

"Okay, but before I leave, you have to tell me where the spheres went."

"They are a distance from here."

"But how did you transport them?"

"If I show you, will you go—and hurry?"

Digger nodded and then followed Zorinthalian back to the bromeliad. The Star Teacher put his finger into the water. Digger could have sworn that one of the tadpoles literally jumped onto his finger and clung tightly as the powerful man moved to another nearby bromeliad. As he placed his finger over the water filling the center of the plant, the tadpole slid off and began to swim merrily.

"There. Dimensions within dimensions. I can't be any clearer than that. Now go," Zorinthalian said with a smile as he firmly nudged Digger toward the steps.

Digger shook his head. He wasn't going to try and figure this one out—at least not now. After one last, baffled stare at Zorinthalian, during which he became convinced the man would not allow him to ask any more questions, or even to stay and watch whatever it was he planned to do to the last remaining sphere, Digger turned and ran down the hill, hoping to outrun the rain that was sure to come. But what really drove him was the desire to find Angélica again. The last twelve hours were like a dream, like a whirlwind of events that had catapulted him off his usual world, and he'd been apart from her for too long. He had so much to tell her... but knowing Angélica, perhaps she already knew everything he would say...

When he came to the stream he slowed down to catch his breath. Several dragonflies danced over his head, bringing a smile to his face as he remembered being with her the last time he encountered these elegant, golden-tipped insects. What was it that she'd told him dragonflies represent? Oh yeah, he remembered, illusion and change.

Veiling all in mist, the heavy, blackened clouds cast a dark shadow over the morning village. His nostrils twitched with the tang of fire and smoke. Surveying the village for Angélica, he saw only *Los Otros*, busy with early-morning duties. No one seemed to be paying much attention to the approaching storm as the wind bunched the heavy clouds together. Women were crushing maize atop grinding stones, or cooking over fires, men were carrying water in clay jars, and children were playing tag with the electric blue Morpho butterflies and the jeweled hummingbirds.

Across the way, Digger saw Winauka walking along the cobblestone path and remembered her beautiful story about the wind, and the way she'd helped him with Gutubo. He was pleased to see her young son nearby, smiling and skipping as he chased a dragonfly. He must have made it all the way around Gutubo, Digger thought fondly.

Darant passed him on her way to the stream, stopping for a moment to greet him warmly and tell him that Mashuba was looking for him. "He is in his stone hut, over there," she motioned. Then she took a few steps along the path to the stream. Chucan and Seentar appeared, predictably, and the three lingered to talk while Digger turned back to find Mashuba.

Just then, a cool gust of wind swept through the village as a lightening bolt crashed, eerily lighting the plots of crops. Looking out over the fields, he saw the familiar woman and young boy tilling the soil.

"So, what is *your* name?" a familiar voice blew in from behind him.

Digger turned and stared into Angélica's incredibly luminous green eyes. Smiling, she formally greeted him, *Los Otros* style, cupping her hands and moving through the elaborate gestures. For the first time Digger felt the true spirit of that greeting. "And what is your name?" she repeated, beaming in expectation.

"I am—" he began quietly. And then without another thought, he reverently blew his chosen name into his waiting, cupped hands, "Too-kashaam."

Bringing his cupped hands close to his chest, he felt a tingling, swirling, dynamic energy. He looked deeply into Angélica's eyes, his self-proclaimed name reverberating within his heart. He had no idea where it had come from; its meaning and origin were, at least for the present moment, lost to him. But he extended to her his treasured epithet and then gently brought his arms back. His hands flowered open, as if they were an exquisite orchid opening to the light of stars. He felt the cool breeze sweep his name, "Too-kashaam," from his gentle grasp and shower it throughout the jungle.

"What does your name mean?" Excitement filled her face with light.

"I don't know," he answered. "The name just flew out of my throat."

"Well, I *love* it." She moved closer to him and then in a demure tone said, "The truth is, I—" Her body suddenly tensed and her eyes riveted on the fields behind him. Digger felt a sickness plunge into his stomach as he saw a look of horror and stark terror pass over her presence.

Chapter 25

"Believe it or not, everything is in Divine Order..."

Startled, Digger looked in the direction of Angélica's shocked stare. Hundreds of razor-sharp arrows were hissing through the air, heading toward the Keepers of the Garden and their apprentices. He shouted, but his voice was lost in a clap of thunder. As he and Angelica watched in helpless horror, one of the arrows narrowly missed the little boy who'd insisted on uprooting plants. Instead, it pierced the leg of the woman nearby. She fell to her side without a sound, her blood seeping into the fertile ground. Seconds later, another arrow slipped into the young boy's back, sending him to his knees, then sprawling in the dirt. The rolling thunder muffled the cries of other gardeners as they fell quickly under a hail of arrows—some wounded and screaming in pain, others falling lifelessly to the dirt.

It all happened so fast, Digger didn't have time to react. It was like he was sitting in the front row of a movie theater, frozen in his seat, feeling the action on the screen but not moving because he knew it wasn't real.

Suddenly he felt Angélica's fingers grip his arm and the sensation of her warm and urgent flesh yanked him back to the present. "Run!" he shouted, grabbing her arm and spinning around, looking for a place to take cover.

"No!" she resisted, pulling him the other way. "I have to take you to—" but her voice choked off in a cough as the air around them filled with smoke. The jungle surrounding the village was engulfed in flames as fire danced quickly up the bark of trees and incinerated the rich canopy foliage. And the black, obsidian-tipped arrows kept falling as if from the stormy clouds, plummeting with deadly fury into the heart of the village.

Who was attacking them? And where could they hide? Thoughts rushed frantically through Digger's mind. The world had gone mad—the land, its people, nature—why was Angélica pulling against him? What was she saying? He opened his mouth to yell at her over the din of flames and thunder, but at that moment a short, sharp flash of light burst from the nearby trees, accompanied by a loud popping sound.

Darant, who'd been talking to Seentar and Chucan just a few feet away, was suddenly flying through the air toward Digger and Angélica. Her body fell backwards, spraying blood on him as she fell with a cry at their feet, her left shoulder splayed by a gunshot. Seentar rushed to comfort her friend, stooping to gather her protectively in her arms. Digger looked up to see Chucan standing in shock in the middle of the open pathway.

"Run for cover!" Digger shouted at Angelica as he lunged for the young husband, tackling and knocking him sideways onto the dirt as an arrow narrowly missed them both. Chucan came to his senses and sat up, opening his mouth to say something, when another arrow sunk into his chest. A gurgly noise wretched from his body as air escaped through the puncture in his lungs. That awful sound lodged in Digger's groin, paralyzing him for a moment as Chucan slumped to the ground. Another loud popping sound jolted Digger again as Seentar screamed—and fell suddenly silent. Digger spun his head around to see that she, too, lay slain and bleeding atop Darant's lifeless form.

The rain of arrows stopped. But as lightning and thunder covered the once-tranquil village, red-and-black-painted men set fire to *Los Otros'* homes with burning torches. The cries and wails of death echoed throughout the crater.

"Over here!" Angélica yelled from several yards away, scooping Vawaha into her arms. Digger struggled to his feet and stumbled away at a staggering run. He followed her into a stone hut whose bamboo roof had just begun to smolder.

"Mashuba!" Vawaha cried as she ran to the elder who greeted them inside.

"There is no time. Go in the corner and I will try to hide you," Mashuba commanded. Angélica and Vawaha did as they were told.

"What about you?" Digger asked.

"Believe it or not, everything is in Divine Order. Now go!" Mashuba threw blankets on top of them, shoving several large, empty clay jars into the same corner to make it look like nothing more than a disheveled hut.

From beneath the blankets, Digger could smell the burning roof. He heard Mashuba walking toward the door of the stone hut, then several natives shouting at the elder as they dragged him away from the entrance. Digger held his breath. Any moment, he feared one of the men would run in and jab a spear through the blankets, killing all three of them. He cradled Angélica and Vawaha closer, breathlessly waiting. He could feel their hearts pounding in unison with his. But surprisingly... nothing happened.

Under the blankets several small holes in the wall brought some light to their darkness. They dared not speak, but Digger could see that Angélica's face held an expression that must have been much like his own: two superimposed images dramatically opposed, one of passionate disbelief and the other of pure terror.

The high-pitched outcry of a young boy cut through all the other sounds of horror outside. Digger peered through a small opening to see Winauka's son fleeing down the cobblestone path. A loud popping sound silenced the boy's voice as he catapulted sideways through the air. His life was over before his frail body ever hit the ground. Screaming in anguish, Winauka rushed toward her lifeless son. Digger gasped and turned away after he saw a war-painted native shoot an arrow into her back.

Digger looked through the hole again when he heard Mashuba's voice. "What do you want from us?" The aged wise man was facing in Digger's direction, about forty feet away from the hut, speaking calmly in the dialect Digger had come to understand. Two harshly painted men on either side of him were holding his arms while another swaggered into position before him, obscuring Digger's view. All he could see now was Mashuba's face.

"Who are these people?" Digger hissed in Angélica's ear.

"It is *them*. The ones who have come from our past," Angélica whispered sorrowfully.

The sinewy man yelled something at Mashuba in a language Digger couldn't understand. "What is he saying?" Digger asked softly.

"They want to know the location of the spheres," she mouthed back as quietly as she could.

"Even if you find them," Mashuba was saying with quiet dignity, "they will do you no good. You do not truly know that for which you seek."

The man hit Mashuba across the face and again asked the location of the spheres.

Mashuba did not answer but continued to look softly into the angry native's eyes.

Digger cursed silently, sweating beneath the blankets. *I have to do something.* He began to throw off the blankets but Angélica grabbed his arm, imploring, "Not now! The right moment will present itself," she whispered urgently.

Digger turned his flaming eyes to look into her earnest face and a cooling sensation passed through him. This time he cursed audibly, then turned against the wall in frustration and looked again through the opening. With a sudden cry that cracked through the jungle, the man unsheathed a long knife with a jade-embedded handle. Flashing the weapon before Mashuba, the warrior spewed out angry words that Angélica translated in a whisper, "'The foreigners will not be so kind to you! They will be here very soon! It will be easier for you if you tell *me*.'" Digger felt Angélica's body tremble as she mouthed the words for him and he drew her closer, meanwhile tightening his grip on Vawaha's shoulder. He glanced down at the little girl; she was so terrified she hadn't made a sound, but clung mutely to both Digger and Angélica for her life.

In the flickering from the burning huts, Mashuba stood silently, gazing compassionately at the man waving a knife in front of his face. Infuriated, the man screamed what sounded like gibberish to Digger and drew the blade back to strike. From the jungle, a deep, masculine voice boomed in Spanish, "*Paren!*" The native ignored the command and began to plunge his knife downwards.

Digger, glued in horror to the sight, saw Mashuba turn his gaze impassively. Digger shuddered with the sudden realization that the elder was looking directly at him. Within that gaze, just as he'd felt during the masked dance, Digger sensed the flow of spirit. That river was filled with love, with compassion, with forgiveness. Then, with the same compassion in his eyes, Mashuba shifted his focus back to his attacker just as the knife blade sank deep into his chest.

Digger threw off the blankets, a low, guttural moan sputtering from his throat. Bolting to the hut's entrance, he saw in agonizingly slow, staccato snapshots the carnage before him: Mashuba's knees buckled as his lifeless body collapsed to the ground; sparks flew as a bolt of lightning struck the base of a nearby ceiba tree; war-painted men scattered as the tall, massive tree began to fall; Mashuba's killer's hands, dripping with blood, held aloft in triumph a clump of red, pulpy flesh. Then the enormous tree crashed to the ground, mercifully blocking the grizzly scene.

This isn't real, Digger told himself. It can't be. He stared blankly at the fallen tree—which had narrowly missed the stone hut.

Angélica rushed to his side, Vawaha still clinging to her hand. "What happened?" she asked frantically, "What happened to Mashuba?"

He answered in stunned disbelief. "They took his heart."

"That is what *they* do," Angélica responded fiercely, angry tears forming in her eyes. Vawaha inhaled a single sharp breath, then buried her face in Angélica's side, shaking with sobs.

A sudden thick, hard wall of rain drove into the village, waking Digger from his momentary stupor. Two of the war-painted men were moving toward them. He quickly scooped Vawaha into his arms and shouted, "Let's go!"

"This way!" Angélica countered as she led them through a billowy cloud of smoke, using it as camouflage. Coughing, they side-stepped burning huts, bushes, and trees. The torrential rain gave little relief, and the smothering fires singed their skin. As they fled through the thick haze, they had to jump over several slain bodies of *Los Otros*. This is strange, Digger thought with a twinge of guilt as he gripped Vawaha more tightly and pushed through the choking brush, that in this moment their bodies bring me no grief, no sadness, no tears; they are just an obstacle, something in my way on my path to survival. Maybe that's what these murdering invaders felt about *Los Otros*? How does one get to that frame of mind, he wondered bitterly, of thinking about another person as an obstacle, as something in your way on your road to survival?

When they cleared the fire line, Digger put Vawaha down. Shoving branches and fronds out of their way, Angélica led them through the thickest part of the jungle. Occasionally, they heard the loud popping of gunfire coming from different parts of the village behind them. The wind, thunder, rain, and fire had all diminished the screams of their friends, which came more sporadically now. Several times they fell on soft and muddy ground, but the trio pushed on breathlessly, determined to escape the nightmare. When they stopped momentarily at the crater wall, Digger noticed the rain cleansing his body of Darant's blood.

Quickly they climbed the steep path that had brought Digger to this serene place a week ago. Angélica led the ascent with Vawaha right behind her. As they hurried their way to the top, rocks tumbled off the steep trail into the valley below. Digger glanced nervously back and saw the two warriors, with spears, scrambling up the path. Then he remembered what Mashuba had told him, when he'd fallen down on his way to the quarry, and quickly turned forward to watch where he was climbing. This was no time to stumble.

Just then Vawaha screamed as she slipped and fell, rolling over the edge. Digger dove to the ground and grabbed her arm as the rest of her body dangled in mid-air. Above him, Angélica quickly grasped a rocky ledge and leaned over to clench Digger with her other hand. Keenly aware of their pursuers, none of them made a sound as Digger lay flat on his belly, grimly clutching Vawaha—but her wet, oily skin was causing his grip to loosen. Desperately, he dug his nails into her arm and with one heave pulled her partially onto the ledge. From there, she was able to swing her leg up onto Digger and pull herself up. Silently, they clutched and kissed each other in relief before hurrying to their feet to continue the climb.

A flash of metal caught Digger's eye and he ducked instinctively.

The native's thrown spear clanked into the rocky wall and then rolled over the steep edge. "Go! Go! Go!" Digger yelled as he backed around several steps to face the two painted men who were rapidly closing the distance. The closest man jabbed a spear at him, barely missing his side. Digger quickly walked backwards, keeping his eye on the path, but also on his two assailants. He had to slow them down to give Angélica and Vawaha enough time to make it to the top. There was no room to maneuver; the warrior jabbed his spear again, thinly slicing Digger's thigh.

"I am here to help you," Angélica cried, slipping carefully by Vawaha and climbing down toward him.

"Get to the top!" Digger yelled at her, keeping his eyes on the two men.

Everything was chaos. Everything was spinning out of balance. He took a deep breath and stood firmly facing the man in front. Like a sword, the painted warrior swung his spear toward Digger's side. But instead of moving back, Digger took a quick step forward. He caught the spear's shaft, which sent stinging pain searing through his hands but he kept a firm grip to prevent it from slicing him. The fierce-jawed man lunged and Digger lunged back as both tried to throw their opponent off the trail and into the jungle below. Suddenly Digger lost his footing, stumbling forward and carrying them both precariously to the edge. They wavered for a moment, holding onto the spear for balance. Then Digger's attacker glanced down at the steep wall below them as Digger intensified his focus on the sweating man.

In a flash, he felt the difference of energy between himself, the spear, the crater wall, the attacker, and the path. Taking a deep breath, he went within and found his balance between the tick and the tock—and then let go. Still holding the spear, the man's painted eyes widened in terror as the momentum of Digger's release flung him to his death.

Digger spun quickly and collided with Angélica, who'd been frozen on the path, unable to help. "Move!" he yelled and they ran up the soaked trail toward Vawaha as the other man plunged up the trail after them in a blind fury.

The pouring rain was creating a small stream that rushed down the rocky path making it more treacherous. Digger kept his focus straight ahead, but he could feel the man rapidly closing on them. Sensing he was just an arm's length behind, Digger purposefully dropped to the ground, landing on his side with his back to the wall and kicking his powerful legs forward. He caught the man's leg just as he lunged and sent him plunging toward the valley floor, screaming through the air until he crashed through a tree below. Stunned, 'Digger's first thought was, "The sound of another leaf falling in the rainforest."

He looked up to see Vawaha and Angélica standing still, looking back at him with fragile smiles that broke through his numbness. "We are almost to the top; let us go," Angélica called back to him, "We will be okay once we get through to the other side of the crater wall."

Lightening sizzled above them accompanied by a deafening clap of thunder. Catching his breath, Digger looked down the path and saw that no one else had followed as his heart still pounded from the adrenaline moving through his body. He looked for any signs of the deadly struggle in the village below. The crumbling granite walls still dripped with lush, green vegetation, the waterfall still plunged into the crater floor, the stream still meandered through the once-peaceful village. But the beautiful trees that filled the crater were being threatened by the flames rising toward the now-empty quarry—he still had no idea where its treasures could have gone, or how. A shriek pierced his thoughts and he looked up to see a Harpie eagle gliding on a vortex of hot air. The enormous bird was flying high above the devastation. Only ones who ride the wind can be assured of safety, Digger thought.

A flare of rage passed through him again—it was senseless, this sudden attack on an innocent tribe of people, people who could have taught his world so much about living, people whose only crime was to throw away what had been expected of them by others. People who had created instead what was expected of them by their spirit.

With the rain still pelting down upon him, Digger turned and cautiously ascended the steep path. When he reached the top, a firm embrace met him as he stepped into the dark crevice leading through the crater wall. Angélica's tears dripping on his neck showered him with warmth.

"Are you okay?" he asked gently, holding her out at arm's length so he could see her eyes.

"Do not leave me! " Vawaha cried, grasping Digger from behind.

He bent down and gave the young girl a loving hug. "I'm not going to leave you. Nobody's following us now, so we're okay. " He wiped the tears from her face. "Are you all right?"

Vawaha nodded, her lips quivering. "But if we lose each other, will you find me? Will you promise to find me?" she asked urgently.

"I promise!" he smiled, then looked up at Angélica, "I promise."

He stood up and enclosed the dark-haired woman in his arms. Just as he had with the Love sphere, he found himself sinking, sinking into her loving embrace, sinking into her light. After a moment, he said softly, "I can't believe this is happening. I don't understand."

"I will explain what I know later, after we are safe," she murmured in his ear. "But right now, we must keep moving. Let us go!"

Chapter 26

"So much senseless dying! So much death!"
"No, Jonathan, so much senseless living! Yet so much life!"

Pushing aside moss and vines, Angélica led Digger and Vawaha through the dark, narrow corridor. Just as Digger stepped out into the torrential rain, a loud, crushing explosion filled his brain and he fell forward, his face sinking into the puddled ground.

Choking as he sucked the murky water, he felt two hands grab his shoulders. They yanked him to his feet and threw him into a chokehold. He couldn't see his attacker, but nausea swept through him as he breathed in the man's unbathed stench. Digger's head throbbed with pain. He looked urgently for Angélica and Vawaha, but the hard-hitting blow had blurred his vision. Squinting, he was able to make them out a few feet away, both being held by strangers in loincloths. They were speaking a dialect Digger couldn't understand. Angélica and Vawaha didn't respond. He struggled to get to them as the man holding him tightened his grip, spewing rapid Spanish at the other two men.

Digger couldn't follow the Spanish, but he sensed an attitude of superiority. Now his captor yelled angrily at Angélica, *"Donde estan las esferas de piedra y ora. Donde teneis el oro?"*

She didn't answer him but said in English, "They want to know where the stone spheres are. These two," she jerked her head at the men holding her and Vawaha, "want to have the spheres' powers. That one"—the man holding Digger—"thinks there is gold inside them."

At a grunt from Digger's captor, one of the other two swung a fist and struck Angélica across the face. Digger struggled helplessly against the Spanish-speaking demon—he felt his flesh jabbed by some hard, metallic ornament on the foul-smelling man's body. Digger's efforts were futile. He couldn't get free. "Tell them that the spheres are gone!" he urged Angélica desperately. "Besides, they are not about gold or power!"

The Spanish-speaking man dragged Digger over so he could yell in

Angélica's now-bleeding face, but she remained silent as the rain continued to pour. He then shouted at the man holding Vawaha.

"NO!!" Angélica shrieked, explaining to Digger, "They are going to take Vawaha back to the village and kill her if someone does not tell them where the stone spheres are hidden!"

The loin-clothed stranger dragged the little girl back into the crevice. She kicked and screamed; Digger could hear the terror in her voice and he struggled desperately to get free, which earned him another crushing response from the man whose face he still couldn't see. The man dragged him toward a nearby tree, forcing him away from Angélica. He couldn't see her anymore but he shouted back at her, "If you know where they are, tell them!"

"I can't," she called back, with an eerie tone of calmness. It sent chills down Digger's wrenched spine. "If I do, they will destroy the spheres and then all will be lost. The spheres are *our* only salvation."

"Tell them, Angélica. Tell them," Digger pleaded, his voice choking in frustration.

Angélica's sudden scream pierced his ears and his heart, and Digger felt the muscles of his captor's arm ease slightly. Quickly, Digger reached back and grabbed at the man's head, clutching a beard. He bent over and dropped to his knees, using all his strength to fling the man over his head. They wrestled on the muddy ground. Angélica, somehow broken free from her captor, jumped onto the bearded man, trying to pull him off Digger.

"Get back to the empty riverbed by the rocky bluff! That's your only way home!" she yelled.

As she pulled at the bearded man's arm, Digger was finally able to break loose. He tried to stand up, but the wound on his head was worse than he'd realized. He fell back down on the muddy ground.

Now the man in the loincloth smashed into Angélica, sending her to her knees. The bearded man swung his arm and hit her on the side of her head, knocking her to the ground. Digger fought his way to his feet. In his still-hazy vision, he could see the bearded man brandishing a knife as Angélica attempted to get up. With a howl of rage, Digger lunged through the air to stop the slicing blade from harming her. Angélica's face turned toward him. He tried to see her eyes. God, he wanted to see her eyes! But before he could reach the man, the knife slashed across Angélica's belly, spilling her red blood into the brown, muddy pools of rainwater.

Digger let out a high-pitched wail and smashed into the bearded man, driving him to the rainforest floor, knocking the bloodied knife into the mud. Digger rolled on top of him and flailed his arms wildly, not knowing if any of his punches were landing, just pummeling in grief and fury. He couldn't see anything, couldn't hear or feel anything—only his rage moving his body recklessly.

The other man crashed sideways into Digger, knocking the air out of his lungs and sending him sprawling face down in the mud. The bearded-Spanish man straddled him and pulled his head back by the hair. Digger caught sight of a shiny knife moving toward his throat. "This is it," he thought. "I'm going to die in the middle of the jungle and no one will ever know what happened to me."

Time suspended as he waited for the final blow. Except for his vision, his senses had now heightened. He felt the cool, muddy water beneath him, the zealous heat of the man on his back, the taste of earth in his mouth, the smell of the dank, humid jungle deep in his nostrils.

Would his death be painful? How would it feel as life oozed from his body? Do I really have a soul? Where will I go after death—anywhere or nowhere? He struggled for one final breath when lightening flashed and an explosion of thunder shook the ground beneath him. He then felt a sudden thud as his head snapped forward again into the puddle of muddy water. He gasped for air and realized no one was on top of him anymore! He quickly scrambled to his feet.

Lightning lit up the jungle again and Digger faintly recognized Zorinthalian, yelling, "*Bastante*—Enough!"

The bearded man momentarily stopped, holding something behind his back. The man in the loin cloth let out a whoop and burst toward the Star Teacher. Zorinthalian quickly turned around and kicked him; the man slumped slowly to the soaked ground.

Now Digger's blurred vision caught sight of the bearded man heaving a sword toward Zorinthalian's back. Digger yelled and leaped toward the man. As the sword swiftly sliced downward he knew—like with Angélica—that his attempt would be too late. Flying through the air, his muscles instinctively tensed as they prepared for impact. Then Digger's sight went completely black and he felt a spray of hot blood cover his body. To his surprise, he landed on the ground, missing the bearded man altogether. Quickly turning back, he expected to see Zorinthalian's mutilated body but instead he saw a black jaguar. The wild cat's teeth were firmly imbedded in the bearded man's throat. The creature was shaking its victim's neck and the blood spewed every-where. Then the animal released its hold.

"Go!" Zorinthalian said sharply. Digger didn't know if he was talk-ing to him or the jaguar, but the animal quickly slipped into the opening of the crater wall and disappeared.

Digger crawled clumsily through the slippery mud toward Angélica, whose blood was still draining from her wound. As the rain poured on her face, he wiped the hair away from her eyes. He tried to see in them what he'd seen in the dance circle, but the glow was faint. She moved to speak but no sound left her lips. Digger cradled her in his arms and began to rock her slowly, mumbling comforts. His eyes never left hers as he eased his lips down to kiss her softly. As he withdrew, the faintest hint of a smile passed over her face. Then the radiance in her gleaming green eyes began to diminish. Each moment brought Digger excruciating pain, as if tendons and ligaments linking them together were being severed one by one.

Just before the light in her eyes extinguished completely, her smile became broader. Then those beautiful, spirited orbs stared off to another place.

"No!" he wailed. "No, no! Life is not supposed to be this way! This is not what it's about!" Digger sobbed as the downpour drenched his body.

"Let us go," Zorinthalian interrupted somberly.

Digger felt as if the light, the life, had extinguished within him. He held Angélica's body more tightly. He was faintly aware that Zorinthalian had put his hand on his shoulder. Then he heard him firmly repeat, "We have to go."

"No! Leave me alone," Digger wept.

Prying Digger's hands off Angélica, Zorinthalian gently laid her body on the saturated earth. Still stunned, Digger remained kneeling beside her.

"We must go *now!*" Zorinthalian urged again.

"We can't," Digger replied hoarsely as Zorinthalian pulled him to his feet. Then the realization that Vawaha might still be alive pushed through Digger's shock-numbed consciousness. He turned quickly to the Star Teacher. "We have to find Vawaha! They're going to kill her!"

"No. She is gone. You have to get to safety now. It is more important than you know. It is more important than her life!" Zorinthalian insisted.

"I'm not leaving without her!" Anger filled Digger once again. He plunged toward the crevice. But Zorinthalian quickly caught up and pulled him back, his huge hands spinning Digger's shoulders around. Rain dripped from their faces as Digger struggled furiously to get out from under Zorinthalian's powerful grasp, raging, "We can't leave her! She needs me! I promised her!" Digger's wrath exploded in anguish as he tried to break away. But the muscular Teacher held him firmly until he stopped resisting. Totally exhausted, Digger fell sobbing into Zorinthalian's arms. "So much senseless dying!" he wailed. "So much death!"

"No, Jonathan," the Star Teacher's eyes burned gently into Digger's. "So much senseless living! Yet so much life!" Zorinthalian let go of Digger's shoulders but he held his gaze. "Angélica, Mashuba, and

Vawaha have earned the right to breathe their last breath. Can you say that of yourself?"

Digger looked at him absently as the impact of his words sank in. But the moaning of the man in the loincloth distracted him—he was trying to get up again.

"You have to trust me, Jonathan. We need to leave *now.* This is Angélica's and Vawaha's place and time. Know that their destiny is their own. It has already been written."

Sheets of rain continued to hail down upon them as Zorinthalian dragged him through the rainforest. Digger was out of breath but his vision had finally cleared. The Star Teacher stopped where several huge, Bird of Paradise plants were growing and, reaching between the seven-foot stems that held the boat-like flowers, he pulled out the green-and-violet Heavens sphere.

"This sphere and the others must remain hidden—at least until the proper time," Zorinthalian said urgently and then asked, "Remember where your journey to *Los Otros* began? In the middle of the river, where you were clinging to a round boulder. Do you remember, Jonathan?" The Star Teacher's eyes drilled in as if to implant the knowledge Digger was too distraught to recall. "The riverbed is straight ahead. Nearby you will find the cavern where the other spheres are already hidden. You must place this sphere with the other eleven—it is very urgent that you take this sphere to that place, Jonathan! The safety of these twelve spheres is more important than I can convey to you."

"Wait a minute—where are you going?" Digger said in a stupor.

"I have to be somewhere else. I will try to lead these men away from you. Jonathan, you must be successful."

"You've got to be kidding! This sphere is heavy, nevermind running with it!" Digger was exasperated—and afraid of being left alone. "Besides—there's no such thing as 'straight ahead' in a jungle! I have no idea where I'm going!"

"You will find the strength, I know it. And I have to trust that you will find the way. Keep your focus and remember, those who have been together at this time shall come together again—as souls do throughout time—but they will be scattered and may not remember. That is why you must help them. *Help the others remember.* These spheres will be their triggers."

"I don't understand. What about you?"

"I, along with others, will come back one last time. The Star Teachers thought this could be the time when all of you awakened, but it was not so. We have spent much time trying to assist you in this awakening process but, as always, it is up to you to recognize and then act on the opportunity. We cannot do it for you; we can only assist you in helping yourselves. Trust me. We will try one more time. Be ready, be open."

Branches cracked. They ducked behind the enormous Bird of Paradise plants and waited silently. Moments passed. Then Zorinthalian whispered somberly, "Digger, don't let all that has happened become your focus. Keep your balance through it all. It is at these times, when your world is appearing to be at its darkest, that you must remember: within the same moment, the light has never shone so brightly!"

Zorinthalian's words faded into the distance as the horror of that morning flooded through Digger.

The Star Teacher continued, "Listen, to me carefully: There will be two triggers that will stimulate remembrances within you. They will help define your past, your purpose, and your tasks. Are you listening?" Zorinthalian lightly shook him. "No matter how strange or difficult those remembrances are to comprehend, allow yourself to feel them deep within, and then make a decision from here"—he patted Digger's chest—"about whether, for you, it is true or not. Whatever it takes to allow the ancient knowingness to seep into your consciousness, it is also the key to unlocking your potential. All I can say is that you are much more than you realize."

Before Digger could respond, Zorinthalian gave him a final look of encouragement and then quickly sprinted out from their hiding place. The rain was so heavy Digger lost sight of him after a few short yards. He then saw several silhouettes move in the Star Teacher's direction.

Fear catapulted Digger back into the present moment. As he picked up the sphere, the *déjà vu* sensation he'd had when he first saw Zorinthalian holding it moved through him again. He dismissed the feeling and started a fast trot in the direction the Star Teacher had indicated. How would he ever find his way?

As he ran, a light in the sky caught his attention. It came from the direction Zorinthalian had run. At first he thought it was a flash of light-ning—but it didn't go away. It illuminated the underbelly of clouds moving rapidly in circular spirals. As the glow persisted, the hair on Digger's body stood on end. It never flickered, but created a steady, incandescent brightness. Then it was gone and the jungle was once again thrown into darkness.

He heard another branch break and increased his speed. His arms, back, and shoulders ached but he finally knew—inside—what Zorinthalian had tried to tell him. He had to make it! All of his emotions—anger, fear, terror, rage—funneled into one clear purpose: survival. Survival of the spheres and himself.

After running what felt like miles, Digger stopped. Panting anxiously, he tried to get a feeling for which way to go. But standing in the endless rain only allowed excruciating images of the massacre to catch up with him. He fought off those visions and recalled the dragon-fly—lessons of change and illusion. *Focus, Digger*, he commanded himself. *Focus!*

As he set off again at a trot, not knowing where he was or where he was going, Digger felt a warm, tingling sensation emanate from the sphere. The pleasant prickling moved through his fingers and up his arms and shoulder. After a while, the weight of the sphere began to lessen. But several times it became heavier on one side and he allowed the weight to steer him in that direction.

Still, after hours of struggling through the jungle, he felt entirely lost. Maybe he'd been going around in circles. For a moment, the sun broke through the clouds. Its rays reflected off what looked like shiny crosses in the distance. Digger couldn't make them out clearly, but he could hear the sounds of metal slicing through the jungle. He changed his direction and picked up his pace.

Mercifully, the rain finally stopped, but he could still hear thunder off in the distance. His legs stung with bloody scratches, his back ached and shot ribbons of pain into his buttocks. He didn't know when he'd begun to shiver, but now he felt his teeth chattering.

He heard rustling in the bushes behind him. Quickly he darted behind a fifteen-foot fern tree, peeking between its enormous leaves. Sauntering deliberately toward him was the black jaguar. As Digger's heart pounded, the stealthful animal gazed directly at him and continued its approach. Digger crouched behind the flimsy leaves and peered back at the black feline. He knew he couldn't run anywhere. But thankfully the animal stopped some ten feet away, sitting on its haunches, licking its paws. Then the jaguar looked straight into Digger's eyes. It was a strange sensation, but he felt like the jaguar was trying to speak to him.

He watched cautiously as the black cat slowly walked by him. Without thinking, Digger picked up the sphere and followed the large animal like a beacon—followed wherever it went.

Finally, exhausted beyond endurance, he pushed aside a branch to discover a steep slope—leading, unbelievably, down to the empty river-bed! Digger put the sphere down and stepped carefully to the edge. Below, he could just make out a slice of a dark cavern's shadow winking up at him ominously. Off to his right, the jaguar sat atop a pile of earth and boulders, calmly licking its paws. He stared at the feline and then looked again at the cavern several hundred feet below him. He felt so tired. If he could just rest for a moment.

Digger froze when he realized that suddenly the only sound coming from the jungle was his breath: no chirping birds, no screeching monkeys, no clicking crickets. The jungle had gone deathly silent.

Several leaves fell onto his head. He looked up in time to see the trees shiver as a tremor moved through the jungle. The ground beneath his feet undulated, knocking him down. He snatched at a low-lying limb while all around him, the earth gave way, sliding hundreds of feet down the steep embankment. The Heavens sphere now began to roll toward the new precipice. In a frenzy, Digger struggled to his feet and caught the colorful ball, but it sent him stumbling backwards as the tremor continued. Regaining his balance, he carefully moved away from the newly-formed ridge and watched in awe as a landslide enveloped the cavern far below.

As the last boulders tumbled to the riverbed, the Earth ceased its tantrum. The jungle was once again chatteringly normal.

What was he going to do now? Zorinthalian specifically ordered him to place the Heavens sphere in the cavern with the eleven others.

Digger winced as the pain from his head wound returned. He thought he heard someone. Frantically, he scanned the area for a place to hide. The jaguar, still atop the pile of boulders, was pacing nervously from side to side. Beneath the feline, Digger spotted a shadow that looked like a small hollow. He moved cautiously closer. It was a cave, about three feet wide and seven feet high—big enough to conceal a man, he decided. Pushing aside his fear, he moved directly toward the jaguar. The feline had stopped pacing and didn't flinch as Digger walked into the dark opening.

The musty darkness felt familiar. Didn't he have a dream about this a few nights ago? He couldn't remember. His whole experience with *Los Otros* was like a wonderful dream and a horrific nightmare all wrapped up together. In fact, his whole life back in San Diego felt like a dream. How long had it been since he was there?

He dropped in exhaustion to the dirt and dragged the sphere to the deepest corner of the small cave. There was a kinship. A kinship between the sphere and him, between the earth and him, between the heavens and him. Suddenly he felt as if he were falling into darkness. His plunging soon transformed into a floating—floating to the moon and then to the stars. He could see Orion's belt off in the distance as he sped toward the cluster of stars known as the Pleiades.

Digger was surprised to find himself standing in a large room with tall walls and no ceiling. In front of him, on a frosted glass, oval table, was a crystal the shape and size of a bowling ball. Six of the seven chairs circling the table were occupied by slightly luminescent, human figures. He didn't recognize any of them but knew that he knew them. No words were spoken but he sensed that he was to "sign his name" on the crystal. Lifting his arm, he discovered a strange instrument in his hand. He leaned over and scribbled his signature amongst many others.

Once again Digger experienced the sensation of falling into darkness. He anticipated the pleasant floating of his last experience but instead felt the heaviness of his body—a body infused with pain.

Above the pounding of his heart, he could hear voices. First, they were speaking a native dialect, then Spanish, then English—a woman's voice that sounded vaguely familiar.

From the back of the mildewed cave, where he lay on his stomach next to the sphere, he tried to look out into the dim jungle but his vision had gone blurry again. He thought he saw a man's bare legs with colorful anklets, and other feet covered with some crude material. But he blinked and the feet were now wearing tennis shoes. In fact, the legs were a woman's. Then the lighted opening of the cave grew more blurry, and the voices and images layered on top of one another.

He closed his eyes and tried to take a deep breath. His throat felt parched and he was suddenly famished, as if he hadn't eaten in days. A pain in his right shoulder throbbed as his breathing grew shallower. Cold. He felt so cold. Someone might hear his teeth chattering, he thought, so he curled up around the sphere for warmth. He couldn't think anymore; he didn't want to think anymore. All he could do was let go… and breathe.

Chapter 27

"With the intent of living your soul's purpose you will find... yourself."

Delivering a biting chill into her bones, Bendi heard the rumblings of thunder emerging from somewhere deep within the rainforest. The stifling, humid jungle brought a heaviness to each of her steps as she and Ortega slowly hiked their way up the hill with a *policía* walking behind them—orders from Manuel. The morning was getting late, so she and Ortega had decided to return to where Bendi had last seen the jaguar.

They climbed the rocky bluff a different way than Bendi had taken the previous day. Half-way up, the *policía* yelled *"Esperenza!"* He gestured to several broken branches dangling from the thick, prickly scrub. They looked like they were coated with dried blood.

"Looks like something big and hurt has been dragged through the vegetation," Ortega said breathlessly. "This could have happened three, maybe four days ago. I do not want to worry you, Bendi, but look over there. Those are big cat prints, maybe from the jaguar."

The *policías* walkie-talkie crackled as he notified Manuel about what they had discovered. Bendi could see his team begin to move toward them. "Come on," she urged Ortega excitedly.

A cool gust of wind blew through the narrow valley, bringing them a moment of relief from the oppressive heat, followed by a flash of lightning. Unfazed by the approaching storm, Bendi pushed up the hill, Ortega and the *policía* close behind. She followed the trail to where she'd last encountered the jaguar, scanning the top of the rocky bluff for anything unusual.

Suddenly the jungle became quiet. She glanced nervously at the others. Then she heard a low rumbling in the distance and the ground began to undulate. All around them, trees and bushes were swaying wildly.

Twenty feet below them, a boulder loosened and tumbled down the ravine toward the cavern and stone spheres. Bendi watched in horror as Ortega's students scattered up the opposite side of the riverbank, their shouts and screams echoing upward. The boulder crushed bushes and knocked down small trees before it slammed into one of the largest spheres the students had been examining. The shaking continued for several moments more and then stopped.

Bendi heard Manuel yelling over the walkie-talkie, "Is everyone all right?" The students had rushed over to assess the crashing boulder's damage.

"One of the spheres has a big crack extending half way around," one of them responded.

"I do not give a damn about the spheres!" Manuel barked back. "Is anybody hurt?"

"No, we are fine down here," the student replied.

"That is it," Manuel's voice screeched. "This is too dangerous! The search is over! All search teams immediately return to the cavern area!"

Ignoring Manuel's orders, Bendi walked toward the pile of boulders atop the rocky bluff where the jaguar had been sitting yesterday. She suddenly came to a halt. Her heart began to race and she felt goose-bumps moving up and down her spine. Something was happening. Becoming dizzy she quickly turned and saw Ortega rubbing his hands over his arms and the *policia* turning from side to side, as if looking for an unseen enemy. The scene in front of her kept changing—rocks, trees, and foliage seemed to move back and forth. Then a hazy image darted into her peripheral vision and she heard faint voices speaking Spanish and another language she'd never heard before.

The ground raced toward her face as she felt Ortega's hand grabbing her shoulder. Regaining her balance, she held onto him for a moment until her vision cleared.

"*Gracias,*" she mumbled. "I felt as if I was falling then everything became blurry. Did you see what I saw?"

"I do not know what was before me," Ortega answered. "It was strange. Things seemed to change before my eyes."

"Did you hear voices?" Bendi asked hesitantly. Ortega nodded. The *policia,* his rifle off his shoulder, was still looking around cautiously. She could hear Manuel shouting over the radio to get down from there. The *policia* motioned for them to comply, looking relieved at the orders.

"No, I'm staying," Bendi told him defiantly in Spanish.

"Bendi, we should go," Ortega urged gently.

"No! You felt something, too, besides the aftershock, didn't you? We can't go now! Digger's somewhere close, I know it."

"Another aftershock could send the whole hillside tumbling down. As much as I hate to admit it, Manuel is right. We should get down."

"*Vamanos!*" the *policia* called impatiently.

Bendi glared at him and started to argue with Ortega, but stopped instead and slowly turned to see the jaguar leap from the underbrush to the top of the boulders. As the *policía* raised his rifle to shoot, Ortega stepped in his way.

Repeatedly, the black feline looked down and then back at Bendi. She followed its gaze to see a small, darkened opening among the pile of earth and rocks, about three feet high and wide. She told herself there was no time to be afraid. She moved cautiously closer.

Now the jaguar held her gaze fiercely—then turned slowly and leaped back into the jungle. Bendi hurried quickly to the opening and dropped to the ground to peer inside. It was a small cave. *The one I dreamed about several nights ago,* she smiled to herself. Fearing snakes, she grabbed a nearby stick and gingerly probed the darkness. She chuckled at herself. *It's okay that I was just face-to-face with a jaguar, but God forbid I find a snake.*

Soon her eyes adjusted to the darkness and she saw a silhouette in the corner. Her heart raced as she crawled closer.

"Help me! It's Digger! He's here!" A heartfelt sob swelled up and out of her as she scrambled over to cradle the unconscious figure in her arms.

Ortega squeezed his portly body into the cave's opening and helped her move Digger carefully into the daylight. Her tears of relief were splashing freely onto his withered face as she pressed closer to listen for a breath. "He's breathing—barely—but he's breathing." His frail body was covered with hundreds of insect bites. Dried blood stained his T-shirt and surrounded a cut on his head and left arm. She smothered his parched lips and forehead with kisses. "Digger! Digger, you're alive. Please come back!" Ortega signaled the *policía* to bring water.

Far in the distance, Digger heard Spanish-speaking voices and then, again, the familiar woman's voice. He tried to open his eyes, but the light brought a sharp pain. When he could finally see, he thought he must be dreaming. Bendi's face was hovering over him, breaking into a slow smile. A stranger pressed water to his lips. "Ben —" he tried, but couldn't talk. The words coagulated in his parched throat and dry, sticky tongue. He didn't have the energy to try harder.

"Ssshhh," she hushed, taking the canteen herself and giving him more water. "Just drink. You're going to be all right," she smiled.

I'm back—I made it back, he realized groggily. But a nagging thought began in the distance of his consciousness. It was quickly accompanied by strong emotions that screamed into his present reality. "They're coming!" he tried to shout in Spanish. "They've got machetes, swords, and guns!"

He tried to get up but Ortega gently pushed him back down. Manuel and more *policías* came running up the hill at that moment, rifles in hand.

"Who has guns?" Manuel demanded.

"*They* do! *Los Otros* needs help. Go! They have already killed Angélica and Mashuba! We have to try to save Vawaha," Digger gasped out in a raspy voice. Again, he tried to struggle to his feet, but he quickly collapsed into unconsciousness.

"He is delirious," Manuel pronounced, looking at Bendi.

"Maybe—but what if he's telling the truth?" she countered.

Manuel shouted orders to the *policías* to look for any signs of *banditos*. With rifles drawn, they moved further up the hillside. Meanwhile, the rescue medic was checking Digger's vital signs. He turned quietly to Manuel. "Call in a helicopter from San José, *ahóra*!"

Ortega asked the question Bendi couldn't, "Is he going to be all right?"

"I do not know, *señor*," the medic replied cautiously. "This man is in very poor condition. It looks as if he has not had anything to eat or drink in days. And look here." He pointed to several holes in Digger's bloodstained T-shirt, then gently slid it off his right shoulder to reveal several deep puncture wounds front and back, surrounded by bright red, inflamed skin. "These wounds are infected. They look like a bite from a very large animal. But the wounds or infection are not the big problem—dehydration is. We need to get him to a hospital, quickly. His kidneys and bowels have probably shut down."

The whirl of the landing helicopter sent birds flying in every direction. They'd carried Digger to the riverbed so the chopper could reach them and now Bendi covered his face with her body to protect it from swirling debris.

A swishing noise slowly brought Digger back to a waking consciousness. He again felt an insatiable thirst as he saw Bendi's worried smile. She delicately lifted his head and trickled water between his cracked lips onto his swollen tongue. He remembered the water tasting delicious just before he drifted away again.

Ortega touched Bendi's arm and pointed up to the rocky bluff. The black jaguar stood there majestically, his chest thrown high. She remembered a dream she'd been having that morning, which Ortega had interrupted. The jaguar was speaking to her, asking what she'd do after she found Digger. Its last words were cut off when she awoke. She remembered only, "With the intent of living your soul's purpose, you will find—" The missing word came to her now: *yourself.*

Nodding, she smiled gratefully up at the mysterious cat.

As the helicopter lifted off, Bendi took one last look at the rainforest below. It was a strange place, filled with life and death, questions and answers, colors and shadows. She looked back toward the rocky bluff, but the jaguar was gone from its perch; it had slipped back into the camouflage of the jungle—alone. Silently, she thanked the beautiful creature for all of its help, although she knew she'd never really understand how or why it came to be.

She turned her attention back to Digger as the paramedics slipped tubes and needles into his ravaged body.

"Don't worry," Ortega patted her arm. "To outsiders, Costa Rica might seem a 'third-world country,' but it is one of the best when it comes to medicine."

"I hope so," was all she could say.

Chapter 28

"They didn't want the truth...
what they really wanted was a story that would fit
the boundaries of their world, their perceptions."

The first twenty-four hours were the most critical, the doctors in San José told Bendi, so she'd spent that first night outside Digger's room in the Intensive Care Unit. She watched helplessly as medical personnel moved in and out, setting up IV lines and a catheter tube, drawing his blood, giving him antibiotics, and checking his vital signs throughout the night. She was grateful when they finally moved him to a private room; she could be at his side. But now it had been three days since they rescued him and Digger was still unconscious.

A few times he'd started to come to, blurting out half-sentences about stone spheres, and the tribe he called *Los Otros*, the massacre he'd been trying to describe to rescuers, and something very strange about "imprinting." Bendi couldn't make sense of any of it. The doctors tried to sound optimistic when they talked to her, but she overheard enough Spanish to know they were concerned about brain damage because of his lengthy dehydration.

She spent most of every day at Digger's bedside. Ortega visited several times, dropping off some archaeological books for her to read. When she'd called the States, Digger's brother Jeff wanted to hop a plane right then, but she talked him out of it. There was nothing he could do, she told him. She also broke the news to Digger's agent, and her own family and friends—all of whom were very worried, as much about her, in a strange country with an injured boyfriend, as they were about Digger. She reassured them that everything would be okay. Privately, she wished Digger would give her some sign confirming that. She sighed and rubbed tired eyes, tying her long hair in a knot at her neck. Then she heard a moan from the bed.

Digger's eyelids fluttered. "Where am I?" he asked in a raspy, weak voice.

Bendi rushed to kiss his blistered lips. "Thank God you're awake!" she breathed in tearful relief. "You're in a hospital in San José." She gently squeezed his hand, then pushed the nurse call button.

Digger's voice was barely audible, but she could hear his urgency. "Did you find Vawaha? Is she still alive? Did any of *Los Otros* survive?"

"Shhh," she tried to quiet him. "No, they haven't found anyone yet. The *policías* searched the whole area and didn't find anyone or any signs of trouble."

A doctor stepped quickly into the room and said cheerfully, "*Pura vida, señor* Taylor." She looked at Digger's charts, then began examining him. "It is a good sign that you are awake. The antibiotics seem to be working. Better than that, your kidneys have begun to function again. We will continue giving you fluids." She aimed a pinpoint light into his eyes. "Do you know how you got here?"

Digger squinted in the painful light. Stifling his grief and horror, he tried to describe his escape from the massacre—leaving out everything about his friends and their deaths; that was simply impossible to think about right now. And he knew he couldn't tell the doctor about Zorinthalian or his orders to carry the small sphere to the cavern. Instead, he told her how he'd crawled into a cave to hide from his pursuers. His heart started to beat faster as he remembered his flight, and the ones left behind...

"You are safe now, Mr. Taylor," she interrupted. Bendi gave her a worried look. "For now, I recommend that you rest as much as you can. Your body needs much recuperation."

Digger smiled faintly at Bendi. Then exhaustion overtook him and he quickly drifted off to sleep.

The doctor turned to Bendi. "I am encouraged. Let us see how he does in the next few days."

"But why is he still delirious? He's still telling these crazy stories..."

"High fevers stemming from severe dehydration can create confusion, excitability, and even hallucinations. Upon awakening, some patients believe their hallucinations to have been real. This usually goes away with time. We will know more in the next few days but everything seems to be pointing to a full recovery." She gave Bendi a reassuring smile.

* * * *

With each passing day, Digger felt physically better but he grew more depressed. Scenes of the massacre and Angélica's death replayed continuously in his mind. If he tried to talk about any of it, the doctors and nurses merely nodded their heads in feigned empathy—while Bendi looked pained and concerned. So he stopped talking. Finally, he was able to convince Bendi that he'd be okay, and that she should spend more time at her hotel, getting some much-deserved rest.

But she was at his bedside one morning when a portly man peered into his room. She introduced him as Ortega, the archeologist who'd been such a help to her during the search.

"*Hóla,* Digger. You are a very lucky man to be alive—and also to have such a woman," he beamed at Bendi. She blushed. "She has told me bits and pieces of your experience in the jungle. I was wondering if you would tell me more," he asked, getting right to the point.

"Why would you want to know?" Digger shrugged. "The doctors say I've suffered from dehydration, a high fever, and hallucinations. None of it really happened." He raised a sarcastic eyebrow.

"People also conclude that I am a little *loco,* so I believe that you are in good company," Ortega laughed. He pulled up a chair and placed it at the foot of the hospital bed. "I am not medically qualified to say the conditions of your health, but from the little I have heard, I believe there is much more of interest in your story."

Digger scrutinized Ortega carefully as the professor explained his life-long passion in working with the stone spheres. He said he was planning to attend a conference soon at which the newly discovered spheres would be a topic of great importance. For this reason alone, anything Digger could tell him might be of significance.

Digger noted that the man had a certain disarming charm, even though he seemed a bit eccentric. But he was the only person who didn't look at Digger as if he were nuts. Plus, if he was ever going to tell anyone the story, shouldn't it be someone with a passion for the spheres? Mashuba, Angélica—they tried to tell him how important the spheres were... it's what they died for, after all... Digger cleared his throat. "Bendi tells me you found spheres scattered along the riverbed," he said slowly. "Did you find any in the cavern?"

"Only one," Ortega responded.

"And how many were in the riverbed?"

"Ten."

This puzzled Digger. All eleven should have been inside the cavern where Zorinthalian said they'd be. And he'd seen the landslide himself, the earthquake that sealed and buried the cavern just before he hid in the cave. But before he explained all that, he blurted the question no one else would listen to—the burning question: "Did you find the twelfth sphere? The one I was holding in the cave where you found me?" He held his breath.

"No." Ortega seemed surprised. "Nothing else was in the cave but you." He glanced quickly at Bendi. She shrugged.

What happened to it? Digger worried. His stomach clenched suddenly as he remembered the Spanish-speaking voices he'd heard. What if they'd found him, left him to die, and took the sphere? He tried to cover his anxiety with another question. "The spheres in the riverbed—they all had luminescent colors and geometric symbols and codes, right?"

"What?" Ortega's eyes lit up. "No—they are plain granite, like all the others discovered over the last seventy years. What do you mean?"

Bendi, remembering her first dream of the colored balls, joined in. "You mean they were painted?"

"Sort of," Digger answered evasively.

"I have only heard legends of the spheres you talk about," Ortega interjected. "Can you tell us where you saw such spheres?"

"In the quarry, next to the village," he mumbled, lost in thoughts.

Bendi looked worried, but Ortega's face was flushed with excitement. "Go on," he urged, "tell us more."

"But they should have been in the cavern. At least, that's what I was told." He looked at Ortega urgently. "They're real, you have to believe me," he implored. Mashuba's dying look—pure compassion—flashed in his mind. "You must help them! You have to go back and search for survivors! *Los Otros* needs our help... we need theirs!"

"Wait," Ortega patted Digger comfortingly. "We will try to help everyone. But we are getting ahead of ourselves. Let us start at the beginning. Please—tell me everything that happened—where you were, who you met, what happened, how you found these colored spheres you speak about."

Digger nodded. He was ready. If it would help *Los Otros*...

The professor stood up, pulled a small tape recorder out of his pocket, and placed it on the nightstand near Digger's head. He returned to his seat and waited eagerly.

Digger told them everything he could remember about his adventure in Costa Rica—everything except his growing love for Angélica, and hers for him. He would tell Bendi about that alone—as soon as he could find the right words and keep the lump out of his throat. But now he just wanted them to find Vawaha—or anyone else still living.

Up to this point, all Bendi had heard were Digger's feverish ramblings. But after hearing his story's elaborateness, she realized that whatever really happened, Digger had a complete conviction that everything he'd just told them was true. But what stunned her the most was her déjà vu experiences the whole time Digger talked about the little girl. It was as if Bendi knew what Vawaha would say or do a second before he spoke it.

Digger continued to tell them as much as he could until he was completely exhausted, mentally and physically. But it felt good, finally, to talk about it.

Bendi sat there speechless.

Not Ortega. "That is incredible!" he stood up excitedly. "I am not a doctor, but I do not think you could call what you just told us as the delusions of someone who was sick with a high fever. It is either the most lengthy, specific, yet grandiose dream ever told—or it did happen. I want to believe you!" He paused in thought for a moment. "But some major discrepancies exist between your story and what we know, at least so far.

"For example, you describe twelve spheres with colors and designs intricately painted onto their surface. And yet we have found only eleven which are plain granite, like the others discovered in Costa Rica. You say you brought the twelfth sphere—the Heavens sphere, is that correct?" Digger nodded. "And you carried it with you into the cave. But it is not there now. You fear someone could have taken it from you when you were unconscious?"

"Yes," Digger replied anxiously.

Ortega began pacing the room. "Then there is your epic chronology of a week's worth of travels—but the medical facts indicate that you were unconscious for a week, that you had not eaten or drunk anything, and that your body suffered from lying on the ground for a long time. The puncture wounds in your shoulder seem to be from a large animal, maybe from the jaguar. It is possible it dragged you up the slope and into its burrow, perhaps as food for later, although that is unusual behavior even for a jaguar. Or more unusual, the animal could have been, in some mystical way, trying to protect you. That is totally up for speculation." Ortega seemed to take delight in this unorthodox reasoning, but he went on, returning to his role as a serious, investigative scientist, "Finally, while you have been recuperating, the *policías* have searched the entire area and found no signs of any people, village, or any such struggle as you describe." He added quickly, "I hope you do not think that I am challenging what you have told me, but these are the discrepancies that we must resolve."

As Digger pushed himself up to a sitting position, he remembered he'd always been thirsty and also how he'd felt a sharp pain in his shoulder during his last few days with *Los Otros*. Could it have anything to do with—but that didn't make any sense to him. He sighed, "Well, just as much as people are confused by my story about *Los Otros*, I'm confused by doctors saying that I was unconscious for a week, and the police saying they can't find the village—or its destroyers!"

"The rainforest is a big place," Ortega offered, "so we could have missed something. But another major point is that there are few indigenous tribes left in all of Central America, and none of them reside in Costa Rica! No one has ever heard of a tribe named *Los Otros*—except for a few pioneering archaeologists like myself." Ortega stopped and smiled as Digger digested his words.

He went on, "As I have told Bendi, I spent much time with the tribes of the Brazilian rainforests. They share in common a myth about a tribe of outcasts who lived in the 'cradle'—you would call that Panama and Costa Rica. These outcasts left their villages, the story goes, because they didn't believe in the traditional ways of their people, gods or religions. They gathered together eventually, like an underground movement that went on for centuries. It was believed they had special powers, and wise Teachers who helped them. Supposedly, these special powers came from the stone spheres—stone spheres with strange markings etched onto their surface." He paused again while his words worked their dramatic effect. Digger listened intently. "What intrigues me—and makes me take your story seriously, Digger—is that our most recent discoveries in Guayabo and Teotihuacan include several paintings we have uncovered. They are crude representations of *multi-colored* spheres.

"Up to now, all we have had are the Brazilian legends. But the paintings give us 'written proof,' in a way of speaking."

"So why has there been no evidence of this tribe before now?" Bendi truly wanted to know. She desperately needed some facts to validate all of her "insights."

"I believe the reason is simple," Ortega replied. "As in any civilization, the presiding rulers try to—how would you say?—*squelch* any hint of something different, of something they might perceive as a threat to their power. In a way it is trying to create a historical amnesia. So I believe that these ancient rulers probably banned any mention of this tribe you call *Los Otros* and tried to destroy all evidence of them. Throughout Central America and the Yucatan, we have found faint traces of engravings that have been 'erased,' more or less. That might have been done by early vandals—but why go to so much trouble when there were treasures to be pillaged? No, what I believe is that they were particular writings, maybe of *Los Otros,* that frightened the Maya, Aztec, and Inca rulers who ordered them to be eliminated. It is like the Church destroying Mayan writings, or hiding away other cultures' controversial books, findings, and manuscripts in dark rooms of the Vatican. Even now in our society and yours—you remember the missing seven minutes of your President Nixon's tape recordings? Or the missing memory of your president about his escapades in the Oval Office? Sorry to say but it is human. Do not many of us 'forget' about certain times of our past?"

Ortega rubbed his hands together eagerly, pulling a chair close to Digger's nightstand where he changed the tape for the third time. "Your experience has brought up a very intriguing question, Mr. Taylor. What if, right now, descendants of *Los Otros* are living in the Costa Rican jungle? What if I could talk to them and record their stories and legends? We might be able to unravel the mystery of the stone spheres, once and for all. We might even learn about their belief in help coming from the Star Brothers—or as you call them, Star Teachers."

"You mean people actually know about Star Teachers?" Digger's eyes widened.

"Of course," Ortega shrugged. "That belief is very common among all cultures, from the beginning of time, you could say. You will find it documented in writings and pictographs, and discussed throughout archaeological studies—and several other disciplines. In fact, it is still common today, although my colleagues like to argue with me that it is not the same. But look at all the information that is now being disseminated about them, the movies, the books, the cartoons—pictographs, no?"

"I don't mean to be the skeptic," Bendi piped up, "but is there any proof? I mean, all we have are legends, beliefs, and writings…" She was trying to be open, but Star Teachers? Wasn't that a little much?

"Well, if you do not think those are proof, if you are asking me to show you the propulsion system of a space ship, I cannot—although many people have made diagrams… But if you think that our governments have told and shown us everything that they know about these things, I would have to say with much fervor, they have not.

"But let us put aside the Star Teachers, for now. Digger, if there is even the slightest possibility that *Los Otros'* descendents are out there, I must pursue it. But I need your help. When you are recovered, will you come with me to find their village, to look for survivors?"

Scenes of the massacre rose before Digger's eyes, interspersed with moments he and Angélica had shared. He shivered involuntarily. "I don't know…" he replied. "Can I let you know?"

Ortega looked crushed—it clearly wasn't the answer he'd been hoping for. Bendi looked at them both sympathetically.

"Maybe I'll feel differently later…" Digger mumbled, settling back into his pillows. "It's been a very long afternoon. Would you mind if I sleep for a little bit now?"

Bendi stood up quickly. "You're right. We shouldn't have kept you up so long. Ortega, let's leave him to his rest." She gently ushered her disappointed friend toward the door, but before they disappeared Ortega stopped and turned back to Digger.

"I am sorry if I have overtired you. Please forgive me. But please also think about what I have asked. Think about what *Los Otros* would want…"

As soon as they were gone, Digger got up and shuffled into the cool darkness of the bathroom. He turned on the light and leaned on the sink.

Thoughts and feelings tumbled through him as he stared at himself in the mirror. It might be easier to just deny it all. It had been over a week since they'd found him and with each passing day, the events seemed more dreamlike. He touched his face in the mirror. Was he real? Which of him was he talking to? The man in the mirror, or the one leaning on the sink? He chuckled sadly, "Don't get too crazy, Digger."

Suddenly exhausted, Digger flipped down the toilet seat and sat, breathing deeply. Who am I kidding? I can't lie—at least not to myself. If I deny any of it, that's like saying the lives and deaths of *Los Otros*—of Angélica, Mashuba, and the others—didn't mean anything. A vision of Vawaha suddenly loomed before him. *Don't leave me!* he heard her young voice pleading. *Los Otros* was now as much a part of him as his arms and legs—maybe more.

He turned off the light and cried quietly in the dark.

What would Los Otros want?

Chapter 29

"... yet another of the wind's many currents touched her with one of its truths. A truth that was ready to be born."

Digger looked out the helicopter window and saw below flocks of multi-colored birds flying over green, yellow, and purple trees. He and Bendi were flying to the tent encampment in the old riverbed, near the cavern, where Ortega's students were preparing studies of all the spheres.

Ortega had called the hospital, insisting that this trip would answer many mysteries for them. Digger had tried to calm the ebullient archeologist, hoping for more information before he and Bendi agreed to the trip. But all Ortega would say was that he had several surprises, and something about new discoveries.

This new friend of Bendi's was definitely eccentric, Digger chuckled to himself but then sighed as he tried to shake off his anxiety about returning to the jungle.

At least this would give him an opportunity to spend some time with Bendi before they returned to the States. He needed to explain things to her; he just didn't know how yet. Guilt still swarmed within him.

Bendi had wanted from him what he wanted to give to Angélica. But Bendi had done so much for him. She found him, for God's sake! If it hadn't been for her, he might not be alive. But he'd felt guilty so many times for so many things.

"I'm tired of it. No more," he mumbled to himself.

"What did you say?" Bendi shouted above the roar of the helicopter's whizzing blades.

"Nothing," Digger shouted back, embarrassed by his unconscious slip.

As they landed, Digger glanced over at her. He had the sudden strange sensation that the Bendi beside him was somehow different than the woman he'd left in San Diego.

"We arrive," the pilot announced in broken English.

Digger stepped out of the cramped cockpit to the familiar bellow of howler monkeys. 'Aaaarrroooo-ooo-oo-gaahhh'—the loudest sound in the jungle, he'd been told. His emotions roiled as he looked down the ancient riverbed which had once held the raging floodwaters of the Río Pacuare, the waters that had swept him deep into the jungle with Angélica three weeks ago. But now the cavern and the strewn spheres were the only remnants of the deathly struggles that had changed his life so drastically, and ended hers.

Digger cleared his throat abruptly, relieved to see a short, middle-aged man in a large-brimmed hat approaching them.

"*Pura vida,*" he called out, then continued in English, extending a hand. "My name is Juan. This is all very exciting, no?" he bubbled.

"What is?" Bendi inquired.

"Oh—Ortega has not told you?" The man looked puzzled, gazing into each of their faces. "I am sorry," he apologized, "I thought you knew."

"Knew what?" Digger was annoyed.

"I am sorry, but if I tell you, the professor will"—Juan made a slashing gesture across his throat. "You know how Ortega likes to tell his stories. He is at the cave and is anxious to see you both." He pointed above the cavern to the top of the rocky bluff.

Digger and Bendi watched as Juan disappeared amidst the numerous students who were busy measuring the ley lines of the spheres.

"So how long do you think he'll keep us in suspense?" Digger wondered, his irritation growing.

"With Ortega, who knows? His surprise could be anything, and it depends on if it's of this world or another," she grinned.

Digger relaxed a little as he laughed at her joke.

Bendi was glad to see a smile on Digger's face. She hadn't seen that for a long, long time. But it soon turned to a frown as he stopped and touched one of the spheres they passed as they made their way down the riverbed.

"It's okay, Jonathan. It'll be all right," Bendi said compassionately and then added, "Is there anything you want to talk about?"

Digger didn't hear her words. He was seeing again the horror of Mashuba's murder. *They took his heart,* he lamented. But not his spirit, came another thought quickly. He remembered the look of forgiveness and understanding that had filled Mashuba's eyes in those last seconds.

Then he heard the echo of Angélica's words, "To live to the fullest, you need to reflect on what thoughts, emotions, and actions of your life brought you to this moment. That reflection can unlock the mystery of the present." A short-lived smile came to him, until he felt the heavy, dull ache of grief sink into his gut again.

Overwhelmed by a new sense of loss, he looked around and saw Bendi gazing at him expectantly. She was waiting for him to say something. What had she been talking about?

"I'm sorry. Did you ask me a question?" He'd been so accustomed to shutting her out.

She lightly touched his arm. "One day, Jonathan, I hope you will talk to *me*, tell me what you *feel* about all you've been through. But not now." She smiled. "You have all the time you need."

She was actually grinning, he realized with surprise, as she turned and started the climb up to the bluff. She had definitely changed.

Alone now, he decided not to follow right away. Instead, he walked into the cavern where he stared absently at the seven-foot sphere. He'd only been able to see the top of it before the monstrous wave had engulfed him, sweeping him out of the cavern and down the flooded river.

Almost to the top, Bendi settled onto a boulder and gazed out over the richness of the rainforest. She realized now how much she had covered over the "real Bendi" with the façade of the fearful and needy child. What she really needed was a personal excavation! She smiled at the thought.

Every new internal discovery challenged her beliefs, her relationships, her career, her dreams—but she loved it. She had so much to tell Digger, but she knew he needed time to be alone with his thoughts. Maybe she did, too. She'd reached a major crossroad in her life. A decision had to be made. And she was petrified.

She breathed in the magnificent scene before her as the evening sky made its preparations for sunset. For the first time she realized that, without certain ingredients such as the horizon, the winds, the clouds, sunrises or sunsets would always look the same. What created the beauty was the contrast—the contrast of nature's various elements and the rhythm to which they flowed.

Now she could see Digger climbing toward her. Surrounded by the jungle, hills, spheres, mountains, and sky, the scene transformed with every step he took. Everything before her was changing; *she* was changing. And because she had changed, what she thought she had wanted for herself had changed.

A wind swept across her face and then gently subsided. With the touch of that breeze, Bendi knew that she would not only survive the death of all her illusions and false personas, but that she would learn from them. She could feel those old perceptions of herself transforming their energy into something more beautiful, more real, more lasting, more truthful, more truly *her*.

From a different direction, another of the wind's many currents touched her with one of its truths. A truth that was ready to be born.

Digger sat down beside her. "I'm sorry I was so quiet back there," he apologized. "I know you've been patiently waiting for me to open up about my experiences. You're right about me holding back, there are things that I have to tell you—that I *need* to tell you about my time in the jungle, about the spheres, about *Los Otros...*" A mixed bubble of pleasant memories and grief began in his chest and moved into his throat. "About the people I met and how I've changed because of them..." Digger choked on his words. He looked helplessly into Bendi's eyes. "But I can't yet. As soon as I'm able, I promise you I will."

Bendi reached over and patted his hands, then held them in hers for a moment.

"You know, Jonathan, you're not the only who's been keeping secrets." Bendi smiled at his surprise. "I know how many times I was angry at you for holding things inside and how much I complained. I felt that you were afraid of being hurt, like you were by your mother. Well, I was also angry at myself—but the joke is, I'd been keeping my secret so hidden I didn't even realize the truth myself until I came to Costa Rica!

"You see, when I was little, I had what they sometimes call 'a gift.' I could see and feel things that other people couldn't. But when I talked about my dreams or insights or precognitions, my parents and later my friends would put me down. It was done by a word, a glance, a gesture, or even by silence. I don't believe they meant to hurt me, but nevertheless it was done in a way that told me to 'step in line, be quiet, don't be different.' And I eventually obeyed."

Her words caught him by surprise. "I didn't know," he said, turning to see her eyes.

"How could you? When I was young, I shut it down and kept it inside, denying it myself. Even though that gift never left me, even though that gift is in each of us, I forgot it was there. But when we were looking for you, searching for you, I discovered it all over again. It began with my dream about the stone spheres before I left the States. And then, because I trusted my dreams, my intuition or whatever you want to call it, more came. They led me to the jaguar and to you. But it was more than just trusting those feelings—it was that I *acted* on them!" Her face glowed with pride.

"It was a battle, though. And the fight wasn't so much in confronting others' criticism or put-downs—that's always going to be there. The fight was with myself. Me battling me. Me trying to overcome my own feelings of discomfort, silliness, and even stupidity for acting on such illogical, emotional, unproven feelings. But as the search continued, my intuition proved to be correct. It was a miracle. My own miracle. Ortega was right."

"About what?" Digger queried.

"The first day I met the professor he told me that many times the treasure we find is not always the one we're looking for. I always thought that treasure was you," she grinned, "but really, it was myself!

"I'm different now," she went on. "I don't even pretend to understand how yet, but that's okay. I do know that there are many things about this universe, about me, that I can't even imagine. Then there was the time, after searching for you all day, that Ortega showed me another side of the jungle—he let me experience the rainforest at night. It was a magical place, filled with the possibilities of fairies and dragons and angels and love—I was ecstatic because I saw this world as the kind of place I want to be living in; a place where the potential for different ways of being is unlimited!"

She turned to him enthusiastically, caught up in the excitement of self-discovery. "There are so many new things I've learned about myself, I don't know how to tell you all of them. For instance, I realized I was such a needy child for my father's attention and love, and I've carried that over with you... and then I've experienced incredible *déjà vu* every time you talk about the little girl of *Los Otros*—Vawaha. There's something more for me to learn about her, and her people, and their way of life... Digger, I don't know how to say this other than to just blurt it out: I've decided to stay," she concluded emphatically.

Digger stared at her in complete bewilderment.

Breathlessly, she explained, "I'm staying here in Costa Rica. Ortega has offered me a six-month archaeological fellowship through the *Universidad*. I'll leave tomorrow morning to settle things with my school, family, and apartment in the States, but I'll be coming right back."

Digger didn't know what to say. He was stunned.

"Surprised?" Bendi asked.

"More like in shock."

"There you are!" Ortega called as he climbed down from the cave above them, huffing and puffing. "*Pura vida*," he bellowed vivaciously as he hugged them one after the other. "How are you feeling?" he asked Digger.

Before Digger could finish a nod, Ortega patted him on the head and said, "I hope your brain can take in *all* that I will tell and show you today." As he turned to lead them back up the hill, he began his speech with a broad gesture, "This is all amazing?"

"What is amazing?" Digger asked, and then thought, lately everything seems amazing!

"All the information," Ortega replied. "It seems to be moving so fast. And everything is changing. I'm not just talking about the 'Information

Age' with computers, but *everything*. Life-changing experiences seem to be happening, one after another. Don't both of you agree?"

Bendi and Digger smiled at each other and kept walking.

A moment later Bendi noticed that Ortega had stopped to tie his boot while Digger kept climbing. This was her chance to tell Ortega her news, she realized. "Wonderful" the professor exclaimed. He was as excited by her decision as Digger was baffled, and his enthusiasm gave her a warm feeling that she'd made the right decision.

"Wait, *señor*! We will catch up," Ortega called to Digger.

As the three rejoined the climb together, Ortega, beaming with happiness, chattered loudly so they could both hear his story.

"Three days ago, I came back to this cave where Bendi found you, where you said you'd left the Heavens sphere. I sat in the deepest corner and tried to remember all of your dreams, Bendi. Then in the darkness, I played the tapes of your story, Digger, the ones I recorded in the hospital." Ortega's eyes twinkled. "The discrepancies between what we know and what you said are still there. But after listening several times, I also noticed minor incongruities within your own story. My premise all along has been that what you have told me is true. So I asked myself, what could account for those inconsistencies?

"Well, I kept playing the end of the tape, from the landslide until the time we found you. I played it over and over again. Then I heard another inconsistency.

"I don't know how my mind made the leap from that discrepancy to my new, unbelievable, earth-shaking conclusion, but the answer was there." He stopped climbing and turned to face them. "My theory explains the mysteries of *Los Otros*, the stone spheres, and your adventures, Digger!" Excited, he picked up the pace again. "You see, I kept replaying the part where you said, 'And then I *walked through the opening* and dragged the sphere to the deepest corner'... 'and then I *walked* through...'" Ortega repeated for emphasis. But Bendi and Digger were confused. He continued, "My theory is totally unacceptable to any scientist, at least any present-day scientist. If I can prove it, it will change the field of archeology—forever. But it won't only change archeology. It will change science, religion—everything!" He gestured expansively, scaring a black-and-yellow cacique from her hanging nest as they reached the top of the bluff.

Two of Ortega's students exited the cave as Ortega finished breathlessly, "Almost every scientist—in fact, *everyone* would have to change their definition of reality!"

Finally, Digger's exasperation peaked. "What is it, Ortega?" he demanded. "What is this theory? What did you find?"

Ortega was undaunted. He continued in his maddening, unhurried pace, enjoying his moment. "I placed a ground-penetrating radar device in the cave, exactly where you said you last held the sphere. The beeps went off! I had my team set up lighting and take pictures of every step of the process. Then I had two students at a time carefully clear dirt from the cave floor, while I took measurements of the height of the opening. Do you see? It was little more than a meter high when you were found— three feet only. But you said you'd 'walked through'! So we dug down one meter. It was perfect! Do you see? It was all perfect!"

Bendi and Digger were thoroughly confused.

"Are you ready to get dirty?" Ortega grinned and took a flashlight from one of his students.

Sighing, Digger followed the crazed archaeologist, carefully stepping down into the small excavated cave. Behind him in the darkness, Bendi recalled one of her dreams and thought she could actually feel the breath of the jaguar on her neck. Meanwhile, Digger was remembering the cold that had penetrated his bones, and the quaking fear of being caught by his pursuers.

Squeezed on his knees between Ortega and Bendi, Digger watched as the archaeologist shined the flashlight on an object resting two feet away. A tingling up and down Digger's spine cleansed all of his fears, leaving him with a sense of awe. He was staring at the Heavens sphere, with its intricate lines and thousands of miniscule indentations amidst fluid shades of green and violet. It was beautiful. It was mysterious. It was reassuring. It was entangled within the roots of a tree.

"I don't understand," Digger said slowly, his voice dampened by the small enclosure. "This doesn't make any sense—this would mean the sphere would have to have been here twenty, maybe fifty years ago!"

"No, Digger, that is not true. That is not true at all. It has not been here for fifty or even a hundred years. More like five hundred years."

Chapter 30

"All the pieces are before us, but ever so subtly."

"Five hundred years?! Are you *loco*?" Digger exclaimed.

Bendi simply stared at the Heavens sphere in amazement.

"Maybe," Ortega laughed from inside the cave. "Go back out and I will explain."

Obediently, Digger and Bendi backed themselves out and stood up beside the cave's low opening. Inside, Ortega had repositioned himself until he was standing upright, looking up at them. "All I am doing is connecting the many scattered dots you have given me," he explained, his voice muffled by the surrounding earth. "According to your own account, Digger, you said that you *walked* into this cave. So it had to be at least two meters—I am sorry, six feet high. Is that true?"

"I kind of remember... yes, I did walk in. But how—?" Digger was completely baffled. The top of the cave opening reached just below his belly.

"Unless you were three feet tall, you could not have walked in!" Ortega continued. "But *five hundred years ago*, the ground was at the level of the Heavens sphere, the level where I am now standing, three feet down, which would make the cave opening just as you said—high enough for you to walk through! You see, over the centuries, animals, wind, and weather dragged leaves and branches into this shelter, which eventually decomposed into soil, and dirt naturally accumulated in the opening. Then there was that beautiful, growing ceiba tree which now holds the sphere in the safety of her roots." He smiled in satisfaction as he climbed out, awaiting their reaction.

Bendi was wide-eyed and silent, but Digger tried to let the implications settle into his brain. His mind kept spitting them back out. "You mean to tell me I just traveled back in time *five hundred years*? And then somehow came back to the twentieth century a week later?"

"Just listen," Ortega smiled patiently. "There is more. Here in the jungle, Digger, you would not have known the difference between past or present, whether it was 500 B.C. or 2500 A.D. There are no streets or buildings to change, and indigenous tribes would look much the same. The jungle is the jungle," he shrugged. "For the little that is left of it, the rainforest is pretty much the same as it was hundreds of years ago.

"Since your rescue, many people have searched this area. There is no evidence of a tribe, a struggle, or even the remains of a village. Now, in your tape recording, I discovered a tiny clue that I originally ignored as a lapse in your memory. It was insignificant then, but in light of your time travel, it is staggering. You mentioned that on your rafting trip, the moon was just a sliver. And for your information, on that date it was a sliver moving to a new moon—no moon at all. *But,* supposedly only one week later, on your last night with *Los Otros*, the night you described 'imprinting' with the Love sphere and having some insight about your shadow, you went into great detail about the *full* moon that created that shadow! The only explanation is that it was a different moon—I mean, the same moon but a different cycle, a moon that was full, *five hundred years ago.*"

Hearing a low grunting noise, Digger spun around. A bald, red ukari monkey stared at the trio before swinging back into the rainforest.

"Okay, now stay with me here," Ortega brought Digger's attention back. "During the massacre, you mentioned you heard gunshots that sounded like popping noises—not rapid fire but singular pops accompanied by a flash of light. You also described shiny reflections coming from different points in the jungle which you thought were machetes."

The mention brought terrible scenes back to Digger's mind. It didn't matter if it was weeks or centuries ago, his emotions were fresh and painful. Noticing his grimace, Bendi touched his back in gentle sympathy.

Ortega went on eagerly, "Now think of this: those reflections were armor, and those popping guns were muskets."

"Wait a minute—you're telling me they were conquistadors?" Ortega's hypothesis tore him out of his melancholy. Could it be true?

"*Si.* When you were captured, you told me, the blow to your head made your vision blurry—but you heard men speaking Spanish."

"Everyone speaks Spanish in Costa Rica," Digger countered.

"Because that is true does not make my statement untrue, no? You also described that as you tried to get away from your attacker you felt your flesh being jabbed by some hard, metallic ornament. He was an armor-wearing, Spanish conquistador, I believe!"

Digger shook his head in astonishment as Ortega continued.

"There are many other clues: you saw cross-like reflections coming from the jungle before you found the cave. For protection, the conquistadors marched with metal crosses held high on sticks. And countless historical records relate how the conquistadors allied themselves with Meso-American tribes in their search for gold. And"—Ortega led them to the edge of the precipice—"before seeking safety in the cave, you stood here and felt an earthquake tremor and watched a landslide cover the cavern, no?"

Digger nodded.

"Where is the landslide?" Ortega continued, not waiting for Digger's reply. "In the twentieth century, we, too, experienced an earthquake in that very same spot—but only one big boulder came crashing down. No landslide, no covering of the cavern as you described. And finally, the biggest clue of all, Digger: why did you not see all of my students filling the riverbed, working on the stone spheres? In fact, you did not even see the spheres! Why not? Because you were looking down at that riverbed five hundred years ago!"

"This is crazy!" Digger exhaled. He dropped down cross-legged in the dust. His legs wouldn't hold him anymore.

Ortega settled awkwardly next to him, replying thoughtfully, "Not really. Scientists have discovered particles of the atom that actually move backwards in time. Time is not on a horizontal continuum, from left to right, past to future. Einstein led us to believe that time is actually a dimension. He talked about it folding back upon itself like a tortilla. You don't have to eat that tortilla from left to right. You can bite it anywhere you want and then take a bite somewhere else," he grinned.

"Now, you said that when you were lying in the cave, you saw images that seemed to be layered over one another. You also heard voices speaking different languages. Bendi and I experienced those same sensations, and we were also near the cave! Do you get it? We tasted the same part of that tortilla, that dimension of time! You, Digger, just savored it a bit longer."

Ortega's self-satisfied smile was lighting up the jungle, but Digger's logical mind tried to reject everything the professor was saying. But another place within him, a deeper place, listened attentively. In that place, all of Ortega's hypotheses and postulations fit into an ancient puzzle. From that deep place within, he tried to listen with an open mind. Nervously, he glanced at Bendi, who'd found a little patch of green so she could sit comfortably yet within earshot. She gave him a puzzled shrug.

"This different concept of time is not new," Ortega was explaining. "The Meso-American cultures most definitely believed in time travel. The Mayas believed that each day of their calendar year had a certain vibrational frequency. For example, the frequency of today would be similar to the same day of last year, or five hundred years before, or even five hundred years into the future. So on this day, the events of all similar days would somehow be accessible. One would be able to feel, heal, and maybe even travel to those days in some way, shape, or form. If I had two similar tuning forks and struck one of them, the other would begin to vibrate—and you would be able to hear it, experience it.

"To put it into your language, Digger, there are basically seven notes which are repeated throughout the keyboard. Each F note is different, yet it has similar vibrational frequencies to other F notes. I believe that, in some way, the stone spheres are a cosmic keyboard, and if certain notes—spheres—are activated, you can sense other times and places.

"Remember when you fell into the river? You described holding on to a round boulder that had a chip out of it. That was one of the stone spheres—we found it later, with your blood dried on it! Holding on to this sphere, this note on the keyboard, you lost consciousness and *magically* woke up, back on land with Angélica. How would *you* explain it?"

Bendi interrupted, "Wait a minute, if what you're saying is true, how did *Los Otros* know English?"

"With the help of Angélica." Ortega's enthusiasm swelled. "Think about it! She had to know how to activate the stone spheres and move through time. She came to this era, the changing of the millennium, probably many times and gathered all the necessary skills and information that it would take for her to lead you to her tribe. That included learning your language, English. She brought that knowledge back and taught it to *Los Otros* long before your arrival."

Digger remembered Angélica describing her chosen name, "Traveler... a traveler between the tick and the tock!"

Bendi couldn't help thinking about her jaguar—or shapeshifting shaman, or whatever it was. Was it possible the jaguar, too, traveled through time? Helping her, then Digger, then her again? And even entering her dreams. Didn't the jaguar always disappear when it *went behind a sphere*? She was almost afraid of what Ortega would say if she asked this question, so she decided to save it for later.

Digger tried hard to imagine that Ortega was right. "Okay," he granted. "Let's say that Angélica, with the use of that sphere, helped me travel backwards in time. But she wasn't with me..." his voice cracked slightly. He cleared his throat. "She wasn't with me when I came back. So how did I return without her help?"

"You forget that you are a man of experience!" Ortega said dramatically.

He looked at the professor dubiously.

"I am serious. While you were with *Los Otros*, you imprinted with the Love sphere, didn't you? Somehow, accidentally or unconsciously, you learned how to use the spheres for time travel. When you were in the cave, the last thing you did was to wrap yourself around this Heavens sphere we've just uncovered. And then—poof! You are back in this time. And there is something else."

"Not anything more, please, Ortega," Digger pleaded.

Undaunted, the archaeologist continued, "One of the Mayan symbols is a pathway that keeps spiraling inwards upon itself: the serpent. According to Mayan writings, one of the meanings and purposes for that symbol is time travel."

"Digger, remember?" Bendi interjected excitedly. "You saw that design on the top of the pyramid at Cobá!"

He nodded reluctantly.

"I have been there," Ortega said, "and I did not see any such symbol. But just recently, we uncovered a mural of what that pyramid looked like back in the thirteenth century. There it was, the serpent painted on the top level!"

"Digger," Bendi jumped up. "You said that day in Cobá that you felt like you'd fallen into a darkness! And you've described that sensation now several times: when you were in the river, holding on to the chipped sphere, when you were in the cave with the Heavens sphere—and me! I had that same feeling of falling into darkness right before I found you!" She looked at Ortega questioningly. "Maybe that sensation is part of time-traveling? Maybe, Digger, you tapped into some kind of time-portal at Cobá—and then did it again with the stone spheres!"

"Exactly!" Ortega agreed, nodding approval at his newest student.

"But why?" Digger asked in exasperation. "Why go to all that trouble to take me to another time?" Before the words left his mouth, he knew at least part of the answer: so that he could meet Angélica. And maybe more importantly, so that he would remember—so that he could help others remember.

"That is your mystery to solve," Ortega answered. He added pensively, "I do find it fascinating, though. It was as if you left one body here in this time period and had another body back there with *Los Otros*. Remember telling us about feeling pains in your shoulder? Well, here, in this time, your body was probably being dragged to the cave by the jaguar at that moment. And remember how thirsty you were during your last few days with *Los Otros*? Your body here was becoming more and more dehydrated. Digger, you somehow played an octave of time, simultaneously."

"How could that be?" Digger shook his head.

"Science is full of paradoxes," Ortega answered. "Especially now that we understand something about quantum physics. If scientists try to explain light, they are faced with two different and opposing theories. They can explain it by defining light as particles, or by defining it as waves. Each explanation perfectly describes light, but at the same time, each theory cancels out the other one."

Ortega got up, brushing the dirt from his hands on his trousers. "Can you not see that everything is right here? All the pieces are before us, but ever so subtly. Okay, I know it is a lot for you to take in all at once. I need to obtain more information to corroborate my theory. But as unbelievable as all of this may seem to you, I believe it is the only explanation that accounts for all the conflicting data. But I know that I am talking about a different way to look at the universe—and our lives!"

Digger's mind was racing, trying to digest all of the professor's ideas.

Ortega beamed with mischief. He looked from Digger to Bendi and then back again, hesitating, then seemed to make a decision. "I have another surprise," he added quietly. "We have just discovered something I think you might like to see, if you feel up to it."

Digger shrugged. "Why not? It can't possibly be as shocking as all this," he gestured back toward the cave.

"Let's go!" Bendi agreed. "This is all so exciting, Ortega."

Digger looked at her strangely for a moment, then got up and followed the two eager archeologists about a hundred feet across the top edge of the bluff, away from the cave. Their feet crunched in harmony with the familiar cheeping and twittering of the jungle's feathered creatures.

Ortega stopped at a pile of dirt, panting for breath in the humid heat. "A student discovered this site. One of the tremors had caused a fissure and when she looked into it, she thought she saw some artifacts. After much digging, we finally discovered this."

Ropes had been strung around the site for protection. Ortega stepped over them and Digger followed, helping Bendi over. He felt her body stiffen as if in fear. He looked to see if it was his touch that had caused the reaction, but she was staring down into a hole about eight feet square, and at least six feet deep. At the bottom, several stone slabs lay neatly beside an array of oddly-shaped bones.

Ortega urged them to follow him down a crude ladder into the pit. Digger agreed, but Bendi graciously declined.

She stayed atop the mound of dirt, uneasy chills moving up and down her spine, as if she were stepping on her own grave. A shudder passed over her at the thought.

"This looks like more than one person's bones," Digger noted calmly.

"Correct. These bones," Ortega pointed reverently as they crouched deep in the grave, "are of an older woman. She apparently died of natural causes. We have estimated that she was in her mid-sixties. These other bones were very unexpected. I have never seen this combination before in any gravesite excavation. They are jaguar bones."

He looked up significantly at Bendi.

Digger followed Ortega's gaze, but his own emotions and memories were bubbling up from deep within. Bendi was still staring, but now she looked very pale.

Ortega pointed at the stone slabs. "We discovered these just after we uncovered the Heavens sphere and have dated the writings as being from the mid-1500s."

"Are they her story?" Bendi finally spoke. Digger thought he heard a trembling in her voice.

"Well, at first they were difficult to translate," Ortega replied. "But I was finally able to decipher them. Yes, they tell of this individual's journey." He looked at Digger pointedly.

Digger grabbed his arm. "The name, Ortega—do you know her name?"

"Look over here," Ortega directed Digger's gaze to several pictographs on the granite tablets. "This is her 'signature.' Her name was not like ours—a Tom, Betty, or Manuel. It is more like the names of your Native Americans—"

"Tell me! Tell me what it is!" Digger interrupted. He was tired of Ortega's games! He could already feel the name forming in his mind...

With a compassionate grin Ortega complied, "The name loosely translates as: 'the wind that touches the wings of a hawk.'"

Digger let out a big sigh as a smile ripened on his face. Stretching out the syllables, he slowly whispered, "Vaawaahhaaa." The image of his little friend formed in his mind, the girl who always smiled, who chased after butterflies, who showed him water fairies, who shared her wisdom.

Ortega moved back up the ladder considerately, leaving Digger alone with his friend and comforting Bendi, who seemed strongly affected by the scene.

"I'll try to keep *Los Otros* alive," Digger whispered to the bones. "I don't know how to do that right now, but I promise that I'll find a way."

As he finally climbed out of the grave, the sky was ablaze with a fiery sunset. Red and purple strokes of light streaked from between the clouds, stretching to the top of the rainforest canopy. Digger moved to the foot of the site and, with cupped hands, extended them towards the physical remains of his friend. Then he slowly opened his arms as a gentle breeze swept through the ancient ruins. The breeze reached deep into his soul and pushed out his lungs, the wind carrying his own name off into the jungle: Too-kashaam.

Chapter 31

"Don't you get it? We don't have any more time."

Digger noticed that the twelve-inch, green-and-violet Heavens sphere was now resting on a table in Ortega's research camp. Several of his students had moved it carefully out of the cave and brought it into the camp for closer study.

After their visit to Vawaha's grave site the previous evening, Bendi had left by helicopter that morning, the first leg of her flight back to the States. Digger was still amazed by her transformation, the depth of strength and determination he'd never seen in her before. But before she left, she admitted that the grave had stirred powerful reactions within her. She couldn't explain what they were, or why she would be so shaken by the grave of a stranger. Maybe that would be the first mystery she'd solve when she returned to work with Ortega, she'd laughed. Digger was glad for the laughter. Their goodbye was tearful but happy, a gentle parting between friends. They'd agreed to stay in touch, and not to let the friendship die even though they'd both come to the same conclusion: that a deeper relationship wasn't meant for them. Digger was tremendously relieved by her understanding—but she seemed to be as relieved at his.

Now Digger turned his attention to the spheres. He felt they had something to tell him. He didn't know what that could be, but the Heavens sphere was beckoning to him from the makeshift table. Maybe it would help him conceive Ortega's outlandish ideas. He laughed at the thought of the stone communicating to him—then realized it wasn't so funny.

"Can I pick it up?"

"You are the *only* one I would ever let touch it," the professor replied seriously.

Digger cradled the familiar sphere in his arms; it felt like it belonged there. But immediately, he saw himself standing again at the oval table with the six luminous figures—and one empty chair. The crystal lay in front of him as it had the first time he experienced this vision. He promptly put the Heavens sphere back down.

"What is it?" Ortega never missed subtleties.

Digger looked up, embarrassed. "Nothing." Looking back down at the sphere, he examined a thin crack running around its circumference. "What happened here?"

"I do not know. That is how we found it. Maybe it was pressure from the ceiba roots. One of the bigger spheres is cracked also, but that happened during our tremor, when the boulder fell from the bluff and crashed into it."

Digger's finger was tracing the patterns on the colorful sphere. "Ortega, with all your theories, how do you explain the missing symbols and colors on the other spheres?"

The professor nodded thoughtfully. "Maybe the first question to ask is, are these the same spheres you saw with *Los Otros*? If we follow your story and my theory on time travel, these should be them. Hypothetically, they were hidden in the cavern until the flood waters washed them out, so they should have been protected. The river only ran down this old bed for a short time, so it could not have wiped them clean through erosion. We have even checked for etchings and flecks of dye— we found nothing," he shrugged. "But do you remember what you described to me about the Love sphere? How, after you 'imprinted' it, the sphere began to spin rapidly, and when it stopped, there were no symbols left?"

"Now I'm not really sure that happened," Digger sighed. "I only saw it for a moment before the white light appeared, and it was so bright I was blinded. Then the Love sphere was gone—along with the rest of them."

"And you were only *told* that they would be in the cavern. You never saw anyone put them here. So despite my hopes, maybe these are not the spheres you saw five hundred years ago. Except for this beautiful Heavens sphere, the others look like the hundreds of plain granite spheres that have been found in Costa Rica."

"*Profesor*," a student cheerfully greeted Ortega as he handed him a manila envelope.

"*Gracias*," Ortega thanked the retreating student. He pulled several photographs of the Heavens' sphere from the envelope, spreading them on the table. "As you can see, your little sphere here has thousands of indentations," he indicated, "but look at these close-up photos! Each tiny hole is infinitely meticulous and unique, varying in diameter and depth from the others." His finger traced one of the etchings on the sphere. "Here you can see that these very thin lines connect five of the biggest holes. I thought that whoever made the sphere might have wanted us to focus on those five points, so I had a photographer place a light directly above each of them and take pictures from those five perspectives."

"The photos look like a white moon with dark craters," Digger observed.

"Interesting is it not? Oddly enough that is how astronomers look at the heavens. They reverse the images, making the background white and the light of the stars, black. It is easier to see black dots on a white background."

Digger looked closely. "Then if these are supposed to be stars, this picture looks familiar. There's Orion's belt—and the Pleiades."

"Very good. That is my theory. I believe the indentations were made to represent varying sizes of stars, at least how we see them from here. If it turns out I am right, by the way, that kind of accuracy cannot be accomplished by hand—by laser, yes—but fifteenth-century tools, no— at least, not using any method we know of." Ortega took the photograph from Digger thoughtfully, holding it over his head. "Yes, you can see that this is what the night sky looks like in Costa Rica; not in Los Angeles, not in Tokyo, not in Capetown, but in Costa Rica."

"So what about the other vantage points? Where are they from?" Digger asked, picking up other photographs.

"Ahh, that is the wonderful mystery before us," Ortega answered dramatically. "Who knows what heavens these pictures will show us? I will send copies of them to a friend of mine who works in the radio physics lab at the *Universidad*. He is an astronomer and has the use of very sophisticated computers. Maybe he will have an answer for you."

As Ortega scrutinized the photos, Digger turned to gaze at the spheres lying "downstream" in the riverbed. He felt a magnetic pull on his right side. Were all of them pulling at him or just one? Excusing himself, he walked the short distance to the cracked, chipped sphere that had, according to his rescuers, been stained with his blood. Placing his hands on the cool stone, he remembered how he'd felt clinging to it for his life as the raging river threatened to pull him away. Now the sphere's tiny silica chips were sparkling in the light of day. He smoothed his palm along the crack. A tingling began in his fingers and quickly moved up to his elbows and then his chest.

"Quick, give me a pen and paper!" Digger called to Ortega excitedly. "This is the History sphere!"

"How do you know?" Ortega yelled back, and then recanted, "Nevermind... I trust you." He hurried into the nearby supply tent and rushed back to Digger with a pad of paper and pencil.

Digger sat down and, from memory, drew the design of the History sphere. By now a crowd of curious students had gathered to watch as he drew a circle with four intersecting arrows, then a strange-looking pendulum, and then the circles that represented the dimensions within dimensions.

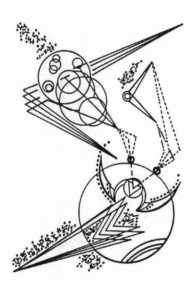

Later that night, Digger tossed and turned on his cot, wide-eyed and wide awake, the constant chattering of crickets and frogs filling the dark forest around him. He was still trying to convince himself that Angélica had been dead for five hundred years—just her body, he reminded himself. He now knew better than most people that, whether it's a day or a millenium, time is not a factor when it involves affairs of the mind, heart, or spirit. But why did he have to meet Angélica and fall in love, only to have her die? She knew so much—did she know this would happen? And if she did, why did she come for him? It didn't seem fair, and it didn't make sense. The thoughts tormented him mercilessly. And he knew of no one who could answer his questions.

Restlessly, he gave up trying to sleep and crawled out of the stuffy tent. Overhead blazed the narrow highway of stars created by the bygone river's cleared path, their faint light illuminating his walk down the deserted riverbed until, exhausted, he settled on a fallen tree. Perspiration dripped from his body. As he sat, the moon slipped into the slender starry opening, bathing his surroundings in a brighter glow. The spheres cast long and distinct shadows toward Digger. He remembered his experience with the light and shadow at the quarry and turned away from the light to see his own dark counterpart. He'd danced in and out of that darkened form for many years, but now that he'd tasted the light, the shadow was no longer comforting.

When he turned back to face the moon, he felt like a volcano holding back the pressure of hot, dynamic energy. He quickly stood up straight as geysers of energy spiraled from the earth up through his legs, into his torso, shooting out the crown of his head. He felt completely rejuvenated!

Now he felt again another ancient stone drawing him into its influence. Ambling through the maze of spheres, he sat down in front of the three foot sphere that had called him, placing his hands over the surface. He immediately felt tingling and a lightness. He knew this rock—intimately. It was the Love sphere. Leaning over, he lay his chest on top of it. Immediately, visions and sensations flew by him as he viewed his and others' imprints. Again, he felt something lacking about his imprints compared to the others. But before his logical mind could grapple with what that distinction could possibly mean, his vision became momentarily blurry.

Now, instead of lying atop the Love sphere, Digger was magically standing before the Heavens sphere. Giving only a dream-like acknowledgement to the impossibility of that, he reached out and cradled the familiar stone. He sat down on the ground, the sphere on his lap, and was immediately absorbed. Falling into its grasp, he was suddenly in a hallway; a place of no yesterdays or tomorrows. As if he sensed the lingering aroma of a familiar friend who'd passed by, Digger knew this to be the corridor for the Keepers of Wisdom. He frantically tried to grip the walls as the end of the hallway slowly dropped.

Sliding through a multi-colored tube of lights, he fell onto a small portion of land surrounded by a vastness of ocean. Digger knew he was on Easter Island as he viewed its monumental stone carvings. But he grew fearful as each megalith pulled at him like a forceful magnet. He resisted. Immediately, he slid through the colored lights and was deposited on top of Ayers Rock with a panoramic view of flat, arid Australian desert. The scene then changed to another desert, but one filled with bright, red-rock formations. In amazement, Digger watched four gigantic and tens of smaller, stationary tornadoes send spiraling waves of energy up into a deep blue Arizona sky. Floating to the center of one of these vortexes, he slid again through the long, multi-colored tube and found himself staring out of a transparent, snow-covered Mount Shasta.

Each place was strongly connected, he realized. And each sacred site pulled at him. But he was afraid—afraid that if he allowed himself to be drawn out any further, he wouldn't know how to get back. So each time he resisted the urge to remain.

From Mount Shasta, he was jettisoned into space, hurtling toward the moon. Looking over his shoulder, he saw he was in the earth's shadow as it eclipsed the sun. He turned back toward the moon and somehow expected warmth from its faint light. But it was cold. The moon is just a reflection, he realized, a reflection of light. He wanted more. His body momentarily stretched like a piece of gum and without warning shot by the glowing orb. Looking down he saw a gold umbilical cord attached to his chest. That filament stretched into the vastness of infinity. Then, to his surprise, he saw several thin, red beams crossing the heavens. As he tried to calm himself by taking deep breaths, the darkness around him filled with these intersecting lines. It seemed that every star was now connected to every other by a red tether.

He turned back, noting that the sun that had been so familiar to him was now just a tiny speck of light amongst millions. He didn't know how he knew, but he knew exactly which star it was.

Again he felt the pull of the golden cord at his chest. The fiber of light stretched him through space and he lost all track of time. When his momentum eventually slowed, he noticed a ball of rock in the sky. At first, lights dotted its surface but as he came closer he could see peculiar architecture piercing the night sky. The futuristic-looking city was vaguely familiar. Pulled closer by the golden cord, he watched one of the buildings become diaphanous. Chills moved up and down his spine as he peered into one of its large and airy rooms. There in the middle of the room was the end, or the beginning, of his golden cord. It was attached to the underside of the frosted glass, oval table surrounded by six translucent figures. In unison, they lifted a small, clear sphere off the table and looking up at him, smiled.

The golden cord disappeared and instantaneously his stomach felt like it had dropped to his feet as he quickly ascended back into the heavens. Thankfully, he rapidly adjusted to the new warp-speed motion but wanting some direction in his flight, he willed himself toward one of the red lines of light. With childlike enthusiasm, Digger used the ray as a slide, travelling effortlessly over its beam. In the distance, he could see the reddish light connecting to a beautiful sphere which reflected impressionistic blues and whites. Emanating from different points on its surface were several golden beams. They stretched across its face, and up and out into the star-lit heavens.

As Digger's momentum slowed, a kaleidoscope of images appeared before him. Splashes of vivid reds, glowing emerald greens, and spiked browns adorned the sphere, while silvery curved lines emptied into shimmering pockets of cobalt blue. Intersecting, darkened paths crisscrossed along its surface, creating squares and triangles of different sizes and shapes. Even more beautiful than the brightly decorated spheres of *Los Otros,* and with more intricate symbols, this dynamic ball in the sky seemed alive.

Hundreds of feet above its surface, Digger slipped off the red beam and onto one of the golden rays that circled the sphere. Traveling along the lustrous light, he finally realized he was traveling above Earth. So beautiful! Amazed, Digger marveled at how it lovingly held so many intriguing inscriptions: from beautiful skyscrapers to flowered meadows, from adorned temples to fluid, interlocking loops of highways, from spiked volcanoes to rolling oceans, from sparsely painted, yellow deserts to sculpted valleys and mountains, from mysterious designs engraved into fields of crops to strange figures etched onto its hardened surface.

Digger enjoyed his ride as the golden light pushed him toward a pyramid in Egypt. Once he touched its apex, he switched to another beam of gold that quickly brought him to the snow-capped mountains of Tibet. Standing briefly in one of its temples, he again slipped through a tunnel of colored lights. Accelerating to another part of the globe, he viewed lush mountains spotted with ancient ruins. Machupicchu rose majestically in front of him, standing in the clouds, with a sweeping carpet of greenery rolling thousands of feet downwards. The sacred site pulled at him, furiously.

Digger's fragile ego screamed loud and clear, "This is different! I have no idea what is happening here! Be careful! Stay where you are! It's what's familiar, what's known! Okay, sometimes it's painful here with me, but heck, you don't know the depth of possible pain that could be out there. I can't protect you if you go!"

Digger deliberately and lovingly sank into the very core of his jabbering ego. At first it was like landing in a bed of nails. But the sharpness gave way to a suffocating quicksand and then to a bearable, unpleasant itchiness. Within those sensations, he discovered that something was missing; his ego was just like the moon, with little warmth or light within its borders! But still Digger felt its purpose and its beauty as his ego played a role within his life, within the universe.

Immediately, light surrounded him. Then, spiraling through the soles of his feet and shooting out the top of his head, pulses of pink and green energy slipped through him like a tornado. The energy then catapulted him backwards, tossing him onto a giant wave that approached a foreign shore. After tumbling within its effervescent surf, he was spit out, sprawled before the Love sphere.

Breathless, he gasped the humid jungle air. After several more deep breaths, he realized that the darkened shadows had long disappeared and the fingertips of dawn were serenely touching the jungle canopy.

Digger stood up joyfully and gazed down the ancient riverbed, which held the stone spheres delicately in its grasp. It's like a giant nest with fragile eggs, he thought, eggs that are filled with life, eggs that are about to be hatched. The chipped sphere again caught his attention. He quietly walked over and touched the cracked surface. To his surprise, energy gushed out from the fracture. Just like spirit flowing out from behind the masks during *Los Otros'* dance, he remembered.

"Where do you go when you the world gets too crazy?" he suddenly yelled ecstatically, although no one else was up yet to hear him. "Where do you go to find the answers?" he called to the treetops, scaring up a flock of colorful macaws. Seized by a crazy, frantic notion, he ran into the equipment tent and grabbed a hammer and chisel. He sprinted back to the sphere and began to pound away.

"Hey, who's over there?" he heard Ortega shout from a tent. "What are you doing?"

"It's inside! It's all inside!" Digger sang back happily.

Still throwing on clothes, Ortega came running, hollering, "*Qué diablos estas haciendo?*" He grabbed at the tools in Digger's hands.

"Let me go," Digger pulled away. "If you want to know the answer, you have to go inside!"

"*Qué la fregada.* Stop it!" Ortega commanded with uncharacteristic vehemence as he tried to wrestle the tools away from the crazy American. "*Hombre! Estas loco.*"

Students came running sleepily out of their tents towards the disturbance, but Digger continued to chisel. The jungle grew restless with the disturbance. Birds flew up in a great commotion, monkeys leaped to the safety of higher branches, and creatures scurried from bushes and burrows.

"Trust me," Digger insisted. "Just let me chip out one very small section..." He pounded harder.

"That is not how it is done!" Ortega bellowed desperately, pleadingly. "It takes weeks, maybe months to uncover simple artifacts! We do it methodically and slowly—very, very slowly!"

"That's just it Ortega. Don't you get it? We don't have any more time." With Digger's next stroke, a two-inch chunk of granite flew off the sphere. Excitedly, he blew the dust out of the opening, partially exposing several intersecting, golden circles. "Yes!" he pumped his arm up and down in triumph. "Yes!"

Ortega stood with his mouth agape. Then without saying a word, he grabbed the chisel and hammer from the dancing American. Ortega's students huddled near as he carefully chipped away at the fracture. Digger just kept dancing, in and around the stone spheres, using every move he'd learned from *Los Otros* to express his joy.

After half an hour of delicate chiseling, Ortega had exposed a two-foot-wide strip around the circumference. He was speechless. Overhead, a low thumping signaled the approach of the helicopter coming to take Digger back to San José. The archaeologist slowly pulled a paper from his back pocket. Digger's memory-drawn design of the History sphere and the newly exposed symbols lined up identically.

Chapter 32

"Death was a necessary step before... rebirth"

A faint glow in the distance brushed aside the darkness below. Soon a few twinkling lights gave way to "America's Finest City." The plane narrowly missed the tops of downtown buildings and quickly descended into the heart of San Diego.

After disembarking Digger picked up his luggage, and hailed a taxi. Plopping down in the back seat, exhausted from the plane ride, he realized he didn't want to go home just yet. He directed the driver to Mister A's restaurant and asked him to wait. Taking an elevator to the twelfth floor, he asked the maitre'd for a table on the outdoor patio, one with a view of downtown and the bay.

Digger sipped slowly on a *Clos Du Bois* Chardonnay and enjoyed the slight chill of the San Diego night. After being in Central America for almost a month, the city felt foreign to him—and any thought of being with *Los Otros* seemed like home. At the same time, his experiences in the Costa Rican jungle seemed like a hundred years ago. He chuckled to himself. *Let's be exact, Digger—five hundred years ago.* He took a big gulp of his wine.

Digger gazed at the beautifully lit skyline. With its multiple, hexagonal towers, the Wyndham hotel projected its iridescent green rooflines, slanted at a ten-story angle, up toward the muted stars. The twinkling lights of the Coronado bridge arched over the bay and merged into the downtown buildings, many of which were also dotted in lights. The panoramic view was illuminated with intriguing squares, triangles, and rectangles. But the scene only triggered a painful ache for *Los Otros*—for Angélica.

He finished his drink and returned to the waiting taxi. Heading north on Interstate 5 towards his home in Cardiff-by-the-Sea, he asked the driver to make another detour. "Take Interstate 8 east to 15, and get off at the Carroll Canyon East exit." He surprised himself. It certainly hadn't been on his mind. Fifteen minutes later, the cab pulled up into a drive-way.

"This is where you want to go? It's closed, Buddy." The driver sounded perturbed.

"Yeah, but let me check it out." Digger jumped out and walked to the wrought iron gates; the sign read: "Closed at sunset." He returned to the taxi and asked the driver to circle around the premises. He'd only been here once but felt he could remember where she was.

After a moment, Digger ordered, "Stop."

Shaking his head, the driver pulled over near the curb. Digger gave him a $20 bill and again asked him to wait. He got out and approached the brick wall, taking a deep breath. Then he jumped, grabbing the top of the ledge and pulling himself up. Why was he doing this? Maybe it was impulse, or maybe intuition, but he felt compelled. Leaping down to the ground, he saw where the road split into three separate paths and knew he was close.

Along the way, Digger tried to read the tombstones. What a strange custom, preserving and keeping the body of the deceased in the ground, he thought, as if the body were that person. He was painfully reminded that Angélica never even had a grave. Her body was probably left to the jungle. Maybe that wasn't so bad, he reflected, looking at the gloomy cemetery in the dark.

He switched his thoughts to the moment his mother had died, remembering how she'd looked—how she'd felt. At that moment of death, it was obvious to him there was nothing left. Call it a soul, or whatever you like, but it had left the body and gone somewhere else. All that remained was the costume she'd used during her journey. Given all of that, he still felt that he needed to be here.

Spotting the new headstone, he heaved a sigh, then stood at the foot of his mother's grave. Trees rustled in the night breeze. It reminded Digger of his trip around Gutubo. The first side had been easy for him, putting things from his perspective, voicing his feelings of being right. His anger had been hidden within that perspective.

Without thinking about what he was doing, he moved to the right side of the grave. The second side was much more difficult: trying to see things from his mother's perspective. The only way he'd been able to do that before was by envisioning himself as a tree and opening wide to the wind. He remembered how long it had taken him. But when he stretched, he saw that, regardless of the mask his mother had worn, she really did want the best for him; she really did care. In Costa Rica, he'd never finished that second step; he knew there was more to see from her perspective.

Digger looked around as a foul smell saturated the cool air. At first he thought it might be a skunk, but as the rank odor continued to waft through the graveyard he knew it was something else; it was the stench of death that permeated his nostrils. He then sensed the crisp bedsheets, and his ears filled again with the loud, gurgling breath escaping from weary lungs. His dying mother lay before him.

Digger had forgotten all about this moment; it happened a few days before his mother died, the last moments she'd been awake. It was so very clear to him now—how could he have forgotten?

At the hospice, his mother's frail body lay there listlessly, except for her hard-fought breaths. She whispered several sounds. Digger softly held her hand as he bent over, trying to catch her words. Her eyes, he thought, God, her eyes are intense! Every other part of her body was dead but her eyes were still filled with life.

"Kieve," she said in a sickly voice.

"I'm sorry, Mom. I didn't hear what you said." He leaned closer.

"Kieve," she repeated.

"Kieve. I don't understand," Digger replied softly.

"Ggieve. Geve," she slowly, strenuously formed the sound. When he repeated back to her what he thought she'd said, he could see her look of frustration.

"Geve, Geve."

"Geve, I don't understand, Mom," Digger apologized. "Geve, geve… oh! You mean give. Give!"

He felt the slightest squeeze from her hand.

"Ehh," she wheezed.

"Give a…" Digger encouraged.

"Geve ehh, ehh, meh," his mother rasped almost inaudibly.

This is too painful, Digger thought. She's using every ounce of energy she has to speak. "It's okay, Mom. Please don't try to speak any more. It's not that important. Just relax."

Her eyes lit up and he knew that look. He'd seen it many times before.

"Meh…," she repeated with more force.

"Mehh, Meh," Digger kept repeating it, hoping his mind would stumble upon the correct pronunciation, "Meh, meeh, me…"

She squeezed his hand again. "Ahhh."

"Give me a… what, Mom? What is it that you want?" He looked around the room for anything that might give him a hint about what she needed: food, a glass of water, Kleenex.

"C-Caasse," she said.

"Case?" he questioned. He thought of all the times that she'd yelled at him, seemingly from blocks away. His steel door would automatically close whenever her voice reached a certain decibel. God, how he'd despised her screaming! What an irony, he mused, that in this moment, with his ear next to her lips, he could barely hear her. That he was using all his concentration to try and understand just one word.

"Ccaasse," she repeated.

He'd seen in her eyes the urgency; the wanting to speak these words, the needing to speak these words.

"Case. Give me a case?" Digger looked again around the room for what she might want, what she might need in this moment. Looking back into her eyes, he brought her veined and bony hand to his lips. She squeezed his hand hard. And in that instant he knew what she wanted. What she needed. What he needed.

He gazed into her eyes and saw they were different somehow. He didn't know it then, but he realized now—now that he was reliving this moment—that they were the eyes of a child. Those eyes had searched for a lifetime hoping to be satisfied, hoping to filled, hoping to be answered.

"Mom, of course," Digger answered his mother's simple question. He slowly bent down and gave her a gentle kiss. An almost unnoticeable smile came to her weathered face as her eyes softened. Then slowly, she allowed them to close for the last time as Digger's salty tears fell upon her dried, cracked cheeks.

Reliving that moment now, in this chilled cemetery, another layer sloughed off. Like the masked dance, like imprinting with the Love sphere, he realized anew that the moments of his life would always appear different when he looked back. But within every moment, if he cared to look, cared enough to be aware, to be open, to let go of the old way of perceiving; within every moment, waiting to be uncovered, there was always love. More love than every person, animal, plant, and thing on this planet could ever hope for.

As a breeze swept through the graveyard, Digger recalled Mashuba's compassionate gaze into his killer's eyes. That look had diminished Digger's horror and rage. Now the memory of his mother's pleading, childish eyes dissipated his anger towards her. The memories now gave way to a river of sadness; a sadness for not having Mashuba or Angélica in his life, a sadness for not having the kind of childhood that he wanted, a sadness for not having the kind of mother that he wanted. The sadness actually brought relief, for it was more pliable, more liquid than the confining, brittle anger. As Digger flowed with that emotion, he was brought to another place, another facet of love—forgiveness.

That's what was missing from his imprints! All of *Los Otros'* imprints with the Love sphere—whether of loving times or challenging times—contained that aspect of love: forgiveness. But within his own, forgiveness accompanied only the loving times, not the challenging ones.

This was the key that would enable him to "see" from another's perspective. He realized he'd have to work on feeling forgiveness—for his mother, for others who he'd perceived had done him wrong, even for himself. But at least he'd begun now.

He needed to feel the forgiveness to complete his circle around Gutubo, wherever 'the tree of many eyes' happened to be. It didn't make any difference whether Gutubo was a tree, a lake, a graveside, his heart, or his mind. All that was important was to make the journey and recognize the treasures within each step.

Several leaves fell to the ground as another gust of wind moved through the graveyard. Calmly, he walked to stand behind the headstone—the third side. Now all he had to do was come up with new perspectives.

He felt good in this moment, but then questioned himself. How can I feel so "good" while I am and have been around so much death? The answer immediately came to him, one he already knew. Death was not what he'd thought it to be. It wasn't the end for those who died, only a beginning, a passage into a natural way of being.

Los Otros showed him that death came, not only in physical form, but also in emotional and intellectual forms. In fact, the end of each journey around Gutubo was a death—a death of the myriad aspects of self. Death was a necessary step before... before what?

As a dark shadow flew over his head, Digger flailed his arms. He remembered Angélica telling him to be open to the messages of the creatures. When the bat circled once more, he felt the word more than he heard it, "rebirth." Death was the necessary step before rebirth.

A horn blared from the taxi. Digger inhaled deeply and gazed upon his mother's grave for the last time.

"Thanks, Mom, for all you've taught me. Whether I wanted to learn that way or not," he chuckled. "Now I realize you did your best. Which I've also done." Digger sighed as the hint of a tear formed in the corner of his eye. He added, "I truly wish you well on your journey, Mom. I wish you love."

Another gust of wind brushed across his body. He remembered Winauka and her story of how the wind gathered and shared its wisdom from all that it had touched with all that it would touch. The wind that knew of the past, but did not linger there. The wind that knew of possibilities of the future, but firmly remained in the present. It was the same wind that had glided over mountains, blustered into cities, and whisked through jungles for eons of time. The same wind that blew through battlefields and also cooled the bodies of embracing lovers. The same wind that, moments before, had skipped the waves of the ocean, then swirled across the sand before it blew into offices and homes. The wind that touched insects, birds, animals, and people before it slipped through the trees and swept across graves. Digger felt its soft caress not only on his body but in his mind, heart, and soul. That gentle breeze touched him and shared with him all that it had learned. In exchange, Digger gave of himself, of his thoughts, of his love, of his spirit. The wind gladly accepted him, and carried his imprint away on its endless journey.

Chapter 33

*"... once those notes are played,
others might discover that my song harmonizes with theirs,
and that this music has been playing for eternity within all of us."*

Six Months Later

As the movie began, Digger's musical score resonated with the crescendo of drums. The trill of flutes seemed to lift the birds from their trees and the violins sang the flowing melody, while a piano repeated an arpeggio, mimicking the sounds of a waterfall.

The film's images sped by, but Digger could only hear the symphony of the Costa Rican rainforest—and its rhythm. The tones and timbres of the jungle had played within him perpetually since his return to the States, inspiring him through the months he spent composing the score.

No more composer's block. Now the music of *Los Otros* and the rainforest was inside him. Melded with a hint of new jazz and a touch of classical, it was a new sound for him, perfect for this film about the rainforests of Borneo.

As the premiere ended and director, producers, and stars gathered in the lobby to congratulate one another, Digger felt his pager vibrate. He looked at the display; an international call—Costa Rica. Smiling, he imagined Ortega's frustration at not being able to tell him about some new discovery. Flipping the pager off, he said his good-byes and graciously accepted congratulations. Quietly, he reminded himself of his score's private dedication: *To Angélica.*

As he handed his ticket to the parking valet, a flood of reporters engulfed him. Since the dramatic revelation of the stone spheres' sacred and beautiful symbols, the spheres had become a worldwide phenomenon. Every major magazine, newspaper, radio, and TV station had presented some theory about the mysterious balls of stone. At public functions now, the media hounded Digger, "discoverer" of the underlying designs. Tonight they were pressing to know about the connection between his music and his jungle adventures.

"No comment," he told the paparazzi. He was relieved to see the valet pulling up to the curb with his car. As he tipped her—clearly an aspiring actress with her hot-pink hair and triply pierced ears —and was about to make his getaway, a tall, slim woman in her mid-thirties shoved her way toward Digger. She stepped boldly in his path, extending her hand.

"Mr. Taylor, I'm Annie Gallagher," she blurted quickly. "I'm an investigative reporter. I don't know if you've ever read any of my —"

"I'm sorry, Miss Gallagher, but I'm on my way home," Digger interrupted politely and slipped into the front seat.

She tossed back her shoulder-length black hair and leaned assertively into his doorway, blocking him from closing the door. "I'm not like the other reporters," she insisted. "I *don't* want to know what happened to you, as much as I want to know how you're different because of your experiences."

"I need to go," Digger apologized, but his eye was caught by a golden pendant with interlocking loops hanging from her graceful neck.

"Please, Mr. Taylor," she persisted. "You have no idea how long I've waited to speak with you! Please, if only I could ask you a few questions. I know I'm a little bold—okay, a lot bold—but if you could just drop me off at my hotel, the Hyatt, it's a few miles west of here, on your way to the freeway, and then we could talk and I wouldn't slow you down at all." She smiled winningly.

"Hey, Annie! You trying to scoop us?" a reporter yelled from the crowd behind her.

"You see, Digger? I really am a reporter," she grinned.

He didn't know why—maybe it was the way she'd just said his name—but he sighed, "Okay, get in."

She stepped around to the passenger door and confidently slid in. Tugging discretely at the hem of her black velvet, scoop-necked dress, she settled comfortably into the leather seat. Then she looked directly into Digger's eyes. "Thank you. Thank you very much. As I was saying, my stories have run in major newspapers around the world. I like to think I cover the things that others miss. What puzzles me is why you won't talk about your experiences, not even at the archaeology conference last month in San José, although your friends there begged you to."

"Miss Gallagher—" Digger began as he pulled into traffic.

"Please, call me Annie," she interjected.

"Annie, that's a long story. As with anything, it's rarely this or that, up or down, wrong or right." Digger glanced over and noticed her eyes widen a bit. It was almost as if she were testing him. Why? But he went on politely, "My most comfortable way of communicating has always been through my music. So to stand in front of people, the press, a convention of scientists, and use my words... well, that would have been a humongous stretch for me. Besides, my experiences transcend, if I can use such a word for the press, beyond *what* happened to me. My experiences touched parts of myself that I didn't know even existed. I'm different because of all that."

"You're right," Annie agreed. "We all have experiences—sad, tragic, happy, heroic. That's not so important as what we do after the experience. How does it change us? How do we then make a better world for ourselves, for others? And that's what I really want to know: how have your experiences affected your life, your future plans?"

This seemed a strange line of questioning for a journalist but Digger decided to play along. He figured she'd make something up if he didn't tell her some sort of true story, so he briefly described his newest endeavor. He told her that, among friends and colleagues, he'd gotten a lot of flack over his latest idea. "First, I had to get over my own barriers, then I had to fend off their opinions. All I heard was, 'Stick to your music, what you're good at,' 'You can't teach an old dog new tricks,' 'Don't try anything new.'"

He laughed and she joined in pleasantly, nodding as if she understood. "So with all that criticism, why did you go ahead?"

"I had to vary my usual method of expression. This film score you just heard only tells a part of my story. Really, this is the first time my music wasn't able to express everything I have inside." He gazed at her thoughtfully for a moment, feeling whether or not he could go on. A familiar, comfortable sensation came over him as he looked at her dark hair under the dim streetlights. He decided to continue.

"After going back in time, if you're one who believes I did, I suspect there were reasons I was helped to return. One of those was to expose the spheres, the other was to bring back my memories of *Los Otros*. But exactly what I was to do with those memories was a mystery until I started this new project a few weeks ago. I thought about the stone tablets found in the grave of a young *Los Otros* girl, Vawaha. I call her young, although she lived to be in her 60s," he smiled fondly. "She wrote those tablets almost five hundred years ago, yet they still tell a story. What a powerful medium!"

Annie smiled broadly. "Now you know why I am a journalist."

He flushed, embarrassed that he'd forgotten who he was talking to. But she made him feel something he hadn't since he'd left *Los Otros*: that he was talking to someone who understood. "Sorry, I get so caught up in my own self-interests. And that's another reason I'm taking this on.

Like those stone inscriptions, my project, on a small scale, anyway, may serve as a trigger that helps people open up to other perceptions, other remembrances, and even other worlds. I realized that any fear I had about telling my story was silly, even stupid. What are we here for, if not to find and then communicate our own truths? I'm certainly not afraid to do that in my music. As a composer, if I kept the notes in my heart, no one else could hear the music. But to truly play the music, I must live those notes in every way: at work, at home, and in my relationships. And once those notes are played, others might discover that my song harmonizes with theirs, and that this music has been playing for eternity within all of us."

"That's quite poetic, Mr. Taylor. Have you always spoken that way, or is this a side-effect of your new career?" Annie teased.

He smiled sheepishly. He'd actually surprised himself; the words just kind of came out. Stopping at a red light he turned to her, noticing for the first time how mesmerizing her green eyes were. Was that why he'd told this stranger more than he'd told anyone else? The only other person who'd opened him up like that was—

"Let me ask a typical reporter's question," Annie interrupted his thoughts. "After you finish this new project, do you believe that you'll have accomplished everything you want? Will it be time then to meet the Keepers of the Gate?"

The light turned green.

"Oh, I don't believe I'm through yet," Digger bantered easily, not catching the oddity of her reference.

"How do you know?" Annie quipped, eyes ablaze.

"A wise man who is very far out—literally far out—once told me that my friends"—Digger gulped for a moment—"that my friends had *earned* the right to breathe their last breath. I don't know that I can truthfully say I have done that yet."

"I wouldn't be too sure about that, Digger," Annie said seriously. Then she kidded, "Not that I'm trying to get rid of you, but from what I know of your journey, I would have to say that you've done a lot. I travel around the world and I've never seen anything like people's fascination with the spheres! And it's not just fascination; somehow those spheres you uncovered are touching people deep inside." She leaned a little closer.

"One early morning in Milan, I sat next to a woman in a *trattoria*. She was reading a newspaper article about the spheres' discovery. As she sipped her cappuccino, she told me that she hated to read the papers, but she couldn't get enough information about those mysterious boulders, that knowing something about them made her happy somehow.

"Then on an assignment in China, two weeks ago, I was walking through the rebuilt Tianamin Square, talking casually with some young people. They told me they were on their way to a friend's apartment where, once a week, they take turns sharing information about a new place, concept, or ideology. It was their week, they told me, and they were taking all the information on the stone spheres they could gather."

As Annie spoke, Digger felt as if he were right there with her, smelling the coffee, seeing the expression on the young people's faces, feeling the street beneath his feet. He slowly applied the brakes as another stoplight turned from green to yellow.

"Once for background," Annie continued, "I was interviewing the street children of Río de Janeiro. When I sat down next to a young girl, she grabbed a newspaper and pointed to a picture of a stone sphere. She said she couldn't read, but would I please tell her about these 'magical stones'?"

At that moment, Digger found himself standing in someone's living room. It felt like the imprinting visions; he could see and sense his surroundings, and also be inside someone's head and heart. He knew he was in Des Moines, Iowa, where a single mom had just put her two children to bed. Flipping on the TV, she watched local announcers describe new information gleaned from the spheres. Tired, she didn't even realize that a slight smile came to her face as she watched and listened.

Then he was standing in the corner of another room where, lying in his bed, an elderly Japanese man reached out for his glasses. Shakily placing them on his face, he peered closely at an article with a picture of the Love sphere prominently displayed. He slowly read each line, savoring the possibility of life being more than just this physical world.

Then Digger was back in his car, listening to Annie talk about the street child. He realized he hadn't even missed a word. The stoplight was just turning from yellow to red.

"The next day I went back to see that child and she told me how she'd dreamt of running through the jungle and seeing people dancing around a fire."

Digger blinked a few times, startled from the sudden change of visions.

"Are you okay?" Annie asked coyly.

Digger nodded uncertainly.

She went on, "Every day in Costa Rica, the lines to see *las esferas de piedra* are several blocks long. Do you know that this very evening, the *Museo Nacional* in San José is holding a special event displaying them? I've seen people's reactions as they stand before the spheres. One person—"

Again, Digger followed her words—literally—and found himself standing in the middle courtyard of the *Museo*. No one seemed to know that he was there, but as before, he knew what they were thinking and feeling.

He watched a man from Poland, who'd spent his life savings to make the trip, stare at a basketball-sized sphere. The ball of stone was colored in blues and indigos with etchings of silver-lined squares and rectangles, along with dots that looked like Morse code. The man bent over the artifact. A tingling went straight to his heart.

A banker from Hong Kong, who'd been standing all day before the Communication sphere, cradled a pad of paper in his arm as he drew a circular design.

A young German boy pointed to several of the geometric shapes on the History sphere. He told stories to his mother of ancient battles, of good guys and bad guys, of flying machines in the sky. His mother listened to the "imagination" of her young son.

Hundreds of people stared at the designs and codes of the stone spheres. They didn't know why. They couldn't explain it, but the designs stirred something deep inside them, just beyond the grasp of their waking minds. They felt different, more alive, more hopeful. And they *wanted more.*

A widowed, elderly woman from Mexico City watched silently as the symbols on the largest sphere pulsed to an unheard song. She smiled as the music echoed gently within her.

Suddenly Digger's attention was captured by a young woman who was also staring at the widow. She turned toward him—it was Angélica. Startled, he pulled back, shrinking into his car seat. Beside him, he saw Annie staring at him.

"Are you sure nothing's wrong?" she asked again.

"I was... you were..." he stammered, looking around the car as the stoplight turned green. "Sorry, nevermind."

He made a left and pulled into the entrance of the Hyatt hotel. He felt an unexpected twinge of disappointment. So soon?

"Thank you so much for talking with me, or should I say me talking to you," Annie was laughing graciously. "It was great to hear your new music—and to hear about your latest endeavor. May I print it? No, you'll probably say no," she grimaced before he could answer. "That's all right. In fact, if you need any help, I do have connections." She handed him her business card. Her eyes sparkled as she added, "*Please,* call me if I can help."

He thanked her for the offer, then watched her walk to the entrance, stop, and turn to wave, smiling, as the bellman opened the door for her. Digger waved back halfheartedly, but he was still stunned by the visions he'd had while she talked about the effect the spheres were having on people. Didn't he need the spheres anymore to experience such visions? Did this woman have anything to do with it?

As soon as she was out of sight and he was speeding on Interstate 405, taking him back to Cardiff, he regretted not saying more, or inviting her out for coffee, or something. Sighing, he remembered Ortega's page earlier and picked up his cell phone to check his messages at home.

Sure enough, he heard the familiar voice, "*Pura vida*, Digger! I just tried to page you. Please call me right away, as soon as you get this message. You will not believe what we have discovered! Oh!... Oh! I can't wait. I will tell you now... You remember the photo of the Heavens sphere that looked like the Costa Rican night sky?"

Digger could hear the excitement swelling in Ortega's voice.

"For the last several months my astronomer friend has been trying to match the unidentified patterns of indentations on the sphere with other places we might view the heavens. He had no luck—until yesterday, when he and I were talking about the astronomical charts of Teotihuacan in Mexico; it was an ancient Aztec city that was laid out on an east-west axis, with the Pleiades on the western horizon—"

"Get to the point, Ortega!" Digger heard Bendi's voice in the background. He chuckled.

"Okay, okay. Well, just for fun we decided to reverse things. My friend programmed the computer to show what a night sky would look like from the Pleiades looking back at Earth. It was incredible! It matched one of the patterns on the Heavens sphere!"

It sounded to Digger like the old guy was choking, he was so excited.

"How could anybody have known what the night sky would have looked like from the Pleiades? Unless they had the help of today's sophisticated computers. Or... unless they were *from* the Pleiades. *Dios mio*! Who knows what other reference points we will find on the Heavens sphere!!"

Digger laughed; the old, deep-down, belly-bouncing kind that hurts afterwards. But it felt great. It had been a long time since he'd really laughed. As Ortega continued, Digger opened the moon roof.

"Also, my friend pointed out to me that the Costa Rican night sky etched into the Heavens sphere was not exactly correct. This bothered him because everything about the star markings was so ingeniously intricate and precise. Then my friend snickered at himself, which does not happen very often, I might add, and he told me that he had become so engrossed into the details of the project that he forgot to take a step back and take in the whole perspective. He had forgotten one of the basic principles of astronomy: the universe is always changing.

"Guess what? The markings on the sphere *are* exactly correct— correct for anyone in Costa Rica who was looking up into the nighttime sky in the 1500s!

"Well, that is only part of my news. Right now, Bendi and I and a half-dozen scientists are crowded around the cracked Heavens sphere, or what is left of it, I should say. I don't know what made me do it; maybe yesterday's discovery, or Bendi's promptings, or maybe witnessing the Digger methodology of excavation," Ortega guffawed at his own joke. "Or all of that. But I decided to chip away at the crack. When I did, an outer shell peeled away exposing an inner core. Are you ready for this? Inside we found a *perfectly symmetrical ball made of crystal,* with minute inscriptions that are so small it is like looking at a huge micro-chip. No one has any idea what it all means, but we know it is momentous."

Digger couldn't breathe. He sat up straight and forcefully inhaled, as all his visions of being in that room with the six translucent figures and the crystal sphere flooded back to him.

"We dated the layer of rock that lay over the crystal by looking at some of the tiny organisms that were caught within its surface." Ortega's voice was rising a pitch with each new revelation. "Those organisms have just recently become extinct, at least in planetary time. It gets more technical, but believe me when I say that we have conclusively dated the earliest—the latest, oh, it all seems so confusing but the evidence is right before our eyes. You are not going to believe this but the inscriptions on the crystal sphere had to be made at least *850,000 years ago.* And you won't believe the rest."

Ortega gasped for air and lowered his voice. "Are you sitting down? Of course you are, you are already sitting down, if not lying on the floor! Well, here it is: When we looked closely at the crystal, some of the inscriptions looked similar to the other geometric designs found on the stone spheres. One area looked like a total blur until we magnified it and discovered thousands of names that looked like they had been etched into the crystal. Next to the names were symbols unlike anything we've seen before. One symbol jumped out at me. It is intriguing, kind of like a pretzel with interlocking loops. I'll fax the image over to you. But what is truly incredible is that this symbol was placed above a name we know.

"Digger, it is your chosen name: Too-kashaam."

Digger pulled into the driveway of his oceanfront home. Walking upstairs, he changed into a pair of shorts and his favorite Costa Rican T-shirt—the one with the rafting frog. Opening all the second-story windows, he allowed the light wind to clear out the stale air while he went out onto the balcony to watch the waves burst into a white foam as they broke on the shore. No moon tonight, no shadows, just the brightly sparkled sky. The cool, moist breeze brought the smell of salt as he looked high above and to the north. There the Seven Sisters, the Pleiades, were playing hide-and-seek with his vision.

He remembered Zorinthalian telling him he would come across two triggers that would help him define his past and his purpose. And although they might be difficult to comprehend, he should be open to all that they had to offer.

Well, Ortega's news had to be one of those triggers. It was actually too much to think about. The implications were staggering. He didn't know if he could comprehend it all.

Immediately, he felt the shallowness of that belief. How limiting can you be? he gibed at himself. "I have room for universes within me," he yelled toward the darkened Pacific.

Walking back into his study, he turned on the desk light and sat down in his chair. Gathering his handwritten notes, he read the first page of his new book:

The notes of death had followed Digger more than three thousand miles into the Costa Rican rainforest. Now they reverberated around him as he stood within the lush jungle enveloping him in an array of colors, textures, smells—and sounds. As the realization seeped into his consciousness, he chuckled to himself: there was no escape. Closing his eyes, he—

Annie Gallagher's intense, sparkling eyes flashed into his mind. Weren't they green?

On an impulse, he got up and retrieved the fax Ortega had sent, showing the symbol they'd found above the name Too-kashaam. He hurried into the bedroom to fetch Annie's business card from his tuxedo pocket. Mouth agape, he walked back to the study and fell into his chair.

There, on Annie's business card, in gleaming gold imprint, was the same symbol as her golden looped pendant, the same symbol that glared at him from Ortega's fax. The same symbol that someone had engraved on the crystal sphere, 850,000 years ago?!

Annie Gallagher
Investigative Journalist
619-698-9462

Internally, he felt as if a huge combination lock with thousands of tumblers was falling through its final spin as he stared at the design. The safe opened—and he suddenly realized that this was the symbol he'd been looking for, ever since that dream-like meditation on the night of his first audition in Hollywood! Could this be Zorinthalian's second trigger?

One of Ortega's ramblings shouted back to Digger: "Everything seems to be moving so fast... everything is changing, life-changing experiences seem to be happening one after another..."

Digger picked up his cell phone and dialed information. Soon a cheerful hotel clerk was putting through his call to the Hyatt's Room 432, while Digger scrambled to find his keys and raced to climb back into his car.

Each ring of the phone was an eternity. Mercifully, someone picked up the phone but before anyone could even say "hello" he blurted, "This is Jonathan... Digger. Is this Angélica? I mean Annie—God, I don't know what I mean."

"Maybe He is the only one who *does* know," she laughed.

"Are you, I mean were you Angélica?" He couldn't bear the momentary pause before she answered.

"Yes, Digger I *was*," she replied softly.

Chills ran over his entire body. His heart was pounding wildly and his mind was struggling to hold on to any scraps of rationality as he maneuvered the streets of Cardiff.

"Have you always known?" were the only words that came out of his mouth but that wasn't what he wanted to ask.

"No," she answered. "Hazy memories of my time in the jungle began about ten years ago. Since then more and more have come back. But it all became clear when I saw the spheres that you uncovered. Digger... the others are anxious to see you."

"The others? They are? Which others?" He was thoroughly confused now.

"When are you going to stop asking your infernal questions and *get over here?*" she blurted, in a way that only Angélica could.

"I'm already on my way!" he reassured her as he pulled out onto the freeway.

They talked through his entire drive back to L.A. Digger could clearly see Angélica's eyes. From the open moon roof, the light of the stars flooded him with memories of all their experiences together, their eyes meeting as he pulled her into the raft, the light that danced over her face as he watched the dragonflies, her touch that night by the blazing *Los Otros* fire—then he remembered the lessons of circling Gutubo.

Strange, he thought, how the one step that ends a journey is the same step that begins a new one. What an exciting step that is, so filled with death yet so much life—a step filled with sadness yet hope. He realized that every sunrise, every song, every feeling, every thought, every new millennium, every book, every slumber, and every gaze into another's eyes was potentially a magical step out of the shadow and back into the Light.

The Sphere

As I felt complete with all that I've done,
My very next step, I wanted to run.

For when I espied your spherical form,
You quickly delivered my most frightful storm.

I thought it was over, ah! but I was a fool,
For there is no end, just delightful renewal.

Now high in the sky, the sun did reveal
All that is true and all that is real.

It was but a glittering sight I beheld,
Man, woman, and child, what a shimmering meld!

Rocks, birds, plants, and creatures, a beautiful tree,
Past, Present, and Future, all of it Me.

I was captivated from the first moment that I viewed Zon-O-Ray's art-transmissions. I strongly feel that her work acts as a wake-up call to our individual and collective journey. For not only do her art-transmissions deliver intrigue, awe, and beauty, they also kindle universal concepts which remind us of our connection to the Light. This remembrance is brought about by the sacred symbols and codes which somehow stimulate, like a forgotten fragrance, the ancient travels—memories—of our soul. If you would like to experience Zon-O-Ray's readings or art-transmissions contact:

Guiding Lights
Zon-O-Ray
PMB 172-2370 W. Highway 89A-11
Sedona, AZ 86336-5349 U.S.A.
e-mail zzlights@hotmail.com

I wish to thank you for reading my book. With every rewrite—over 20—I have learned a little more about writing, a little more about myself, a little more about my past. I trust that the time and energy you have put into this book has brought you some entertainment, maybe even some insight, or hopefully both. Your readership is what enables me to continue my writing. Thank you again.

If you would like to make comments or inquire about workshops, lectures, or products, please contact:

Creativeic@aol.com
http://www.tomyoungholm.com
Creative Information Concepts
P.O. Box 1504
Lemon Grove, CA 91946

Tom Youngholm lives in San Diego. Along with coaching other visionary writers, he also lectures, writes, and presents seminars that promote balance—Physical, Emotional, Intellectual, and Spiritual—for individuals and organizations. He has worked as an adolescent and family counselor, restaurant owner, training specialist, business consultant, and is a sports enthusiast and musician.

Order Form

Visit our web site at http://www.tomyoungholm.com for further information or to order any of our products.

You may also send a check to:
Creative Information Concepts, P.O. Box 1504, Lemon Grove, CA 91946

Please send me the following materials.

Books if you would like them autographed please print your name

		Quantity	
In the Shadow of the Sphere	$14.95	____	$_____
The Celestial Bar	$12.95	____	$_____

Audio

Return to Gutubo   **2 cassettes** $16.95   ____ $_____
Revisit *In the Shadow of the Sphere* through the authors' viewpoint to discover how this mythic story can assist you in healing your past. The author read passages, personal revelations, and explanations will reveal the many subtle messages of this profound book.

The Celestial Bar   **2 cassettes** $16.95   ____ $_____
Author read audio book

T-shirts

In the Shadow of the Sphere $14.95   ____ $_____
Imprint of the art-transmission which is in the book and also on back cover (black starry background with the design in gold and silver) including the title and the quote from the heading of Chapter 24

Celestial Bar $14.95   ____ $_____
Colorful imprint of the illustration on the original cover of the book (piano keys winding up into the starry heavens) including the quote, *"I've Been To The Celestial Bar."*

Choose: ____ Large ____ X Large

Subtotal	$_____
Sales Tax Add 7.75% (CA only)	$_____
Shipping	$_____
Total Enclosed	$_____

Shipping $3.95 Please allow two weeks for delivery
Outside USA (except Canada) Global Priority $9

Offer good only while supplies last. Prices subject to change.